The Witching Voice

Thou know'st that thou hast formed me
With passions wild and strong;
And list'ning to their witching voice
Has often led me wrong.

– Robert Burns
    from "A Prayer in the Prospect of Death"

The Witching Voice

A Novel from the Life
of Robert Burns

Arnold Johnston

WingsPress

San Antonio, Texas
2009

The Witching Voice © 2009 by Arnold Johnston

First Edition

ISBN-10: 0-916727-44-0
ISBN-13: 978-0-916727-44-4

Wings Press
627 E. Guenther
San Antonio, Texas 78210
Phone/fax: (210) 271-7805

On-line catalogue and ordering:
www.wingspress.com
All Wings Press titles are distributed to the trade by
Independent Publishers Group
www.ipgbook.com

Library of Congress Cataloging-in-Publication Data:

Johnston, Arnold.
  The witching voice : a novel from the life of Robert Burns / Arnold Johnston. --
1st ed.
     p. cm.
  Includes bibliographical references.
  ISBN-13: 978-0-916727-44-4 (alk. paper)
  ISBN-10: 0-916727-44-0
  1. Burns, Robert, 1759-1796--Fiction. 2. Poets, Scottish--Fiction. I. Title.
  PS3560.O387W57 2009
  813'.54--dc22

                              2008052080

For Debby

Acknowledgments

I wish to express my thanks to Western Michigan University for awarding me a sabbatical leave that allowed me to complete much of the work on this novel. Like anyone who tackles a biographical or historical subject, I'm indebted to the research of many other scholars and writers, some of whose names may be found at the end of the book in a list of works consulted. I also owe special gratitude to my friends and colleagues Richard Katrovas, Stuart Dybek, Robert Eversz, and Ted Kistler, as well as to Bryce Milligan for his talent, his vision, and his commitment to literature, poetry, and song. And as always, my thanks to Debby. Though this is, of course, a work of fiction, I've tried to build it on historical fact; where I depart from history, I do so either through my own error or creative license. Such liberties as I've taken with conventions of Scots dialect are intended to increase readability for an international audience.

Contents

❧ **1784** ❧

Dr Cousin,

I would have returned you my thanks for your kind favor of the 13th Dec. sooner had it not been that I waited to give you an account of that melancholy event which for some time pas[t] we have from day to day expected. – On the 13th Currt I lost the best of fathers. Though to be sure we have had long warn-ing of the impending stroke still the tender feelings of Nature claim their part and I cannot recollect the tender endearments and parental lessons of the best of friends and the ablest of instructors without feeling, what perhaps, the calmer dictates of reason would partly condemn. –

I hope my father's friends in your country will not let their connection in this place die with him. For my part I shall ever with pleasure – with pride acknowledge my connection with those who were allied by the ties of blood and friendship to a man whose memory I will ever honor and revere. – I expect therefore, My Dr Sir, you will not neglect any opportunity of letting me hear from you which will ever very much oblidge

My dear Cousin, yours sincerely,

ROBERT BURNESS

Letter to JAMES BURNESS, Montrose
17th February 1784

Chapter One

The two ponies move steadily, one after the other, along the road to Alloway Kirk. The rhythmic slide of their brown haunches sets a measured pace for the line of riders strung unevenly behind them. Slung between the ponies on two long poles, a plain deal coffin sways from side to side.

Astride his own horse at the head of the procession next to the minister, Robert holds the lead pony's halter. What is left of his father lies in the coffin, a pathetic rickle of flesh and bone that scarcely burdens the two animals. Robert glances back at the swinging box and catches Gilbert watching him. His brother's eyes are red-rimmed with fatigue and grief, but something in that stare, a glaze of ice, a slight raising of the brows, recalls their father's frequent expression of doubt and disapproval.

Nodding shortly at Gibby, Robert looks behind him, where Willie Muir, the miller, black crape ribbon fluttering from his bonnet in the raw damp wind, is drawing a caup of ale for John Rankine of Adamhill from a small cask strapped to his horse's saddle. And farther back, fat Bob Aiken, the lawyer from Ayr, takes a quick swallow – Kilbagie, like as not – from his silver flask before passing it to the banker, John Ballantine. Among the other riders, Willie Paton hardly cuts a notable figure, his hodden grey farmer's clothes ill-hidden under a dark cloak. Willie has journeyed from Lairgieside to attend the funeral of his daughter's employer, a more than usual courtesy. Robert finds himself wondering whether Betty may have said ought to her family. And suddenly the image of Betty takes shape, the white of her shoulders, the damp strands of hair at the nape of her neck that first time after haymaking, and the thought turns him uneasily toward the road ahead.

At the sudden movement beside him, John McMath reaches out to grip Robert by the arm. "Steady on, lad. It'll a' come right."

Unwilling to meet the minister's eyes, Robert hunches his shoulders. "Aye. It's come as right as it ever will for my father."

McMath makes no reply. And the bitterness in his own voice causes Robert to lapse again into silence. He has no real wish to speak, or to hear comforting phrases, even though McMath is a good man, able and willing to ride the four miles between Tarbolton and Alloway over wet and boggy roads to honor a dead man's wish. Not many ministers would do so.

A stumble of hoofbeats and Bob Aiken is beside Robert, proferring the silver flask. "Have a swallow or two, Rab. It'll warm ye."

Robert shakes his head. "Thanks, Bob. I've nae stomach for drink the now."

He half expects open laughter from the lawyer at the notion of Rab Burns turning aside from the taste of Kilbagie, but mindful of the circumstances Aiken nods sympathetically. "Aye, well, ye'll know your own mind, Rab." He reins in his horse and falls back to his place.

Robert knows the men in the funeral party must take his dour silence for simple grief. But grief is merely one of the emotions that crowd his brain, their conflicting claims seeming to cancel each other. Like the white glare of the sun behind the clouds that hang over the sea to the west, he feels blank and pitiless. The old man is gone, taking with him his disapproval of pleasure. No more will Robert have to leave the house either in shame or anger for the sake of a drink or a dance. But no more will he cradle the hope of astonishing his father with some accomplishment that might end – no, not end their toil, but at least see it decently rewarded. And he knows, too, that William Burns has died without seeing a lifetime of unending labor repaid by so much as one good harvest. And now Robert – and Gibby – must take up that gloomy stewardship where the old man has left off, providing for Agnes, their mother, and their five brothers and sisters. A line from his own Commonplace Book rises amid Robert's confusion: "How welcome to me were the grave." And its simplicity now strikes him as a deal more eloquent than the epitaph for his father, folded in a pocket of his coat, that has cost him far more time and tears.

And now Alloway Kirk lies before them, a gray squat ruin. A small building, roofless and long-abandoned, it seems to Robert a stolid mass, built to hunch down and suffer, rather than aspire above the earth it stands on. The little kirkyard is soon cramped, somber with men standing uneasily in their dark clothing. The February air is sharp with the mingled salt tang of the nearby coast and the damp of fresh-dug clay. Robert and Gibby supervise in silence the unslinging of the coffin from between the ponies and take their places at its head and foot until it is laid under the mort-cloth at the graveside. As the service begins in the flat tones of Dr. William MacGill, the minister from neighboring Ayr, Robert's eyes wander, to the gravedigger leaning on his spade near the kirk itself, shivering in the chill air, to the horses shifting and clattering, dropping their steamy dung outside the stone dyke that William Burns himself mended just before leaving Alloway.

Here, it occurs to Robert, his father enjoyed his best days. William first came to the Lowlands from Dunottar in the northeast, up near Aberdeen, too long a journey for any of his family to have made now for the funeral. Tenant farmers for generations, the Burnses suffered in the aftermath of the Stewart rebellion because of their feudal ties to the Earl Marischal, who was misfortunate in backing the sad young man the English seem pleased now to call The Pretender. And afterward, William and his kin fought a doomed fight, too, trying to scratch a living from the thin skin of arable soil that clings to the granite braes of Clochnahill. But William was long past thinking of Prince Charlie's lost dream when he and his brother set out for Edinburgh: "I'll tell ye," he said one day when Robert wanted to know what had brought him south, "I was after nothing mair than decent work and a guid wife."

Work he found in Edinburgh, but no wife. The proud folk of the Scottish capital had not just been to his liking, Robert knows, and the stink of Auld Reekie's streets repelled his country-bred sensibilities. So William set off again, tramping west to the clean sea wind and low green hills of Ayrshire. And there he found work fit for a countryman, and met the woman such a man needed to share a life tied to the land and the seasons. At the age of thirty-six, ten days before Christmas in 1757, he wed Agnes Broun of Kirkoswald, a sturdy lass of twenty-five. They settled immediately in Alloway, where William set up as a nurseryman and market-gardener, working besides as an overseer on Provost William Fergusson's estate close by.

And here, in Alloway, on William's first rented land, a mere seven acres, Robert, Gilbert, Nancy, and Annabella were born. The old clay two-room cottage, which William built almost unaided, is an easy walk from the kirkyard, and Robert's mind stirs now with images: the homely wooden stool in the chimney-corner; the rack of good china plates, their faces leaning down over him, stained by firelight, like a row of harvest moons; his mother's spinning wheel, with its wonderment of moving parts, that he dared not meddle with. There he can remember his father's face creased with its rare smiles, and the occasional sound of his laughter. There William made provision to educate his two elder sons as best a poor man could, to prepare them for the better lives he hoped they might someday lead.

But that was before the needs of a growing family caused William to rent the first of several farms, and sour soil and poor harvests forced him on to another, and yet another. And now, finally, exhausted by his efforts to battle a dishonest landlord, William lies dead, deceived at the end even by his own sons. For Robert and Gilbert are now ready to shift the family to one more new farm, Mossgiel, near Mauchline, rented in secret while the old man still lay dying.

" . . . twenty-five years and more a member of the Auld Kirk in Ayr," Dr. MacGill is saying, passing from ritual to personal observances, "and in those years tasked wi' many a sair dunt. But a man that faced it a' wi' staunch faith and unwavering fortitude. A man that took a just pride in his family, and provided for them as best he could." The minister sighs in a great puff of steam. "Now those living must take up the burden that William Burns has laid down. And as we pray for his departing soul, sure of his everlasting salvation, so we pray that his sons will find the strength to live as he would wish, and as he did, an example of man's patient goodness here on earth."

As MacGill moves on to his closing prayer, Robert, conscious of the bowed heads around him, regards the minister sharply. It is as if the man was at his father's deathbed in those final hours, for his sentiments are like an echo of William's own.

"Robert," his father said, voice labored and indistinct, breath already like a dry exhalation from the grave, "I fear for ye. Ye're my eldest. And ye have strength in ye, . . . muckle strength. . . . But will ye put it tae use . . . for the best? I can only hope . . . and fear."

Unable to answer, blind with tears, Robert turned away then. Only his mother was near at hand, her face unreadable through the salt smirr in his eyes. And as he turns now from MacGill, Robert sees the eyes of the gravedigger, rheumy in the cold wind, lift to watch him incuriously for the space of a few heartbeats, then drop.

A few more gentle words, this time from John McMath, repeating some of the service he spoke earlier in the day at Tarbolton for the family, and the funeral is virtually at an end. But now McMath is looking at Robert. "Gibby tells me ye've written an epitaph for your father's stone. Maybe we could close wi' that if ye feel . . ." McMath trails off and all eyes fix on Robert.

He feels no desire to speak, let alone read. But this is no occasion for shuffling and hanging back. "Aye," he says. And taking the sheet of paper from his pocket, he unfolds it and reads, forcing his voice to ring with a warmth that, genuine enough at the writing, now feels calculated and shabby. "O ye whose cheek the tear of pity stains, draw near with pious rev'rence, and attend! Here lie the loving husband's dear remains, the tender father, and the gen'rous friend; the pitying heart that felt for human woe, the dauntless heart that fear'd no human pride; the friend of man – to vice alone a foe;" – Robert pauses momentarily – "for even his failings lean'd to virtue's side. – " As he finishes reading, a few large raindrops strike the paper in his hands, their spatter loud in the stillness.

A squall is moving in from the sea, wind and stinging rain. In decent haste, with little more talk, the coffin is lowered and the mortcloth removed. Stiffly, Robert and Gibby scatter some of the kirkyard's stony clay into the grave. Then, with the chunk, thump, and clatter of the gravedigger's spade at their backs and the cold pelt of rain in their faces, the funeral party mount and ride back toward Ayr and Simson's Brigend Inn.

Simson's seems full of warmth in contrast to the dreich rattle and soak of rain outside. The air around the fireplace is steamily pungent from the damp weeds of the mourners, and tongues are loosening in the rising glow provided by a few drams of rough-edged Ferintosh or, for those who can afford it, the smoother Kilbagie.

"So you and Gibby are agreed wi' Gavin Hamilton on the Mossgiel farm, eh, Robert?" John Ballantine, the banker, a slim man in his late thirties, dressed elegantly but with fitting sobriety, claps a hand on Robert's shoulder. Bob Aiken, eyes brightly alive in the chubby face that can never quite manage solemnity, stands close by, poised as if to propose a toast.

"Aye, we are, Mr. Ballantine." Robert shifts to look at the two men squarely. "And I may say we're grateful to both of you for your sound counsel through this damnable tangle o' legal jiggery-pokery wi' yon bugger MacLure."

Ballantine sips at his whisky. "I must admit, Robert, I never knew the depths David MacLure had sunk to, trying to make good his own losses by cheating your father. I merely suggested the means o' recourse any man has a right to in a business dispute."

"Aye," says Aiken, moving forward, "but ye'll no' see many tenants willing – and able – to take on a landlord in an action before the sheriff. I advised your father to come to some agreement wi' MacLure, mysel', but damned if he would."

Robert nods. "He was a proud man, and no' one to bow to injustice if he had the means to face up to it."

Aiken raises his glass in admiration. "Aye, and did he no'? He faced MacLure, a' right – and beat him!"

Gilbert is standing nearby with John McMath, Willie Muir, and John Rankine, whose farm at Adamhill lies close to Mulr's Tarbolton mill. "Four years he fought," Gibby says to the lawyer, his voice low, constricted with unfocused anger, "and a' it's won him is a plot in Alloway Kirk."

Chastened, Aiken lowers his glass and purses his lips momentarily. "Ye're right, of course, Gibby. He might have done better to settle wi' MacLure, after a'. But as Rab says, it wasna in his nature."

Robert, surprised to find himself doing so, speaks up to break the tension. "Aye, Gibby, and if he hadna fought, and if Bob here hadna ta'en an interest, what would we be up against now?" Even as he speaks, though, Robert feels a surge of affection for his brother. Gibby's bitterness mirrors his own, but Gibby seldom lets his feelings out, and it warms Robert to see this sign of the kinship he sometimes fears goes no farther than the flesh.

Willie Muir steps in, too, blunt in his effort to turn the company to thoughts less sour. "I've known the Burnses since early days in Tarbolton, so I think I may speak to the point. William Burns was a man among men, Gibby. Every one o' us maun admire him. It's as Rab said in yon grand lines for the stone – whatever failings your father micht ha'e had, he ploughed a straight furrow through this life. I drink to his memory – and the twa fine sons that stand here afore us!"

Muir drinks off his whisky emphatically, and the rest of the company upend their own glasses amid a chorus of agreement. Gilbert acknowledges the miller's good intentions with an attempt at a smile, his eyes glistening, and Robert moves to him, calling to the landlord. "Another dram for my brother, Mr. Simson. Aye, and one for me, as well – for here's a toast that takes us a' in."

Simson puts a drink in Gibby's hand, then turns to Robert, who takes the other glass and raises it. "The past is bad, and the future hid, its good or ill untried, O. But the present hour is in our pow'r, and so we maun enjoy it, O!"

The men around Robert raise a general din of assent, but he sees that Gibby, though obviously still moved by brotherly feeling, has found the sentiments a bit too irresponsible for his taste. If only Gibby could let go, get roaring drunk, and forget now and again how much his father's son he is.

"Rab, what's that from, lad? It's something o' yours, is no'?" Willie Muir's blue eyes are narrowed under beetling white brows as he searches his memory, now none the better for a deal of ale and whisky.

"It's a wee bit o' paraphrase from 'My Father was a Farmer Upon the Carrick Border,' Willie. I first sang it for ye up at the Mill a couple o' years ago, no' long after I wrote it." Robert waves in self-deprecation. "My singin' likely gave ye ample cause to forget it."

"Nothin' o' the kind, Rab. My auld head's addled wi' drink, that's a'. I just hope the wife and me havena heard your last new sang at the Mill, now that ye're bound for Mossgiel,"

"Ye needna worry about seein' us in Tarbolton. Mossgiel's near enough – and we wouldna forget good friends." Robert glances at his brother. "But I'm the new head o' a muckle family, and I'll soon ha'e the runnin' o' a new farm. So when it comes to songs – or poems, either, for that matter – I'll have little enough time for singin' them – aye, or scribblin' them. And if ever I'm inclined to forget mysel', I've nae doubt Gibby will put me to rights soon enough."

Before Gibby – or anyone else – can speak, Bob Aiken steps forward. "If ye ask me, Rab, ye'd do well to keep at the scribblin', as ye ca' it. For to my mind, your verses and songs might well do more to provide for your family than any farm. Ye've a fertile mind – and ye need to cultivate that, as well as the land. I'm sure Gibby agrees wi' me there."

Gibby, flushing a bit, says, "I'd never suggest that Rab lay aside his poetry – as he well knows."

Robert, thoughtful, nods to Gibby a moment before Willie Muir throws his arms around the two brothers' shoulders. But as the noise of conversation swells around him, Robert's mind is no longer occupied with Gibby, nor even with his father. Can Bob Aiken possibly mean that poetry might provide a way to put want and uncertainty behind them?

Later, as he and Gibby ride together on the cold road home, saddles creaking beneath them, the notion comes to Robert again. "Well, Gibby, I may say I'm glad that's by us. We'll be back to auld clothes and porridge, the morrow. But we'll no' be confused wi' drink or good-hearted friends into thinkin' there's an easy road before us."

Gibby turns to him, hands braced on his horse's neck. "Bob Aiken's a bit inclined to enthusiasm, a' right. And it's a lawyer's way to say what he thinks folk would like to hear. But as for what he said about your poetry, I wouldna argue wi' that. Whether or no' ye ever turn a penny from it, Rab, your verse deserves to be read and your songs to be sung beyond these hills and fields." He reaches across and grips Robert's arm. "Never let it be said that your ain brother couldna see that."

That night, Gibby eases into place on the familiar lumps of the mattress he shares with Robert. Tucking his nightshirt down around his knees against the cold, he looks over to where Robert, still fully dressed, stands at the entrance to their sleeping-loft, staring out at the farmyard below.

The farm is quiet now, save for the shifting and snorting of the livestock. All the tears have been wept for this day. Early on, the widowed Agnes fell into a deep exhausted sleep downstairs in a bed now painfully spacious. The rest of the family, though drained by grief, have been tense all evening with anticipation of the impending move to Mossgiel. But now all are settled for the night: the three sisters – Nancy, Bell, and thirteen-year-old Isa – crowded into the spence along with Betty Paton; and the two younger boys – Willie and thin, sickly John – sharing a bed set up near the kitchen fireplace. Only Robert, staring out from the head of the ladder, has not yet given to fatigue.

Gibby raises his head. "Are ye no' comin' to bed, then?"

Robert turns, his eyes transformed by the bedside candle into points of flickering light. "No. I canna sleep now. I'm away out for a stamp in the night air."

Gibby says nothing for a few moments, measuring his response in even breathing. "I'll douse the candle then," he says finally.

Robert swings a foot onto the top rung of the ladder. "I'll find my way back," he says, and descends into the night outside.

Gibby moistens his thumb and forefinger with the tip of his tongue, pinches out the candle-flame, and lies on his back in the sudden darkness. An argument would have been useless at this point, and on such a day. Their father is gone, and Robert is the new head of the family. And Robert has been careful till now. But if Gibby knows, others will soon guess. How can Nancy and Bell have failed to see? And how can Robert take risks with their future for a lassie as plain-faced and common as Betty Paton? Gibby rolls over on his side, hot with shame at the swiftness of his own response to the thought of those plump warm breasts that will soon be pillowing his brother's head.

In the stable-loft, the air heavy with the sweet strong smell of hay and sleeping beasts, Robert pulls Betty down to his chest and loses himself for a time to the feel of her open mouth on his own.

At last she leans her head on his shoulder and speaks in a breathless undertone. "One o' these nights Nancy or Bell will hear me when I come out to ye, Rab."

He squeezes her companionably. "Even if they hear ye get up, they're no' to know what ye're gettin' up for. And they'll soon go back to sleep. Anyway, here ye are, so all's well."

"But what about Gibby? Was he no' awake?"

"Aye. I told him I wanted a breath o' air." He peers at her in the dim starlight. "What's troublin' ye, Betty?"

After a pause, she speaks in the matter-of-fact tone that first suggested to him, months ago, that this plain young girl with the well-shaped body might know more about the ways of a man and a maid than he did himself. "Gibby looks at me," she says, "when he thinks I don't see him. I thought he might know about us."

He leans to kiss the top of her head. "Never worry, lass. I've taken care. Gibby suspects nothing. Or if he does, he's too close a lad to let on. More likely he has a notion o' ye, himsel'." A thought strikes him. "Your father was at the funeral, Betty. You havena said ought about us to him or your mother, have ye?"

Sitting up she grasps his hands tightly. "I'd never do that, Rab. Surely ye don't think that?"

He pulls her down next to him again. "No, lass. It'll be my own bad conscience talking. That and the thought o' my father in that box at the graveside."

"I'm that sorry about your father, Rab." She touches her fingers to his cheek, then kisses him lightly. Lying back, she says, "I don't like kirkyards much. They frighten me."

"Nothing but dust, lass. Grass and earth and dust. And nothing beyond."

"You mean ye don't believe we go to Heaven – or Hell?"

For a time he breathes the cool silence around them. "No, Betty. I don't. The grave is a' we can look for. That and what we have now."

"But what about . . . ghosts, Rab?" She tugs at his sleeve. "Alloway Kirk's a ruin, is it no'? And I've heard tales . . . about what happens there at night."

He chuckles, the closest he's come to laughter all day. "Oh, I've heard them mysel'. About Alloway's haunted kirk. About Shanter's mare, that lost her tail savin' her master from a troop o' spirits they'd interrupted at their dancin' one market-night. A grand story, that."

"And ye're no' feart to have your father buried in sic a place?"

For a time he pictures the lonely kirkyard with its fresh grave under the cold stars, and a shiver runs through him as he realizes himself truly alone. No more judgments. No more dependence. Despair sits on his shoulder like the shadow of a hoodie crow. But despair will never do.

"My father never feared a thing," he says at last, "living or dead." He draws Betty close, pushing her nightgown down from her full breasts. "And if it come to that," he adds, this time forcing a chuckle, "yon spirits had better watch themsel's. For if I know my father, there'll be damned little dancin' at Alloway Kirk from this day forward"

Alloway Kirk and Graveyard

. . . Shenstone observes finely that love-verses writ without any real passion are the most nauseous of all conceits; and I have often thought that no man can be a proper critic of Love composition, except he himself, in one or more instances, have been a miserable dupe to Love, and have been led into a thousand weaknesses & follies by it, for that reason I put the more confidence in my critical skill in distinguishing foppery & conceit, from real passion & nature. . . .

– from the first *Commonplace Book*
April 1784

Chapter Two

The River Ayr undulates in a lazy sweep westward through its own broad valley to the Firth of Clyde. On a treeless ridge on that valley's north slope lies Mossgiel Farm. Robert stands in a field above the freshly-thatched and whitewashed buildings, looking a mile or so down the road to the south where the village of Mauchline huddles, tidy and grey, under threads of reek that hang twining in the wind; and farther yet, across the meandering sparkle of the river, he can see the Dalmellington hills at the other side of the valley, blue-green and misty, with a faint dust of snow about their crests.

Robert fills his nostrils and his chest with cold air, his ears singing to the quick rush of blood. The soil under his feet, he knows already, is little better than the poor earth he's worked these seven years at Lochlea Farm. But he'll be his own master now, he and Gibby partners in a new enterprise, and the fresh breeze infuses him with a hope no less real because he knows it will pass soon enough.

And he realizes, too, with sudden confidence, that he will write here: the surge in his veins makes him eager for the scratch of pen on paper and the lilt of a song. With the confusion of the past months, his father's death, the removal from Tarbolton, the work to put the new farm in order, he's taken little thought for poetry, except the pleasure he's drawn from reading Bob Fergusson's verses. Fergusson wrote the kind of stuff a man would be proud to set his name to, cast in the broad Scots to catch the life of the plain folk that spoke it, and full of their earthy humor and pleasure in homely sights, sounds, and customs. Much good it had done him, lying now in a pauper's unmarked grave in Edinburgh, where of all places such a writer should have been honored, but where the gentry and the literati had scarcely bestirred themselves to note his passing. Well, if Scotland treated its poets little better than its peasants, no one could deny them the pleasures of the language, its pungent words and rhythms that had substance on the tongue, like bannocks and honey, enlivened by the old tunes and inspired by a dram or a lass, aye, or both.

Robert sets off for the house, striding down the slope of the field with the tune of "Green Grow the Rashes" bubbling out of him. And he sings, unashamed of the voice his brother Willie has likened to the grate of a corn-crake, for pure pleasure of the song, not the new verses he wrote himself last year, but the old, bawdy words:

> The down bed, the feather bed,
> The bed amang the rashes O,
> Yet a' the beds is no' sae saft
> As the bellies o' the lasses O.

In the farmyard, Gibby stands among the boy-laborers, Davie Hutchieson, Willie Patrick, and John Blane. Robert can't hear what Gibby is telling them; he can only make out out the bailiff's tone that seems to creep into his brother's voice whenever he talks to the lads.

"Mind what he's telling ye, ye wee brocks, or it'll be skelps on the backside and nae porridge the night!" Robert delivers this broadly enough to be rewarded by laughter from the boys and a frown from Gibby at the interruption.

Robert tips Gibby a wink and crosses the yard to where his brother William and his cousin, Bob Allan – hired on as a ploughman from his home nearby Kilmarnock – are mending harness outside the stable. He arrives in time to take the big needle from Bob and complete the final difficult stitches through the double thickness of leather at the ring of a breast-strap.

"Where's your brother John?" he says to William, tying off the thread and handing the needle back to Bob.

William's habitually cheerful face darkens. "In by," he says. "Mither said he was lookin' too peely-wally to be out here. He's likely in his bed, or sittin' beside the fire."

Bob Allan shakes his head. "Poor wee laddie. He has a right sair time o' it."

"Maybe the spring will bring him round." Robert has no wish to let Bob, cousin or not, see the real depth of his concern for John's health. Many of William Burns' Tarbolton neighbors regarded his decline and death as a consequence of failure, and saw the family's removal to Mauchline as a flight from that humiliation and from the demeaning public exposure brought on by the legal battle against MacLure the landlord. The Burnses now look on any family misfortune as vaguely shameful, something to be kept within the walls of Mossgiel.

Robert decides to look in on John before resuming work in earnest. But as he starts for the house, Betty Paton emerges from the door, eyes puffy and cheeks glistening. She glances at him wildly, then, looking away, hurries toward the byre and disappears inside. After a moment's hesitation, Robert walks slowly to the house and pokes his head in at the door. His mother, Nancy, and Bell are standing just inside, in attitudes of surprise and indignation, while Isa sits on a stool at the ingle, arrested at the task of sewing a button on a shirt.

Robert raises his eyebrows at the scene. "What's up wi' Betty, then?" he says, hoping to sound no more than ordinarily curious.

Agnes Burns looks at her son, the dark eyes under her broad forehead almost as penetrating as his own. At fifty-two, despite having borne seven children, Agnes retains the red hair and glowing skin of her youth. "She's needed back wi' her folk at Lairgieside."

"What?" Robert is startled and annoyed. In the weeks since the move to Mossgiel, Betty has said nothing of this. "What do ye mean?"

Agnes sniffs. "When she was hame Sunday last, her faither tellt her. Her mither's poorly, and she's wanted there. She said nothing till the day. She had some daft thought o' keepin' it to hersel', at first. Then she thought if she spoke up, we'd tell her faither she couldna be spared."

Robert looks at the four women. "And what's happened, then?"

Nancy, eldest of the girls, plain-faced and strongly-built, speaks up. "Mither just tellt her the truth, Rab."

And Agnes continues: "I tellt her she was as well at hame, anyhow. Now that your faither's no' here, I've o'er much time on my hands. I canna thole idleness, and we canna afford to keep her if I'm back in the fray."

"Ye'd think she'd sooner be at hame wi' her ain," says Nancy. "I know I would."

"Aye," says Bell in her soft tones. "Especially wi' her mither no' weel."

Robert feels a flush spreading up from his neck, and hopes that the dim light of the house will hide it. "She's good-hearted," he says. "She's shared the family's sorrows these past months. And I expect she just likes it here, as well."

Agnes bobs her head impatiently. "Aye, she's goodhearted enough, and a decent worker. But she's a silly lassie."

"And a bit coarse," adds young Isa, sewing ladylike at the fireside.

Agnes shoots her a look. "Wheesht, you," she says.

Robert takes a deep breath. He can't allow his feeling to boil over now. Elaborately casual, he says, "I'll ha'e a talk wi' her."

Walking to the byre, he has time to think. His first notion on seeing Betty's distress was that she had somehow betrayed, or the other women had guessed, their intimacy. At least he's spared that squabble for the time being.

Betty looks up sullenly as he enters. She is half-kneeling, half-sitting in the hay, one hand clutching the rim of a milk-pail as if that might hold her to the farm.

"I'm no' goin' hame, Rab," she says.

Standing above her, he speaks gently. "I fear it has to be, Betty. Ye'll know best yoursel' how much your mother needs ye, and it's true that we're gey sair-pressed here."

She rises in a single motion, a note of panic in her voice. "But ye wouldna need to pay me, Rab. I'd work for nothing – only bed and board – just to be here!" She looks at him steadily, the stare of sexual promise undermined by her tear-swollen eyelids. "You want me here, don't ye?"

He takes her by the shoulders. "It canna be, Betty. Ye know that, yoursel'."

Fresh tears form and saturate her dense lower eyelashes, then spill over in two large drops that course down her face and drip, first one, then another, on her bosom. Her voice is a thick whisper. "I'll never see ye again."

He draws her to his chest, smelling the wetness of her tears mingled with the slightly acrid, smoky fragrance of her hair. "Aye, lass. You'll see me. Lairgieside's no' so far. We'll find ways to meet. Never fear."

She looks up. "As long as I can see ye now and then, Rab, I'll be a' right." A new note, calmer, enters her voice. "I know I can never look for ye to wed me. But I didna want to lose ye yet – no' as soon as this."

"Now, lass, dinna fash yoursel' about things like that. You're a' the lassie I care for, Betty." He hugs her again, then disengages himself, looking down at her. He lays a finger on her cheek. "Now, draw yoursel' thegither, and away back to the house wi' a smile on your face."

The corners of her mouth twitch unconvincingly as she moves to the byre entrance. Then she turns back. "Will I see ye the night, Rab?"

He smiles and nods. "Aye. When they're a' sound asleep. It'll be you and me, Betty, and the howlet's cry for a song."

As he watches her walk away, though, he thinks of what she said about the future, and he realizes she has instinctively grasped what he has ignored himself since their first embrace months ago: she is not the woman for him, not ultimately. And he recognizes suddenly that Betty's imminent departure for Lairgieside is tied somehow to the vista he saw before him from the high field: not just the sprawl of the valley and the town, but the accompanying sense of freedom, the stirrings of possibility.

"So ye're well settled at Mossgiel now, are ye, Rab?" Gavin Hamilton, square, solid, and confident in his rich blue coat and breeches, leans forward in his heavy oaken chair, drink in hand, handsome face creased with good humor.

Robert, seated in another of the carved-oak thrones, balancing his own whisky on his knee in a fine cut-glass tumbler that reflects its amber highlights on his hand, feels less uneasy now in Hamilton's study than on his first few visits. But he is still painfully conscious of his peasant's hodden gray clothing, the coarse woolens woven by Nancy and Bell; they chafe his skin here as they never do in spence or byre or field at Mossgiel.

"Aye, Mr. Hamilton. The house, as I've told ye before, is grand, better far than Lochlea. Ye did proud by us there. And if the seed I've laid in proves as good as it looked, we'll ha'e a muckle harvest. God knows we've worked hard enough. I've spent that many hours atween the plough-staves, I can feel them in my oxters as I sit here."

"Aye, I know ye've toiled hard and long, Rab. But don't look for too much this first year. Establishing a productive farm calls for a byornar deal o' patience." Hamilton sits back and drains his glass. "Is that no' right, Bob?"

Bob Aiken, who's been nodding in agreement with both men, sets his empty glass down on the small table nearby his chair. "Of course," he says, "Rab will know his own business better than any lawyer could. But there's little doubt that what ye say is the conventional wisdom, Gavin."

Robert shifts in his seat. "Fine I know it. Patience is a crop any poor farmer had best cultivate along wi' his corn, Mr. Hamilton."

Hamilton colors slightly, a bit discomposed by Robert's frank and pointed wit. He takes up the stone jar of whisky at his hand and rises. "Ha'e another dram, the pair o' ye." As he refills Robert's glass, he says, "And ye needna stand on ceremony, Rab. We're no' met here as landlord and tenant the night. We're three friends that relish good drink and good talk. Never mind the Misters – it's Bob and Rab and Gaw'n." Resuming his chair, Hamilton regards Robert cannily. "Ha'e ye formed any opinion yet on the local guardians o' our religious well-being?"

Robert falls silent for a bit. He knows from Tarbolton gossip that Hamilton has been at odds with the Mauchline parish minister, the Rev. William Auld, and his kirk elders, doubtless on the subject of the Auld Licht-New Licht controversy that currently divides the Church, at least in Ayrshire. The forces of conservatism, the Auld Lichts, cling implacably to the orthodox Calvinist faith that man is preordained to salvation or damnation, while the liberal New Lichts have the temerity to insist that a man might help himself into Heaven through a good heart and good works. Aside from some reform clergymen, most of the ministers and their Sessions – the Councils of Elders – hold with the Auld Lichts; but many of the younger gentry – like Hamilton and Aiken – and others tainted by a bit of secular education, are likely to embrace the New.

"I've had no dealings wi' Mr. Auld," says Robert carefully, "save for the day when I presented the Mauchline Session wi' our family's certificates o' character from Tarbolton parish. He seems a vigorous man for his age, stiff-necked like many another o' his cloth. But he was civil enough to me. He's given me little cause to doubt he's as fair-minded as a man might be that wears the Kirk's blinders."

Hamilton chuckles. "'The Kirk's blinders.' An apt phrase, right enough, Robert. I just hope ye never run afoul o' him. Auld he may be – in name and age – but when he – or his elders – fancy they've sniffed out a sinner, he's as zealous to mete out retribution as ever he was."

Winking at Robert, Bob Aiken pokes a stubby finger at Hamilton. "Gaw'n can tell ye a thing or two about Auld's zeal, a' right. The good minister's had his chief scourge o' sinners, Holy Willie Fisher – "

"Mean-spirited hound that he is!" Hamilton brings down his glass sharply on the arm of his chair, spilling a few drops of whisky. Then, more calmly, he turns to Robert, as if alarmed at the depth of his own feeling. "Fisher – and his crony James Lamie – comb the parish on Mr. Auld's behalf, spyin' out sin and passin' on full details to their master. Pigs howkin' for acorns couldna enjoy their work mair!" He glances at Aiken. "I beg your pardon for the interruption, Bob."

"Not at all, not at all." Aiken looks again to Robert. "Anyhow, Rab, as ye may have gathered, Auld has set Holy Willie and Lamie after Gavin. Aye, and they havena been idle. They've dug up such evidence o' sin as Gavin's settin' off on a journey to Carrick on the sabbath, and two or three other offenses near as black." He chortles, but then shakes his head ruefully. "And when they've satisfied their master wi' a lang enough list o' trivialities, I think they mean to bring Gavin before the Kirk Session to answer them."

Hamilton snorts. "It'll no' be the first time." He turns to Robert. "Auld wasna pleased to ha'e an apostle o' the New Licht as collector o' the stent for relief o' the poor, so he as much as accused me o' bein' a thief. He couldna win that case afore the Session, so now he's set his minions on me to gather such other sins as they might."

Aiken shakes his head. "And a' because Gavin has the spirit to disagree wi' them as concerns the right road to salvation."

As Aiken leans back in his chair, Robert realizes that his own opinion is called for. Hemming and hawing is a course he regards with contempt, so he resolves to speak his mind. "I don't know if there is such a place as Heaven," he says. "And if there is, I canna doubt there must be more than one road to it. But as for Auld Licht or New Licht, it seems to me the world's in sair need o' good hearts and good works. And the Kirk's far too full o' narrow-minded zealots so sure o' bein' among God's Chosen that they can sin day and daily and never smell the stink o' their ain hypocrisy."

"Well said, Robert! Well said!" Hamilton springs to his feet and replenishes their glasses again.

Robert sips his whisky and feels its warmth probing through his limbs. "Whatever licht may guide ye, Mr. Hamilton – New or Auld – I hope it'll shine bricht enough to blind Daddy Auld and his hounds."

Hamilton reaches out and slaps Robert's knee. "Gavin, lad – ca' me Gavin." Then a crooked smile spreads slowly across his face. "Daddy Auld and his hounds. They're blind enough, a'right. And by God, one o' these days their sniffin' will maybe lead them somewhere they'd sooner no' be. Eh, Bob?"

Aiken grins broadly, chuckling. "Aye, I'd gi'e a shillin' or twa to see Fisher stick his lang neb into a bees' nest."

In laughter, the three men toast the idea. Then Robert sets down his glass and rises to his feet. "I'm grateful for your hospitality," he says to his host, "but I'd best get back to Mossgiel. For there's ample work yet to be done, and I mauna leave Gibby to it while I sit at my leisure."

"Och, sit a minute an' gi'e us a sang, Rab," says Aiken. "Do ye no' ha'e anything new for us afore ye go?"

Robert claps Aiken on the back. "Another time, Bob. Ye ken I wouldna leave good drink and good company if I didna ha'e good reason."

"Let the lad alone, Bob," says Hamilton. "He knows his own mind." Then, walking with Robert to the study door, the landlord adds, "Bob's right, though, Rab. Next time we'll ha'e some o' your new verses – a far cheerier subject than Willie Fisher and his ilk."

Robert shakes hands with both men. "I'll see what I can do, Gavin. Though I fancy the foibles o' the Kirk might afford a subject worth a rhyme o' two, and maybe a couple o' laughs, as well."

Aiken wags a cautionary finger. "Just mind ye keep clear o' Willie Fisher, Robert. He's no' a man to thole bein' laughed at without nursin' a grudge."

Robert gives the lawyer a parting grin. "Never fear, Bob – he'll no' get me."

Walking out through Hamilton's public law office, Robert pauses at the clerk's desk, where John Richmond is hard at work copying legal papers with a grey goose quill. Richmond is in his mid-twenties, about Robert's age, fine-featured, with black hair, clear blue eyes, and a sensual curl to his lip. He and Robert have exchanged words once or twice before, and now he lays his pen down and gives Robert an appraising, but not unfriendly look.

"Well, Mr. Burns. You and Mr. Hamilton seem to ha'e found a lot in common."

Not quite sure how to take this, Robert responds guardedly. "We're both friends wi' Bob Aiken, if that's what ye mean – and we share a taste for poetry and good conversation."

Richmond smiles suddenly, showing a mouthful of healthy teeth. "Dinna take offense, Mr. Burns. I ken you're a poet. I've even heard some o' your verses and songs – and admired them. Mr. Hamilton likes nothing better than to pass the time in good talk – no' just idle clatter. I'm no' surprised he finds ye a welcome visitor."

Robert unbends, smiling himself. "Mr. Hamilton's a fair land-lord. And he's no' o'erimpressed wi' his position, like far too many o' the gentry. As ye say, I do a bit o' scribblin'. And it's a welcome relief after slavin' ahent a plough to share a dram and a blether wi' folk that relish a rhyme and a tune."

"And do ye never gi'e a thought to the lassies?" Richmond cocks his head and raises his eyebrows, blue eyes innocently wide.

Robert chuckles. "More than a thought, as ye'll know if ye've read my verses. I just havena had time latterly to do much about it. I suppose Mauchline has its fair share o' beauties?"

"An ample sufficiency. Aye, ye'll maybe find the Mauchline belles are worth a song or two before ye're done."

"Very likely. Maybe ye'd consider showin' me the sights, so to speak."

Richmond sits back on his high stool with a laugh, then extends his hand to Robert. "Done. And ye might just look in the night at Johnnie Dow's Whitefoord Arms at the Cowgate. Ye'll find there's more than a few folk in Mauchline wi' a ready tongue and a sharp wit."

Robert shakes Richmond's hand. "The Whitefoord Arms it is. And ca' me Rab – or whatever ye like, as long as it's no' Mr. Burns."

"And I'm Jock."

The outer door suddenly swings open and a young woman enters the office, carrying a small parcel. Dressed neatly and plainly, she is tall and fair-haired, with blue eyes as clear as Richmond's, but shading toward violet.

"I beg your pardon," she says, approaching Richmond, "but here is the sealing-wax Mr. Hamilton said he was wanting."

Her fluting voice carries the quaint formality and the lyrical rise and fall of the Highland tongue. As she hands over the parcel, Robert senses a momentary tension between her and Richmond, and he notes, too, her fine slim body, so different from Betty Paton's sturdy frame. A sprinkling of tiny pockmarks high on either cheek mars the girl's face, but its planes are cleanly-modeled, and she moves lightly, without self-consciousness.

While Richmond thanks her shortly, she looks at Robert, neither feigning shyness nor betraying interest, and without disdain for his peasant's clothes. "It is sorry I am for interrupting," she says, and turns to leave.

Unwilling to see her go, Robert opens his mouth and allows his tongue to lead his thoughts. "If I could be sure they'd aey come wi' such sweet sounds and such pleasant form, I might wish for a lifetime o' interruptions."

Turning back, she smiles at him. Her teeth are prominent, a bit uneven, though not unattractively so, and her lower lip is full, like a ripe berry. "I can see it's a flatterer you are," she says, and quickly leaves the office by a door that leads to another part of Hamilton's spacious house.

Robert looks at Richmond, who seems a trifle less jovial than before the girl's appearance. "Who is she?" he asks.

Richmond glances at the door. "Mary Campbell," he replies. "She's a servant to Mrs. Hamilton."

"A sonsie lass," says Robert. "I see you're right about the Mauchline belles, if she's anything to go by."

Richmond sniffs. "She's nae belle, that one. She kens the road to the broom, a' right."

Robert can't ignore a pang of disappointment. But he fights it down and laughs knowingly. "There's worse faults a lassie can have than the will to lie down to a likely lad." Then, carefully, he adds, "Ye'll maybe ha'e ta'en her that road yoursel'."

Caught, Richmond reddens. "No, worse luck." His voice drops and he nods toward the study door. "I suppose she didna want to foul her nest here wi' the Hamiltons. They're gey canny, yon Hielan queans." Then, brightening, he says, "Besides, I've my ain lass. And ye'll find far bonnier and mair likely lassies in Mossgiel than Mary Campbell – just you wait and see."

A short time later, Robert stands in the Backcauseway, just past the Carrier's Quarters on the outskirts of the village. Should he make directly for Mossgiel, he wonders, or cross over to the back and take a caup of ale at the Elbow Inn against the walk?

Before he can decide, though, he realizes that someone is standing near him. Turning, he confronts a thin, bony man of about fifty, who is watching him with moist eyes and a pinched mouth. The man, dressed in grey, though not the coarse hodden weave that Robert wears, gives a vaguely familiar clerical impression. Then Robert's memory jars. The Mauchline Kirk Session. This is none other than the worthy whose very name threw Gavin Hamilton into such a passion.

"Good day," Robert says, balanced between curiosity and irritation. "Mr. Fisher, is it?"

The man's eyes fix on a spot over Robert's shoulder, and he wets his thin lips before speaking. "Aye," he says. "William Fisher, Elder o' the Kirk. And you'll be Mr. Burns."

"That's right." Amused by the man's unease, Robert waits for what might follow.

Though still unwilling to meet Robert's eye, Fisher adopts a hectoring tone. "I see ye've just left Gavin Hamilton's."

Robert stiffens. "You're very observant, Mr. Fisher."

Fisher straightens his stooped shoulders momentarily and passes his watery gaze over Robert's face. "It's my duty as a Kirk Elder. Ooh, aye. My sworn duty."

Robert smiles ironically. "Then ye'll be well aware that Mr. Hamilton is my landlord."

"I am," says Fisher. "Ooh, aye. And I suppose that canna be mended. But I can tell ye've ta'en strong drink there. Ye'd be weel-advised, Mr. Burns, to confine your relations wi' that man to what's needfu', for he's no' a fit companion for Godly folk."

Anger swells inside Robert, but he checks himself with an effort and speaks lightly enough. "I'm grateful for your vigilance, Mr. Fisher. But I'll take a drink whenever it suits me. And I feel well able to judge for mysel' between fit and unfit companions. Good day to ye."

And having spoken, Robert turns and walks quickly in the direction of Mossgiel, leaving the speechless Elder gaping after him.

As the farms and the long ridge at its back come into close enough view for Robert to see Nancy and Isa hanging out the wash, his indignation fades, and he finds himself thinking of Jock Richmond's enthusiasm for the belles of Mauchline. He hasn't seen Betty for some weeks, and the thought of her stirs his body. But he knows that part of what excites him lies at his back, in the village. Possibility, unknown and enticing. And for all he tries to turn himself to the image of Betty, or the vaguer attractions of women yet unmet, he cannot help but admit to himself that, here and now, possibility wears fair hair and violet eyes.

Mossgiel

. . . I think the whole species of young men may be naturally enough divided in two grand Classes, which I shall
call the Grave, and the Merry; . . .

The Grave, I shall cast into the usual division of
those who are goaded on, by the love of money; and those
whose darling wish, is, to make a figure in the world. –
The Merry, are the men of Pleasure, of all denominations;
the jovial lads who have too much fire & spirit to have
any settled rule of action; but without much deliberation,
follow the strong impulses of nature: the thoughtless, the
careless, the indolent; and in particular He, who with a
happy sweetness of natural temper, and a cheerful vacancy
of thought, steals through life, generally indeed, in poverty
& obscurity; but poverty & obscurity are only evils to
him, who can sit gravely down, and make a repining com-
parison between his own situation and that of others; and
lastly to grace the quorum, such are, generally, the men
whose heads are capable of all the towerings of Genius,
and whose hearts are warmed with the delicacy of Feeling
. . .

from the first *Commonplace Book*
April 1784

Chapter Three

"**A**ye, she is, a' right!"

At the sound of raised voices, John Burns, seated at the fireside ingle with a blanket drawn around him, awakens from fitful sleep, his breath coming in shallow gasps. He sees his sister Nancy standing at the kitchen table with a knife in her hand, poised over a partly-sliced loaf of bread. His mother and Bell are nearby, but Isa is nowhere to be seen. John holds still, knowing that so long as he does the women will talk as if he isn't there.

"And where did ye hear this, if I maun ask?" Agnes Burns pauses in the midst of carding wool and fixes her dark eyes on her eldest daughter.

"It's no' something I'd want to bring up if I could help it," says Nancy, her eyes wide and her face flushed a mottled pattern of scarlet and white.

"It's true, Mither," chimes in Bell. "We got the news o'er by, in Mauchline. It was common gossip. We thought we should let ye know so ye could ask our Robert about it."

"And what body in Machlin would ken onything aboot a lassie that's been awa' in Lairgieside these three months?" Agnes compresses her lips and looks at each of the girls in turn.

John senses that his mother is close to outright anger, but whether at his sisters or at someone else, he can't tell. He knows that the Lairgieside lassie must be Betty Paton, though, and he wonders what she can have to do with his brother Rab.

"Lairgieside's no' that far awa', Mither." Nancy speaks with unaccustomed quietness. "And bad news doesna sit long in one place."

Agnes rises, dropping the wool she's been working at. "Aye," she says. "Well, we'll see aboot this." She crosses to the table. "I'll just take your brithers their breid and cheese."

"But that's my job," says Isa, who has just come in unnoticed at the door. Before the youngest daughter can speak more, Agnes silences her with a look.

"Mither," says Bell. "He canna marry that ane! She's no' fit to be part o' this family."

Agnes glowers at her. "That brither o' yours has already ta'en her intae the family, by the sound o' things."

And as his mother leaves for the high field, carrying bread, cheese, and beer in a bag, John looks around at his sisters.

"What's up, then?" he asks.

"Never you mind," says Nancy. "Go back to sleep."

Robert and Gibby stand side by side among the other workers, harvesting corn on the high rig, shirts soaked with sweat in the raw November air. Normally, their sisters would be here, too, working beside them; but the harvest is so poor and so late that they have no need of the women. This should be a time for song and laughter, a time to celebrate the just rewards of their year's labor. But instead they toil in silence, cutting and gathering the dwarfish, meager-eared stalks, Gibby keeping his thoughts to himself as usual, and Robert miserable in the knowledge that this harvest is the product of the seed he bought so hopefully months before.

Gibby pauses, hands on hips, then points down the slope toward the farmhouse. "It's Mither," he says to Robert.

Robert straightens, bringing his shoulder-blades together to relieve the burning ache between them, and follows where Gibby's finger picks out the small figure making its way toward them. "Bringing us a bite to eat, by the look o' it," he says.

"I wonder what's up wi' our Isa?" says Willie Burns. "That's usually her job."

Frowning, Gibby looks at Robert. "The laddie's right. It's seldom Mither ventures up this length."

"Aye." Robert passes his forearm across his wet brow. Something about his mother's stiff-backed walk tells him that she doesn't intend to cheer them up.

When Agnes arrives among the men, she sets the bundle of food down on a cart. "There's your bite, lads," she says to the workers. Then she turns to Robert. "I want a word wi' you," she says. As she begins to move away from the others, she adds to Gibby, "You'd better hear this as well, I suppose." And when Willie Burns makes to follow his brothers, she snaps at him: "You get back to your food!"

When they've moved down out of earshot on the damp stubble, Gibby says, "Well, Mither, what is it? Bad news?"

Snorting ruefully, Robert bobs his head, indicating the fields around them. "Aye, Mither. What could be worse than what ye see up here?"

Agnes glares at him. "Aye. Ye have the face to say that to me at sic a time. I daresay ye'll ken weel enough what brings me up here."

Robert feels himself redden and his stomach turns over. "Is it Betty?"

His mother's mouth tightens into a small bitter smile and her eyes seem to darken. "Aye," she says. "Betty."

Gibby looks from one to the other of them. "What about Betty?" he says at last.

His face hot with shame, Robert says, "She's expecting a bairn."

"His bairn," Agnes informs Gibby needlessly.

Gibby shakes his head. "For God's sake, Robert. As if things werena bad enough already." He throws his arms in the air, then folds them, sighing gustily. "I canna say I'm surprised, as long as the pair o' ye ha'e been at it."

Robert looks at his brother in shock. "You knew about Betty and me? And ye never let on? You're a cool one, I must say."

Gibby stares back at him. "Let on to who? To you? What good would it ha'e done me?"

"Nae mair good nor it ever did his faither to bring him up short for his misdeeds." Agnes shakes her head, looking at Robert with eyes that could wither the poor corn still unreaped. Then she turns on Gibby. "Ye might ha'e let on to me. I'd ha'e minded him o' his obligations, even if you couldna bring yoursel' to it. And maybe then we wouldna ha'e needed to get the first word o' his shame in the streets o' Machlin." She swings back to Robert. "I wish the seed ye'd sown about these fields had been as fertile as what ye ploughed into yon silly hizzie."

"Mither!" says Gibby. "Ye canna gi'e Robert the blame for everything. The seed he bought looked fine to me, as well. None o' us could ha'e done mair to help this harvest!"

"Weel," says Agnes, "there'll be plenty to gi'e him blame now. Willie Paton and his wife. And the Tarbolton Session. And dinna think this'll pass unnoticed in Machlin Kirk, either. Your sisters'll be shamed before the town." Her outburst subsides. "There's nothing for it. Ye'll just need to do the right thing by the lassie."

"Rab marry Betty Paton?" Gibby's voice rises in disbelief. "Och, Mither, ye canna be serious."

"And what else do ye think he should do?" Agnes demands. "Lea'e the lassie to shift for hersel'? He's ta'en his pleasure o' her, and now he maun take responsibility."

Gibby bows his head. "I suppose you're right, Mither," he mutters. "That'll help a bit if he's to be compeared afore the Tarbolton Session."

Robert feels his pulse race with sudden anger. "Ye're as sanctimonious as a Presbytery, the pair o' ye!" he says. "Ye've judged a' that's to be judged without so much as a thought for what I want – aye, or what Betty might want, hersel'!"

"Ye'll no' stand there," says Agnes, "and tell me that lassie wouldna want ye to wed her at sic a time! And as for what you want, I fear that's plain enough!"

"Mither!" says Gibby, ever the mediator. "We canna settle that here and now. We'll need to wait till we can sit and think it a' out."

Angered even by his brother's good sense, Robert says, "The two o' ye can sit and think a' ye like. But afore ye settle matters to your satisfaction, I'll thank ye to let me do a bit o' thinkin' o' my ain!" And so saying, he brushes past Gibby, stays well clear of his mother, and moves off down the hill toward the farmhouse, leaving them to stare at each other open-mouthed.

The Reverend William Auld looks expectantly across his writing-table at his two most useful Elders, James Lamie and William Fisher. "Well, gentlemen, and what have ye to report today?"

Lamie, plump and red-faced, leans toward the minister and speaks as if he fears being overheard. "Hamilton's keepin' his horns weel-in this weather. I fear we've nothing to add to what we ha'e already."

Auld shakes his head impatiently. "The matter o' Hamilton is well in hand, I trust. Once the Presbytery kens the extent o' the man's iniquity, we'll maybe see his heretical influence curbed in this parish. If he – "

"Ooh, aye." Unable to restrain himself any longer, Fisher breaks in. "Ye may be sure we'll get him, noo, Mr. Auld."

"It's never been our object to 'get' anybody, Mr. Fisher." Auld compresses his lips briefly, then adds, "We're merely exercising the authority God grants us to remind folk o' their duties before Him. Hamilton has brought himsel' to this pass."

"Ooh, aye, Mr. Auld." Fisher waves his hands before him, as if warding off the minister's displeasure. "It's as you say. But Hamilton's surrounded himsel' wi' heretics and fornicators, now, so we should ha'e nae bother showin' the Presbytery the extent o' his iniquity, as ye ca' it."

"What heretics and fornicators do ye mean, Mr. Fisher?"

"That's just what we maun tell ye, Mr. Auld." Fisher looks to James Lamie for corroboration "It's right what I'm sayin', Jeems, is it no'?"

Lamie coughs nervously, then spreads his hands and shrugs. "It's true we've had our eye on Hamilton's clerk, Jock Richmond, an' the lassie Surgeoner."

Auld fixes Lamie with his grey-eyed stare. "Fine I know that Richmond's been keeping company wi' Jenny Surgeoner. Do ye have anything material to report on their conduct?"

Lamie shakes his head. "No' yet, Mr. Auld. But I've nae doubt we'll see results afore lang."

Auld swings his attention to Fisher. "I fail to understand, then – "

"Aye, but Mr. Auld" – Fisher's hands are trembling before him, now – "ye maun hear this. Robert Burns o' Mossgiel – this new tenant o' Hamilton's – the verses he writes, wi' his landlord's hearty approval, are heretical enough by a' accounts. And now he's branded himsel' a fornicator and a', wi' some lassie frae Lairgieside. We maun ha'e him on the cutty stool for that!"

"I've heard tell o' the matter," says Auld. "Betty Paton is the girl's name. It's regrettable that this Burns should go astray so soon after his arrival hereabouts. But I doubt that his sins wi' Betty Paton began in Mauchline parish, or for that matter that they had much to do wi' Gavin Hamilton's influence. In any event, the case belongs to Tarbolton, so it's there that Burns maun take the cutty stool."

Fisher's eyes widen and his mouth opens and closes several times. "Aye, but Mr. Auld – "

Auld continues. "More to the point, Mr. Fisher, what about these verses ye speak o'? What form does their heresy take?"

"Weel." Fisher wipes a hand over his lips before saying more. "Ye'll ken, Mr. Auld, that sic folk as pass these verses frae hand to hand would scarcely let Jeems or me ha'e a look at them if they could help it. But there's nae doubt that this Burns attacks the very Kirk itsel'. Is that no' the way o' it, Jeems?"

The plump Elder reddens a bit more behind his usual high color. "Now I couldna just say that, Willie." Turning to Auld before Fisher can interrupt him, Lamie goes on, "But the few scraps I've heard folk comin' o'er surely gi'e ample cause for worry about Burns' effect on the moral and religious well-being o' the parish."

In a deliberate show of strained patience, Auld lays both hands palm down on his writing table. "But what is it ye've actually read – or heard?" he says.

"Weel," says Fisher, "there's ane sang Jeems has heard that starts aff, 'Nae churchman am I to rail and to write,' and ends up ca'in' a man o' the cloth 'an auld prig.' Jeems?"

"Aye." Lamie warms to the subject. "And the sang does nothing but praise strong drink, even to the length o' ca'in' it the equal o' Heaven."

Fisher, mouth working away, again turns his watery eyes on Auld. "What do ye think o' that, eh? It's a' sangs in praise o' drink and loose women for that fellow, wi' nae regard for the Kirk or them that values it."

Auld shakes his head. "A line or two from a drinking song is scant evidence against the man. Especially without further proof that he even made it up. And it certainly adds nothing to the case against Hamilton."

Fisher sputters. "But Mr. Auld – "

"Gentlemen!" Auld cuts him off. "I have little doubt that if Burns is as black as ye paint him, his nature will come to light in due course. Meantime, I recommend patience and continued vigilance."

Sensing that the minister's own supply of patience has dwindled, Fisher glances at Lamie, who has backed a step or two toward the door, face crumpled into a tight smile. Backing away himself, Fisher nods and says, "Just so, Mr. Auld. Ooh, aye. Just so. Ye may rely on us, never fear."

When the two Elders have left and closed the door behind them, Auld looks at a wisp of cobweb on the low ceiling of his small study and draws his breath in through his teeth. Robert Burns will keep for another day, he knows. But he cannot suppress a twinge of regret that Fisher and Lamie are the instruments likely to bring about his inevitable confrontation with the young man. Ah, well. He mauna question the ways of the Lord.

Robert makes his way toward Mauchline through a grey haze of drizzle, keeping as best he can to the grassy verge instead of the boggy road. His hair, tied back in its customary queue, is soaked, letting a steady trickle of water run down inside his collar. His clothes cling to him like a frog's skin, and the sheen of rain on his face feels more real to him than the air he breathes.

As he walks, he thrusts a hand into his coat pocket and fingers the letter folded within. It came to him yesterday, from John Rankine of Adamhill Farm near Tarbolton, warning him that word of Betty's condition was out and giving him at least some preparation for his mother's ire. Rankine is far from being a gossip, but he does have a wide circle of acquaintance in Tarbolton and beyond, and a taste for convivial fellowship that keeps him well abreast of local talk. That taste, in fact, brought Rankine and Robert together for the first time only months before William Burns' death, when the young man had need of an older friend who knew firsthand the trials of a farmer. At William's funeral Rankine had kept to the background, and later at Simson's he had damped his ready wit, Robert knows, in deference to the occasion and the many friends with prior claims.

But now Adamhill has roused his wit to tax his young friend. For the letter Robert carries in his pocket is not merely a warning: Rankine has made Betty's trouble and Robert's certain discomfiture the occasion for a few coarse observations in Scots on the conduct of young men and the maids they entice "amang the rigs o' barley"; the reference is to a song of Robert's written to commemorate his dalliance with Rankine's youngest daughter, Annie, in a field near Adamhill after he'd enjoyed an evening of drink and talk with her father.

The thought makes Robert squirm inwardly as he walks, not so much because Rankine obviously knows about his night with Annie, but because the older man has more than once made clear his hope that the poet might someday be his son-in-law. Rankine cannot help but be nettled at the news of Betty, but he has characteristically chosen humor as his weapon: "Ye ha'e herried the wrang nest this time, my lad," the letter reads, "and noo the game-keeper and the poacher-court maun ha'e their due. Though I canna say but it's seldom the poacher leaves eggs where there were none afore! But ye may be sure that your bonie wee hen will want whatever chicks may hatch to ken their faither."

Robert's face feels hot enough to turn the rain to steam. Why must everything come down on him at once? A bad harvest is surely enough to contend with. But he can hear his mother's rejoinder already. "Ye've done this to yersel', my lad. It's your ain blame." And he can scarcely argue with that. But is he never to have so much as a taste of good luck? When he does wrong, he always pays at the final reckoning; fair enough, maybe. But even his best-laid schemes seem doomed by ill-fortune.

And now what? Marriage to Betty, as his mother would have it? He wipes a drop of rain from the end of his nose. No. Whatever may lie ahead, it won't be marriage to Betty, any more than to Annie Rankine, bonie as they both may be. The child must be provided for, of course. But he must keep some freedom, such as it may be, or he can look forward to nothing but the same obscure drudgery and death as his father. And in that realization, bleak as it seems, Robert feels a surge of warmth and strength go though him like strong drink. He looks through the rain at the trees beyond the road, where on a low branch a thrush sits with its wings hanging down on either side to shed the water; and as he watches, he hears the bird loose a sudden ripple of song, as if to remind itself what it was put on earth for. The simple sound sets music dancing in Robert's own veins, and the squelch-squelch of his boots on the sodden grass gives background to the defiant words forming in his head as reply to Rankine:

> 'Twas ae night lately, in my fun,
> I gaed a rovin' wi' the gun,
> An' brought a paitrick to the grun' –
>   A bonie hen;
> And, as the twilight was begun,
>   Thought nane wad ken.

The poor wee thing was little hurt;.
I straikit it a wee for sport,
Ne'er thinkin they wad fash me for't;
      But, Deil-ma-care!
Somebody tells the poacher-court
      The hale affair.

Some auld, us'd hands had ta'en a note,
That sic a hen had got a shot;
I was suspected for the plot;
      I scorn'd to lie;
So gat the whissle o' my groat,
      An' pay't the fee.

But by my gun, o' guns the wale,
An' by my pouther an' my hail,
An' by my hen, an' by her tail,
      I vow an' swear!
The game shall pay, o'er muir an' dale,
      For this, neist year

The Elbow Inn stands ahead of him now. He'll find paper there to write on with the old pencil-stub he always carries with him. He'll work the lines in his head into a letter in verse for Rankine; though it may take a while, he knows it will come. For whatever else happens, the song is always there, just waiting to be sung, as near at hand and undeniable as the thrush warbling in the rain.

Hughie Meldrum, the Elbow's landlord, looks up from where he's been feeding peat into the fireplace. Seeing Robert on the threshold, dripping wet, Meldrum rises. "God, Mr. Burns, ye're like a drookit rat. Ye didna fa' in a dub, did ye?"

"No, Hughie." Robert wipes his face with his handkerchief. "I've just been out for a turn in the fresh air."

Meldrum laughs. "A turn in the fresh air, eh? Weel, come awa' in an' warm yoursel' at the fire, laddie. An' ye maun heat your insides wi' a dram, an' a'."

"Aye. And some sheets o' writin' paper, if ye please." Robert crosses the room and sits on a stool at the ingle-nook, where he can watch the blue and orange flames shift and dance in the fireplace, and let the heat get at his rain-soaked clothes.

The Elbow, on the outskirts of the village, is seldom full at the best of times, and so early on a dreich day like this it is all but empty. Apart from himself and Meldrum's wife Sarah, Robert can only see a pair of old fellows nursing pints of ale in the snug. That suits him fine in his present mood, for he feels like writing, not talking. And write he does, finishing Rankine's verse epistle and two fragments that, inconsequential though they may be, help him to put a better light on things as they stand.

At length, laying down his pencil, he thinks of what lies ahead: a conference with the Patons, surely, to discuss what will become of Betty and the bairn; and the cutty stool, of course, likely as not in Tarbolton parish, where the lovers' sins commenced. Better to endure chastisement there than in Mauchline, where he'll have to face folk Sunday after Sunday. It'll be bad enough, in any case, even if Tarbolton's aging minister, the Reverend Dr. Patrick Wodrow, will let his assistant John McMath handle the compearing. McMath will still have to give both Robert and Betty a sound moral drubbing to satisfy Wodrow's ecclesiastical conscience.

Ah, well, it must be endured, he supposes. But what would they have a young man do? Live like a damned monk, never taking a chance, doing nothing but work and pray? And pray for what, since the black bonnets leave nothing on earth to be enjoyed or savored? Maybe Gibby can thole day after day like that, but not Robert. He shivers with a deep inner chill that neither whisky nor the crackling fire have quite dispelled.

"Hughie!" he shouts. "Another dram."

As the landlord moves toward him with the whisky bottle, Robert sees a man with a coat over his arm emerging from the private room opposite the snug. The man, about fifty by the look of him, is square-faced and florid, with a hard-looking paunch, and he carries himself with a military air. Looking around him as if used to giving orders, the newcomer eyes Robert appraisingly, nods once to the landlord, then pulls on his coat and walks out of the Elbow into the rain.

Meldrum fills Robert's glass and looks at him conspiratorially, laying a finger along his nose. "Captain Montgomerie," he says, inclining his head toward the door. "Lord Eglinton's brother, d'ye ken?"

Robert grunts noncommittally, though he is mildly surprised. What might attract his Lordship's brother to the Elbow Inn? He looks at the door of the private room, which tells him nothing. But he's loathe to indulge himself by speiring at Meldrum; a man's affairs should be safe from idle gossip. He drinks off his whisky and rises, pocketing pencil and paper. "I'd best be away, mysel'," he says to Meldrum, handing the little landlord several coins. "I think the rain's nearly stopped."

But as he opens the outside door to leave, Robert hears a sound behind him. He turns to see a fair-haired young woman approaching him from the back of the inn. Her violet eyes open wider as she recognizes him, and she stops, glancing around her in apparent confusion.

"Mary Campbell," he says.

She looks at him, blinking once or twice. "Good day, Mr. Burns."

Impulsively, he holds a hand out to her. "Can I see you back to Mr. Hamilton's?"

For a moment, watching her face, he's convinced she'll refuse his offer. But she finally says, "It's very kind you are," and moves toward him.

And looking into her heather-hued eyes, he realizes that this puzzling young woman will always keep part of herself secret, untouchable, just as whatever makes him write verses will continue to separate him from those around him. And he knows, too, as she takes his elbow, that he and Mary Campbell are destined to share secrets yet unspoken.

Song
Tune: "Black Joke"

My girl she's airy, she's buxom and gay;
Her breath is as sweet as the blossoms in May;
    A touch of her lips it ravishes quite.
She's always good natur'd, good humor'd & free;
She dances, she glances, she smiles upon me
    I never am happy when out of her sight.
Her slender neck her handsome waist
Her hair well curl'd stays well lac'd
Her taper white leg with an et and a c,
for her a, b, c, and her c, ? t,
    And O for the joys of a long winter night.

        – from the first *Commonplace Book*
        September 1784

Chapter Four

As you go forth from this place to other parishes, as I know both of you will, think on the shame you've endured here, and remember the sins of the flesh that brought you to such a pass. You should be well aware that fornication is ever despicable in the eyes of the Lord, and that His laws mauna be flouted. No decent Christian need be reminded that the only proper union between man and woman is the one sanctified by the Kirk in the holy bond o' matrimony."

Pausing in the flow of his rhetoric, John McMath looks down from the pulpit, first at Betty Paton and then at Robert Burns, as they sit cramped and awkward on the absurdly short-legged cutty stools before the Tarbolton congregation. The position must be doubly difficult for the girl, the minister knows, with the now obvious burden she carries before her. And pity briefly softens the hard lines into which McMath has set his face for these final moments of ceremonial rebuke. As his hesitation lengthens, he sees the Reverend Dr. Patrick Wodrow, whom he serves as assistant, frowning at him from among the other expectant faces in the front row, and he makes himself go on.

"You, Robert, and you, Elizabeth, must now resolve to cleave to the path of righteousness, and to remove the stain from this unborn soul, the product of your transgression, by providing the loving home and Godly upbringing to which it is entitled."

McMath looks at Robert, barely four years his junior, whom he would far rather be facing over a drink at John Simpson's, and attempts to give some sign of fellow-feeling; but Robert's eyes seem directed past him, or through him. And as Robert's head finally bows, the young minister wishes for a moment he could shake his friend by the shoulders, make him understand that McMath, too, is suffering, and that a man must endure such moments patiently.

Clearing his throat, McMath speaks directly to Robert: "As a man, with a man's strength and a man's wisdom, you must bear the lion's share of responsibility both for this misconduct and for the child's future. And may your life from this day forward serve as a true example of virtue that will far outshine the blackness of the sin we charge you with here, the occasion of God's just wrath and the righteous ire of His congregation. Go forth and sin no more!"

Breathing deeply, McMath descends from the pulpit, relinquishing it to Mr. Wodrow for the closing prayer. And as he sits listening to the drone of the old man's voice, he realizes that, even though he would like to abolish the grotesque and humiliating ceremony of the cutty stool, he would nonetheless have wished as a minister to have offered some good counsel to Robert at such a time. But he knows that his words from the pulpit were far from what he would have said; and he reflects, too, that within Robert Burns lies a place essentially unreachable, not merely by his fellow man, but by God himself.

"And what way do ye ettle to mak things richt, then, Mr. Burns?" Willie Paton sits with Robert on a low stone dyke, broken and tumbled, outside the Patons' mean cottage, while Betty and her mother wait inside. "Ye may ken there's nae keepin' a bairn here wi' Mrs. Paton no' weel, an' little enough siller to keep us a' as it is." Paton briefly massages the back of his neck with one hand, then flattens both hands palm down on the knees of his coarse woolen trousers and looks at Robert.

Robert glances at the cottage, where he can see Betty standing in the shadows near the window, hands clasped over her swollen belly. He feels a sudden surge of affection and pity for her, but he turns back to Paton. "Ye'd hardly want to lose Betty, then," he says, "for I'm sure she gi'es her mother the best o' care."

"But whit aboot the bairn?" Paton's bulbous nose wrinkles, and he wags a finger to emphasize his point. "Betty canna weel attend to her mither wi' a babby to run after."

Robert marvels, as he has before, that a well-formed lass like Betty, plain-faced though his sisters may call her, can have sprung from the Patons, both of whom are squat and lumpish. "Ye needna worry about the child, Mr. Paton. I'll see that it's provided for."

Paton shakes his head, unconvinced. "But how, Mr. Burns? How? That's the question."

"Well," says Robert, "when the bairn arrives, I'll come and take it to Mossgiel where my mother and sisters can care for it. It's mine. I freely acknowledge that. And I'll take full responsibility for it. If Betty's agreeable, of course." Robert's confident tone gives no hint of the heated Burns family discussions that preceded his offer.

Paton nods, considering. "Ye'll no' wed Betty, then," he says at last. And with some bitterness, he adds, "My dochter wouldna mak a fit wife for ye, nae doubt."

Robert rises abruptly, dislodging a few small stones from the dyke, and walks a few paces before turning back to Paton.

"Your daughter's a bonnie lass, Mr. Paton," he says, measuring the pitch of his voice. "She'd mak any man a grand wife, and I've little doubt she will, someday. But, as ye've said said yoursel', she's needed here. And I've far too many obligations o'er by at Mossgiel to let me aspire to the status o' a married man."

He pauses, looking at a scatter of water-worn pebbles around his feet, still carefully choosing his words. "I ken ye may feel a single man has little defense for meddlin' wi' a young lassie, however willin' she might ha'e been, and ye'd be right to say so. And ye needna think I havena heard that from my ain family, for I have. But we maun think o' what's best for two families here, even if it's no' just what the Kirk might tell us." He looks Paton in the eye. "So what do ye say, then, Mr. Paton?"

Paton rises and walks over to Robert. After a moment or two, he extends his hand. "It's fair enough, what ye say, Mr. Burns, . . . Robert, if I may ca' ye that. It's no' what I micht ha'e wanted for my lassie, but it's fair enough."

The two men shake hands. Then Paton inclines his head toward the house. "Ye'll want to see Betty yoursel', noo, I fancy." Robert nods, and the little man starts for the cottage door. "I'll just send her oot, then."

Robert sits back down on the broken wall. When Betty emerges from the house after a short time, he rises to meet her.

"Well, lass," he says, holding out a hand to her.

She looks up at him steadily, but doesn't take his hand. "My faither tellt us," she says, her voice flat. "So that'll be that, I suppose."

He takes her gently by the arms, feeling her muscles tighten at his touch. He is acutely conscious of the Patons' presence behind the cottage window. "I've never deceived ye, Betty," he says quietly. "Ye kennt from the start we were never meant to be man and wife. But that doesna mean I dinna care for ye, lass."

She steps back from him. "When the bairn comes, and ye tak it to Mossgiel, I'll never see ye again, will I?"

Again he speaks as tenderly as he can. "I've said I never deceived ye, Betty. And I'll no' deceive ye now. What ye say is as like as no'. I'm no' the man for marriage, and aiblins I never will be. And it wouldna be right to stand in open defiance o' the Kirk's minions. But I'll never regret the times we've had thegither. Far from it: I'll aey prize them. And I can only wish that the bairn may inherit its mother's handsome looks and grace, and that it'll be kept free o' its father's failin's."

Betty shakes her head and clicks her tongue, seeming already like the mother she's to become. "Rab, Rab," she says softly, "ye've a voice that would charm the birds oot o' the sky, so ye have. Thae Mauchline lassies had best stick to their spinnin' wheels as lang as you're aboot, I'm thinkin'."

He gathers her into his arms as best her condition will allow. How well she knows him, he thinks. And how much he'll miss her earthy frankness. He kisses her temple, feeling under his lips the pulse that beats there, beats for two hearts together. "Never mind Mauchline or its lassies, Betty," he whispers in her ear. "Come and tak a walk wi' me amang the heather afore I have to go."

Robert looks around the large central room of Willie Muir's mill, at the light from the fire dancing in the eyes and on the whisky-flushed faces of Muir and John Rankine. "It's no' right!" he declares, pounding his knee with a fist. "I've tellt the Patons I'll take in Betty's wean. Now that's responsibility. But no – yon sanctimonious set o' prigs o'er by could only be satisfied wi' seein' the pair o' us shamed afore them!"

"Ca' canny, Rab," says Willie Muir. "I was there mysel', as ye ken weel enough, an' so was John, an' no' because we wanted to see ye shamed. A man needs frien's aboot him at sic a time."

Robert waves his hand impatiently. "I ken ye meant well, the pair o' ye. But there's no' much can help a man on that damned stool. It's bad enough to hear yoursel' sniggered about in country clatter, but to sit still for what John McMath had to say – and him a frien' and a' – well, it's a sair dunt, I can tell ye."

John Rankine leans forward to squeeze Robert's arm. "Ye ken John McMath had his job to do, Rab. And at that ye maun be thankful ye got him instead o' auld Wodrow, for he'd ha'e gie'd ye hells-fire, right enough."

Robert empties his wooden cup, swirling the whisky around his mouth before swallowing. "Ye're right, nae doubt, John. But I'd fain mak a bonfire out o' every cutty stool in Scotland – aye, and maybe wi' a wheen o' black bonnets to help the blaze."

Muir and Rankine chuckle at Robert's vehemence, and he finally gives them a grudging smile, himself. Muir refills Robert's coggie. "Anither swallow or twa o' this'll fuel your ain bleeze. An' aiblins ye'll ha'e the best o' the black bonnets afore a's said an' done."

"Aye, and written," says Rankine, "if what ye've sent to me's onythin' to go by."

Muir pours more whisky for himself and Rankine. "We'll drink to a better future, then." But before they can act on the toast, he holds up a hand. "Na, ha. Haud on. Rab – what was yon toast ye came o'er at Simson's on the day we buried your faither?"

"The present hour," says Robert quietly, touched that Willie has remembered.

"Aye," adds Rankine, "and present company, and a'."

"That's it." Muir smiles broadly. "The present hour, and present company!"

As the three men raise their coggies, they hear a knock at the mill's door. "What's this, I wonder?" says Muir as his wife hurries to answer the summons.

Mrs. Muir opens the door and admits John McMath, who stands just over the threshold. "I kenned ye'd be here before the journey hame," he says to Robert, "so I thought I'd just drop in for a minute." He looks at Willie and Mrs. Muir. "Begging your pardon for the presumption."

Willie bounces to his feet and crosses to the door. "Now, now, now," he says, taking the minister by the arm, "dinna talk rubbish, John. Ye maun save that for the pulpit! Now come awa' in."

Amid the general laughter at this, he leads McMath to a chair at the fire, and gestures to Mrs. Muir. "Anither coggie for Mr. McMath, Mither. An' aiblins a whang o' kebbuck an' a'."

When Mrs. Muir has brought McMath a cup and set out bread and cheese, Willie pours the minister a generous measure of whisky, then breaks the silence that has fallen. "We were juist aboot to drink a toast, John," he says, raising his coggie. "The present hour and present company."

McMath raises his own cup. "That's a rare toast, Willie, one I'll gladly drink to."

Robert can't forbear a comment. "Even wi' sic a notorious fornicator, John?"

McMath flushes. "If I didna want to drink wi' ye, Robert, I wouldna be here now," he says. "Fine ye ken I admire ye. As I admired your father, and a'. The Kirk makes demands on every one o' us – on you as well as me – and we mauna shirk our duty."

Again, Robert feels he must speak. "Nae doubt ye're right, John. But I think ye maun agree there's demands the Kirk needna mak on any o' us – demands that ha'e less to do wi' the Lord's will than the mean-mindedness o' them that act as if what they think must be what He thinks."

McMath sets down his cup and looks at the two older men, then at Robert. "The cutty stool is a custom I could well do without. And I could wish for a bit more enlightenment from a good many o' the shepherds that lead the faithful hereabouts, and a'. The Kirk's at odds wi' itsel', and until that struggle's settled we'll a' need to watch how we go – like your landlord Gavin Hamilton, Robert. And whatever I can do to come between honest folk and abusers o' the Kirk's power, ye may ken I'll do it." He swallows some whisky, then addresses Robert again, frowning and shaking his head. "But I canna do a thing if I turn my back on my duty."

"Well said, John." Robert leans across to McMath and offers his hand.

And as the two men shake hands, John Rankine says, "That's the spirit, lads. And now, Willie, what about that toast?"

Later that week Johnnie Dow's Whitefoord Arms is cheek-by-chow with folk, their heads buzzing with strong drink and the sound of their own voices. And ranged about the inn's back room, where they can at least hear each other, are Robert, Jock Richmond, Jamie Smith, William "Tanner" Hunter, and John "Clockie" Brown.

Robert and Jock Richmond have been in Dow's, drinking steadily, since finishing their day's labor, Robert in the fields and Richmond at Gavin Hamilton's office, and they are already light-headed with whisky and defiance of convention. The two friends have been drawn closer to each other by recent events, for Richmond will soon face the same agenda of clerical abuse that Robert has just endured. But now Robert is bent over a sheet of paper with his ever-present pencil stub, while Richmond rails again at the Elders.

"Yon sleekit buggers trailed after Jenny and me for weeks, be damned to them." Richmond runs his fingers through his thick black hair as if trying to keep anger from escaping directly through his skull. He looks over at the little Mauchline draper, Jamie Smith. "I'll tell ye, Jamie," he says, "yon stepfather o' yours had best no' run afoul o' me on a dark nicht onywhere near deep watter."

"Ye needna think the drownin' o' that ane would gi'e me cause to greet, Jock," says Smith, who has often borne the marks of James Lamie's heavy Calvinistic hand. "Just watch he doesna batter you the way he's battered me."

"Nae fear o' that," says Richmond. "Wallopin' a wee laddie's no' juist the same as contendin' wi' somebody that's able for him."

Robert looks up from his writing and shakes his head. "For a pillar o' the Auld Licht's temple, Mr. Lamie seems gey worried about folk's conduct o' their life on earth."

"He's no' worried aboot himsel' or yon bugger Willie Fisher," says Tanner Hunter, the village shoemaker, another object of the Elders' vigilance. "Him an' his ilk are saved frae the start. It's only the likes o' us that needs watchin' – till they bring us to heel."

"Aye, well they'll damned well no' bring me to heel!" says Robert. "They can keep their salvation if they're any taste o' what we maun spend eternity wi'. I'd sooner pass my days among beggars and gangrels."

Sandy Dow, son of the Whitefoord's landlord and driver of the Kilmarnock coach, has put his head in at the door. "Gin ye want to pass your time wi' the folk aff the road, Rab, ye maun hie yoursel' o'er to Poosie Nansie's, for that's where they gather."

Robert laughs. "Aye. We'll maybe just do that afore the night's by, Sandy."

Reaching up to clap a hand on his son's shoulder, Johnnie Dow, short, fat, and ruddy, feigns gruffness. "For God's sake, Sandy, ye wouldna tak custom awa' frae your ain faither, would ye? An' to the benefit o' yon den o' iniquity o'er by, an' a'. Think shame on yoursel'."

"Dinna fash yoursel', Johnnie," says John Brown, the clockmaker, laughing breathily. "We'll gi'e ye ample custom afore we gang."

"Aye, Johnnie," says Richmond. "What aboot anither roond for the Bachelor's Club, the now?" He pokes Robert's shoulder with a finger. "An' aiblins we'll get the bard, here, to let us hear what he's been scribblin' awa' at a' nicht."

Johnnie Dow bawls out the order to Meg the servingmaid, then turns back to Robert. "A new set o' verses, is it, Rab? Or a sang?"

Drink and fiery talk have made Robert feel reckless, and the writing has given him more pleasure still in turning tapsalteerie the humiliation of the cutty stool. "It's a new song, Johnnie, to an auld tune – 'Clout the Cauldron.'"

"Then lea'e us bloody well hear it!" shouts wee Jamie Smith.

Robert rises and waves down the clamorous demands for performance. "A' right, a' right," he says. "But in view o' the subject, we'd best keep it amang the members o' the Bachelor's Club." Then, forestalling Dow's objections, he adds, "And yoursel', of course, Johnnie."

"A pity we've nae fiddler aboot, the nicht," says Clockie Brown.

"Aye," says Robert, "an' ye'll soon be sorrier when ye hear the sound o' me singin'."

Richmond sticks out his tongue and makes a farting noise. "Nae excuses!" he says. "Juist sing."

So Robert sings the new song as best he can, making up for his musical shortcomings by giving each line its full dramatic value, and stamping his foot to keep time:

> Ye jovial boys who love the joys,
>   The blissful joys of Lovers,
> Yet dare avow, with dauntless brow,
>   When the bony lass discovers,
> I pray draw near, and lend an ear,
>   And welcome in a Frater,
> For I've lately been on quarantine,
>   A proven Fornicator

Before the Congregation wide,
    I passed the muster fairly,
My handsome Betsy by my side,
    We gat our ditty rarely;
But my downcast eye did chance to spy
    What made my lips to water,
Those limbs so clean where I between
    Commenc'd a Fornicator.

With rueful face and signs of grace
    I pay'd the buttock-hire,
But the night was dark and thro' the park
    I could not but convoy her;
A parting kiss, I could not less,
    My vows began to scatter,
My Betsy fell – lal de dal lal lal,
    I am a Fornicator.

But for her sake this vow I make,
    And solemnly I swear it,
That while I own a single crown
    She's welcome for to share it;
And my roguish boy his Mother's Joy
    And the darling of his Pater,
For him I boast my pains and cost,
    Although a Fornicator.

Ye wenching blades whose hireling jades
    Have tipt you off blue-joram,
I tell you plain, I do disdain
    To rank you in the Quorum;
But a bony lass upon the grass
    To teach her esse Mater,
And no reward but fond regard,
    O that's a Fornicator

Your warlike Kings and Heros bold,
    Great Captains and Commanders;
Your mighty Caesars fam'd of old,

And conquering Alexanders;
In fields they fought and laurels bought,
And bulwarks strong did batter,
But still they grac'd our noble list,
And ranked Fornicator!!!"

When Robert has uttered the last explosive word, shouting and swinging his fist for emphasis, the back room is silent. All the men have been glancing at each other throughout the song, eyes wide and mouths half-open, poised between shock and laughter at this defiant celebration, frank and personal, of what the Kirk condemns regularly, but what goes on unabated in every secluded corner of the land. And after a moment, as if on cue, the company breaks into a great roar of delight.

As he walks across the Cowgate with Richmond and wee Smith, Robert can't seem to find level footing on the cobblestones, and his head feels only loosely connected to his body. The rest of the Bachelors' Club have declined to enrich their lives by leaving Dow's for the riskier pleasures of Poosie Nansie's, but Robert's determination – and his new song – have inflamed Jock and Jamie with the zeal of explorers and conquerors.

Pausing before Poosie Nansie's door, Smith puts a hand out to lean on Robert's shoulder, finding it a less than steady support. "God, Rab," he says, "it must be grand to ha'e the gift to write sangs like yon. The black bonnets canna thole bein' made cods o', but they canna stop folk frae thinkin' – aye, or laughin'. An' a guid sang travels faster than Holy Willie Fisher can hirple." The little man lurches sidewise, loosing a great belch.

"The black bonnets will ha'e plenty to occupy themsel's in the days to come," says Robert, "if the Muse has anything to do wi' it." He props Smith against the wall and opens the door of the notorious inn.

Immediately, his senses are set whirling in the light from the great central fireplace and the candles flickering from sconces and tables, in the mingled reek of smoke and sweat, whisky, and stale beer, in the cacophony of drunken voices shouting and singing against the squeal of an ill-tuned fiddle and the thump of many feet keeping many different measures. And in a moment, flanked by Richmond and Smith, Robert stands in the midst of the moiling splore.

Before them, lying next to the fire in the stained remnants of a soldier's red coat, they see a greasy-haired man with startling eyes and a crusty grey stubble of beard. His left arm ends in a rusty hook, and thrusting from the left leg of his tattered, once-white breeches is a wooden peg. In the crook of his right arm a woman lies sprawled, her drink-ravaged face upthrust to give her warrior a loose-lipped, smacking kiss.

"That ane's got a mou' on her like an aumons dish," says Richmond at Robert's ear.

Before he can reply, a stout woman wearing a mutch and a white apron approaches the three companions, her face gleaming with sweat. "Sit ye doon, lads, sit ye doon," she says, gesturing at a vacant table. "Dinna be feart. Ye're aey amang frien's at Nansie's."

This is the locally-fabled "Poosie Nansie" Gibson, whose establishment takes regular abuse from the Mauchline pulpit. But despite such attacks, she and her black-bearded husband George preside more or less serenely over their own dispossessed and vagrant congregation. And now she gathers Robert, Jock, and Jamie to her ample bosom, settling them at a scarred and smoke-blackened table near the door.

"Aggie Wilson!" she cries. "Get on your feet, ye hizzy, and attend to these braw laddies. D'ye no' see we've got a weel-kennt spinner o' rhymes amang us?"

The woman lying at the fireside detaches herself from the grip of her one-armed, one-legged soldier and struggles to her feet. She staggers over and sways before Robert and the others, her once-red hair a white-fuzzed tangle and her gash of a mouth spread in a gap-toothed smile. "What are yiz drinkin', then?" she says, her voice hoarse and blurred by drink.

"Aggie!" The roar sounds above the general din. "Come awa' here to me!" The old soldier has propped himself upright against the wall and now beckons to his tipsy wench.

Poosie Nansie turns on him. "Sit ye doon and haud your wheesht till she sees to these young fellows."

The battered warrior shakes his rusty hook. "I've gi'ed an airm an' a leg at Gilbraltar for the likes o' them. Aye an' focht in Canada an' Cuba an' a'."

Robert speaks quickly to forestall an angry rejoinder from the landlady. "We'll a' ha'e a dram, Aggie," he says. "And bring ane for yon sodger as well. We'll drink the health o' them that fight for glory round the world."

Mollified, the soldier sinks back down among his bags of oatmeal, the main alms given to beggars all over Scotland, serving them both as food and as the currency they exchange for drink. And when Aggie has served them all, and couched again with her sodger laddie beside the fire, Robert raises his coggie to them: "To a' the sons o' Mars, whate'er their uniforms, that march to the sound o' the drum!"

The entire company pauses in its clatter to raise coggies or pint stoups to Robert's toast, echoing its final phrases. The soldier drinks off his dram with a flourish. "Aye!" he roars. "An' wi' the drum soundin' in my ears an' a gill o' whisky in my belly, I could face down a troop o' Hell!"

A pockmarked young woman emits a high-pitched giggle that ends in a snuffling cough. One of three doxies posed like a tableau of sluttish Muses at the far side of the fireplace, she responds to the soldier's glare with vacant eyes and a crooked smile.

"Racer Jess," says Smith, leaning over to Robert, his voice low. "She's Nansie and Gibson's dochter."

"Aye," adds Richmond in an undertone. "She's half-witted. She'll run onywhere for a ha'penny – whether it's to carry messages or juist to race wi' the weans."

Robert nods. He has seen Jess, himself, running through the village streets, her skirts kilted up past her knees, surrounded by laughing children or jeered by idlers on corners. He knows that the Kirk Elders must look on her addled state as a judgment on the Gibsons for their evil ways. Everywhere he looks seems to reveal a new reason to question the smug righteousness of those who feel they can tell others how to live. He sips his whisky and gives himself over to the sensations of this time and place.

Suddenly, the inn's noise grows louder with the sound of angry voices. A little fiddler, well-known for plying his trade at markets and fairs, has evidently been pleading his case with an old girl nearly half again his size. And now a rival has declared himself, a hulking tinker who grasps the little fellow's beard in one hand and a corroded rapier in the other.

"I'll spit ye like a roastin'-fowl, ye damned gutscraper!"

The tinker forces the fiddler to his knees, bringing a howl of delight from the company, none laughing louder than the contested object of the pair's affections.

"Oh, dinna break my fiddle, man!" pleads the fiddler, sheltering the instrument and its bow behind him.

"Then play the damned thing," bellows the tinker, "an' lea'e the wenchin to them that's able!"

With that, the tinker tumbles the little man on his arse, then staggers off with his blowsy conquest to sink in an embrace among a heap of rags. The spurned lover, meanwhile, is left to content himself in a corner with the delicate shape of his fiddle, the stroke of horsehair on gut, and the sting of whisky in his gullet. And before long he is drinking the health of his rival and eyeing another prospect.

The prodigality of the scene fills Robert with pleasure, and he laughs aloud, his head spinning with affection for Richmond and wee Smith, who have the mettle to share a night like this. "D'ye see, Jock?" he says. "They're juist like us! They want what we want. To drink when they ha'e a drouth. To sing or dance or come to blows when the mood takes them. The only difference is, we worry about a' the rest o' it. The Kirk, the Crown, the courts, the seed and the harvest, the clink o' gowd and siller. But them" – he flings his arm in an arc around him – "they don't care a fig for ony o' that. And that's real freedom. Whether they're cauld or wet, ragged or penniless – they don't bloody care!"

Suddenly lines begin to sing in his head: "A fig for those by law protected, . . . Liberty's a glorious feast. . . . Courts for cowards were erected, . . . Churches built to please the priest!" And he knows he will write about this evening, something beyond the simple songs and verses he's done before. He'll let these jolly beggars sing for themselves, in their own voices, and stitch it together with whatever lines he needs to set the scene, a description to bring alive the place, the people, and their actions. By God, he will.

And this will be no more than the start. The words and images crowd his brain. If only he can make time to set them on paper. He delves into his pocket for his pencil.

"Here now," says Richmond. "Ye scribbled damn near a' nicht at Dow's. Ye'll no' do it here as well. For God's sake, gi'e us a sang!"

"Aye," says Smith, drumming his palms on the table. "Gi'e us 'The Fornicator' or whatever the hell ye like, as lang as it's lively!"

Poosie Nansie, overhearing the exchange, whispers to her husband. And Geordie Gibson shouts for attention from the rabble. "Order! Order! Order for a sang frae Poet Burns!" He advances on the little fiddler, who is smothered between the breasts of another doxy. "Come on, Tam!" he thunders. "Ye maun squeeze and blaw yon bagpipes efter ye've played for the bard. And for Christ's sake, man, tune that bloody fiddle!"

Robert rises, while the beggars and gangrels – crippled, blind, malformed, homeless as they may be – crowd merrily around to hear what song he'll give them. And he touches a hand to his coat pocket, feeling the hard stub of pencil nestled there, ready to give line and form to what his brain has already stored of this night. And he knows that as long as there's a world to be caught and brought to life on paper, he – like these vagrant souls whose smell rises rank in his nostrils – will always be free to roam beyond the lockstep of convention, beyond the long furrow that most men plough directly to the grave. And he opens his mouth to sing.

1785

John Barley corn was a Heroe bold
    Of noble enterprize,
For if you do but taste his blood
    'Twill make your courage rise. –

'Twill make a man forget his woe,
    And heighten all his joy;
'Twill make the widoe's heart to sing
    Tho the tear were in her eye. –

Then let us toast John Barley corn
    Each man a glass in hand,
And may his great posterity
    Ne'er fail in old Scotland. –

– from the first *Commonplace Book*
June, August, 1785

Chapter Five

On this spring evening a few of Mauchline's windows already show the shifting yellow gleam of candlelight as Dr. John Mackenzie steps out of his surgery onto the Backcauseway. He is due shortly at Gavin Hamilton's, whose house lies virtually across the narrow street, but almost without thinking he glances left to the market cross. His heart gives a loup as he sees Helen Miller standing there in the gloaming with her sister Betty and two other lassies, Jeany Markland and Jean Armour. The girls are talking with Robert Burns, who stands over them, turned out handsomely in tan coat, white breeches, and riding boots. Mackenzie knows that Robert, too, must soon present himself at Gavin Hamilton's, so he strolls along to join the poet and the belles, though his eyes fix themselves chiefly on Helen Miller and the way her green dress sets off her red hair and white skin.

"Good e'en, ladies. Rab." The young doctor inclines his head politely, not missing the nudge that Betty Miller gives to her sister at his approach.

He can see that Burns, too, hasn't missed the sisterly exchange, for as the lassies respond to his greeting with a scatter of words and laughter, the poet's mouth widens in a knowing smile. "A pity we maun soon turn our backs on sic beauty, eh, Doctor?"

"Ye'll no' get the chance to turn your back on us, Rab Burns," says Jeany Markland playfully, raising her her eyebrows. "Or if ye do, ye needna think we'll be heartsore for lang." She turns to Jean Armour, a well-formed eighteen-year-old lass with a tumble of mahogany-colored hair. "Is that no' richt, Jean?"

For answer, the Armour girl simply glares at her friend. Mackenzie senses that the favorite daughter of Mauchline's foremost builder has more than a merely flirtatious interest in Robert; and as he has before the doctor envies the poet his easy manner with the lassies. If only he could have Robert's way with words for an hour or so to open his heart and mind to Helen. But then he reflects on the younger man's recklessness in the matter of Betty Paton, who will soon bear the fruit of that illicit union; he recalls, too, Robert's dour, detached silence two years ago in the spring of 1783 when he first attended William Burns at Lochlea Farm. And he knows that in Robert Burns, who can charm you with wit and knowledge that belie his station, lives a darker companion, who can risk everything on the curve of a plump breast, or turn distant and suspicious, with no wish to interest or please anyone.

Mackenzie suddenly realizes that Helen Miller is smiling at him. Feeling the need to respond in some way, he tries for a compliment: "May I say, Miss Miller, I ha'e never seen you look lonelier."

Helen's eyes widen in shock, and Jeany Markland lets out an unladylike keehaw of a laugh as the other girls titter behind their hands. Puzzled at first, Mackenzie looks at them and at the grinning Burns, then realizes what he has said. "Lovelier!" he exclaims. "You've never looked lovelier, I meant to say."

Helen's mouth softens into a pleased smile; then she, too, begins to laugh. Mackenzie feels a deep flush rising from his neck to his scalp. "Well, Robert," he finally manages, "we dinna want to be late at Gavin Hamilton's."

Burns grins at him a moment longer, then evidently takes pity. "Aye. We mauna be late." He makes a sweeping, vaguely Oriental gesture with his hand. "Well, ladies, I'm sure we'll find ye as lovely the morrow as ye are the nicht."

As he and Robert walk up the Backcauseway toward Hamilton's, past the drift of music from Ronald's ballroom, they can still hear the girls' laughter trailing them, and Mackenzie says, "Ye'll no' mention this to Gaw'n or Bob Aiken, will ye, Rab?"

Robert chuckles. "Dinna fash yoursel', John. I'll keep it under my bonnet." Then he nods back at the cross. "But I'm no' so sure ye can depend on yon lassies to do the same."

When Robert and Dr. Mackenzie arrive at Hamilton's, they find their host and Bob Aiken in considerable glee over a quarrel lately broken out between two celebrated Auld Licht clerics from nearby towns, the Reverends John Moodie of Riccarton and John Russell of Kilmarnock.

"And what's it a' aboot?" asks Mackenzie.

The doctor, as Robert knows, tries to hold himself somewhat aloof from religious disputation, obliged as he is by his practice to treat all comers alike. But Mackenzie is Ayrshire-born, for all his education at Edinburgh University, and understands how deeply feelings run in these airts, especially as regards Hamilton's relations with Daddy Auld.

"Something to do wi' parish boundaries," says Hamilton. "The pair o' them want to haud sway o'er as muckle a congregation as they can gather, and they'd argue a black craw white to do it. When the case came up afore the magistrates in Kilmarnock, Russell had to be kept frae throttlin' his holy brither."

"Aye, he wanted Moodie's guts out," chortles Aiken.

"I'll tell ye this," says Hamilton, settling Mackenzie and Robert in chairs near the fire with glasses in their hands, "it does my heart good to see the orthodox fa'in' oot amang themsel's. The feck o' them are that busy findin' faut wi' folk that dinna share their views, they seldom notice each other's shortcomin's."

Robert, smiling broadly, draws several folded sheets of paper from his coat pocket. "Here's a few thoughts on the matter I penned the other day. They'll maybe spice the discussion a wee bit." He looks at Hamilton and Aiken. "I told ye the Kirk could provide subjects in plenty for the likes o' me."

Aiken takes the sheets from Robert and reads aloud. "'The Twa Herds,' it's ca'd. 'Or the Holy Tulyie – An Unco Mournfu' Tale.' And here's an epigraph frae Pope: 'Blockheads with reason wicked wits abhor,/But fool with fool is barbarous civil war.'"

Hamilton and Mackenzie break into laughter at this. "Come on, then, Rab," says Aiken, proferring the sheets. "Gi'e us the rest o' it."

Robert waves him off. "What about yoursel', Bob? I canna think o' a better man to gi'e tongue to my verse."

Aiken needs no encouragement, for he prides himself on the eloquence and vigor of his recitations. He stands before them, his small, stout frame seeming to grow as the rhetorical mood comes on him, and begins to read:

> "O a' ye pious godly flocks,
> Weel fed on pastures orthodox,
> Wha now will keep you frae the fox
> Or worrying tykes?
> Or wha will tent the waifs an' crocks
> About the dykes?

The twa best herds in a' the wast,
That e'er gae gospel horn a blast
These five an' twenty simmers past –
    O, dool to tell! –
Hae had a bitter, black out-cast
    Atween themsel.

O Moodie, man, an' worthy Russell,
How could you raise so vile a bustle?
Ye'll see how New-Light herds will whistle,
    An' think it fine!
The Lord's cause gat nae sic a twistle
    Sin' I hae min'."

Robert sits back in his chair, closes his eyes, and savors the rise and fall of Aiken's sonorous voice declaiming his ironically solicitous account of the affair. His pleasure in the sound and cadence of the lines, in their clever Scots rhymes, spreads through him like the warmth of the fire and the whisky. He feels as if he's never heard the poem before, and his admiration rises for the little lawyer. He realizes that "The Twa Herds" may have little more than its local significance; but if his verse can impress such men as these, who knows where it may end? And the poem does impress them: as Aiken reaches the climax, in which the speaker gives ironic voice to the Auld Lichts' wish that common sense be banished like a dog to France, Hamilton and Mackenzie sputter and yip with delight.

"Aye," says Hamilton, after Aiken finishes reading, "ye've caught the truth o' it right enough, Rab. They'd hang knowledge on a tree and chase common sense oot o' the country if they could."

"Aye, and they'll hang you if they can, and a', Gavin," says John Mackenzie, "if Daddy Auld and Holy Willie ha'e onything to say aboot it."

"They havena just got the noose round my neck yet, John," says Hamilton, splashing more whisky into Mackenzie's glass. "For if they do ought, they'll need to do it afore the Presbytery in Ayr, and no' afore a Kirk Session that Auld can twist aboot his finger."

Robert has heard from Jock Richmond of Hamilton's intent to appeal to the Presbytery, composed of all the district's ministers. "But are ye no' worried about havin' to deal wi' the likes o'

Alexander Moodie there?" he says.

"As your poem says, Rab, Moodie's o'er busy wi' his ain squabblin' to gi'e much thought to mine. An' there's a wheen o' good liberals in the Presbytery and a' – William MacGill that helped bury your faither, William Dalrymple, and your frien' John MacMath, amang others. Besides, I'll maybe gi'e them a surprise or twa, as well."

"What kind o' surprise, Gaw'n?" says John Mackenzie.

A crooked smile spreads slowly across Hamilton's face. "I'm thinkin' I'll maybe just exercise my rights and take legal counsel along wi' me." He grins at Aiken. "Eh, Bob?"

The lawyer is visibly startled, his round face suddenly shiny. "What? Me?" He laughs uneasily. "I'd ha'e thought you were a' the lawyer ye would need, yoursel'."

Hamilton sets down the jar of whisky he's been holding. "Ah, but think, Bob. Think o' the dance the pair o' us could lead yon sanctimonious crows. Besides, ye know yoursel' my practice seldom goes beyond drafting and verifying documents. I'm just a law writer, after a'. You're the man for an eloquent plea and elegant tactics. What d'ye say, Bob?"

Aiken, his poise recovered, gives a derisive snort. "We'll need little in the way o' tactics or eloquence, Gaw'n. Your character's the best defense we could muster, as the gentlemen o' the Kirk would know themsel's if they werena blinded wi' pure malice and envy at the way folk heed your counsel."

"Save that for the Presbytery, Bob." Hamilton pours each man a fresh measure of drink. "For we're no' here to strategize, the nicht."

Robert senses that Aiken's natural conviviality makes him reluctant to give offense to anyone; despite his oratorical gifts, the lawyer's instinct is to minimize differences and soften hard feelings, rather than demolish the opposition by argument. Perhaps he can do the same before the Presbytery. "Here's to your success, then, Gaw'n," he says, raising his glass. "Ye canna go wrong wi' Bob at your side."

Whatever their private doubts may be, the four men toast the prospect of victory over Daddy Auld and his reactionary lieutenants. "Maybe I'll ha'e the chance to scribble a line or two on that subject and a'," says Robert.

Hamilton shakes his head. "For my ain part I wouldna do onything different," he says. "But if I were you, Rab, I'd think a bit afore layin' mysel' open to the malice o' the Mauchline Kirk Session."

"They maun girn and pray a' they want," says Robert. "But they can hardly keep a man frae honest expression o' his feelin's – or frae scratchin' his thoughts down on a bit o' paper."

Aiken, back in high spirits, shouts them down. "As Gaw'n says, we maun save it a' for the Presbytery, Rab. In the meantime, we needna spare the black bonnets anither thocht. Gi'e us a sang or twa frae 'The Jolly Beggars,' Rab!"

Mary Campbell sits in the dark of the old tower next to Gavin Hamilton's house, looking down at the law writer's front door. The Hamilton weans, her young charges, have been asleep for an hour or so, leaving her free to wait here in the Castle of Mauchline, as the townsfolk call it, which her employer first bought, then sold, and now leases from the Earl of Loudon. As Mary watches, shivering a bit in the evening chill despite her shawl, Hamilton's door opens, and the spill of light from within reveals the dark figures of four men, one of whom, she knows, is Robert Burns.

A brief hubbub of goodnights echoes in the Backcauseway, then Mr. Hamilton closes the door on himself and Lawyer Aiken, who is staying the night, and Robert and Dr. Mackenzie are left in darkness to shake hands and go their separate ways. But Mary knows, and her breath quickens at the thought, that Robert will soon be here in the tower beside her.

She rises with the sound of a quiet footstep at the bottom of the stairs, and holds herself still, heart rattling at her ribs, waiting. Her excitement puzzles her, for she knows she cannot afford to indulge her emotions: she has her job with the Hamiltons to consider, and her relationship with Captain Montgomerie already puts her at some risk; but the Captain does at least provide some return for her favors, whereas she can look for little from Robert Burns save the pleasure of his company. Nonetheless, when she encountered the young farmer earlier on his road from Mossgiel, and he asked her to meet him in the tower tonight, she found herself unable to refuse him outright, even though coyness has never been her way. And now here she is, heart fluttering, like a silly lassie.

"Mary?" Robert's hoarse whisper rings unexpectedly loud in

the narrow stone stairway.

Mary makes no answer, for fear someone might hear them. Instead, she watches with eyes grown used to the chamber's gloom, and after a few moments she sees the pale oval of Robert's face in the doorway's darker shadow.

She can smell him now, whisky and peat smoke and an underlying sweetness like fresh-mown hay, and the small room seems warmer for his presence. His teeth gleam momentarily in the faint milky light coming through the window from the moon and stars.

"So ye're here, after a'," he says his tone betraying pleasure, but with no hint of the off-putting self-satisfaction Mary can often hear in the Captain's voice, as if she were at Montgomerie's command for himself alone.

"Aye. Here I am," she says. "Though I am not sure I could tell you why."

Robert moves closer to her. Though not the worse for drink, he must have refused little of Hamilton's whisky, for Mary can hear that climbing to the top of the tower has made him pant a wee bit. "I ken why I'm here," he says, his voice soft with unspoken meaning.

"I wonder at you," she replies, backing away until her legs press against the old chair she's been sitting on. "A man who is soon to be a father, talking in such a way."

He takes a sharp breath, then blows it out again. But when he speaks, his voice remains gentle. "Soon to be a father, aye," he says. "But no' a husband. For there's nae lass has claims on me, Mary, beyond the birth o' the bairn."

As Robert leans nearer, Mary finds herself pressed down into the chair. He kneels beside her, a warm hand on her left thigh. "And what about you, lass? If it comes to it, we both ha'e our entanglements, eh? But would we be here if they bound our hearts? And forbye that, do they matter now? This minute? Does anything matter in this place, except for you and me?"

His hand moves from her lap to one of her small, high breasts. The suddenness of his touch makes her gasp, turns her blood to warm water that seems to run directly from the nipple under his hand to where her thighs meet, yes, her cunt, as they call it, and sets her head spinning as well. She reaches up to put her hand over his, not to pull it away, no, and as she does so he leans in to kiss her, first on the mouth, his tongue moving warm and soft on hers, then on the side of her neck, the heat of his breath there making her feel too weak to hold up her head. The darkness now fills her as well as the room, and without knowing how, she feels her arms clasping him as his envelop her, and then they are lying on the straw-covered floor, her body half-cushioned by his, and her free hand caressing his hard thighs, feeling his thing, his cock, stirring through his breeches at her touch as if she were giving it life of its own.

"God, Mary," he murmurs, pressing his face to her cheek. He runs his fingers lightly down her body, finally spreading his hand flat on her stomach, making her writhe, a cry strangling in her throat. Images from memory whirl in her mind: other faces floating above her, other mouths on hers, other hands moving over her body; but not like this. This feeling impossibly blends urgency and lassitude, making her want him now, without waiting, but filling her with the need to savor each moment as it passes.

Then he tugs at the front of her dress, and her own hands move quickly to assist him. Soon his mouth, his tongue, are on her breasts, circling her small, firm nipples, and she moans, worrying only vaguely about the Hamiltons below, and fumbles at his breeches. When the hard warm shaft of his cock is in her hand, she herself pulls the dress up around her hips and opens her thighs to him, trembling not from the cold air, but from the welter of heat and chill generated in her own body by his touch.

But as he slides into the wet depth of her, she remembers herself for a moment. "Ye'll not finish inside me," she manages to whisper. "Please."

The next few minutes are lost to thought, however. And so many times do her own mind and body break into a confusion of passion, like the rain and ragged clouds of a sudden storm, that when at at last they settle quietly on Robert's coat, her head resting on his shoulder, she recalls her final turbulent and breathless heavings only in flashes, like moments left with her from the white light of a dream.

This was not what she expected at all. Not from a night's tryst with a young farmer, poet or no. Her family has begun to depend on the little she can send them, and Captain Montgomerie's occasional gifts make that possible. Now what will she do? She whispers at his shoulder, her lips brushing his neck, "Where have you come from, Rab Burns? Where have you come from?"

Robert staggers a bit, tightening his grip on the plough-staves, as the coulter glances off a buried stone. His first impulse is to cry out in irritation at Gibby, who is tramping just ahead and to the left of him, clearing clay from the mould-board when necessary, and making sure that the coulter cuts cleanly through the soil, rather than merely scraping the surface. But Gibby can hardly be expected to see every stone in this poor ground before the blade strikes it, so Robert holds his peace. They've been hard at it all day harrowing in the oats, Robert and Bob Allan taking turns seeding and toiling behind the plough, with young Willie Burns driving the horses, and soon they'll be trudging down the rig back to the farmhouse for a well-earned meal. Then Robert will wash and dress himself before going down to the village for an hour or two's fellowship with the rest of the Bachelors' Club.

His mood has hovered for some time between elation at the memory of his night with Mary and anger at what happened a few evenings later, when he and Richmond and the other fellows saw her walking on the green while they were making for Johnnie Dow's. Robert, eyes full of her fair and slender beauty, stopped to speak with her and found her uneasy, confused-seeming, unwilling to commit to another tryst, and anxious to be on her way.

When she walked off, erect and handsome, Richmond let out a low chuckle and turned to wee Smith. "When she gets where she's goin' she'll no' be standin' up for lang," he said.

"Aye, nor sittin', neither," Smith responded, snirtling like a schoolboy.

Angry as he was, Robert did what he could to divert them from that line of talk without giving himself away, but he's afraid that his interest in Mary was all too obvious. Even now with Betty Paton's time fast approaching, everything seems to remind him of Mary, and nothing more than the heaving of the plough under his hands and arms as it cleaves through the wet earth.

"That'll do for the day, lads," he says as they reach the end of the rig nearest the house.

Willie takes hold of the lead horse's bridle and brings it to a halt, while Robert moves away from the plough to stretch his cramped muscles and Bob Allan walks about in a circle, stamping his feet.

"No' such a bad afternoon's work," says Gibby, shading his eyes and looking back over the neatly-furrowed slope.

"Aye," says Robert. "I hope to hell this crop turns oot better than the last."

The two elder brothers carry the plough back to the house as Willie and Bob lead the horses. When the plough is put away, Robert and Gibby leave the other two to care for the animals and cross the yard to the house. Nancy and Bell meet them at the door and sit them down at the kitchen table to bowls of savory broth with barley and beans and coggies of fresh milk. Plates of mutton and a heap of oat-cakes stand waiting, too. And while they sup, Robert notes his mother glowering at him from her seat beside the fire, as she champs tatties in a pot for them with butter, milk, and salt. She'd think better of him if he married Betty; but then his sisters would be ill-pleased. What would they think, he wonders, if he brought Mary home on the heels of Betty's bairn? He spreads butter thickly on an oatcake and cuts a slice of good white cheese to go with it.

"Come and have a bite to eat, laddie," he calls to John Burns who is sitting at the fire opposite his mother, wrapped in a woolen blanket with only his pale face and hands visible.

"It's nice beside the fire," the boy says, his voice faint.

"I'll bring ye o'er a bannock wi' a whang o' cheese," says Robert.

"Do ye no' think we've asked him ony number o' times if he wanted ought?" says Nancy sharply. "We're no' just sittin aboot a' day while you're oot in the fields, ye ken."

Nancy, like her mother, has been looking through Robert for weeks, angry not at his refusal to wed Betty, but at his ever having touched what she's called "yon coarse hizzy." But he knows, too, that his sister shares his concern for John, and he makes allowance for that.

"I'll no' dispute your hard work," he says mildly, "or the way ye care for the lad. But I can surely talk to him, can I no'?"

"Say whatever ye like." Nancy crosses the kitchen, takes the pot of tatties from her mother, and sets it down with a bang on the table. "There ye are," she says. "Maybe ye can get him to eat some o' these."

"I'm no' hungry, Rab," says John, smiling with a slight, painful twitch at the corners of his mouth.

At that moment, Willie Burns and Bob Allan walk in through the front door to join Robert and Gibby at the table, and the kitchen fills with noisy, convivial talk. Robert, himself, eats in silence until, finally, he drains the last swallow of milk from his coggie, pushes his chair back, and rises.

"A fine meal, as usual," he says addressing the women generally.

Nancy softens at this. "Ye earned it," she says. "You and the other lads."

He smiles at her, then crosses the room to John. "Mind ye take some nourishment, laddie. It'll gi'e ye strength." He ruffles his brother's hair gently, feeling how damp and warm the boy's head is, and a sudden memory stirs of the fevers that afflicted him in his own childhood, and which still devil him from time to time. Perhaps John will be luckier. "Well," he says, "I'm off for a wash."

"And then what?" says his mother, speaking for the first time since Robert entered the house.

He stiffens, but looks at her without rancor. "Then I'm away down to Mauchline for an hour or twa."

"Aye," says Agnes Burns, and the single word speaks volumes.

Jock Richmond, Rab Burns, Jamie Smith, and Tanner Hunter make their way up the Backcauseway toward the Elbow Inn. For the past hour or two they've been at Johnnie Dow's Whitefoord Arms, and normally they'd have stayed there till closing time. Tonight, though, Jock has a point to make.

At the Whitefoord, he and the other two were chaffing Rab about his way with women. But he was brimming with even more confidence than usual, quoting them a song he'd written to parade his own roguery:

> "O leave novels, ye Mauchline belles,
>   ye're safer at your spinning-wheel;
> Such witching books are baited hooks
>   for rakish rooks like Rob Mossgiel;
> Your fine Tom Jones and Grandisons,
>   They make your youthful fancies reel;
> They heat your brains, and fire your veins,
>   And then you're prey for Rob Mossgiel.

Beware a tongue that's smoothly hung,
    A heart that warmly seems to feel;
That feeling heart but acts a part –
    'Tis rakish art in Rob Mossgiel.
The frank address, the soft caress,
    Are worse than poisoned darts of steel;
The frank address, and politesse,
    Are all finesse in Rob Mossgiel."

Something about the performance rubbed Jock the wrong way, but before he could say anything, Jamie Smith spoke up: "And what ane o' the belles d'ye ettle to set your trap for next, your bardship? My sister Jean says Jean Armour's had her eye on ye."

"Och, I've scarcely spoken to the lassie, Jamie," said Rab. Then he smiled. "But I canna deny she's a beauty."

"Does that mean ye've gi'ed up on yon hielan' quean?" said Hunter, an innocent smile brightening his lantern jaw.

Robert looked at the skinny shoemaker, his own smile fading, then glanced at the others. "If ye mean Mary Campbell," he said, "she's a fine-looking lass. But I dinna ken where ye got the notion I had ony byornar interest in her."

Tanner just widened his eyes at Jock and Jamie. Jock wondered at "Rob Mossgiel's" denying any amorous exploit. But then he reflected that the poet was much more likely to do a bit of posturing in verse before or after the fact. While an affair was in progress he could be close-mouthed enough. In this case, though, the signs were unmistakable. And again Jock felt a touch of resentment, since Rab knew well how he felt about Mary Campbell.

"Ye're as well to keep clear o' that ane, onyhow," he said. "An' it's no' the first time I've tellt ye that."

But Rab continued to defend the Campbell lass as he had on the green a few days earlier. And Jock, who's had to be careful of his own activities since taking the cutty stool with Jenny Surgeoner, decided that his friend's eyes needed opening. So now, at his urging, the Bachelors' Club is about to reconvene at the Elbow, where he's sure the truth will emerge.

As usual, the Elbow's cramped interior is more than half-empty, at least what Jock can see of it, since of its three rooms only the central kitchen and the snug are evidently in use for casual trade. Jock's interest, though, is the shut door of the private room opposite the snug. Nodding his head toward it, he tips a wink to Jamie and Tanner. Moments later he sees Rab, too, give an uneasy glance in that direction amid his jovial greetings to Hughie Meldrum the landlord.

But after they've been talking and drinking for a while, Jock begins to think he's made a mistake, for he sees neither comings from nor goings to the private room, nor does he hear ought from within. Rab seems aware of Jock's intent, and as time passes without incident, he relaxes more and more visibly, returning to his earlier brash, bantering mood.

When, as it often does among them, the talk turns to sexual misconduct – or houghmagandie, as Tanner likes to say – Rab takes out a pencil and writes rapidly for a minute or two. Then, with a wicked smile at wee Smith, says, "Here's an epitaph for ye, Jamie. We'll save this to bury ye wi'." And while Jamie grins in mingled pride and discomfort, Rab reads:

> "Lament him, Mauchline husbands a'.
>   He aften did assist ye;
> For had ye stayed hale weeks awa',
>   Your wives they ne'er had miss'd ye.
>
> Ye Mauchline bairns, as on ye press
>   To school in bands thegither,
> O tread ye lightly on his grass, –
>   Perhaps he was your father!"

A salvo of laughter greets Rab's extempore versifying, and Jock gives himself over to enjoyment of the moment. Suddenly, though, the door of the private room opens and Mary Campbell walks a few steps into the kitchen, her dress looking hastily-fastened and her flaxen hair in disarray. Catching sight of Rab, she stops, bringing a hand up to her face in confusion. Rab, arrested in the midst of his delight, stares at her open-mouthed.

Jamie Smith, never one to let an opportunity escape, says, "Good evenin', Miss Campbell. Ha'e ye ta'en a wrang turnin'? Hamilton's is doon the road. Or do ye work here, and a'?"

To Jock's surprise, the Campbell hizzy blushes like a virgin and looks down at the floor. Then she lifts her eyes to Rab and seems as if she might speak. Finally, though, she turns away and hurries back into the private room, slamming the door behind her. During all of this, Rab sits without moving, eyes fixed first on Mary Campbell, then on the door that hides her.

"Well," says Jock at last. "I tellt ye the kind she was, Rab. We a' did."

Rab blinks at Jock, as if clearing his eyes. "Ye ken nothing aboot her," he says. "Nothing at a'."

And at that moment, the door to the private room swings open again, this time disclosing Captain Montgomerie, dressed in shirt and breeches, his red face gleaming. He takes in room with an incurious sweep of his eyes, then shouts to Hughie Meldrum. "Beer, landlord! And bring some cheese and oatcakes, as well." So saying, he pivots on his heel and disappears again with a bang of the door

Jock looks at Rab, his feelings an admixture of triumph and unease, in time to see his friend's face coloring deeply and his neck seeming to swell at the collar of his shirt. Rab's lips draw together, compressing for an outburst, and Jock begins to wonder if he's been wise in arranging this confrontation.

But when Rab's mouth finally does open, no shout issues forth, nor does he throw his caup or kick over a chair. "Damn it!" is all he says, spreading his hands flat on the table before him. But his voice, no more than a hiss, conveys more depth of feeling than might have shown in a less temperate display.

Rising, Rab looks down at his three friends. "I'm away home," he mutters.

Dropping a few coins on the table, he turns and walks out of the Elbow into the night, leaving Jock to consider the possibility that there may be more to Mary Campbell than he's ever dreamed.

Mauchline

However I am pleased with the works of our Scotch Poets, particularly the excellent Ramsay, and the still more excellent Ferguson, yet I am hurt to see other places of Scotland, their towns, rivers, woods, haughs, &c. immortalized in such celebrated performances, whilst my dear native country, the ancient Bailieries of Carrick, Kyle, & Cunningham, famous both in ancient & modern times for a gallant, and warlike race of inhabitants; a country where civil, & particularly religious Liberty have everlasting found their first support, & their last asylum; a country, the birth place of many famous Philosophers, Soldiers, & Statesmen, and the scene of many important events recorded in Scottish History, particularly a great many of the actions of the GLORIOUS WALLACE, the SAVIOUR of his Country; Yet we have never had one Scotch Poet of any eminence to make the fertile banks of Irvine, the romantic woodlands & sequestered scenes on Aire, and the heathy, mountainous source, & winding sweep of Doon emulate Tay, Forth, Ettrick, Tweed, &c. This is a complaint I would gladly remedy, but Alas! I am far unequal to the task, both in native genius & education. – Obscure I am & obscure I must be, though no young Poet, nor young Soldier's heart ever beat more fondly for fame than mine –

from the first *Commonplace Book*
August 1785

Chapter Six

my God, ye should ha'e seen her!"

Robert's smile illuminates his already handsome features, and Nancy Burns cannot help but share some of his excitement, her chest tightening as if she'd climbed to the crest of the high field outside. Her brother has just returned to Mossgiel from Lairgieside, where Betty Paton has borne him a daughter. And now he looks around the kitchen at the assembled Burns family, his face transformed by amazement at the life he and that servant-lassie have brought into the world. Nancy shakes her head at the sight of him, affection warming her.

Looking at young John, whose face has taken on a deceptively healthy-seeming glow at his elder brother's arrival, Robert holds his hands a short distance apart and says, "She was nae bigger than than this, Johnnie. And ye've never seen a bonnier wee thing."

John's rare laughter ends in a fit of coughing. Moving to lay a comforting hand on the back of boy's neck, Nancy sees her mother stiffen in her chair.

"And what's it to be cried, this bairn?" says Agnes Burns. She thrusts out her lower lip, waiting.

Robert, still looking full of his joy, responds quickly. "Elizabeth. She's to be ca'd after her mother."

"Aye," says Agnes, leaning forward with her hands on her knees, "but what's the last name to be?"

"Mother!" says Nancy, taking her hand from John's warm neck and holding it before her.

Agnes wheels around. "What?" she demands, biting off the word.

Nancy sees the familiar widening of the dark eyes, but she meets her mother's challenging stare. As she opens her mouth to answer, though, Gilbert speaks from his place at the kitchen table.

"There's nae point to this, Mither," he says, setting down his teacup. "We've been a' o'er it afore."

"Burns," says Robert suddenly. He fixes their mother with the eyes whose color and fire they share. "When we bring the wee lassie home to Mossgiel, from that day she'll be Elizabeth Burns. Our wee Bess."

Nancy smiles at his tone of pride and affection. But their mother is not to be disarmed. "Ours," she says with a sniff. "Aye, ours she may be. But she's gey dear-bought if ye ask me."

Robert straightens his shoulders and sighs. "She's dear-bought, right enough, Mother. And I ken how ye may feel." He looks around him at the family. "But she's worth the price, to me, at least. And I'll do what I can to ease the burden, as far as money goes." He looks again at Agnes. "But I'll no' argue wi' ye, Mother. No' the day, onyway." He moves to the foot of the stairs to the garret. "I'm away up to ha'e a bit scribble," he says, and soon disappears.

Nancy hears the scrape of his chair in the garret's tiny central room, where he and Gibby sleep and where he retreats to write. She imagines him up there, sitting at his table, pencil in hand, poised over a clean sheet of paper. Surely he'll make something wonderful out of his pride and delight in his new wee daughter.

"Well," says Agnes Burns to her own daughters, "I suppose we maun shift to put some meat on the table, for we canna a' sit aboot wi' a pencil in oor fist." She rises and moves toward the press to begin laying out food and crockery.

Nancy follows close behind, smelling the yeasty odor of fresh-baked bread that always seems to cling to her mother's clothes. She wishes she could find words to put things right between her mother and Robert. But whatever those words might be, she knows they will not come from her. "When will we see the wee lassie?" John Burns' thin voice breaks the silence. He looks from Gilbert to Nancy to his mother.

Agnes Burns, turning from the press, thrusts a stack of plates into Nancy's hands, then glares in John's direction. But when she speaks her tone is surprisingly gentle. "Soon enough," she says. "Soon enough."

At his table in the garret, Robert hears the homely tympany of dishes and cutlery and pots. But he can give no thought to food, for his heart and head are full of the day's events, of the baby and its mother.

Betty was as lovely as he'd ever seen her, lying in bed with the bairn in the cramped kitchen of Paton's but and ben. She was wan from her ordeal, and her hair clung damply to her cheeks and forehead, but the effect charmed him, making her look uncharacteristically soft and helpless, like the child itself.

The baby curled a tiny hand around Robert's finger, its eyes opening and closing drowsily, its wee pink mouth and tongue working at Betty's breast, which was swollen nearly translucent with its burden of milk.

Betty looked at him, smiling. "We made her well, did we no', Rab?" she said, placing her own hand lightly on his and the baby's.

His heart seemed to grow larger, causing his breath to catch in his chest, and his eyes blurred with tears. He passed his free hand across his face and sniffed. "Aye, Betty," he said at last. "We made her well, richt enough. I doubt any lad and lass ever made better." And he bent, first to brush his lips over the baby's fragile head, then to place a tender kiss on Betty's mouth.

And now, remembering, he feels the tears brimming again. He sets down his pencil, takes out his handkerchief, wipes his eyes, and blows his nose. Then, after breathing deeply, he lifts the pencil again and begins to write.

Later, as he sits with pen and ink copying what he has written, smiling with pleasure at the flow of words across the page, he hears footsteps on the stairs. In a moment or two Nancy appears, carrying a mug of steaming tea and a plate heaped with mutton, bread, and a wedge of their mother's good sharp cheese.

"Here's a bite for ye." She sets the food and drink on the table, well clear of his ink bottle and paper. Preoccupied, he mumbles his thanks while she takes a knife and fork from her apron and lays them next to the plate. Then, as he completes the final lines, she steps back and looks down at him. "What is it ye've written?" she asks. "Something aboot the wean?"

"Aye," he says. Then he grins at her. "Would ye like to hear it?"

"Of course I would," she says, sitting down on a nearby stool and resting her back against the wall. "If it's fit to be heard."

Robert chuckles and takes a sip of his tea. Then he picks up the pages he's just copied. "It's ca'd 'A Poet's Welcome to His Bastart Wean,'" he says, and he begins to read:

"Thou's welcome, wean; mishanter fa' me,
If thoughts o' thee, or yet thy mamie,
Shall ever daunton me or awe me,
My bonie lady,
Or if I blush when thou shalt ca' me
Tyta or daddie.

Tho' now they ca' me fornicator,
An' tease my name in kintry clatter,
The mair they talk, I'm kent the better,
E'en let them clash;
An auld wife's tongue's a feckless matter
To gi'e ane fash.

Welcome! my bonie, sweet, wee dochter,
Tho' ye come here a wee unsought for,
And tho' your comin' I hae fought for,
Baith kirk and queir;
Yet, by my faith, ye're no unwrought for,
That I shall swear!

Wee image o' my bonie Betty,
As fatherly I kiss and daut thee,
As dear, and near my heart I set thee
Wi' as gude will
As a' the priests had seen me get thee
That's out o' hell.

Sweet fruit o' many a merry dint,
My funny toil is now a' tint,
Sin' thou came to the warl' asklent,
Which fools may scoff at;
In my last plack thy part's be in't
The better ha'f o't.

Tho' I should be the waur bestead,
Thou's be as braw and bienly clad,
And thy young years as nicely bred
Wi' education,

> As ony brat o' wedlock's bed,
> > In a' thy station.
>
> Lord grant that thou may aye inherit
> Thy mither's person, grace, an' merit,
> An' thy poor, worthless daddy's spirit,
> > Without his failin's,
> 'Twill please me mair to see thee heir it,
> > Than stockit mailens.
>
>
> For if thou be what I would hae thee,
> And tak the counsel I shall gie thee,
> I'll never rue my trouble wi' thee,
> > The cost nor shame o't,
> But be a loving father to thee,
> > And brag the name o't."

Robert lays the pages on the table after reading the last short line, then looks over at Nancy. Her brows are drawn together and her mouth is set in what looks like a scowl, but whether her expression signals concentration or disapproval of the poem's improprieties, he cannot tell. He pushes his chair back and rises to stretch his legs. "Well," he says, "what did ye think o' it?"

Nancy, too, rises, shaking her head, her mouth twitching, hands twisting at her apron . "Ye're an awful' man, Rab Burns," she says at last, "so ye are."

But, having spoken, she crosses the tiny room and throws her arms around him, pressing her head to his shoulder. And as he draws breath against the force of his sister's embrace, Robert marvels as he has done so many times before – reading Fergusson or Ramsay or Henry MacKenzie, or in the act of writing his own verses – at the power of mere words to stir the heart.

The rise and fall of Mr. Auld's hard-edged voice echoes from the granite walls of Mauchline Kirk above the usual restless noise from the congregation: the shifting of feet and bodies, the low buzz of whispered gossip, the barking of churchgoers' dogs at the open door. For Jean Armour, seated between her mother and her young brother Adam, Auld's sermon separates itself only occasionally from the other sounds. Now she turns and cranes her neck to Jeany Markland sitting among her folk in their own pew. Jeany catches her eye and smiles, inclining her head toward the door, then makes a face in the direction of the pulpit. A giggle escapes Jean.

"You get turned round in your seat, my girl." Jean feels her father's heavy hand on her shoulder and spins quickly about. James Armour, leaning past his wife, is staring balefully at her. "And see that ye stay like that," he says in a loud whisper, then settles back into his place.

Jean sees Mr. Auld shooting a glance of annoyance their way, though she wonders how he can pick out any pocket of disturbance amid the general noise. Likely everything bothers him these days, still smarting as he must be from his humiliation – his and Holy Willie's – before the Ayrshire Presbytery over the Gavin Hamilton business. Her mother's elbow suddenly jabs her and she jerks upright in her seat. Behind her, she hears a snirtle of laughter, Jeany Markland's by the sound of it, followed by an angry parental hiss.

Resigning herself to sitting still and quiet for the remainder of the sermon, Jean lets her eyes wander along the back of the oaken pew, idly noticing familiar shapes in the grain of the wood, or faces, like the man with the big nose and the misshapen wig that always reminds her of Auld, whose own large and ornate wig seems to her typical of his old-fashioned views. Distracted momentarily by the fidgeting of her brother, she frowns him into at least temporary immobility. And as she looks at Adam, she catches sight of Robert Burns seated across the way with his family, leaning intently forward as if he's really listening to the sermon.

Jean feels the blood fluttering at her throat. Silly, she knows, for Rob Burns is dangerous, already father of an illegitimate bairn by yon lassie Paton, and compeared for it in Tarboton. And didn't Jean Smith hear her brother Jamie link Burns with Mrs. Hamilton's nursemaid, Mary Campbell? Very big with the servant hizzies is Robert Burns. But for all that, he's the one her friends talk about, the one they watch for on the street or at fairs and markets. And he's the one she thinks of herself whenever she imagines a man's lips pressed on hers, or a man's hands on her body. Jean quickly returns her gaze to the back of the pew, her face warming with guilt at such thoughts in the kirk itself.

Mr. Auld's sermon finally concludes, and Jean looks up, hearing the fresh outbreak of rustling and murmuring as folk begin putting away their Bibles and hymnals, and adjusting their coats and hats for the road. The minister brings the flat of his hand down on the pulpit, though, the smack resounding above the brattle of the congregation and causing more than one head to snap upright in startled attention.

Mr. Auld looks down, lips compressed and eyes asklent, looking from face to face. "My psalm for today is the Eighty-third," he says, "the word of Asaph. And as ye go forth, remember – as some of ye ha'e good reason to do – that the Lord despises them that oppress the Kirk!"

At this, Jean sees folk begin to look over at the pew where Gavin Hamilton sits with his family. And from his place near the pulpit, a hand covering his mouth, Holy Willie Fisher hums and nods his agreement with the priest. But as lips move close to ears and the buzz of comment rises, Hamilton's face remains calm and expressionless, save for a quick glance when someone – Robert Burns, Jean suspects – makes much of clearing his throat.

"Attend!" says Mr. Auld loudly. "Psalm Eighty-three!" And he begins to speak, barely glancing at the Bible before him, his voice throaty with feeling.

"Keep not thou silence, O God: hold not thy peace, and be not still, O God, for lo, thine enemies make a tumult; and they that hate thee have lifted up the head. They have taken crafty counsel against thy people, and consulted against thy hidden ones. They have said, Come, and let us cut them off from being a nation; that the name of Israel may be no more in remembrance. For they have consulted together with one consent: they are confederate against thee . . ."

Jean's attention falters as Mr. Auld begins to come over a list of unfamiliar names – Gebal and Amalek and Oreb and such – and she looks again at Rob Burns, whose eyes are moving back and forth from the minister to Holy Willie as if watching a game of pitch and toss. Suddenly, though, Mr. Auld thunders out again in homelier language:

"O my God, make them like a wheel; as the stubble before the wind. As the fire burneth a wood, and as the flame setteth the mountains on fire. So persecute them with thy tempest, and make them afraid with thy storm. Fill their faces with shame; that they may seek thy name, O Lord. Let them be confounded and troubled for ever; yes, let them be put to shame and perish: That men may know that thou, whose name alone is Jehovah, art the Most High over all the earth!"

Arms lifted and hands spread, trembling, Mr. Auld looks up to the ceiling as if he might see might see Jehovah there. Composing himself, he addresses the congregation in a softer voice and pronounces the blessing.

Outside the kirk, James Armour turns to his wife, his round face flushed. "I'll tell ye, Mary, it was high time Mr. Auld gi'ed it to that ane, never mind what yon Presbytery may say. Aye, an' Lawyer Aiken, an' a'. It's nane o' their affair onyhow, if ye ask me."

Mary Armour puts a hand on her husband's arm and nods. "Aye, Jeems," she says, clicking her tongue at the thought of so many clergymen misguided into siding with Gavin Hamilton by the glib pleadings of Bob Aiken.

Jean cares little for any of them, with their disputes that leave ordinary folk shaking their heads. Maybe a master mason like her father, whose business involves the very building of kirks, needs to know the ins and outs of it all. But the world is more than prayers and preaching, she thinks, looking at the clouds blowing across the bright sky like sheets torn from a clothesline, and at the shifting green hues of grass and trees around her. She sees Jeany Markland, Jean Smith, and the Miller sisters, standing with Chrissie Morton in the shade of a yew tree, and she hurries over to them, though she fears they, too, will be caught up with talk of Auld and New Lichts.

But she needn't have worried. Jeany Markland laughs at her approach and says, "Wait till ye hear what Chrissie an' Jean Smith heard frae Rabbie Burns the other nicht!"

Jean sniffs. "It must ha'e been a wonder, richt enough, for ye to think I would care about it."

"Och, dinna talk rubbish, Jean Armour," says Betty Miller, her pug-nosed face lit up with good-humored exasperation. "We ken how little ye care for Rab Burns, a'richt."

Leaving Jean no time to respond, Chrissie Morton holds up a graceful white hand. Chrissie's hands are her best feature, Jean thinks, which is why she uses them often in conversation. "We were at the dancin'," says Chrissie, gesturing vaguely in the direction of Ronald's ballroom, "an' we saw Rab Burns sendin' his collie Luath awa' back to Mossgiel. And Jean, here" – she indicates wee Jean Smith – "says to him – "

Wee Jean interrupts, giggling as she speaks. "I says to him, 'Mr. Burns,' I says, 'what'll ye do now for a dancin' partner?'" She pauses for the laughter, then resumes. "And do ye know what he says to me? He says –"

Chrissie takes up the tale again, holding up a finger for attention. "He says, 'That dog just followed me a' the road frae Mossgiel. I just wish I could find a lassie as faithful.'"

Again the girls erupt into laughter. "Would ye credit that?" says Jeany Markland breathlessly. "As faithfu' as his collie dog, if ye please." Then her mouth forms a circle and she bobs her head. "My God, here he comes the now."

Jean's own laughter dies, her throat seeming to swell shut, and again, as in the kirk, she feels herself reddening. In the space of a moment or two, Robert Burns stands before them, resplendent in his blue coat, white breeches, and riding boots, looking hard and sturdy and, as always, faintly amused. Bowing slightly to all of them, but with his eyes on Jean, he says, "And how are ye this fine Sunday, ladies? Well, I trust."

Jean feels rather than sees the other girls looking at her, and realizes she must find some response. Before she knows it, her mouth opens and she says, "We're grand, Mr. Burns. And what about you? Ha'e ye found a lassie yet to equal the devotion o' your dog?"

She hears the other girls drawing in sharp breaths, holding back their amusement, and she sees Rob's eyes widen as if he's just noticed her. Then he throws his head back and lets out a roar of laughter that the girls soon join in chorus, causing folk to turn and take notice all across the kirk green.

"Jean!" Her father's voice carries loudly as he strides toward her, glaring. "Get you o'er here, my lass," he says, stopping short. "It's time we were awa' hame."

"Aye, Faither," she says quietly, her heart thumping, mortified, and she falls into step beside him as they walk toward Mrs. Armour.

"Adam!" James Armour shouts over his shoulder, and the boy comes at a run from where he's been jouking among the trees with some other laddies. "Stop your caperin'," he says to Adam when the boy is nearby, "an' walk at a decent rate. It's the Sabbath. And you," he adds, turning to Jean. "Don't let me see you takin' onything to do wi' yon blackguard again."

"But Faither – " she begins.

"Haud your tongue!" says James Armour. "Rab Burns is nae fit company for ony lassie. Aye, nor for ony man, neither."

Within the week, Robert takes himself into the village to buy ink and paper and to get one of the ploughhorses shod. At Hughie Woodrow's smithy, he waits while the blacksmith and his apprentice Archie Millar bend to the fire. As if tranced, he watches the reddening of the metal in the shifting flames, and listens to the soughing of the bellows and the clink of hammer and anvil as the first shoe takes shape. Then he holds the bridle with one hand and strokes the mare's soft nose with the other while Hughie secures the shoe on her right front hoof with a few deft strokes.

Before long, the job is done. "Aye, there ye are, Mr. Burns," says the smith, passing a forearm over his dirt-smeared brow, then giving the mare's flank a clap. "Them shoon'll see her doon mony a furrow."

"Thanks, Hughie," Robert says. He fishes some coins from his pocket and drops them in Woodrow's outstretched hand. Then he leaves the smithy with the patient animal clopping behind him at the end of its bridle.

Later, after having bought a new supply of paper and India ink out of the frugal seven pounds yearly pay he allows himself, Robert starts for home along Loudon Street. He's about to lead the mare across the kirkyard up toward the Backcauseway when, glancing toward the Cowgate, he sees Jean Armour coming out of her house, which lies directly behind Dow's Whitefoord Arms. On impulse, he keeps to the street, and before he's gone very far Jean looks in his direction. He half-expects her to hurry away on whatever errand she's bound, but she slows her pace and lets him catch up to her.

"Good day, Miss Armour," he says, retreating into formality. "I trust ye're as well as ye look."

The normal pink of her cheeks deepens. "However I look, I'm weel enough, Mr. Burns," she says after a few moments. Then she notes the ploughhorse and her eyes take on a merry glint. "Do ye no' ha'e a saddle for your mount, then?"

Robert chuckles at her sally, then essays one of his own. "The best mounts," he says, giving her a direct look, "dinna need a saddle."

"Mr. Burns!" she says, her face scarlet. But just as he fears he's gone too far, Jean's ample chest begins to heave with the effort to suppress her laughter. When she's composed herself, she tries for an expression of severity. "Ye must think I'm an awful hizzy to say a thing like that."

Looking at her full, well-made figure, at the contrast between her dark eyes and hair and her fine pink and white complexion, Robert feels gooseflesh rise on his arms. "I'll tell ye what I think ye are, Jean," he says. "Ye're the bonniest o' a' the bonnie belles in Mauchline. And if ye'd consent to walk out wi' me on ane o' these fine summer nichts, ye'd mak me the happiest man in the West o' Scotland." He moves closer to her, his nostrils filling with her clean, sweet scent. "What do ye say, lass? Will ye do it?"

Jean looks guiltily toward the Armour house, then back at Robert. "Aye," she says, her voice scarcely audible. "I will." She glances again at her front door. "I'll need to go now, or my mither'll see us. I'm supposed to be awa' up to meet Jean Smith at Jamie's shop."

"I'm on the road back to Mossgiel, mysel'," Robert says. "I'll walk wi' ye as far as Wee Smith's. If that's no' too wicked a pastime for broad daylight."

Jean colors again, then laughs and nods her assent. And as they walk up to Jamie Smith's haberdashery, where the Backcauseway runs into the market cross, Robert feels himself strong enough for any challenge, ready to make good use of the ink and paper in the bag that hangs across the mare's broad back. Here beside him is a lassie a man might lead a life with. Not like Betty Paton, who airy and buxom though she might be and mother of his child, has about her a coarseness, aye, a servant's demeanor, much as his own snobbery pains him. Nor like Mary Campbell, with her secret heart and her unaccountable attachment to a man who can only shame her. And remembering that night at the Elbow, Robert feels his insides knot. He looks down at Jean, suddenly aware that they're standing before Wee Smith's, and that she's watching him as if trying to read his thoughts.

"Well, Jean," he says. "When will I see ye?"

"Friday next," she says softly, but without hesitation; then she turns quickly and disappears into the shop.

As he starts up the Backcauseway for Mossgiel, Robert marvels at how quickly his own moods can change, from joy to dark depression and back again in the space of a few breaths, and all over the curve of a white shoulder or a red lip, whether in memory or standing before him. And as if to underscore his thought, Gavin Hamilton's door opens and out walks Mary Campbell, fair and slim and lovely.

Seeing him, Mary stops short, and for a moment their eyes meet. Robert swallows against the rush of emotion that seems to congest his throat, and looks down at the road before him. Then, straightening his shoulders, he resumes his stride, looking off into the distance toward Mossgiel.

Passing Mary almost close enough to touch her in the narrow street, he hears her draw a sharp breath. "Robert," she says quietly. Then again: "Robert."

But he keeps walking, and soon all he can hear at his back are the mare's hooves, clip-clopping in time with the beat of his own heart.

The kitchen at Mossgiel

A Fragment.
Tune: "I had a horse & I had nae mair"

When first I came to Stewart Kyle
    My mind it was nae steady,
Where e'er I gaed, where e'er I rade,
    A mistress still I had ay:
But when I came roun' by Mauchlin town,
    Not dreadin' any body,
My heart was caught before I thought
    And by a Mauchlin Lady –

from the first *Commonplace Book*
August 1795

Chapter Seven

Striding along the road to Mauchline, Robert feels dazed, his head and heart full of the late summer evening. To the west the setting sun is a red stain on the horizon, giving way to pale gold among the layers of cloud high above the sea. To the east the sky is nearly cloudless, with a silver crescent of moon riding a field of pale blue like a shadow on snow. Gulls and rooks are circling, mere silhouettes in the mild air, and lapwings skim low over the fields. Robert can scarcely believe that this same land could have brought forth such bitterly disappointing crops last year, and may well do so again.

The move to Mossgiel has brought a mixed result, he reflects: the joy of fatherhood, tempered by the prospect of another mouth to feed and by the humiliation he and Betty endured at Tarbolton Kirk; and the rich harvest of poetry, composed with a facility that seems to mock the family's torturous planning and exhausting labor, as yet unsuccessful, to make the farm productive. And now he sees the Castle of Mauchline looming ahead, a place he'll never again walk past without a confusion of longing and regret. Nonetheless, looking around him at the wheeling birds and the darkening sky, he feels strong and full of life, eager for what lies ahead. Especially this evening.

In the Whitefoord Arms, Jock Richmond, Jamie Smith, and Tanner Hunter are ranged about the table in the back room, pint stoups of ale in hand.

Jock has been in an ill mood for months, ever since he and Jenny Surgeoner were brought to the cutty stool as fornicators. And with Jenny carrying his child, he feels his shame aggravated by the need to act: he must marry her or endure the continuing scorn of the village, the constant pressure from Jenny and her parents, and the persistent gripe of his own conscience like an aching tooth. He sits hunched over his stoup, staring at the shifting patterns of foam on the dark ale as if he might read some answer there.

Jamie Smith, whose stepfather James Lamie helped Holy Willie Fisher expose Jock and Jenny, knows well how his friend must feel. But his natural energy breaks out in impatience, and he brings the flat of his hand down on the table. "What aboot a sang, for God's sake? Ye'd think we were at a bloody wake." He winks at Hunter and nods in Richmond's direction. "And I ken who the corpse is."

Hunter cranes his neck around at the door. "Where the hell's Rab? That's what I'd like to know. A grand night like this, ye'd think it would bring him into Mauchline."

Smith laughs. "Aye, if he's no' oot daffin' amang the heather wi' some hizzy already." He gives a shout. "Johnnie! What aboot anither pint?"

Johnnie Dow enters the room carrying a jug of ale, his bulk filling the narrow doorway, his red face split with a grin. After filling the three stoups, he moves to the broad fireplace, where a pile of peats and logs is already laid. He sets them ablaze, then rises with a flaming taper and crosses to the table, where he lights the large tallow candle hanging in its black iron sconce from the low ceiling. "There. Maybe that'll brighten ye up a bit. Ye're a gey sorry set o' revelers the nicht. Now, what aboot a dram to go wi' your pints?"

"The very thing," says Smith, "an' see if we canna raise the deid here."

Richmond drains his pint in two long swallows, then sets it down and glowers at Smith. "Ye're a daft bugger, Jamie."

Smith refuses to be offended. "Maybe I am. But we're here to enjoy oursel's, no' to girn an' moan. Johnnie," he says, as Dow sets coggies of whisky before them. "Start us aff on a sang – something bawdy, wi' a good noisy chorus."

As Robert enters the Whitefoord arms, nodding to Mrs. Dow, he hears familiar voices lifted in unison. They are singing "Tail Todle," an old ditty with a bawdy chorus he's been toying with, himself, lately, adding two new verses to the surviving fragment of the original.

He steps into the back room, where Smith, Hunter, and Johnnie Dow are on their feet, repeating the only verse they know. Before they can break to greet him, he gestures for them to continue and joins in the chorus, noting Jock Richmond seated with a dour face amid the hilarity.

The chorus ended, Robert holds up a finger for attention and sings out one of his new verses:

> "Our gudewife held o'er to Fife,
>   for to buy a coal-riddle;
> Lang ere she came back again,
>   Tammie gart my tail todle."

Then, after leading them in the chorus again, he sings his second stanza:

> "Jessie Mack she gi'ed a plack,
>   Helen Wallace gi'ed a bottle,
> Quo' the bride, "Tis o'er little
>   For to mend a broken doddle.'"

And breathless with laughter, they sing a final chorus:

> "Tail todle, tail todle,
>   Tammie gart my tail todle;
> At my arse wi' diddle doddle,
>   Tammie gart my tail todle."

Johnnie Dow crosses to Robert with a coggie of whisky. "Here ye are, Rab, lad, get get this down ye – for God knows ye've earned it. That was a rare auld sang to start wi', but, man, ye've improved its wit tenfold." Dow laughs, a deep rumble from his massive belly. "To mend a broken doddle.' Oh, man, that's great." He squints at Robert with a sly smile. "And I'll warrant ye'll gar some poor lassie's tail todle, yoursel', richt enough, gin this nicht's o'er."

Jamie Smith points at Robert. "Damn it, Rab, I've said it afore and I'll say it again: ye're better far than ony o' them – Ramsay, Fergusson, the lot!"

Robert smiles, but shakes his head. "Thanks, Jamie, but I've little enough to recommend me. A handfu' o' scribbled verses to pass amang friends. I doubt I'll ever see good black print."

Johnnie Dow lays a hand on his shoulder. "Dinna forget, Rab, a good sang and a good friend are their ain reward."

Touched, Robert nods. "Aye, Johnnie." Then with a chuckle, he says, "But some days a man can do wi' a bit help frae a drap o' Kilbagie, eh?"

Jamie Smith raises his coggie. "Aye, Johnnie. Let's ha'e anither roond to loosen our pipes."

As Dow fetches more drink, Robert sits on the edge of the table at Richmond's elbow. "What's up wi' you, then, Jock?" he says.

Richmond looks up, his blue eyes hooded, scowling. "We can talk a' we want aboot sangs and Kilbagie, Rab. But you know and I know that a man needs mair. Aye, and mair even even than a lass in the bracken. He needs a bit o' respect – and recognition." He gulps at his whisky. "He needs to be free frae constant want and poverty. And nane o' us will ever be free o' that, scratchin' away here in Mauchline. Sangs or nae sangs."

Robert slides from his perch on the table and draws a chair next to Richmond. In a lowered tone he says, "I hope that doesna mean ye're ready to abandon Jenny Surgeoner, Jock. Man, she needs ye, wi' her time nearly on her. And ye did promise to marry her, did ye no'?"

Eyes flashing, Richmond glares at Robert. "And what aboot Betty Paton?" he demands. "I didna see you rushin' to wed her!"

Robert glances about the room, then leans forward. "That was different," he says, his voice constricted to a whisper. "Betty knew we were never meant to wed. And I made her nae promises. But at least I've made provision to tak in the bairn."

His indignation suddenly gone, Richmond leans his elbows on the table. "Och, to hell, Rab – it's nae use. How could I hope to support wife or child clerking here for Gaw'n Hamilton? He's a good enough master, a' richt – though no' as good as you gi'e him credit for. But there's nae living here – it's too galling." He sits back, breathing deeply. "I'm for Edinburgh, Rab. And so should you be. There's where a man can hope to mak his fortune."

"But responsibility, Jock, responsibility." Shocked, Robert can scarcely keep his voice down. "I've a family to look after. And now so do you."

"It's nae use, Rab." Richmond waves a hand dismissively. "I've already gi'ed Hamilton my notice. I'm aff next week."

Robert is stunned, both by the magnitude of Richmond's decision and by the prospect of so suddenly losing one of his best friends. "Ye never let on," he says at last.

Richmond shrugs, embarrassed. "I'm sorry, Rab. I had to think it oot for mysel'."

With mixed emotions Robert glances at the window, thinking of the house that lies beyond it and what awaits him there at the back yett. "We'll need to talk mair, Jock. But no' here, no' now. I have to be aff in a few minutes."

Richmond's face brightens with piqued curiosity. "An assignation?"

Reluctantly, Robert nods. "Aye."

"Wha is it this time?" Richmond leans forward eagerly. "Betty Miller? Jeany Markland? It's surely no' still Mary Campbell. I thought ye'd ta'en the rue at her for good when ye saw her wi' Captain Montgomerie."

Robert speaks quietly. "No, it's no' Mary." Then, unable to contain his ebullience, he smiles broadly. "It's only the fairest creature in Mauchline!" he says, his voice rising. "Our first tryst. Oh, man, she's lovely."

Richmond pounds the table triumphantly. "Jean Armour!"

Reluctant again, Robert finally acknowledges the fact. "Aye," he says, nodding. "But dinna proclaim it to a' and sundry."

"At least ye dinna ha'e far to go," says Richmond, jabbing his thumb at the window where the Armours' prosperous house stands fewer then twenty steps beyond. "Man, James Armour'll skin ye alive. Ye'll ha'e heard what he thinks o' your Kirk satires, pillar o' sanctity that he is. And if he kenned his favorite dochter was dallyin' wi' ony man – let alone Robin Burns – he'd ha'e an apoplexy!"

Robert drains his coggie. "He'll just no' need to find out aboot it."

Johnnie Dow leans across the table with the stone whisky jar and refills Richmond's coggie, but Robert puts a hand over his own and lays some coins before him.

Tanner Hunter shouts from the ingle, where he and Wee Smith have withdrawn to give Richmond and Robert privacy. "Dinna let him aff that easy, Johnnie! And ha'e ane to yoursel'. Come on, Rab. Tak a dram and gi'e us a poem!"

Robert moves away from the table. "Och, I'm just awa' the now, Tanner."

"For God's sake, Rab," says Wee Smith, "ye've hardly had time to warm your chair. Pour the man a gill, Johnnie."

As Dow complies, Hunter steps toward Robert. "Do ye no' ha'e onythin' new for us? Ye've been writin' at a hell of a rate these days."

Robert eyes the four men in turn, Hunter, Smith, Dow, and Richmond. "Aye," he says finally. "I'd thought to save this for Gaw'n Hamilton and Bob Aiken, since it concerns the two o' them. But I think ye'll a' appreciate it – and it'll maybe even cheer up Jock, here. It's ca'd 'Holy Willie's Prayer.'"

Richmond is on his feet immediately at the mention of the man who was the chief agent of his humiliation. "By God, Rab, I hope ye gi'ed him what for, hypocritical crowl that he is. Sneakin' aboot layin' bare other folk's misfortune – an' a' the time sinnin' away in secret, himsel'."

Johnnie Dow laughs. "Aye, and as for the fornication he's aey sae zealous to condemn, I'll warrant some o' the serving-lassies aboot yon farm o' his could tell a thing or twa on that score." He moves to the door. "But wait, Rab, till I tell the rest o' the howff – they'll a' want to hear this!"

Dow soon returns with a number of folk, including his son Sandy and John Brown the clockmaker. As they jostle their way into the small room, Robert greets them. "Sandy, Clockie, a'body. This is a poem in the voice o' Willie Fisher at prayer – just after Bob Aiken and Gaw'n Hamilton got the best of him an' Daddy Auld afore the Ayrshire Presbytery.

"There's an Argument first," he says, striking a declamatory pose the way Bob Aiken might do. "'Holy Willie was a rather oldish bachelor elder in the parish of Mauchline, and much and justly famed for that polemical chattering which ends in tippling orthodoxy, and that spiritualized bawdry which refines to a liquorish devotion – '"

Laughter rises around Robert, but before he can go on, Mrs. Dow hurries into the room. "Johnnie," she says to her husband, "it's Willie Fisher, himsel' – and he's just comin' in the front door."

"Aye, well," says Robert with a sigh, partially relieved that he can be on his way. "That's that, then."

But Richmond, delighted, takes hold of his arm. "Rab, Rab, this is too good a chance to waste." Richmond motions for quiet, then hurries into the front room, reappearing moments later with the startled and reluctant Fisher in tow. "Come awa' in, Mr. Fisher," he says. "Come awa' in and ha'e a dram."

Casting a disapproving eye around at the company, Fisher shakes his elbow loose from Richmond's grasp. "Na, na," he says in his thin quaver, "nae drink for me. I just came in to warn respectable folk o' the lateness o' the hour. I hardly need to tell you the penalties for excess and recklessness, Jock Richmond."

Richmond's face reddens, and he takes an angry step backward. But before he can speak, Johnnie Dow steps in. "Now, now, Mr. Fisher," he says, playing the jolly innkeeper to the hilt, "this is a place to shed cares and bury disputes."

Recovering himself, Richmond takes Fisher's arm again. "Aye, Mr. Fisher, Johnnie's richt." He leads Holy Willie to the table. "Come on, now, John, a dram for Mr. Fisher."

Dow pours a coggie of Ferintosh and sets it on the table next to Fisher, who sits, eyeing the whisky in greedy fascination. Bending to his ear, Richmond says, "Rab Burns is just aboot to recite a new poem for us."

Fisher looks up, suspicious. "A poem. What kind o' poem? I'll listen to nae scurrilous bawdry."

Catching Richmond's mood, Robert moves forward, glancing around him at the expectant company. "No, no, Mr. Fisher. Far from it. It's a poem about" – he thinks for a moment – "about the glories o' Eldership in the Scottish Kirk."

Fisher raises an eyebrow, curious, but still doubtful. "Ooh, aye? I wouldna ha'e thocht to hear verses like that frae you, Rab Burns." Finally, though, thirst overcomes suspicion, and he picks up his coggie slowly, sipping the whisky at the side of his mouth, as if he might some-how avoid notice. "Weel, aiblins I'll hear a couple o' lines. On ye go."

After breathing deeply, Robert begins to recite, in a fervent, pious tone:

> "O Thou that in the Heavens does dwell,
> Wha, as it pleases best Thysel,
> Sends ane to Heaven an' ten to Hell
>   A' for Thy glory,
> And no for onie guid or ill
>   They've done before Thee!

I bless and praise Thy matchless might,
When thousands Thou hast left in night,
That I am here before Thy sight,
      For gifts an' grace
A burning and a shining light
      To a' this place. . . ."

Fisher breaks in, beaming, "Now there's verse for ye," he says to Johnnie Dow. "Ooh, aye." Then he turns to Robert. "A better class o' thing a'thegither than I've heard ascribed to ye, Mr. Burns."

On a whim, part playfulness, part caution, Robert says innocently, "Oh, it's no' mine, Mr. Fisher." He winks above the elder's head at Richmond, and adds, "I hear it was written by a lad up in Kilmarnock. But I think ye'll agree that he kens weel what he's about?"

"Ooh, aye," says Fisher. "It's a fair treat to hear ane o' the Kirk's elders gi'ed his due. Come awa', then. I'm listenin'."

As Fisher sips again at his whisky, Robert resumes, moving about confidently as he recites:

"What was I, or my generation,
That I should get sic exaltation?
I, wha deserv'd most just damnation
      For broken laws,
Six thousand years ere my creation,
      Thro' Adam's cause!"

This piece of transparent rationalization, so characteristic of Fisher's own shiftiness, causes a ripple of amusement among the listeners, but from Holy Willie himself it elicits only a nod of pleased agreement. Then Robert continues:

"When from my mither's womb I fell,
Thou might hae plung'd me deep in hell
To gnash my gooms, and weep, and wail
      In burning lakes,
Where damned devils roar and yell,
      Chain'd to their stakes.

Yet I am here, a chosen sample,
To show Thy grace is great and ample:
I'm here a pillar o' Thy temple,
    Strong as a rock,
A guide, a buckler, and example
    To a' Thy flock!"

"Ooh, man, Rab, that's wonderful!" Fisher drinks off his whisky. "'A pillar o' Thy temple!' Ooh, aye, that's marvelous. I wonder who could ha'e made that up?"

Behind Fisher, Smith and Hunter are clutching at each other in an attempt to stifle their laughter. But the rapt Elder notices nothing except Johnnie Dow refilling his coggie. Taking the wooden cup in hand again, he says, "Could ye no' just come o'er that last bit again? Ye'll need to pen me a copy o' this, Mr. Burns – I hear ye write a fine clear hand."

Robert lays a finger to the side of his nose. "Well, Mr. Fisher, maybe we'll just go on and see what else our anonymous bard has to say." He perches himself on the table, his feet on a chair.

"Oh, Lord, Thou kens what zeal I bear
When drinkers drink, an' swearers swear,
An' singin' there an' dancin' here,
    Wi' great and sma';
For I am keepit by Thy fear
    Free frae them a'."

Fisher continues to nod smugly, his eyes shut in bliss, and Robert goes on:

"But yet, O Lord! confess I must:
At times I'm fash'd wi' fleshly lust;
An' sometimes, too, in warldly trust,
    Vile self gets in; . . .'"

At these lines, so near the bone, Fisher's eyes open and focus warily on Robert, only to close again, doubt momentarily lulled by the next two lines:

"But Thou remembers we are dust,
        Defil'd wi' sin."

What follows, however, is far more disturbing:

"O Lord! yestreen, Thou kens, wi' Meg –
Thy pardon I sincerely beg.
O! may't ne'er be a livin' plague
        To my dishonor,
An' I'll ne'er lift a lawless leg
        Again upon her."

At this mention both of fornication and the name of a maidservant at his Montgarswood Farm, Fisher shifts uneasily and glances at the now open amusement on the faces around him.

Sensing that the game will soon be up, Robert recites the next verse in a tumble of words:

"Besides, I farther maun avow,
Wi' Leezie's lass, three times I trow –
But Lord, that Friday I was fou,
        When I cam near her,
Or else, Thou kens, Thy servant true
        Wad never steer her."

Horrified at the mention of his neighbor's maid, fully aware now of how he has been duped, Fisher leaps to his feet, throwing down his whisky and tumbling the chair behind him.

"Ye'll roast in hell for this, Rab Burns! Ye're a damned blackguard – a damned blackguard! That I should live to hear sic filthy blasphemy!"

The company erupts into boisterous laughter, and Fisher, all but paralyzed with rage, eyes bulging, stumbles toward the door. "Hell, Burns!" he shouts. "Ye'll gang straight to hell, ye infernal blackguard! The Session'll hear aboot this! Aboot the whole damned lot o' ye!" Then, to a redoubled shout of mirth, Holy Willie Fisher slinks out of the Whitefoord Arms like a drenched tomcat.

The sound of Mauchline Burn mingles with the rush of his own blood in Robert's ears as he sits with his back propped against an oak tree, Jean Armour seated on the grass before him. The full brilliant scatter of the Milky Way arches over them in the clear night, its splendor obscuring the thin pale rind of the new moon. Jean's skin seems to glow in the starlight, set off by her dark eyes and the soft black fall of her hair about her shoulders.

"So," Robert says softly, "ye're out wi' Jean Smith the night, are ye?"

"Aye," Jean says, sounding troubled. "I don't like to lie to my mither. But I've never been oot wi' a man like this afore. And if my faither should hear tell . . ."

"And especially if he should hear it was Rab Burns, eh?" Robert's tone is ironic, but he feels somehow injured at Armour's evident condemnation of a man he scarcely knows.

"He doesna like ye," says Jean simply. "He thinks ye're irreligious – maybe even an atheist. And he thinks ye're a bad influence on Jean Smith's brother Jamie."

Stung, Robert leans forward. "Because I speak my ain mind! For some folk, ony belief other than theirs is nae belief at a'."

"And he thinks ye're a deceiver o' lassies, as weel," Jean goes on. "If he kenned I was here, he'd kill me – and maybe you and a'."

"I'm no' feart for him – or ony man. And I'd brave ony number o' trials to be here wi' you." And as he speaks, Robert realizes he is touched by Jean's beauty and her soft straightforward manner in a way that seems fresh, beyond the hyperbole of such courting declarations. Suddenly he feels the need to justify himself. "And what lassies does he think I've deceived, eh, Jean?"

"I don't know," she says quietly. "There's Betty Paton."

Robert is on his feet, pacing toward the burn. Turning, he says heatedly, "I'm no' ashamed – neither o' Betty nor her bairn! They can ca' me fornicator or what they like. But love begot that child. And I've provided for it and a'."

"And what aboot the mither?"

"Betty's happy enough," he says. "I made her nae promises – and she asked for nane!"

Jean rises, too, and walks to the burn's edge, her feet leaving small, dark patches of shadow on the star-silvered grass. "I wouldna ha'e ye feel ashamed afore me," she says. "Only ye needna think I'm to be anither . . . conquest, even though ye ha'e a great name for your poetical flattery o' the lassies."

Robert turns to her. "I've never yet praised a lass wi' less than a whole heart." And he recognizes, beyond the moment, the truth of what he's said, that he has revealed more of himself than he intended, perhaps more than he has known. But he knows, too, that he must go on. "Sometimes a lad and a lass need nothing mair than each other, Jean. A poet can counterfeit – even go beyond – life. But he canna do without it. And sometimes it wants nae words at a'."

Jean looks up at him, her dark eyes wide, her expression grave. "Ye're o'er clever for me, Rab. But I wouldna want ye to leave me for anither."

"So ye agree wi' your faither, after a'?" His voice is sharper than he intended. "Look, Jean, if ever I make a vow, I keep it! Do ye think my word's worthless? Is that it?"

Jean looks down at her clasped hands. "No, Rab, I think nothing like that. I'm just feart ye'll get tired o' me."

He takes her by the shoulders and, bending, kisses her brow. She raises her face to him, lips parted, and he kisses her again, on the mouth, the scent of her enveloping him in the gently moving air. Bringing his cheek against hers, he speaks into her thick hair. "I couldna tire o' you, lass. No' in a lifetime."

"Oh, Rab," she murmurs, "I love ye – for as long as ye want me."

He knows that, virgin as she undoubtedly is, her decision has been made, and he leads her to the shadow of a hawthorn hedge. He spreads his coat on the grass, feeling the now-familiar weakness in his own chest, always new, always exhilarating. And as they sink down together, without awkwardness, he marvels at the emotional pendulum of his attitude toward the act itself: from pleasure in the artful language and ritual of courtship; to comic delight in bawdy song and tale, with their plain and natural frankness, their celebration of houghmagandie or simple rue at its consequences; to coarse pride among his cronies, strutting head high like a ram after serving a ewe; to the tenderness and wonder of a moment like this, when he feels poised, as if in the space between some cosmic breathing. And to feel it all at once, to be lost in the contradiction. A wonder.

His laborer's fingers feeling coarse and ungentle, he unlaces Jean's bodice, allowing the rise and fall of her quickened breathing to spill her heavy breasts from her loose underblouse. He moves his face between those smooth billows of flesh, runs his tongue over their taut dark nipples. She whimpers breathlessly in pleasure and moves her fingers lightly on his neck. Now he kisses her, his open mouth on hers; then he takes her hand and moves it down to his stomach. Tentatively, but unselfconsciously, she trails her fingers over his groin, and he trembles, his cock taking life at her touch.

"What now, Rab?" she whispers, ingenuously eager. He reaches down and unbuttons his breeches, allowing his cock to stand away from his belly in the cool night air. Her hand brushes against his skin, sending a shiver through his body.

"Take it in your hand, lassie," he says. "Feel it. For your pleasure as well as mine."

As she grips the thick warm shaft, he is conscious through his pleasure of a snippet from an old song: "Weel she lo'ed it in her fist, / But better when it slippit in." And he brings his own hand up under her skirts, between the satin curve of her inner thighs to the already damp nest of her cunt.

At the touch of his fingers parting its warm lips, Jean cries out and presses herself against him, gasping in release. "Oh, Rab," she moans. And then again, "Oh, Rab."

"There's better to come, Jean," he whispers, pushing her dress above her waist and kneeling between her legs. "Raise yoursel' up a bit."

And as she does so, he lowers his body and moves forward, guiding his cock into her. Meeting with the initial resistance he expected, he says, "Never fear if ye feel some pain at first, lass. Ye'll soon go ayont that."

And with a quick thrust he is deep inside her, the tight warm clasp of her surrounding his cock, her brief shout of pain echoing in his ear. They both begin to move, thrusting against each other in the ancient, nearly involuntary rhythm, seized by the moment, their minds dark and yet full of light as the star-shot night around them, until their cries of fulfillment split the quiet air, echoed moments later by the hoot of a swooping owl.

In the stillness that follows, gazing at the wheeling galaxy above them, Jean's head cradled in his oxter, her arm over his chest, Robert says softly, "Are ye a'richt, lass?"

She tightens her arm around him. "Mair than I could ever have guessed, Rab. Mair than I ever hoped for."

Later, as they walk back toward the village, arm in arm, the burn a faint hiss behind them, Jean begins to hum softly, an old country air her mother had sowthed over her when she was a wee lassie. She can scarcely believe the way she feels, linked to this strong dark presence, the smell and taste and touch of him now no longer a dream.

"It's a rare tune, that," Robert says. "And sweeter yet for your voice singing it."

Jean gives his waist an affectionate squeeze. "I've nae words for it," she says. "I dinna even ken if it has a name."

Robert runs his hand up and down her arm, and a pleasurable chill moves through her. "'Miss Admiral Gordon's Strathspey,' it's ca'd." And after a brief silence, he adds, "One day I'll put words to it for ye."

"Will ye, Robin?" she says. "I'd love that."

"Someday," he says at last. And she hears the tender irony in his voice as he goes on, "When we know each other better, I'll know what words to write."

Silhouette of Jean Armour

. . . it has often given me many a heart ake to reflect
that such glorious old Bards – Bards, who, very probably, owed all their talents to native genius, . . . and, O
mortifying to a Bard's vanity, their very names are "buried
'mongst the wreck of things which were." –

. . . O ye illustrious Names unknown! who could feel
so strongly and describe so well! the last, the meanest of
the Muses train – one who, though far inferiour to your
flights, yet eyes your path, and with trembling wing would
sometimes soar after you – a poor, rustic Bard unknown,
pays this sympathetic pang to your memory! Some of you
tell us, with all the charms of Verse, that you have been
unfortunate in the world – unfortunate in love; he too,
has felt all the unfitness of a Poetic heart for the struggle
of a busy, bad world; he has felt the loss of his little fortune, the loss of friends, and worse than all, the loss of the
woman he adored! Like you, all his consolation was his
Muse – She taught him in rustic measures to complain
– Happy, could he have done it with your strength of
imagination, and flow of Verse! May the turf rest lightly
on your bones! And may you now enjoy that solace and
rest which this world rarely gives to the heart tuned to all
the feelings of POESY AND LOVE! . . .

from the first *Commonplace Book*
September 1785

Chapter Eight

It's no' richt, Mr. Auld, no' richt at a'." Willie Fisher paces, pigeon-toed, before Auld's desk, his agitation growing as he speaks. "We canna keep up wi' a' the black sinnin' that goes on in the parish these days." He darts a glance at the minister's firm-set mouth and clear grey eyes. "Meanin' nae disrespect to yoursel', of coorse. Na, na. But it's a disgrace a' the same." He pauses, waiting to see how Auld will take his outburst, which he found himself unable to contain long enough to exchange greetings with the old man.

Auld sets down his pen and closes the Bible before him, marking his place with a thin ribbon of purple silk. "And just what is it in particular, Mr. Fisher, has brought you to such a pitch this morning?"

Fisher can see rain coursing down the small window at Auld's back, and he shivers in the damp cold that fills the Manse. He feels the need for caution now, but his anger pushes him on. "It's ever since yon godless Gaw'n Hamilton escaped the Lord's just wrath through the glozin' lies o' Bob Aiken, and the ill judgment o' the Ayrshire Presbytery." He starts to wag a bony finger at Auld, then thinks better of it and rubs the tip of his nose instead. But he continues: "They've made us a laughingstock. Folk think we canna touch them noo."

Auld frowns and looks down at his desk as if suppressing a hasty response. Fisher notes the dusty crown of the minister's wig, and wonders if he's said too much. When Auld looks up again, his words come forth measured, but with an edge of rebuke. "I've told ye before, Mr. Fisher – God's will's been done in that matter. There's little use in railing now at Lawyer Aiken or the Presbytery."

The minister pauses, and Fisher himself feels a stab of irritation. Where was all this resignation to God's will the other day when Auld was thundering the Eighty-third Psalm at the congregation? But the old man is speaking again, tapping the desk with his forefinger for emphasis, and Fisher twists his mouth into what he hopes looks like a deferential smile.

"If there was ought wanting," says Auld, "it was the strength o' our evidence against Hamilton's heresies. Evidence you gathered, Mr. Fisher."

Fisher raises a hand defensively. "Ooh, aye," he says, "but – "

Auld is not to be deterred from completing his thought. "We must simply redouble our efforts in the Lord's cause."

Fisher clasps his hands before him and bobs his head in perturbation. "Aye, but Mr. Auld," he says bitterly, "it's no' easy. No' wi' abuse and insult bein' heaped daily on God's servants, instead o' the praise that's their due!"

The minister shakes his head. "To do God's work is enough, Mr. Fisher. Ye should ha'e little use for praise and the sin o' pride it fosters." Then he fixes Fisher with his steady grey stare. "But what's this about abuse and insult? Who's been doing such things?"

"It's yon Jock Richmond. And Hamilton's tenant at Mossglel – Rab Burns!" Fisher spits out the names like a mouthful of lye. "Jeems Lamie an' I ha'e tellt ye aboot them afore noo."

"That's richt, Mr. Fisher," says Auld calmly. "And thanks to your vigilance, we've had Richmond on the cutty stool for his sins wi' the girl Surgeoner. As for Robert Burns, ye offered little but the intelligence that he writes poems and songs. Irreligious, I believe ye ca'd them."

"Aye, Mr. Auld, ooh aye, that's just what I mean." Fisher's legs are trembling under him. "Folk copy his scribbles and pass them roond. And noo he's turned his pen on the very Kirk itsel'!"

Auld snaps upright in his chair. "In what way?"

"Wi' a scurrilous set o' verses aboot mysel', for ane thing!"

"And do ye ha'e a copy o' these verses?" The minister leans back in his chair, waiting.

A pang of alarm strikes Fisher as he considers the substance of the poem Richmond tricked him into listening to at the Whitefoord Arms. And his anger cools at the thought of Auld's actually hearing the lines he's heard himself. And God knows what more yon bugger Burns regaled the company with after his own departure, for the poem must have been far from ended. He looks at the minister, who looses an impatient sigh. "No. No, I dinna ha'e a copy, Mr. Auld. But they're a wicked slander, a' the same."

Auld's eyes widen, causing his wig to rise up like a badger. "Lies and unfounded allegations, is that it? Well, what do they say about ye?"

Fisher backs away from the desk a step or two, his stomach squirming. "Weel," he says, thinking quickly, "I canna just come o'er them like that, Mr. Auld."

Auld's eyes close briefly, then snap open again, and Fisher can tell that his chance is slipping away. "And I canna condemn a man on just hearsay," says the minister. "We've had o'er much o' that lately. In any event, until such time as Burns gives substantial cause for censure, I'll leave the watching of him to you, Mr. Fisher."

"But – "

Auld's look stops Fisher's tongue. "The matter is closed, Mr. Fisher," he says. "And now, if ye've nothing further to discuss, I must give attention to my sermon." The old man bends to his desk and opens his Bible, then begins to shuffle through the papers before him.

Fisher, nettled by his summary dismissal, moves a step closer. "Ooh, aye," he says, in a carefully placating tone. Getting no response, he adds, "Weel, then, Mr. Auld, I'll just bid ye good day. I'll keep an eye on Burns, never you fear."

Without raising his head, Auld takes up his pen and dips it in the inkwell. "Good day to ye, Mr. Fisher," he mutters, obviously preoccupied.

Fisher backs away, narrowing his eyes at the minister's bobbing wig. "Aye," he says, opening the door to the study. "I'll be on my way, then."

Outside, sheltering from the cold and driving rain as best he can under the eaves of the Manse, Fisher shivers, then looks about him quickly. Seeing no one on the street, he reaches inside his coat and withdraws a small silver flask. Covering it with both hands from any unseen watchers, he opens it and tips a burning draught down his throat, then hurriedly puts it away. He pulls his collar up, draws his coat tightly about him, and starts across the muddy green toward Bellman's Vennel; he'll maybe just need to take shelter at the Sun Inn until the rain plays itself out. As he reaches the Vennel's narrow path, water dripping from the end of his nose, he glances back at the Manse, where the Rev. Mr. Auld will be writing away obliviously, heedless of Willie Fisher's efforts on the Kirk's behalf, or of his injuries.

"Damn it to hell!" he says, then turns and begins squelching his way toward the Sun.

"Lord, mind Gaw'n Hamilton's deserts;
He drinks, an' swears, an' plays at cartes,
Yet has sae mony takin arts,
            Wi' great and sma',
Frae God's ain priest the people's hearts
            He steals awa'.

An' when we chastened him therefor,
Thou kens how he bred sic a splore,
An' set the warld in a roar
            O' laughing at us; –
Curse Thou his basket and his store,
            Kail an' potatoes."

His back to Gavin Hamilton's fireplace, Robert recites confidently, with just a hint of Willie Fisher's nasal quaver, and his effort is rewarded by loud guffaws, particularly from Hamilton himself, who presides over a semi-circle of men, including Dr. John Mackenzie, Bob Aiken, Jamie Smith, and the guest of honor, Jock Richmond. Buoyed by the laughter, Robert goes on with the prayer that Holy Willie did not stay at Dow's to hear completed.

"Lord, hear my earnest cry and pray'r,
Against that Presbyt'ry o' Ayr:
Thy strong right hand, Lord, make it bare
            Upon their heads;
Lord visit them, an' dinna spare,
            For their misdeeds.

O Lord, my God! that glib-tongu'd Aiken,
My vera heart and flesh are quakin',
To think how we stood sweatin', shakin',
            An' piss'd wi' dread,
While he, wi' hingin' lip an' snakin',
            Held up his head.

Lord, in Thy day o' vengeance try him,
Lord, visit them wha did employ him,
And pass not in Thy mercy by 'em,

Nor hear their pray'r,
But for Thy people's sake destroy 'em,
An' dinna spare.

But, Lord, remember me an' mine
Wi' mercies temporal an' divine,
That I for grace an' gear may shine,
Excell'd by nane,
And a' the glory shall be thine,
Amen, Amen!"

Bob Aiken bounces to his feet and crosses to Robert, beaming. "By Jings, Rab," he says, pumping Robert's hand, "if that's no' Willie Fisher to the life, I dinna ken what's what!"

"Aye," says Hamilton, "I wish I'd been at Johnnie Dow's to see it. Holy Willie hooked like a trout." Rising from his chair, he refills Robert's glass from the shimmering, multifaceted decanter he's brought out for the occasion. "I just hope the Session doesna start in on you next." He turns and tops Richmond's glass. "Jock here needna worry, for he's off to Edinburgh, but if I were you I'd ca' canny for a while."

Robert sets his glass on the mantelpiece. "The Session's wrath hauds nae terror for me, Gavin. There's nought but truth in what I write, and truth's a powerful witness – as you yoursel' found. The narrow mind's o' orthodoxy are too sair-taxed wi' argy-bargyin' among themsel's to face a foe wi' common sense at his back. The only sinners their zeal can expose are the poor thoughtless lads and lasses they chastise as fornicators on the cutty stool."

"Ye maun watch yoursel' on that score an' a', Rab," says Jamie Smith. "For they've driven Jock oot o' Mauchline, richt enough – an' for nae mair than fornication."

Both Robert and Richmond redden at this, especially since it comes from such a dab hand at the game as Wee Smith. And Richmond says, "They've done nae sic a thing, Jamie. If I'm ever to make a mark in the world, I canna do it here."

Hamilton frowns and sets the decanter down, then turns back to Richmond. "Trying to better yoursel' is one thing, Jock, but I canna say I approve your leaving the lassie Surgeoner at sic a time."

"I mean to do right by her when I can!" says Richmond, and Robert can see the whisky shivering in the glass his friend holds.

"More like 'if' than 'when,' I fancy," says Hamilton. "Edinburgh's no' just the far end o' the rainbow, ye ken. Ye'll find it hard enough to shift for yoursel' there, let alone put by the odd shilling for a wife and child."

Richmond looks at the floor, saying nothing, but Robert feels that some response is called for. "Ye're talkin' common sense, nae doubt, Gavin," he says. "But it seems to me that if the poor were a' to heed common sense in amorous affairs, there'd be damned few bairns born in Scotland. And for a' their pride o' place, the rich and power-ful need a plentiful supply o' poor folk to keep them there." He sips at his whisky, then speaks again. "Wise or no', Jock's maybe as well to try Edinburgh, where he can at least try to reach for a life, and no' ha'e it forced on him."

Richmond looks up at Robert, his eyes glistening, then drains his glass. Hamilton clears his throat, takes the decanter from the mantelpiece, and pours Jock another dram. "I certainly wouldna ha'e ye clerking here against your will, Jock. Ye maun do what your ain conscience tells ye." He moves around the company with the whisky, then looks again at Robert. "As for your other point, Rab, there's nae doubt the upper classes should recognize the mutuality o' the obliga-tion between themsel's and the working folk."

Now Robert feels the need to soften the tension he hears in his landlord's voice. "I fear there's few men o' means that share your gener-ous spirit, Gavin."

"Noblesse oblige," puts in John Mackenzie. "The rich maun gi'e the poor their due."

A sudden rush of impatience fills Robert, not precisely at Mackenzie or Hamilton or Aiken, but at the very order of things. "Aye, it's a fine phrase, John," he says. "But sometimes I think the poor will never get their due till they demand it."

Hamilton raises a cautionary finger. "I'd be very careful aboot talk like that if I were you, Robert. I ken fine your poetic sentiments carry ye awa' now and again into expressions that smack o' radicalism. Ye're amang friends here. But it wouldna do for everyone to hear sic stuff."

"Gaw'n's richt, Rab," says Bob Aiken, winking at Robert as if sharing a secret with him.

"Besides," Hamilton goes on, "ye canna seriously support Revolution, can ye? Turning things upside down is hardly the way to improve them."

"As ye well know, Gavin, I'm a loyal Scot." Robert straightens his shoulders, his head swimming slightly. "But I'd applaud anything that bettered the lot o' the common man, be it Royalty or Revolution!" He empties his glass with a flourish, and sees Richmond do the same. Then, embarrassed by his own vehemence, he says, "And now, by your leave, gentlemen, I think I'd best be on my way, for it's late."

Richmond rises quickly. "I'd best be awa' mysel', Mr. Hamilton, if I'm to make an early start the morn."

"Aye," says Hamilton. He extends his hand to Richmond. "Well. The best o' luck to ye in Edinburgh, Jock. I hope ye prosper." When Richmond has expressed his thanks for the good wishes, Hamilton shakes Robert's hand. "We'll need to delve further into the subject o' Revolution anither nicht, Rab," he says. "It could weel provide us wi' a spirited discussion."

Having said their goodnights and farewells to the others, Robert and Jock find themselves alone in the street outside Hamilton's house. Robert looks at the closed front door. "Spirited discussion!" he says in an exasperated undertone.

"Aye," whispers Richmond. "I tellt ye there were limits to Hamilton's liberality an' open-mindedness." He takes a small leather-covered flask from his pocket and gestures toward the old tower. "Come on, Rab. We'll ha'e a last dram thegither."

Robert eyes the tower uneasily, but he follows Richmond to its dark doorway. Jock hands him the flask, then sits down on the stone steps. "Here's to success, Jock." Robert opens the flask, tips it to his lips, and feels the pleasurable burn of whisky in his throat.

Then he gives the flask back to Richmond, who raises it like a glass. "Success, Rab, for you as well as me." Jock drinks, then caps the flask and replaces it in his coat pocket. "Dinna look sae glum, man. What's wrang wi' ye?"

Robert looks down at his friend, his eyes glazing over with tears. He'll be sorry to lose Richmond as a boon companion, but his own emotion surprises him. "Well, Jock," he says, "there's many a thing I'd sooner say to ye than farewell."

"Ach, Rab, I'll be back." Richmond heaves himself up from the stairs. "Edinburgh may no' be the far end o' the rainbow, as Hamilton says, but it's no' the other side o' the world, either." He slaps Robert's shoulder. "An' maybe ye'll see me sooner than ye think. For if ye had ony sense, ye'd mak for Edinburgh yoursel'."

Robert chuckles bitterly. "I fear there's little chance o' that. But if I ever do leave, it'll maybe be oot o' Scotland a' thegither." Again, Robert has surprised himself, this time with a sudden vision of turquoise water surrounding a green-sloped tropical island, a picture he owes to Richard Brown, the young sailor he met in Irvine some five years ago, when he spent an unhappy six months there in an attempt to learn flax-dressing. Robert shakes his head to clear it. "Onyhow," he says, "the best o' luck to ye, Jock."

He extends his hand, and Richmond grips it warmly. "Thanks, Rab. And the same to you." Richmond embraces Robert awkwardly, then moves back, clasping his shoulders. "We'll keep in touch through the post. An' ye'll need to be sure an' send me a wheen o' your verses now and again."

As Robert watches Richmond walking away down the road toward his lodgings, he recognizes the source of his high emotion at his friend's imminent departure. Richmond has made himself free now, as Dick Brown was free, with no horizons but his own, free to find – or make – a future for himself. And Robert feels how far he is from such freedom, from the audacity to turn his back on all ties and obligations, to strike out on his own.

When Richmond, after a last wave, has moved out of sight, Robert turns to start for home. But as he does so, he hears a rustling from behind him. Looking in the direction of the sound, he sees a dark shape rounding the corner of Hamilton's house, and the hair stirs on the back of his neck. But then he hears his name spoken by a familiar, lilting voice, and the shadow resolves itself into the slender form of Mary Campbell. Robert stiffens at her approach, but finds that tonight he cannot ignore her and walk away.

Soon Mary is near enough that he can smell the heathery scent of her. Little shorter than he, she looks into his eyes, a troubled half-smile on her lips. "It is a stranger you are these days, Robert."

"Ye ken weel enough why that is," he says.

She looks down at the ground between them. "Captain Montgomerie," she says, her voice dropping nearly to a whisper.

"Aye." Robert cannot bring himself to say more.

Still unwilling to meet his eyes, Mary raises her voice a bit. "You and I made each other no vows," she says, and her words bring him a pang of recognition. "And you cannot understand the way it is with me. My family depends on the little I can spare to send them. And I could spare nothing of the little the Hamiltons pay me. And Captain Montgomerie . . ."

Mary's voice trails off, and Robert flushes with sudden anger. "He pays ye weel enough, I'll warrant."

Mary flinches and turns away. Looking at the curve of her slim shoulders, Robert feels the anger leave him, to be replaced by a gnawing, sick emptiness in his stomach, and he wishes he could make himself reach out and touch her.

Finally, though, Mary speaks. "The Captain gives me . . . gifts. He . . . knows about my family. You may say I am wrong. A woman alone . . ." Again, she lapses into silence.

Now Robert does brush his fingertips on her shoulder. "I've nae right to judge ye, Mary." He withdraws his hand. "But I thought ye cared about me. And I was angry."

Mary turns quickly and grips his arm. "I do care for ye, Robin." She looks up, her face pale in the cloud-hung night. "I'll not be seeing the Captain again."

Robert shakes his head. "I fear it's too late, lass."

"It will be Jean Armour, I'm thinking," says Mary quietly.

"Aye," he says. Then, surprising himself yet again, he adds, "I love her."

Mary looks at him steadily, her eyes glistening. "You might have been telling me that in time."

He takes her by the arms. "It wasna to be, lass," he says gently. Then he attempts cheerfulness. "But dinna vex yoursel, Mary – it's no' worth it. We've had some grand times thegither, you and me, and that's as much as need be said. It's no' as if we were blushing virgins, either o' us."

Suddenly she wraps her arms around him and presses her face to his shoulder. "A lass may be a maiden in her heart, if not in her body," she says with effort. Then, almost inaudibly, she adds, "And it is my heart that will always be with you, Robin."

Robert's own heart quickens, and he clasps her to him. "Oh, Mary, Mary," he says. "I didna ken it was like that." They stand, embracing, for what seems like minutes, as if life might overlook them there; then Robert breaks away and takes her by the shoulders. "I canna deny I think o' ye often," he says, choosing his words with painful care. "A man couldna hope to find a sweeter lass than you. But my heart's elsewhere now, Mary, and I canna deny that, either." He withdraws his hands slowly and steps back from her. "Ye wouldna want me to."

She looks at him for a time without speaking. "No," she says at last, her voice soft. "I would not be wanting such a thing. If ye could do that you would never be Robin." She backs away from him into the shadow of the house. "Goodbye, Robert," she says, raising her hand as if to wave; then she turns quickly and is gone.

"A Braw Wooer"

Tho' Cruel Fate Should Bid Us Part

Tune: "The Northern Lass"

Tho' cruel fate should bid us part,
    Far as the pole and line,
Her dear idea round my heart,
    Should tenderly entwine.
Tho' mountains rise, and deserts howl,
    And oceans roar between;
Yet dearer than my deathless soul,
    I still would love my Jean.

Chapter Nine

John Burns is dying. Agnes can tell by looking at her son, by seeing the way his skin seems to glow, as if the life within him is burning itself out like the last flare of a guttering candle, just as life left William Burns nearly two years ago. John lies now in the spence, in the curtained bed, with the curtains drawn so that Agnes can watch over him as the hours pass, helping him to sup broth and hot toddy, administering powders from Dr. Mackenzie, or supervising the lassies in the laying on of poultices or hot and cold cloths. From her chair she can almost feel the heat radiating from the frail body, and she finds her hands twisting and retwisting the fabric of her apron like creatures separate from her, spiders trying to weave or unweave her son's fate.

"Mither?"

For a moment the word seems to have formed itself in Agnes' mind, but with a start she realizes that John has spoken, turning his head slightly toward her. She places a hand on his, feeling the bones and sinews so thinly covered by his hot, dry skin. "What is it, laddie?" she says softly.

"Is somebody greetin', Mither?" John's voice is husky, indistinct, and as Agnes strains to hear him she recognizes again how her thoughts have been drifting as she keeps this vigil; for now she hears the strident wail of the bairn from the kitchen.

"It's the wean, son. Wee Bess." Agnes squeezes John's hand slightly.

"Bess," he repeats, uncomprehending, then turns to the wall with a sigh.

Agnes feels as if the blood were slowly draining into her feet, leaving the rest of her empty, at the thought of Robert's child coming into the family without its rightful mother, just as her own son is fading from her. But it maun be tholed, as the Reverend McMath said, decent young body that he is, when Rab brought him in to visit John the other day. And soon enough, Agnes knows, McMath will be burying her boy as he buried her man.

She rises quickly and puts her head in at the kitchen. "Nancy!

Bell!" she calls quietly. "Can ye no' mak yon wean wheesht for the sake o' your brither?"

Isa hurries across to the crib before her sisters can respond. "I'll see to her, Mither," she says, kneeling to cluck at the wriggling baby.

Turning away, Agnes wipes her eyes with the hem of her apron, then resumes her place at John's bedside. He seems to be asleep now, so she settles back in her chair and closes her eyes. Rab and Gibby and Willie are out in the fields with the other men at the autumn ploughing, burying the last traces of yet another disappointing harvest. She cannot find it in her to rail at her eldest son, for she knows that no man could have planned more carefully, nor labored harder, to make this farm productive. And it is, after all, a shared enterprise, stocked by the property and savings of the whole family, with each member drawing ordinary wages for work performed and taking joint responsibility with the rest for whatever befalls them.

The baby's cries have quieted to happy crooning and gurgling, and as Agnes watches the uneven rise and fall of John's chest, Isa slips into the spence and sits at her knee. "Is John no' ony better, Mither?" she asks.

Looking down, stroking Isa's hair, Agnes reflects on the close facial resemblance between her two youngest children, and on the maddening contrast between Isa's robust good health and John's ebbing life. Unable to speak, Agnes merely shakes her head, causing tears to spill down her daughter's cheeks.

Isa rises, moves to the bed, and presses a tender kiss on John's brow. The boy stirs and opens his eyes, then raises his hand, which his sister takes and draws to her breast. Agnes sits watching them for what seems like a space of minutes until she hears the noise of arrival outside, followed by Robert's appearance in the spence. He has obviously come straight from the plough, still wearing his dirty, sweat-stained smock and trousers, though he has likely left his mud-caked boots at the front door. He holds a notebook in one hand and a three-legged stool in the other. He nods toward the bed, and again Agnes simply shakes her head.

But John is shifting beside his sister. "Is that you, Rab?" he asks breathily.

"Aye, laddie. It's me." Robert steps to the bed and, as Isa moves back to Agnes' knee, he puts the stool down and sits. "How are ye, John?" he says.

John looks at his brother. "Sometimes," he says, "I dinna feel as if . . . I'm here at a' Rab. As if I was . . . high up, watchin' . . . mysel', . . . an' Mither . . . sittin' beside me." He falls silent, his breath rasping with the effort at speech, and Agnes grips Isa's shoulder tightly.

"Just lie quiet, laddie." Robert touches John's hand as he might a dried flower. "I'll read ye a new poem." He fumbles his notebook open with one hand. "I've just written it up on the rig, after turnin' a wee mouse out o' its nest wi' the plough. I stopped then and there and sat down on a big stane wi' my pencil and tablet, while Gibby and the other lads ca'd me for everything."

John smiles up at his brother. "A mouse?" he says. "I'd like that, Rab."

And, as word of the new poem spreads through the household and other family members quietly gather around Agnes in the spence, Robert begins to read:

> "Wee, sleekit, cowrin, tim'rous beastie,
> O, what a panic's in thy breastie!
> Thou need na start awa sae hasty,
>> Wi' bickering brattle!
> I wad be laith to rin an' chase thee,
>> wi' mur'dring pattle!
>
> I'm truly sorry man's dominion
> Has broken nature's social union,
> An' justifies that ill opinion,
>> Which makes thee startle
> At me, thy poor earth-born companion,
>> An' fellow-mortal!
>
> I doubt na, whiles, but thou may thieve;
> What then? poor beastie, thou maun live!
> A daimen icker in a thrave
>> 'S sma' request;
> I'll get a blessin wi' the lave,
>> An' never miss't!"

Quiet sounds of agreement and pleasure surround Agnes, and she nods in agreement, herself, at the idea of a greater Power that might relent in the face of such helplessness. If only such a power could think to spare John. All at once Agnes knows that Robert sees into the heart of their situation, aye, and maybe into her own heart, too; and she sits listening, her bitterness somehow eased, as he goes on:

> "Thy wee bit housie, too, in ruin!
> Its silly wa's the win's are strewin!
> An' naething, now, to big a new ane,
>   O' foggage green!
> An' bleak December's winds ensuin,
>   Baith snell an' keen!
>
> Thou saw the fields laid bare an' wast,
> An' weary winter comin fast,
> An' cozie here, beneath the blast,
>   Thou thought to dwell –
> Till crash! the cruel coulter past
>   Out thro' thy cell.
>
> That wee bit heap o' leaves an' stibble
> Has cost thee mony a weary nibble!
> Now thou's turn'd out, for a' thy trouble,
>   But house or hald,
> To thole the winter's sleety dribble,
>   An' cranreuch cauld!"

Pausing now, looking down at John's wide eyes, Robert passes a hand over his own mouth. Agnes is aware that Isa and the other two girls are weeping quietly, their faces bright with tears. She turns her head and sees William standing rapt, his eyes fixed on Robert; and from behind her she hears Gibby's rueful-sounding sigh. She swallows with difficulty herself as Robert resumes reading:

> "But Mousie, thou art no' thy lane
> In proving foresight may be vain;
> The best-laid schemes o' mice an' men
>   Gang aft agley,
> An' lea'e us nought but grief an' pain
>   For promis'd joy!

Still thou art blest, compar'd wi' me!
The present only toucheth thee:
But och! I backward cast my e'e
           On prospects drear!
An' forward, tho' I canna see,
           I guess an' fear!"

As Robert finishes reading, John smiles. "I'm glad ye let the wee mouse go, Rab," he says, then closes his eyes and lies back, his breathing quiet and shallow.

Agnes rises from her chair and moves behind Robert. She puts a hand on his shoulder, the first tender gesture she's allowed herself toward him in months. Robert glances at her, then covers her hand with his own, and mother and eldest son look down at the dying boy.

"But what's to become o' us if I were to ha'e a bairn, Rab?" Jean's dark eyes repeat her question, ingenuous but inescapably demanding, from where she sits on some boxes of fabric, her skirts spread about her like a fan, in the storeroom at the back of Jamie Smith's shop.

"Dinna fash yoursel', Jean," he says. "We'll tak good care that doesna happen." But even as he speaks he knows he is less confident than his words suggest.

Jean, too, shows little sign of reassurance. "But what if it does happen?" she asks. "It happened to Betty Paton."

His face growing warm, Robert looks away from her. "I know," he says quietly. He wishes he might say more, but everything that occurs to him seems either false or empty, so he remains silent, examining a jagged crack in the whitewashed wall before him.

But Jean persists. "Ye said ye made her nae promises. Ye've made nane to me, either."

He turns to her quickly. "I love ye, Jean. Ye ken that weel enough."

"And I love you, Rab," she says. She pushes herself from the boxes of fabric to a kneeling position on the stone-flagged floor, hands clasped at her waist. "But if the worst happened, what would I tell my folk? And what would the town think?"

"The town?" he says hotly. "A lot o' cantin' hypocrites, maist o' them." Seeing he has wounded her, he adds, "I'd marry ye this very day, Jean." Then a sick, helpless feeling wells up in his stomach, and he spreads his hands before him. "But I canna bring a wife into Mossgiel now, lass. Ye ken how it is wi' my brither John. And wi' a new bairn amang us, and anither ill harvest to contend wi', every inch o' pallet, every sup o' meal is spoken for – and God knows it's little enough." Again he finds himself unable to face her, and he moves to the wall, leaning on it with the flat of his palms, bitterly reflecting that it is no less blank nor hard than his view of the future.

He hears Jean rise to her feet, and when she speaks he can tell she is close to tears, her voice thick with emotion. "Then it's just the same as Betty Paton!" she says. "Ye'd let me bear . . . a bastard wean!"

He thrusts himself angrily from the wall and glares at her. "I said no such bloody thing!" he begins. Then, seeing her turn away, stricken by his vehemence, he catches himself. He moves to her and reaches out a hand, but stops short of touching her.

When he speaks again, his tone is gentle. "No, lass," he says. "I'll no' let pride and anger blind me to the love that's between us."

Now he does touch her shoulder, but she flinches and moves away a few steps. He looks at the floor around his feet, where a jumble of twisted thread seems to mirror the tangle of half-formed thoughts in his head. He feels the need to act, to do something, not only for Jean's sake, but for his own, something to defy the dictates of mere prudence.

"Look, Jean," he says at last, his mind seeming to form words and thoughts simultaneously, "I've said I mauna bring a wife into Mossgiel the now. But that doesna mean we canna marry."

Jean turns, her eyes wide, and Robert fumbles in his coat pocket, finally withdrawing a folded sheet of paper and his trusty stub of pencil. He holds them up before her. "These have stood by me many a time when Nature moved me to write," he says, "but I've never been inspired to write better nor truer than this."

He strides across the room to where a small wooden table stands against the wall, piled with Jamie's old ledgers. He reaches under it and draws out a stool. He gives its dusty surface a swipe with his hand, then sits down and, spreading the paper on the table before him, begins to write swiftly and decisively, while Jean watches him, uncomprehending.

"What are ye doing, Rab?" she says. "What is it?"

Pausing, Robert holds up the sheet of paper. "Listen to this, lass," he says, and begins to read. "'This certifies that I, Robert Burns, farmer in Mossgiel, and Jean Armour, spinster of the Cowgate, Mauchline, do hereby take and acknowledge each other as husband and wife; and that we do so in full knowledge of the solemnity and sanctity of the occasion. Signed this 12th day of November, 1785, Mauchline.'" He lays the paper back on the table and signs it with a flourish.

Jean shakes her head. "But, Rab, . . ." she begins uncertainly.

He holds out the pencil to her. "Here, lass. I've fixed my name on it. It only wants your signature to bind us thegither beyond a' the powers o' law to part us. Then we can ca' Jamie in to witness it."

She bends near him to look at the paper, and the scent of roses on her skin swirls about him. "Will this really mak us man and wife, Rab?" she asks at last.

"Aye, lass," he says warmly, "it's fully legal." He has heard that the civil authorities usually recognize such a written declaration as common-law marriage, however much the clerics might girn and howl. "The blackbonnets o' the Kirk might ca' it 'irregular,'" he says confidently, "but they canna deny it."

Handing her the pencil, he rises and begins to pace, gesturing around him. "What need ha'e we o' muttering priests and scribbling clerks, onyway? Our love maks this place mair hallowed than a' their kirks. And we couldna want a sweeter choir than the rustle o' the wind in the thorn-tree out there."

Jean sits on the stool and stares down at the paper. Robert knows she can read only slowly and painfully. He crosses the room and kneels beside her. "The only thing we have to fear is want, Jean," he says. "But if ye can just hang on in your faither's house for a bit, I'll mak some provision for us – I swear it! We'll be thegither soon!" As he speaks, he has no idea what that provision might be, but he knows he cannot resist the declaration, and that he must make it good, even if it means taking Jean out of Scotland, mayhap as far as the plantations of the West Indies.

Jean bends to the paper and signs it, then looks at him. "There," she says, "it's done." She tumbles the plank to the floor, tosses the paper and pencil aside, and throws her arms around him. "Oh, Rab," she says, pressing her face to his shoulder, "I love ye so much!"

And whispering into her thick dark hair, he says, "And I love you, Jean. My bonnie Jean."

Gilbert Burns lies on his pallet in Mossgiel's dark attic, listening to Robert's restless shifting across the room. "Can ye no' sleep at a'?" he says at last.

After a brief silence, Robert responds. "I'm no' sure I want to, Gibby. Lying here in the dark, I keep thinking about poor wee John, and where he lies the now, in the final darkness, doon the road in yon cauld kirkyard." He sighs. "If it were within my power," he says, "I think I'd never shut my eyes to sleep again."

As always, the depth of Robert's emotion dismays Gibby, making any response seem inadequate. But he feels he must speak. "The lad's better off out o' his suffering," he says. "And ye heard John McMath – and Mr. Auld an' a'. John's awa' to a better place."

"God knows that wouldna be hard," says Robert shortly. Then, after a pause, he adds, "And ye maun believe it if ye like."

Gibby digests this in silence. He knows better than to engage Robert on such a point, especially on such a day, when the whole family have shed so many tears and when reality seems to mock hope. And Robert, who had remained dry-eyed at their father's funeral, was unable to hold back his grief today at Mauchline Kirkyard, as if John's youth and helplessness touched some particular chord within him.

Gibby now finds his own thoughts tuned to the past, to a night from his childhood, back in 1768, when his mother was still carrying the unborn John and they lived in the old clay cottage in Alloway. John Murdoch, the young schoolmaster who taught Gibby and Robert as youngsters, was moving to Carrick and had come to pay a farewell visit to the Burns family and his favorite pupils, bearing as gifts a grammar book and a copy of Shakespeare's *Titus Andronicus*. And when Murdoch thought to entertain the family by reading aloud from the barbarous tragedy, Gibby recalls how raptly they attended him, even through their tears at its strange mixture of nobility and brutality and at the summary deaths of innocents; but when the barbarian queen's sons brought in Titus' daughter, the beautiful Lavinia, with her hands chopped off and her tongue cut out, asking her to call for sweet water to wash her hands, Gibby and the other Burns children had all cried out for Murdoch to stop reading.

Annoyed by the outburst, William Burns had said to them, "Weel, if ye'll no sit and thole to hear it oot, there'll be nae need for Maister Murdoch to lea'e the book when he gangs awa'."

And at that, Robert, not yet ten years old, had stood and declared, "If he does lea'e yon book here, I'll take it and put it in the fire!"

Mortified, William had risen to cross the room and give Robert a skelp, but Murdoch had interceded. "Dinna fash yoursel', Mr. Burns," he'd said. "It's no failing for a lad to ha'e so much sensibility." And Murdoch had produced another play, a comedy called *School for Love,* as replacement for the offensive tragedy.

That had been the first of many moments when Gibby can remember Robert's tender sentiments overwhelming him, like yon poem about the mouse the other day, that was enough to make him drop the very plough in the field. Maybe Murdoch was right, Gibby thinks, but he can't help his own conviction that sensibility is a luxury ordinary folk can ill afford.

"Sometimes, Rab," he says, breaking his thoughtful silence, "I wonder if ye dinna feel things o'er much. Aiblins it lets ye see things to write aboot that the feck o' folk would miss, but it seems to me like a mixed blessing."

"On a day like this it's mair like a bloody curse," says Robert. "Sometimes I think we were meant for nothing else but to mourn."

Lines from Robert's poem, "Man Was Made to Mourn," shape themselves in the darkness behind Gibby's eyes. Written a year ago, amid the first disastrous harvest at Mossgiel and the news about Betty Paton, its gloomy sentiments are no less apt now, with its ironic conclusion hailing the relief from mourning that the poor man will find in his own death. But again Gibby cannot fully share Robert's view of things.

"God knows we ha'e ample reason to mourn, Rab." Gibby props himself up on one elbow. "And it's true death was likely a 'blest relief' for John. But we surely canna allow oursel's to think o' death as 'the poor man's dearest friend'. We maun thole whatever life taxes us wi' – and keep at it."

Gibby half-expects a quick, perhaps angry rejoinder from his brother. Instead, he hears Robert breathe a deep sigh and turn heavily. Then, after another space of silence, Robert speaks, his voice low, almost as if he grudges giving expression to his thoughts.

"We maun keep at it, a' right," he says. "For we've nae ither choice. But there's times I look about me at the hills and fields, as bonnie as they may be, and I wonder how sic beauty can hide sic misery. For neither seed nor dung, thought nor toil, seems enough to mak a difference on these rigs, wi' their soil fu' o' stanes and clay, and weather ye can only depend on to confound ye."

Gibby can think of nothing to say that one or the other of them hasn't said before. But Robert goes on without waiting for a response. "We maun keep at it, as ye say, for we've the family to think o'. But maybe we'd be as well to look to something ither than farming to help mak ends meet."

Gibby's stomach begins to churn. "Like what?" he says.

"Christ, Gibby, I'd do damn near onything if it could ease the burden on us. Maybe even try my hand as a tax collector."

"But what put an idea like that into your head, Rab?" Gibby is unprepared for this turn of events. "Surely it's no' so easy to get a job like yon?"

Robert speaks quickly, an edge to his voice. "I'm as weel-educated as many's the gowk that does sic jobs – and mair willing to work, if it come to that. Bob Aiken's said as much. He could maybe help me to get an Excise commission, and a'."

Aware of his own panic, Gibby can think only of objections. When can Robert have been thinking such thoughts? "What about the farm?" he says. "How could I run it without ye?"

Robert again answers quickly and confidently, as if he's prepared for the question, though Gibby knows his brother is quite capable of improvising in situations like this. "Wi' the extra money a job might bring in," Robert says, "running the farm might be a hell of a lot easier than it is the now."

`Gibby remains silent for a time. "I dinna ken," he says finally. "We've aey been farmers. I canna think o' onything else."

Again Robert's response is swift. "Well, I can," he says. Then, after another interval during which the only sound is the two men's breathing, he adds, "And even if farming's what we maun do, there's other places a man can go, where the sun aey shines and the soil aey bears, even if it's no' the crops we waste our lives on here."

His heart beating at a gallop in his chest, Gibby lies in the dark room, waiting for Robert to say more, yet hoping his brother's wild talk comes of nothing more than the strain of grief and anxiety. And as time stretches into minutes, and Robert's breathing becomes quieter and more measured, Gibby himself begins to grow calmer, to surrender to his own weariness and to the comfort of drowsy oblivion.

POEMS,

CHIEFLY IN THE

SCOTTISH DIALECT,

BY

ROBERT BURNS.

THE Simple Bard, unbroke by rules of Art,
He pours the wild effusions of the heart:
And if inspir'd, 'tis Nature's pow'rs inspire;
Her's all the melting thrill, and her's the kindling fire.

ANONYMOUS.

KILMARNOCK:

PRINTED BY JOHN WILSON.

M,DCC,LXXXVI.

❦ 1786 ❦

My dear Sir,

I have not time at present to upbraid you for your silence and neglect; I shall only say I received yours with great pleasure. I have inclosed you a piece of rhyming ware for your perusal. I have been very busy with the Muses since I saw you, and have composed, among several others, The Ordination, a poem on Mr M'Kinlay's being called to Kilmarnock; Scotch Drink, a poem; The Cotter's Saturday Night; An Address to the Devil, &c. I have likewise compleated my poem on the Dogs, but have not shewn it to the world. My chief patron now is Mr Aiken in Ayr, who is pleased to express great approbation of my works. Be so good as to send me Fergusson, by Connel, and I will remit you the money. I have no news to acquaint you with about Mauchline; they are just going on in the old way. I have some very important news with respect to myself, not the most agreeable, news that I am sure you cannot guess, but I shall give you the particulars another time. I am extremely happy with Smith; he is the only friend I have now in Mauchline. I can scarcely forgive your long neglect of me, and I beg you will let me hear from you regularly by Connel. If you would act your part as a Friend, I am sure neither good nor bad fortune should estrange or alter me. Excuse haste, as I got yours but yesterday.

I am, my dear Sir, Yours,

ROBT BURNESS

letter to JOHN RICHMOND, Edinburgh
17th February 1786

Chapter Ten

mary Armour looks down, hoping she has misheard, to where her daughter sits at the kitchen table. But the expression of misery on Jean's face leaves little doubt. Mary feels her own plump features harden into an angry scowl, and she clenches her hands to keep them from trembling. "It's true then, is it?" she says.

"Aye," Jean replies, almost whispering the word.

The flames dancing cheerily in the fireplace across the room remind Mary of moments from Jean's childhood that now seem irretrievably lost. "Oh, ye stupid wee bitch!" She raises a hand as if to strike, but drops it again when Jean recoils. "To think a dochter o' mine would sully hersel' in sic a way!"

Jean pushes her chair back and rises. "But Mither, I'm no' sullied!" she says, speaking with surprising force.

"Haud your tongue!" says Mary, pacing back and forth, annoyed at Jean's unexpected defiance. "Oh, my God Almighty, this'll kill your faither. He'll gi'e ye sic a through-puttin' ye'll wish ye'd never – " Mary suddenly turns toward Jean. "The faither! Wha was it? What damned sly coof o' a gangrel did this to ye?" She glares at Jean, waiting. "Answer me this minute or ye'll hear me on the deafest side o' your heid. Wha is he?"

Jean sinks back onto her chair and speaks quietly and haltingly. "Robert . . . Burns."

"Robert Burns!" Mary almost screeches the words. This is worse than she could have imagined. Then, almost to herself, she adds, "God save us, your faither'll die." Mary can see all her hopes for Jean vanishing. If only Rabbie Wilson, the young weaver Mary has always fancied as a son-in-law, still lived in Mauchline, instead of having moved away to Paisley. And anger seizes her again. "Whatever could ha'e possessed ye to do sic a thing?" she demands. "To let sic a glib-gabbit, thowless scoundrel even touch ye, let alone steer ye like a common trollop. And fill ye wi' his bastard whelp!"

Again Jean raises her voice in unexpected protest. "No, Mither, no! He didna use me so." Then, beginning to fumble in the pocket of her apron, she says, "We're married."

Mary looks at Jean for a moment or two, open-mouthed. Then she says, "Married? Married? What infernal rubbish has yon black-guard been filling your silly heid wi'? What do ye mean, 'married'?"

Jean holds out a folded sheet of paper. "Here," she says. "It's our marriage lines."

Mary takes the document as if it were a dead mouse, and eyes it without trying to read it. "And where did ye get these?" she demands.

Jean bites her lower lip as if she can scarcely bring herself to speak, but she finally says, "Rab wrote them out."

"Married!" says Mary, her mouth twisting with scorn. "That blackhearted scribbler's made ye nae better nor a common whore!" She throws the paper on the floor, then points at it. "Oh, that ye should be so stupid as to think a scrap o' trash like that could stand for a marriage!"

Before she can say more, Mary sees her son Adam poking his head in at the kitchen door, eyes wide with curiosity. Though Adam is only a few years younger than Jean, Mary senses the sudden gulf that life has opened between brother and sister; and with Robert Burns safely out of her reach, Mary sees in her own mischievous boy a target she cannot resist firing at. She waves an arm dismissively. "Get away oot o' here, ye impident wee rapscallion! Can ye no' see we're o'er busy to put up wi' your nonsense? Sneakin' aboot where ye've nae business to be. Just you wait till I see your faither!"

Adam shrugs. He glances at Jean, then back at Mary. "That's what I came to tell ye, Mither. My faither's just comin' the now."

The boy ducks away out of the room, and Jean looks at Mary in panic, then shuts her eyes tightly, as if trying to imagine herself elsewhere. Mary sits abruptly on a nearby chair. "God save us," she murmurs. She shakes her head, momentarily at a loss.

Jean suddenly throws herself forward on the table, face buried in her hands. Stirred into action, Mary rises and crosses to her daughter. She pulls the girl to her feet, then pushes her toward the stairs. "Quick now," she says, softening her tone to calm Jean into obedience. "Away ye go up there. I'll . . . talk to him."

When Jean has gone, Mary crosses to the table and sits, trying to compose herself before her husband appears. Looking about her, she can sense how her daughter must have felt in breaking the news to her, for now she feels stained herself by guilt and shame.

The familiar clump of her husband's feet sounds outside. When James enters the kitchen, he seems to take possession of it, his thick body making the room seem suddenly smaller. He brushes a few strands of grey hair from his ruddy brow and crosses to the fireplace to warm his hands. Then he glances irritably at Mary.

"What's up wi' ye, then, woman? This fire'll soon be as cauld as a grave. Have ye no clashed a pot or a pan a' day, and me oot slavin' like a blackamoor since dawn?" Turning to the fireplace, he says, "Well? Can ye no speak at a'?"

Mary considers briefly how to break the news, but she can think of no way to approach it indirectly. "It's Jean," she says. "She's . . . been got . . . wi' child."

James turns slowly. "What?" he demands. He crosses to the table, walking as if his feet have turned into blocks of granite, and faces Mary. "What do ye mean, 'child'?" he says. "What the bloody hell are ye haverin' aboot?"

Shocked by his language, Mary says nothing. His already high color has risen, and the tension of his body makes her fear that some sort of seizure may be imminent. Apparently maddened by her lack of response, he kicks aside a chair and bellows, "Do ye hear me? What the hell do ye mean?"

Mary flinches, but realizes that she must keep control, that someone must. "It's true, Jeems," she says quietly. "It canna be altered. She's got wi' child."

"The damned sly ungrateful bitch!" In his frenzy, James half-paces, half staggers back toward the fireplace; then he turns on Mary again. "Wha did this? What bugger o' hell did this? Answer me!"

Feeling the words like filth in her mouth, Mary pronounces the name. "Robert Burns."

"Burns!" James's voice is hoarse and weak with fury. His head jerks toward the ceiling and, suddenly, his body stiffening, he sinks to the floor beside the hearth, tumbling the fire irons with a clatter.

Mary rises. "Oh, God," she says, "he's killed! He's killed!"

She crosses the room and bends over him, her head spinning. Flat on his back, James is breathing, at least, though in a stertorous rasp. As she plucks at his collar, Mary hears a sound at the door. Looking up, she sees Adam standing there, mouth open in amazement. Startled into action, she says, "Don't just stand there gaping like a slack-whanged gomeral! Run away o'er to Johnnie Dow's and fetch a cordial for your faither. Can ye no' see he's sick?" Then, thinking of the stir she might cause, she says. "Wait! Just get him a caup o' water. An' hurry yoursel'!"

Adam hesitates, then points at a small wooden cabinet. "There's a cordial – or something – in the bottom o' the wee press there."

"What kind o' nonsense is that?" says Mary. "There's nae drink under this roof."

Adam moves to the press. "Look – I'll show ye," he says. He kneels, opens the door, and rummages within, soon withdrawing a small bottle of brandy. "It's Faither's," he says, bringing it to her. "I've seen him – "

Mary seizes the bottle from him. "Never mind what ye've seen, ye wee devil!" Her heart racing, she opens the bottle and starts to raise it to her own lips. Then, remembering Adam, she bends to the supine James and, raising his head, pours some of the liquor into his mouth.

He jerks convulsively and begins to splutter and cough, then sits up abruptly and glares at her. "Are ye trying to choke me, then?" he demands. He raises himself unsteadily to his feet, shaking off Mary's attempts to help him. "Stand away frae me, woman!" he says. Then he eyes Adam, who runs out of the room before hearing another word.

"Are ye a'richt, Jeems?" says Mary anxiously.

James turns on her. "Whaur is she?" he says, ignoring her question, his voice trembling with ill-stifled rage. "Whaur is she?"

And, as Mary points dumbly at the upstairs door, it swings open, and Jean edges into the room. "Here I am, Faither," she says, her voice small and fearful.

"You damned whorin' hizzy!" James crosses the room in three steps and gives Jean a backhanded slap across the face. She sinks to the floor, weeping uncontrollably.

Mary hurries over to her daughter and kneels beside her. "Jeems!" she says. "For God's sake!"

James glowers down at her. "Haud your tongue, woman!" He points at Jean. "And shut her up an' a', afore I gi'e her the thrashin' she deserves – lyin' bitch that she is!"

Mary manages to help Jean to her feet, then walks her over to the kitchen table and sits her down, where she continues to sob. Mary puts a protective hand on her daughter's shoulder as James approaches and stands over them.

"Do ye hear me?" he says to Jean. "Haud your wheesht!" Then, as

Jean's crying subsides a bit, he says, "Weel. What do ye have to say for yoursel'?"

Jean sniffles for a moment or two longer. Then, without looking up, she says, "I . . . I love him, Faither."

Mary cringes as James's face turns a deeper red. The eruption comes soon after. "I want to hear nothing at a' aboot yon worthless gowk!" he thunders. "It's bad enough ye care so little for yoursel' as to let a fleechin' bummle like yon disgrace ye, and shame your mither and me. But that ye should ha'e the face to sit there whingin' aboot love – it's damnable!"

Jean raises her tear-stained face and shakes her head. "But we're man and wife, Faither. We –"

"What?" James holds a silencing finger up to Jean and turns to Mary. "What's she on aboot, woman?"

Mary walks around him to where the marriage lines still lie on the floor and picks them up. She hands them to James, who reads them in open-mouthed incredulity. Thinking quickly how to make the best of things, Mary swallows her disappointment over Robert Wilson and says, "Would it maybe no' be best for the sake o' appearances to –"

"Be quiet!" James shouts. "There's nae dochter o' mine will ever wed a menseless scoundrel like yon!" Then, holding up a hand as if to calm himself, he adds more quietly, "We'll send her to your sister in Paisley, till we think what to do. And if this hizzy kens what's good for her, she'll mak hersel' agreeable to young Rab Wilson, afore she's o'er far gone."

Mary brightens momentarily. "Aye, Jeems," she says. "Aiblins that's the best thing."

"But Faither," says Jean, straightening her back and raising her voice, "we're married!"

James leans over his daughter. "You shut up, ye stupid bitch!" he says, his voice nearly a growl. He waves the marriage lines in front of her face. "This damnable bit o' rubbish is nae mair nor anither sleekit way to trick you and mak fools o' us a'." He stands up. "Weel, he'll work nae mair mischief in this family." He glances at Mary. "Send Adam to fetch him." Then he turns back to Jean. "Ye'll tell him these mean nothing to ye. That ye want nothing mair to do wi' him."

Jean's face twists in anguish. "But it's no' true!" she says. "I love him!"

Before Mary can intervene, James cuffs Jean across the face again, this time with the flat of his hand. "And that's what ye'll get every time I hear anither word aboot love or marriage or that whorin' scribbler!" He glowers at Mary, as if daring her to speak, then looks back down at his daughter. "Ye'll say what I tell ye to say, or ye'll be oot on the street this very day. Then we'll see how soon your 'husband' lives up to his 'marriage vows'!" Jean begins weeping again, and James turns his attention to Mary. "I thocht I tellt you to send Adam to fetch yon blackguard."

Troubled, Mary leans toward him and speaks in an undertone. "But what aboot these marriage lines?"

James sighs impatiently, but then falls silent, thinking. "Aye," he says finally. "We'll maybe just wait till I've ta'en a ride o'er to Ayr and seen Lawyer Aiken. He'll soon set things richt on that score."

Mary frowns. "But is he no' a great cronie o' Burns?"

James chuckles, the first time he's shown any satisfaction since walking into the room. "Aye," he says. "They're cronies richt enough. But Bob Aiken's no' a fool. It's folk like Burns he may drink and gab wi'. But it's folk like us that pay his fees."

"Married?" Gibby's face crumples in mixed irritation and puzzlement, and he looks first at Robert, then at his mother. The whole family is assembled in the Mossgiel kitchen, called together by a reluctant Robert to hear the news.

Robert nods now, conscious of the disapproval that radiates from everyone around him, except perhaps young Willie, for whom his eldest brother can do almost no wrong. "Aye," he says, "we're married, Gibby. It's irregular – I wrote the lines mysel' – but we're married for a' that."

"Anither wean!" says Nancy, who is holding the squirming Bess to her breast.

"Anither hizzy!" says Bell, folding her arms, her mouth in a scowl.

Before Robert can respond, his mother speaks up angrily. "And what way do ye think ye'll look after her, this wife o' yours – and twa bairns? We canna pay the rent on this place as it is, without your bringin' doon mair misfortune on us."

Robert holds up his hands. "Mither, Mither, I've planned it a' oot. Ye needna fash yoursel' aboot it." He turns to Gibby and, as he speaks, he realizes his decision is made. "Gibby, this hasna been an easy thing to come to, but I think ye'll ha'e some notion o' what I mean to do."

Gibby moves toward Robert, his eyes narrowed. "For God's sake, Rab, what is it?"

"I canna offer Jean her ain but an' ben, though it's what she deserves." Robert looks meaningfully at Bell and Nancy. "But I mauna bring her under this roof, either – for a' our sakes." He rubs the back of his neck in exasperation. "Ach, Gibby – Jock Richmond was right when he said there's nae life scratchin away here for a man that hopes for better. You and I – the lot o' us, if it comes to that – ha'e planned and toiled and sweated o'er this place as much as onybody could. But what wi' poor soil, diseased crops, and weather as ill as a curse, we're nae further forward than we were at Tarbolton."

Gibby spreads his hands before him. "But what's your answer, man?"

Robert shakes his head. "Good luck to Jock, but it's no Edinburgh. A man needs to be where his fortune's his ain to make – no thrust on him by birth and circumstance. To mince nae mair words, I mean to try my luck in the Indies."

"The Indies!" says Gibby, stunned. "I didna think ye were serious aboot that. Ye surely canna mean to turn slave-driver?"

"I maun do what's needfu'," Robert says, though Gibby's words cause a sick knot to form in his stomach.

Nancy and Bell stare at each other, sighing and shaking their heads, and Isa dabs at her eyes with a handkerchief. Only Willie seems favorably impressed. "Can I go wi' ye, Rab?" he says.

"And what's this Indies, if I maun ask?" says Agnes.

"They're islands, Mither," says Nancy bitterly. "The West Indies. Jamaica. Three thousand mile across the ocean."

"They've been a haven for many an exiled Scot afore me," says Robert.

Agnes snorts. "Naebody's made an exile o' ye but yoursel' if ye choose it."

"Fortune, Mither," says Robert. "That's what's done it. Ill fortune. It's aey taigled us." He finds, almost with desperation, that he craves her approval, or at least her acquiescence; and crossing to where she sits, he looks down into her unwavering dark stare. "Ye'll be better off without me here, onyhow," he says. "And once I get myself established I'll be able to send ye money."

"That'll be little enough wi' a wife and bairns to keep," says Agnes, unmoved. "And how will ye pay passage to this Jamaica? Ye'll no' sail three thousand mile for nothing."

Robert takes a deep breath before he can trust himself to speak. "I dinna ken, Mither," he says. "But I'll manage." He turns and walks away from her. "There's plenty ha'e said my verses could maybe turn a penny," he says to Gibby. "I think I maun see what worth they are at last."

Gibby raises his eyebrows, then nods. "They've gained a deal o' praise, richt enough, Robert."

"Folk are aey gey generous wi' what costs them nothing," Agnes puts in dryly.

Robert's face grows warm. "That's as may be," he says. "But I'll no' need much for one passage."

"One passage?" says Nancy. She looks at her mother, who merely shakes her head.

Robert crosses to the table and sits. He folds his arms self-protectively and leans back in his chair. "I'll need to go to the Indies mysel' first," he says, "and send for Jean and the bairn when I've got on my feet."

"Exile!" says Agnes, her voice rich with contempt. "Exile frae responsibility, if ye ask me. Your ain faither feared for your character on his very deathbed!"

An uneasy silence falls in the room, broken only by the burbling of wee Bess. Robert rises, momentarily speechless with hurt and anger, readying himself to lash out at his mother's seeming blindness to reason or compassion. As he opens his mouth to speak, unsure of what he intends to say, there is a knock at the front door.

"What next?" says Agnes.

Gibby crosses to the door and opens it, revealing the small figure of Adam Armour. Breathing hard, Adam brushes past Gibby and confronts Robert. "My faither says ye're to come to oor hoose richt away." The boy runs back to the door and stands waiting on the threshold.

"Aye," Robert mutters to himself. He looks at Gibby. "Armour'll ha'e found out, then." He crosses to Adam and takes his coat from a peg at the door. "I'm sorry, Mither," he says "We'll need to ha'e this out later." Without waiting for Agnes to react, he claps Adam's shoulder. "Come on. laddie. I'll saddle up my pony and we'll be on our way."

Robert brings his pony to a halt outside the Whitefoord Arms. Adam Armour, who has been riding at his back, slips down to the ground; then Robert himself dismounts and hitches the pony to a post near the inn. Together, they make their way around to the Armour house, where Adam opens the front door and walks into the parlor, trailed uncertainly by Robert. James and Mary Armour are standing in the center of the room, which for Robert emphasizes by its furnishings and ornaments the economic gap between the master mason's prosperous household and his own.

Adam gestures at Robert. "Here he is, Faither. I've brought him."

"Aye," says James Armour dourly. "I ha'e eyes, worse luck." He waves at Adam. "Awa' ye go now."

Robert watches the boy out of the room, then nods stiffly to the parents. "Good day to ye, Mrs. Armour. Mr. Armour."

Ignoring Robert, James Armour turns to his wife. "Mary," he says, and nods at the door to the kitchen.

Mary Armour leaves the parlor without a word, glowering steadily at Robert until she is out of sight. James Armour then points to a chair. Feeling at a decided disadvantage, Robert sits. Armour remains on his feet and, looking down at Robert, says, "I'll waste nae civilities on ye, sir. Ye'll ken why I've sent for ye."

"Aye," says Robert. "It'll be Jean."

Armour's burly frame quivers with sudden emotion. "Aye, indeed," he says. "Jean. I ken fine that sic as you couldna care less aboot the black burnin' shame ye've brocht on my dochter – or yoursel' for that matter." He glares at Robert and stabs a finger at him. "I just ha'e this to say. Ye'll ha'e nae further chance to disgrace her. I'm sendin' her away the morn." The volume of Armour's voice rises. "And if ye value your worthless skin, ye'll keep clear o' me and mine frae this day forward!"

Checking the impulse to rise, Robert presses his hands on his knees. "Jean's my wife, Mr. Armour!" he says. "I ken ye've had a shock, and I mak allowances for that. But Jean's nae longer yours to bid."

Armour's mouth drops open. "Nae longer mine to bid!" His face twists into a sneer. "Aye," he says, his voice heavy with sarcasm, "but ye'd let me ha'e the keepin' o' her, I fancy. And the ill-gotten get she's to bear ye!"

Robert does spring to his feet now, hands clenched at his sides. "I'll no' hear such insults, Mr. Armour! I mean to provide for Jean as a man should!" With an effort, he softens his tone. "I mean to emigrate to Jamaica." He grimaces self-consciously, then adds, "I ken I'm at a disadvantage now, Mr. Armour. But if ye could just bear wi' me, I'll send for Jean and the child as soon as I can."

"You worthless blackguard!" Armour moves a step or two toward Robert. "Ye'll never lay so much as a finger on my lassie again – no, nor see the day when ony wean o' hers'll ca' ye 'faither.' You drunken, slanderin', whorin' rhymster!" He points at the front door. "Now get to hell oot o' here, or I'll see the reddest o' ye!"

Robert draws himself upright, his ears filled with the rushing sound of his own blood. "Dammit, Armour," he says, "I wouldna stand for abuse like that frae ony man, but for Jean's sake. I'll remind ye again, sir – she's my wife!"

Armour snorts derisively. "If ye'd thocht o' her sake, ye'd never ha'e put a filthy paw on her." He fishes a folded sheet of paper from his trouser pocket and shakes it open. "And if ye think this maks a marriage, the mair fool you! Like a' your writin' it was never mair nor a worthless scrap o' trash. And now it's less than that."

Armour crumples the paper and tosses it contemptuously on the floor at Robert's feet. Robert picks it up and smooths it out; he quickly recognizes the marriage lines he gave to Jean. But something is wrong: wherever Jean's name or his would appear, they have been neatly cut away. "Who the hell mutilated this?" he demands.

"Bob Aiken!" says Armour, his expression almost gleeful. Noting Robert's shock, he adds, "Aye, that's richt. Your great frien', Lawyer Aiken. So ye micht as well change your tune. Wife o' yours Jean never was, nor never will be!"

Robert looks from the damaged document to Armour's face. "I don't believe ye," he says. "Bob Aiken wouldna do sic a thing." He throws the useless sheet on the floor again. "Besides, ye canna change the law that easy. Nor can ye change the love o' a man and his wife." He speaks with growing confidence, realizing that both reason and emotion are his allies. "What has Jean to say aboot this? She'll no deny me – whatever jookery-pookery you can try."

Armour lets out a burst of triumphant laughter. "Oh, will she no'? We'll soon put that to the test." He crosses the room to the kitchen door. "Jean!" he exclaims. "Get in here!" He folds his arms and waits for a moment or two, then speaks again. "Do ye hear me? Get in here this minute!"

Armour steps back as the door opens and Jean enters, propelled from behind by Mrs. Armour. Though beautiful as ever, Jean looks thoroughly cowed and miserable, her face pale and her eyes swollen and downcast. She steals one brief shamed glance at Robert, then bows her head again.

Robert starts toward her, but Armour gestures angrily. "Get back, sir!" As Robert moves away a few steps, Armour turns to Jean. "Well, Jean," he says, "tell this fellow what ye think o' his claims o' marriage. Tell him just how much ye care aboot the glorious chance to be Mrs. Burns." Jean flinches but remains silent, and Armour advances on her. "Weel? Do ye no' hear me speaking to ye?"

Without raising her head, Jean finally responds, softly and piteously. "It's . . . it's . . . true. Whatever my faither says, Rab." She glances up at her mother, who gives a peremptory twitch of her head. "It's true what he says," Jean finishes lamely.

"There," says Armour, rounding on Robert. "What mair do ye need?"

Robert looks at Jean, trying to will her to meet his eyes. "Ye don't mean it, Jean," he says. "It's no' you talking, is it?"

Jean does finally look up at him, her dark eyes liquid with pain. "I . . . I canna help it," she murmurs. "It has to be."

Now Robert's shock begins to give way to anger. "Do ye mean to say ye deny me?"

"Weel, go on," says Armour, obviously pressing what he feels is his advantage. "Tell him."

Jean again looks wildly at her mother's plump, impassive face, then back at her father. Waiting, Robert feels slightly breathless, with an empty space in his chest. Finally, Jean turns to him and speaks. "I think . . . it would be best," she says haltingly, "if we werena to see each ither again."

Robert is furious. "Christ Almighty! What the hell are ye saying, Jean?"

Robert's words produce an immediate response from Mary Armour. "You heard her!" she shouts, her face nearly scarlet. "She wants nae mair to do wi' ye!" She looks to her husband. "Jeems, are we to listen to sic blasphemy under oor very roof?"

This sanctimonious posturing drives Robert into a frenzy. "Blasphemy!" he repeats, pacing back and forth, rattling china figures on a small polished table. "Blasphemy!" He glares at the Armours, mother, father, and daughter. "How the hell can ye cant aboot blasphemy when ye've just made a mockery o' the sacred vows o' marriage? You damned lot o' stinking hypocrites! Ye'd sooner see your ain daughter a whore oot o' hell than an honest woman. Damn ye a' and your devilish rotten pride!"

Weeping, Jean turns toward the kitchen door, and Robert strides over to her. Armour moves to intervene but, at a savage look from Robert, stops short. Robert bends closer to Jean's gleaming dark hair, dimly conscious of her enveloping sweet fragrance.

"I'll trouble ye nae further in the name o' love," he says, his voice low and intense. "But mark this and mind it well. That's my bairn ye're carrying, and it aey will be mine. And it'll never be a bastard, whatever your attempts to deprive him o' a name. And there'll come a time when ye'll wish he had Rab Burns to cry 'Daddy' to. But ye've robbed him o' that day – forever!"

Jean's shoulders heave and a ragged sob breaks from her. For a moment, Robert's anger threatens to dissipate; but then he catches sight of the grim, self-righteous faces of James and Mary Armour. He strides to the front door and, opening it, flings it back against the wall. Somewhere in the room he hears the crash and tinkle of breaking china, then an intake of breath by Mary Armour. The moment resonates for him, and he turns to look at the senior Armours and at Jean's shuddering back.

"To hell wi' the whole bloody lot o' ye!" he shouts. "And ye can roast there forever before I'd waste spittle to cool the flames!"

And, leaving the door standing open, he walks out of the house into the fresh damp air and turns his steps toward the welcoming sanctuary of the Whitefoord Arms.

Mary Campbell is on her way down Castle Street toward the Hamilton house when she sees the brown pony tethered at the door of the old tower. A lovers' tryst, she thinks, with a twinge of envy. Passing the dark doorway, she puts a hand out to touch the animal's warm neck, and as she does so a shadowy figure moves on the steps within the tower. Startled, she cries out softly.

"Mary? Is that you?"

She recognizes the slurred voice immediately and, as her eyes adjust to the doorway's darkness, she sees him seated on the stairs, rubbing a hand over his mouth. "Aye, Robert, it is," she says noncommittally, smelling the drink on him from where she stands. "I hope you are well."

He squints up at her. "Are ye mocking me, then? I didna think ye'd be so cruel, Mary."

She can only think to treat him playfully, to protect herself, especially with the condition he is in. "Whatever are you saying, Robert? I meant nothing more than I seemed to, I'm sure. Are you sick, is it?"

"Aye, lass," he says, his voice thick and maudlin. "Sick at heart."

Despite herself, Mary feels a pang of – what? Sympathy? Hope? But she makes herself respond skeptically enough. "Is it a falling-out you've had wi' Jean Armour, maybe?"

Robert rises, stumbling, and braces himself on the door-jamb. "Never mention that name to me again!" he says loudly, and she glances around her, for fear someone might hear him. "Oh, Mary," he says, leaning toward her, "I rue the day I ever took up wi' her." Then, more softly, he adds, "It's you should ha'e had my heart frae the start, lass."

Mary backs away a step or two. "Oh, Robin," she says defensively, "you'll not be wanting me on your conscience when you rise up tomorrow to mend a lovers' quarrel wi' Jean Armour."

He advances on her, quietly vehement. "I'm telling ye, lass – it's nae lovers' quarrel. She and I are finished for all time!" He looks around him and waves an arm at the street. "And I'm done wi' this place and a', wi' its narrow-minded sniveling hypocrites – where a man's true worth's hid ahent the clouds o' birth and worldly gear." He turns back to her. "I mean to print my poems, Mary. And if I make ought by that, I'm away to hell oot o' here!"

Taken aback by his outburst, Mary can scarcely find words to respond. "But where, Robert?" she says at last.

He straightens himself upright and squares his shoulders. "The Indies!"

"The Indies!" she repeats, with awe and approval. Then, as she realizes fully the magnitude of such a move, she adds sadly, "As far away as that?"

"Will ye miss me then?" he says, peering as if to see inside her.

Hurt by the seeming lightness of his tone, she says, "It is fine ye ken how much I care for ye, Robert."

His face is lit by a sudden grin. "Then come wi' me, Mary!" He gestures around him. "We'll fly this midden thegither!" He peers at her again. "Well, lass? What do ye say?"

"Oh, Robert," she says, her heart beating as if to escape her chest, "if it's serious you are, there is nowhere I wouldn't be going wi' you!"

And with a cry of joy that sweeps all doubt from her mind, he enfolds her in his arms and swings her off her feet as the pony shifts and whickers gently beside them.

The Betrothal of Burns and Highland Mary

Honored Sir,

My Proposals came to hand last night, and I know you would wish to have it in your power to do me a service as early as any body, so I inclose you half a sheet of them. – I must consult you, first opportunity, on the propriety of sending my quondam friend, Mr Aiken, a copy. – If he is now reconciled to my character as an honest man, I would do it with all my soul; but I would not be beholden to the noblest being ever God created, if he imagined me to be a rascal. – Apropos, old Mr Armour prevailed with him to mutilate that unlucky paper yesterday. – Would you believe it? tho' I had not a hope, nor even a wish, to make her mine after her damnable conduct; yet when he told me, the names were all cut out of the paper, my heart died within me, and he cut my very veins with the news. – Perdition seize her falsehood and perjurious perfidy! but God bless her and forgive my poor, once-dear, misguided girl. – She is ill-advised. – Do not despise me, Sir: I am indeed a fool, but a knave is an infinitely worse character than any body, I hope, will dare to give

the unfortunate ROBT BURNS

letter to GAVIN HAMILTON, Mauchline
15th April 1786

Chapter Eleven

Jamie Smith watches as John Wilson straightens himself on his high stool and leafs through the proposal and the sheaf of poetry that Robert has just laid on the desk in the Kilmarnock printer's shop in the Star Inn Close. A small, sharp-featured man with fine sandy hair and pale eyebrows and lashes, Wilson is the publisher recommended to Robert by several of his friends and acquaintances, including Gavin Hamilton, John Ballantine, the banker from Ayr, and Robert Muir, a Kilmarnock wine-merchant Ballantine consulted on Robert's behalf. Now, as Jamie stands in Wilson's small office with Robert and Gibby and hears the printer hemming and hawing over Robert's manuscript, he wonders about those recommendations.

Jamie imagines that Wilson is only a few years older than himself, and certainly no older than Robert; but the printer's demeanor is far different from Rab's, as if he means to emphasize the gap between successful businessman and importunate writer. As the party from Mauchline waits for the little man to react, Jamie glances about the cramped office, his nose smarting with the sweetly pungent smell of ink from the printing shop beyond, and his ears tickled by the buzzing of a bluebottle at the small dusty window behind Wilson's back.

"I dinna ken," the printer says at last in his high-pitched voice, setting down the proposal and the stack of poems. "An edition o' six hundred odd volumes. It'll tak a byornar deal o' thocht, a job like this."

Robert's shoulders stiffen, and when he speaks Jamie can tell he is choosing his words carefully. "I'm no' just sure what difficulties a job like this might pose, Mr. Wilson."

"Aye, weel," says Wilson, "ye'll maybe no' ken the ins and oots o' the book trade, then, Mr. Burns. It's no' sae easy sellin' books as pennin' them aff." At this, Robert darts an exasperated glance at Jamie and Gibby; but Wilson ignores the exchange and continues. "And ye may ken that sellin' poetry is a gey chancy business, onyhow," he says. "Folk that put doon guid siller for a book want substance – maybe a grammar, or a history, or the like."

Before Robert can respond, Gibby speaks. "It seems to me there's many a book o' poems aboot, Mr. Wilson. Somebody must buy them."

Jamie feels he must voice his own support of Robert, whose confidant he has become since Jock Richmond left for Edinburgh. "I'm a businessman, mysel', Mr. Wilson," he says. "And I ha'e seen folk crowdin' a room to hear the maist o' yon poems on your desk – aye, and beggin' for copies after they heard them and a'. I'd say they'll mak a sound investment."

Wilson's head jerks upward, not quite a nod. "Nae doubt ye're richt, gentlemen." He eyes Gibby. "But as your brither may fin' oot, Mr. Burns, there's very few books o' poems written in the Scots. I think I may say frae experience that folk want what ye micht ca' refined sentiments and formal expression when they turn to poetry at a'." Then, turning his attention to Jamie, he adds, "And I'm aey pleased to hear a bit verse mysel', Mr. Smith, like the feck o' folk. But whether the feck o' folk'll be willin' to pay for what they micht get for naethin', weel, that remains to be seen."

Jamie notes Robert's ears reddening as Wilson delivers these observations. And when the printer has finished speaking, Robert steps forward and scoops up his manuscript. "Aiblins I'll need to talk wi' anither publisher, then," he says, taking a step or two back from the desk. "I'm sorry to ha'e ta'en up your time, Mr. Wilson."

Wilson's eyes widen at this, and he slides down from his perch on the stool, waving his hands in front of him. "Now dinna be sae hasty, Mr. Burns. I didna say we couldna come to an agreement. I merely said it wad tak a bit o' thinkin'. It's the question o' the invest-ment aforehand, d'ye see, and the sellin' o' the books when they're ready." Wilson reaches out to take the poems back. "The subscriptions, d'ye unnerstan'?"

Robert hesitates, the manuscript still in his grasp. "We'll ha'e subscriptions enough, I think," he says. "I propose to mak money enough to allow me to emigrate to Jamaica."

"Aye," says Wilson, nodding, "just so. But afore we maun talk o' profits, there's aey the costs to be met." He extends his hands again, and this time Robert allows him to take the manuscript, which he shakes gently, gauging its size. "Say one volume, octavo," he mutters, "weel-stitched and printed." He looks up at Robert. "We'll no' do that for much less nor forty pound. Yon's a deal o' money." He purses his lips, considering. "To mak a decent profit ye'd need to charge three, four shillings a copy."

Gibby breaks in at this. "Folk'll pay the price for Rab's poems, never fear. I'll tak sixty or seventy books and dispose o' them, mysel'."

"Aye, says Jamie, "and so will I. So there's o'er half o' your costs guaranteed afore ye lift a finger."

Momentarily speechless, Robert looks at Jamie and Gibby, eyes shining with gratitude. But if Robert is grateful, Wilson is nearly ecstatic. "Guaranteed!" he says, his sharp face transformed almost to boyishness by a wide grin. "Noo ye're talkin', lads. Aye, guarantees – that's what we need. And the mair, the better! The minute you let me know we ha'e twa hundred and fifty subscriptions, we can start work!" Laying down the poems on his desk, he takes Robert's hand in both of his and pumps it vigorously. "Ye maun let me hear frae ye as soon as ye can, Mr. Burns."

"Come on, Rab," says Jamie, suddenly eager to be out of the printer's grimy den. "We'll awa' o'er to the Star and ha'e a drink to the future o' your book." As an afterthought, he says, "Will ye join us for a dram, Mr. Wilson?"

Wilson vaults spryly back onto his stool. "Thank ye, Mr. Smith," he says. "I fear I ha'e o'er many matters to attend to here. Mayhap anither day."

Jamie exchanges a look with Robert and Gibby. They've all learned sufficient about Johnnie Wilson for one day, expert printer though he might be. But, as they start for the office door, having made their polite farewells, Wilson offers one last observation.

"Mr. Burns!" he calls, glancing through the poems on the desk. "Anither wee bit o' counsel."

Arrested on the threshhold, Robert rolls his eyes at Jamie, then turns back to the printer. "What's that, Mr. Wilson?"

Wilson taps the end of his nose with a finger, then wags the finger at Robert. "If ye mean to gain the widest possible audience for these verses, ye maun consider weel whether some o' them micht gi'e offense to delicate sensibilities on moral or religious grounds. Aiblins ye micht tak oot a wheen o' lines here and there, and maybe even do withoot ane or twa poems a'thegither."

"I'll think on it, Mr. Wilson," says Robert shortly. Then, turning, he leads Jamie and Gibby out through the shop, past the clatter of the printing press, into the damp spring air.

"Mrs. Burns, your cheese is grand, as usual."

Gavin Hamilton, seated between Gibby and Robert at the kitchen table in Mossgiel, slices a whang of cheese and places it on a bannock. Gibby glances from Hamilton to where his mother stands near the fireplace, characteristically unwilling to join the men, but loathe to move out of earshot.

"It's aiblins no' as good as some, Mr. Hamilton," she says. "We just try to do what we can."

"Nonsense, Mrs. Burns," says Hamilton. "Ye mak the best cheese in Mauchline – and ye can say I said it!"

"Aye," Robert puts in, flashing a smile, "Mither's a great hand at the cheese-making."

Gibby notes the impatient twitch of his mother's mouth. She clearly wants none of Robert's attempts to placate her. She turns her back on the men and, picking up the poker, jabs at the coals in the fireplace, causing an upward dance of sparks. As the awkward silence lengthens, Gibby wishes he might say something to put matters right.

But Robert himself finally speaks. "Can I pour ye a drop more, Gaw'n? We didna mak the beer, but it's good enough, a' the same."

Hamilton holds out his stoup while Robert pours more beer. "I'll take some, Robert," he says. "But only to drink to your health, and the future o' your book. And from the sound o' it, ye should ha'e enough subscriptions now to assure its success."

"Thanks in good part to your guarantee for forty copies," says Robert. "But as I'm sure ye ken, Gaw'n, a man canna ha'e too many guarantees to suit Johnnie Wilson."

Hamilton nods, then reaches into his coat pocket and withdraws a folded sheet of paper. "For my part, I'm happy to do what I can for verse the like o' yours, Robert. And it's little enough, I fear. But I fancy this will ease your mind a wee bit."

He hands the sheet to Robert, who opens it and reads, then looks up, bemused. Gibby glances questioningly at his brother, then at Hamilton.

"It's frae Bob Aiken, Gibby," says Hamilton. "He guarantees to take a hundred and forty-five copies o' Robert's book."

"My God," says Gibby. He says no more, for he can't be sure how much Hamilton knows about Robert's embroilment with the Armours, or Aiken's role in the matter, though he suspects the landlord is better informed than he lets on.

Hamilton beams at Robert. "That'll stand ye in good stead, eh, Rab?"

Robert shakes his head wonderingly. "I canna say but it surprises me, Gaw'n." For a moment Gibby thinks his brother means to broach the question of the mutilated marriage lines with Hamilton. But after taking a deep breath, all Robert says is, "It's nearly as if he felt an obligation."

Hamilton responds quickly and heartily. "As much as admiration and friendship can impose, I'm sure." Then, after a look at Gibby, who feels obliged to nod in polite agreement, the landlord moves to what he evidently considers a less touchy subject. "When do ye go to see Johnnie Wilson aboot final arrangements?"

"I'll be awa' up to Kilmarnock next week," Robert says. "I've nae doubt Wilson'll be delighted to see the new guarantees. They'll maybe mak him less sweirt to print some o' my poems." He chuckles bitterly. "I fancy the promise o' cash will help to ease his moral scruples."

Hamilton laughs. "I wouldna worry, Robert. The important thing is to see the book in print." He raises his stoup. "Here's to the future!"

After echoing Hamilton's toast, both Gibby and Robert join the landlord in drinking deeply from their own mugs. Then, his mouth still watering from the tang of the bittersweet ale, Gibby says, "Do ye think Rab's verses'll do well richt enough, Mr. Hamilton?"

"Better than that, Gibby," says Hamilton, bringing his stoup down on the table with calculated emphasis. "I think they'll assure his fame."

At this, Gibby hears his mother stir in her chair at the fireside. "Will that mean ocht in the way o' siller, then, Mr. Hamilton?" she says.

Hamilton turns to her, teeth gleaming in his square jaw, voice rich with promise. "Silver and gold and a', I'm sure, Mrs. Burns."

"And fame into the bargain," Agnes mutters, her eyebrows twitching.

Undaunted by her skepticism, Hamilton flashes another smile. Then, frowning briefly to signal a change of subject, he turns back to Robert. "I can only wish ye'd take thought to protect your own interests, Rab," he says. "Especially if ye still mean to emigrate."

Robert glances at Gibby, then back at Hamilton. "How do ye mean, Gaw'n?"

The landlord rises from his chair. He places his hands on his sides and stretches his back, then moves a few paces from the table, as if he feels the need to formulate his next utterance carefully. "Well, Robert," he says at last, "I'll risk giving offense in the name o' friendship. James Armour has been asking round the town aboot the prospects for your book. Is there ony reason for him to feel he has claims on ye?"

Gibby darts a look at Robert, who rises from his own chair, his eyes narrowing warily, and speaks in a low voice. "Has he said ought?"

Hamilton purses his lips, then responds carefully. "No. But his daughter Jean's been away at Paisley a good while now, and there's been some talk." The landlord reddens a bit. "I ken ye'd been keeping company wi' her."

"She's nothing to me now!" declares Robert hotly. Gibby hears his mother shifting again in her chair at this, but to his relief she remains silent.

Hamilton spreads his hands as if disclaiming any threatening intent. "I say nothing nor mean nothing, Robert. But if Armour's beard's in a blaze wi' mair than ill-nature, ye'd best be on your guard."

As much to forestall any hasty response from Robert as to show his agreement with the landlord, Gibby speaks quickly. "Ye're as well maybe to heed Mr. Hamilton, Rab."

Without looking at Gibby, Robert nods. "What is it ye suggest then, Gaw'n?" he asks.

Hamilton clears his throat and smiles first at Gibby, then at Robert. "Well," he says, moving as he speaks, "if ye still mean to set sail for Jamaica, ye'll need somebody to see to your affairs hereabouts." He pauses, then resumes, circling the table until he stands over Gibby. "To my mind, ye couldna do better than sign o'er your rights in Mossgiel to Gilbert, here." He claps Gibby on the shoulder. "That way ye'd guarantee your interests would be well looked after. And it would forestall ony claims that Armour – or onybody else – might make."

Gibby is dumfounded, his heart racing. He watches, holding his breath, as Robert moves slowly away from the table, starting first toward the fireplace, then turning back as his mother gazes steadily up at him from her chair. "Aye," he says. "That sounds sensible." He looks at Gibby. "We'll need to see to that, then, just to be on the safe side."

Gibby glances sidewise at a movement from Hamilton, who seems almost to flinch under his and Robert's eyes. "Well," says the landlord, clapping his hands softly and sniffing, "I'll leave ye to it, then, for ye'll ken your ain minds better than onybody else." He smiles at them. "If I can help at a', just say the word." He turns then to their mother. "Mrs. Burns," he says, "I'm obliged for your hospitality."

Agnes rises from her chair. "It wasna much, Mr. Hamilton," she says without great warmth. "But such as it was, ye're welcome to it."

Hamilton nods at the three of them. "Well, I'll be on my way."

Gibby, having shaken hands with the landlord, seats himself again at the table and allows Robert to see Hamilton out of the house. He looks at his mother without speaking, and together they listen to the sounds of farewell from out in the yard, and the thump and clatter as Hamilton starts his horse on its canter back to Mauchline, back to the douce household Gibby knows will never fall under the threats their own must face.

Robert reenters the kitchen and pours more beer for himself from the cool depths of the brown stoneware jug on the table. He sits and takes a long draught from his stoup. Then, setting the beer down, he passes a hand over his mouth and eyes Gibby.

"Weel, Rab," Gibby manages to say. "What do ye think o' that?"

Robert runs his finger around the rim of his stoup. "I dinna ken, Gibby," he says. "Hamilton's a grand heid for business. It seems sound enough advice to me."

Agnes Burns sniffs loudly and resumes her chair beside the fire. "Aye," she says. "It's a sound enough way for him to look after his ain affairs, wi' you stravaigin' awa' o'er the sea to Hell's Glen."

Gibby, wearied by his own habitual peacemaking impulse, raises a hand. "I'm sure Mr. Hamilton's got Rab's best interests at heart, Mither."

"Aye," says Robert before Agnes can respond. "But Mither's richt. Hamilton's no' above having a care aboot his rent. It doesna matter, though. His advice is still good. It'll see you protected – and keep

Armour's claws off whatever money there micht be."

But Gibby can see by the set of her lips that his mother will not be diverted from her underlying concern. "Ye're abandoning this 'wife' o' yours, then," Agnes says to Robert. "Is that it?"

Robert closes his eyes for a moment or two as if in silent prayer, then opens them. "No such thing, Mither," he says in measured tones. "It's she's abandoned me."

"One way or the other," says Agnes, "it's a' the same. Ye've shamed the lassie, and now ye deny responsibility."

"Damn it, Mither!" Robert leaps to his feet, nearly overturning his chair. "I'll no listen to any mair o' this!"

Outwardly unperturbed, Agnes blinks at her eldest son. "Aye, that's richt," she says. "Curses and pride and evasions. It's a' ye ken!"

His face warming with irritation and embarrassment, Gibby rises. "Mither!" he says. "There's nae point in – "

But Robert cuts him off. "No, Gibby!" he says, almost shouting. Then, more calmly, he adds, "We'll need to ha'e this oot."

Gibby looks from the one to the other, seeing the two matched pairs of hard dark eyes, sensing his own inability to oppose two such implacable wills, and angered by the realization. He shakes his head in bitter resignation. "Then I'll no' stay and hear it," he says, and starts for the door.

After watching Gibby stride out of the house, Robert turns again to Agnes. "Well, Mither," he says quietly. "Ye'll be rid o' me soon enough."

Agnes rises from her chair. "Rid o' ye?" she says, moving away from Robert to the spence door, where she stops with her back to him. "Aye, ye can say that to your ain mither and mean it." She sniffs contemptuously. "I still dinna ken what ye want wi' traipsin' awa' to this Jamaica or whatever ye ca' it."

"We've been o'er that afore." Robert stares at his mother's straight back, her squared shoulders, willing her to look at him. Giving up the effort, he finally says, "There's nothing here for me only poverty and obscurity. Aye, and shame."

"Ye'll no escape that," says Agnes, "wherever ye may gang. And like as no ye'll fin' enough wild foreign jads to disgrace yoursel' wi'."

Pain and anger carry Robert a few paces toward Agnes. "For God's sake, Mither!" he cries. "Do ye hate me, then, to talk like that? Do ye never ha'e a kind word for me? It's sma' wonder I feel forced to lea'e Scotland – when my ain mither's scunnered at the sight o' me!"

Agnes stiffens, then turns slowly toward Robert. For a long moment she looks at him steadily, even fiercely, her dark eyes wide. Then suddenly, unexpectedly she draws in a sharp breath, stifling what is obviously a sob, and speaks with difficulty. "Robert," she says, her eyes glistening. "Son. Do ye no' ken how much I love ye?"

Robert's own eyes blur with tears. He crosses to his mother and throws his arms about her, transported momentarily back to childhood by the scent of fresh-baked bread that always seems to cling to her. "Mither, Mither," he says, his throat swollen with emotion. "What would ye ha'e me do?"

Agnes tightens her own grip on Robert. "It's no' for me to tell ye now," she says quietly. Then she leans back from him and looks up into his eyes. "But ye canna live oot your life leaving women in tears, nor denying what ye are – and a' because the world isna yours for the asking."

Robert releases his mother and backs away from her, shaking his head at the gap between them that not even love can seem to bridge. "It's no' the world I want, Mither – only my due. It's the world that denies me what I am – aye, and treats every common man the same." He follows Gibby's path to the threshold of the farmhouse door, then turns back. "The only freedom we have," he says, "is the freedom to dream."

He looks at his mother's face, but reads no understanding there, and no softening. With a sigh he turns heavily and walks out into the muddy yard.

Agnes looks at the door where her eldest son has just stood, and from which he has moved beyond the sound of her voice and the force of her feeling. "The best o' your verses are no' dreams, Rab," she says, as if whispering to the child she still remembers. "The life they talk aboot's real enough. And ye'll no' live the best o' your life in a dream, neither."

My Dr Friend,

   . . . I have waited on Armour since her return home, not by – from any the least view of reconciliation, but merely to ask for her health; and – to you, I will confess it, from a foolish hankering fondness – very ill-plac'd indeed. – The Mother forbade me the house; nor did Jean shew that penitence that might have been expected. – However, the Priest, I am inform'd will give me a Certificate as a single man, if I comply with the rules of the Church, which for that very reason I intend to do. –

Sunday morn:

   I am just going to put on Sackcloth & ashes this day. – I am indulged so far as to appear in my own seat. Peccavi, Pater, misere mei. – My book will be ready in a fortnight. – If you have any Subscribers, return me them by Connell. – The L . . . stand wi' the Righteous –

Amen Amen

ROBT BURNS

      letter to JOHN RICHMOND, Edinburgh
      9th July 1786

Chapter Twelve

Sing it for me, Robin."

Mary Campbell looks up at Robert from the soft mossy bank of Mauchline Burn, supporting herself on hands outstretched behind her. The late May afternoon shifts around them in a dapple of sun and shade, and Robert, seated on a large smooth stone, reaches out to touch the sprinkle of tiny pockmarks high on Mary's cheek, marveling at the fairness of her skin against the myriad shades of green in the grass and trees, and in the spread skirts of her muslin dress.

"Aye, lass," he says. "Though I've nae voice, as ye'll soon hear."

"Sing it," she says softly, extending the sheet of paper that Robert gave her only minutes earlier.

He gives her wrist a squeeze. "Keep it," he says. "I ken the way it goes."

As he looks into her violet eyes, he suddenly thinks of the last time he saw Jean, in the Armours' parlor, a strand of dark hair clinging to her tear-swollen cheek. And he hears in his mind the lilt of the Strathspey – "Miss Admiral Gordon's" – he promised to set words to for Jean, words he has no more notion of now than he knows of Jean herself, still sequestered at her aunt's in Paisley. He closes his eyes briefly, then smiles down at Mary and begins to sing.

> "Will ye go to the Indies, my Mary
> And leave auld Scotia's shore?
> Will ye go to the Indies, my Mary,
> Across the Atlantic's roar?
>
> O sweet grows the lime and the orange,
> And the apple on the pine;
> But a' the charms o' the Indies
> Can never equal thine.
>
> I ha'e sworn by the Heavens to my Mary,
> I ha'e sworn by the Heavens to be true;

And sae may the Heavens forget me,
     When I forget my vow!"

Mary takes his hand. "It is lovely, Robin," she says, then shakes her head. "The very thocht o' limes and oranges. I still cannot believe it is real."

Robert slides down from the stone so that he is on his knees beside her. "It's nae dream, Mary," he says, and he hears the note of pleading in his own voice. Then, more quietly, he adds, "Or if it is, it's one we'll mak come true."

He bends to her, taking her in his arms, and presses his lips on hers. Mary's own arms encircle him and she opens her mouth, her tongue warm and wet on his, her breath quickening and her fingers moving lightly on his neck and shoulders. They sink down to the springy turf, and for a time Robert thinks of little save the feel of Mary's lithe body, the white and perfumed hollow at her collarbone, the flesh of her small breasts, taut but soft, like ripe pears.

When they lie back together, her head cradled on his shoulder and the sound of the burn returning to his ears, Mary says, "When is it to be, then, Robin?"

"Soon, lass," he says. "Afore ye ha'e time to weary at hame in Stairaird, the passages should be booked. We're likely to set sail in August, on the brig *Nancy*, under Captain Andrew Smith – bound out from Greenock for Savannah-la-Mar in Jamaica." He moves his shoulder gently from beneath her head and sits up. "Are ye a' ready for leaving?"

"Aye, Robin." Mary, too, sits up, hands clasped around her knees. "My chest is a' packed and stored awa' in the cart-shed, ready to catch the morning coach out o' Mauchline." She looks down at the tumbling water. "It is sad I am at parting from you. But it will be good to see my family again before we leave Scotland."

"Aye, lass," Robert says. He thinks again of the Armours' parlor, of James Armour's rage-congested face and the sanctimonious purse of his wife's lips. "I only hope your folk dinna try to turn ye against me, as some might do."

Mary touches his arm. "Robin, it is no sheltered child I am. I have been out in service since I was fourteen. My mother and father may counsel me, but they could never be turning my heart from you, nor keeping me from your side."

"Mary, Mary," Robert says, "ye're a grand lass." And again he cannot close the image of Jean from his mind, or keep down his anger and confusion at her weak-willed acquiescence in the face of her father's pride and hypocrisy. Aware of the continued pressure from Mary's fingers on his arm, he nods at her, saying, "There's no' many that ha'e your faith and courage."

Mary withdraws her hand. "As long as you are sure it is me you are wanting."

Stung by her facility in sensing his thoughts, Robert rises to his feet. "Mary, I'm pledged to you now. There's naebody else comes into it." He reaches into his coat pocket and draws out two small books. "Look, lass" – he waves the books at her – "we said we'd pledge oursel's wi' Bibles. This is the Old Testament." He kneels beside her and opens the first volume to its flyleaf. "Do ye see what I've written here?" He recites more than reads the inscription. "'And ye shall not swear by my name falsely, neither shalt thou profane the name of thy God.'" He gives Mary the book and opens the other one. "And here, the New Testament" – again he reads – "'Thou shalt not forswear thyself but shalt perform unto the Lord thine oath.'"

Handing Mary the second volume, Robert rises and looks down at her. "That's the words o' Leviticus and Matthew," he says. "And I've sung ye a pledge from my heart." He takes her hand and gently pulls her to her feet. "Now, for good measure, we'll mak our parting vows across running water. Auld wives' superstition it may be, but it's apt enough. The next time we see each other we'll be crossing the water thegither, as man and wife."

He leaps easily to the other side of the burn, exhilarated by the brief flight and by the bounce of the turf beneath his feet. Then he reaches back to Mary over the clear, tea-brown water. "Tak my hand across the burn, lass." Smiling, Mary leans toward him and clasps his hand. "I give ye my heart, my hand, and my love, Mary," he says. "Till the mortal stroke lay me low."

"And I give myself to you, Robin," says Mary ardently, "for as long as I may live."

Robert jumps back across the burn and takes Mary in his arms. "There, lass. Our troth's been plighted through the words o' God and man, and the formless song o' Nature's joy."

Her lips at his neck, Mary murmurs, "The trinkle o' a brook or a burn will always be reminding me of your song and this day, Robin."

Then, breaking from him, she moves away, looking a bit disconsolate. "The Bible I thocht to be giving you is steeked away in the chest wi' my belongings."

Robert reaches out and hugs her to him. "Never mind, lass," he says. "Ye maun gi'e it to me when we meet again at Greenock afore we set sail. I'll write to Stairaird and let ye know when I get fixed on the ship and the date."

Smiling, Mary says, "Aiblins I'll just be going on to Greenock anyway, for I have an uncle there."

"Aye, yon's a stroke o' luck." Robert grins back at her. "Aiblins it's luck we're in for frae here on."

"Oh, I hope so, Robin." Mary tightens her arms around him and presses her body to his.

Robert glances at the sky and sighs. "I ha'e work to do back at Mossgiel. And by the look o' the sun we'd best mak haste, lass."

Mary chuckles and touches Robert's neck, feather-like, with her tongue. "I did not think it was haste a man should be making while the sun shines," she whispers and, laughing, draws him down with her to the soft grass.

Robert looks at the hoe, then at his brother William. "It's nae use, Rab." Willie shrugs, his eyes widening. "I canna work wi' this. Can ye no fix it?"

Robert takes the implement from Willie and hefts it, hearing the clank of the blade on the handle. The bent nail that has served as a makeshift fastener has finally worked loose. "There's no much I can do wi' it, lad," he says. "We maun tak it in to the smithy the morn. Hughie Woodrow'll soon put it richt. In the meantime, ye'd sooner whistle a tune oot o' your arse as howk totties wi' this." Willie laughs, delighted as Robert knew he would be at sharing a bit of man's coarseness with his elder brother. He tousles Willie's hair. "Now awa' in," he says, "and see if ye can fin' the hammer. I'll gi'e it a dunt or twa, onyhow."

As his brother disappears into the house, Robert becomes aware of a grey figure watching him from the edge of the yard. "Good day, Mr. Fisher!" he calls, putting as much irony in his greeting as he can manage. Holy Willie moves closer, walking as if his feet hurt. Robert eyes the sharp-faced elder for a moment or two, then says, "I'd never ha'e thocht to see you on sic unhallowed ground."

Fisher sniffs, glancing about him like an exciseman. "I'm aboot the Lord's work," he says. "I can weel imagine the work you've been at, Rab Burns."

Robert stiffens, tightening his grip on the hoe, and backs away a step or two. "What I've been at's nane o' your affair, Fisher."

Fisher advances gleefully. "I wouldna just be sae sure o' that if I was you." He narrows his eyes at Robert. "Jean Armour's back frae Paisley."

Unwilling to let Fisher see his shock at this, Robert turns his back on the elder. "And what's that to do wi' me?" he growls. "Or wi' you either, for that matter?"

Behind him, he hears Holy Willie chuckle and shift his feet, full of nervous energy. "Ye needna set aboot to damn yoursel' further wi' lies," says Fisher. "I havena been idle these past weeks. Na, na. I've made certain calls on the Armours."

Robert turns quickly, gripping the hoe like a quarterstaff. "What the hell calls are ye haverin' aboot, ye sleekit bastard?"

Eying the hoe nervously, Fisher still manages to summon a tone of truculent righteousness. "Aye," he says, "'bastard.' Yon's a word that comes easy enough to sic as you, that has ample occasion to use it. Ooh, aye." He points a bony finger at Robert. "It's enough for me to say that my vigilance has been rewarded. We'll ha'e ye on the cutty stool noo, a' richt."

"What's goin' on here?"

His face burning with shame and anger, Robert looks around at the sound of his mother's voice. The whole family – Agnes, Gibby, Willie, and the three lassies – are clustered outside the farmhouse door. "It's a' richt, Mither," he finally manages. "Dinna fash yoursel'."

He turns again toward Holy Willie, who obviously relishes the prospect of an audience. But Fisher's delight fades quickly as Robert advances on him. "Keep awa', ye blasphemin' blackguard! I'm talkin' to ye as an Elder o' the Kirk."

Robert closes in on Fisher until he has backed the cringing elder against the farmyard's stone dyke. "Ye'd best no' add violence to your list o' misdeeds," says Holy Willie, his voice quavering more than usual. "I'm warnin' ye!"

Robert stares at Fisher for a long moment, then speaks in a scathing whisper. "I wouldna foul my hands wi' ye!" He swallows the anger that congests his throat and adds more evenly, "What is it ye want, then?"

Fisher's eyes quickly lose their hunted look and his tone regains a measure of its earlier smugness. "Mr. Auld wants words wi' ye," he says. "He sent me to fetch ye." The Elder draws himself up to his full height, looking over Robert's shoulder toward the rest of the family, and he raises his grating voice. "And Jeems Armour's seeking a warrant on ye," he crows in triumph. "For child support!"

At the sharp rap on the study door, the Rev. William Auld looks up from his desk. He removes his spectacles and pinches the bridge of his nose between thumb and forefinger. "Come away in," he says.

The door opens just enough so that William Fisher can put his head into the room. "He's here, Mr. Auld." Fisher's thin, blue-tinged lips twist his narrow face into what Auld takes to be an expression of satisfaction. "I've brocht him."

Auld raises his eyebrows. "Robert Burns, is it?"

"Aye," says Fisher. "Ooh, aye. That's just what I'm saying, Mr. Auld."

"Thank you, Mr. Fisher." Auld nods at the elder. "Show him in, if ye please."

"Ooh, aye."

Fisher disappears momentarily. Then the door swings open to disclose both Fisher and young Burns, the former looking almost merry, the latter grim-faced. Well, thinks Auld, glancing down at the papers before him, there might be more than one set of teeth gnashing before the day is out. "Thank you again, Mr. Fisher," he says. "Please wait outside."

Fisher's face crumples with displeasure. "Ooh, but Mr. Auld, wait till I tell ye how this fellow received me oot at Mossgiel."

At this, young Burns turns toward Fisher, his fists clenched and his brows drawn down over his dark eyes. Auld holds up a cautioning hand. "I'll speak to ye in good time, Mr. Fisher. Please shut the door behind ye."

"Ooh, aye," says Fisher, licking his lips and glancing nervously at Burns. "Just so, Mr. Auld." He starts out of the study, then turns back. "I'll be richt outside, then, Mr. Auld, if ye should need me."

"I'm sure ye will, Mr Fisher," says Auld, putting a slight edge on his voice to help impel Fisher out of the room. When he is alone with Burns, Auld gestures at a chair, but the young man shakes his head. He has not said a word since Fisher admitted him to the study, and Auld wonders whether the silence comes from sullenness or shame or both, mayhap?

"Weel, Mr. Burns," says the minister, waiting. Again, Burns fails to respond. Auld clears his throat and takes a sheet of paper from the desk. "This is a letter addressed to me," he says, and begins to read aloud. "'I am heartily sorry that I have given and must give your Session trouble on my account. I acknowledge that I am with child, and Robert Burns in Mossgiel is the father. I am, with great respect, your most humble servant, Jean Armour.'" Auld replaces the letter on the desk. "And what do ye say to that, Mr. Burns."

Burns colors further under his farmer's sunburnt complexion. "As to its truth," he says, speech obviously coming hard, "I wouldna dispute that."

"That, at least, is to your credit."

Burns stares at the minister for a moment, then speaks, his voice low, straining for control. "But I could well dispute the sense in owning a man the faither o' your child when ye've denied him the rightfu' name o' husband." Having said this, the young man sits on the chair near him, as if he felt the need to tether himself to something.

Momentarily at a loss, Auld looks down again at the letter from Jean. This is hardly the response he expected from Burns. He fingers the hand-copied poems James Lamie brought him earlier today while Fisher went to summon the poet from Mossgiel. They've prepared Auld for many possibilities – arrogance, stubbornness, defiance, forthrightness, wit, intelligence, even remorse – but not this. Nor have the Armours given any hint of more between Jean and Burns than the victimization of an innocent young lassie by her seducer.

"Come, sir," the minister says at last. "What's this talk o' husbands? Do I understand ye to be claiming marriage to the girl?"

Auld reinforces his words with a frown he hopes will dispel further attempts at evasion. But Burns looks back at him unflinchingly. "You do, Mr. Auld," says the young man. "She and I were married in March. But her pinch-minded folk – my betters! – wi' their bit o' gowd by them, and their property and their pride – they set to work on her. And she was easy enough led to deny me – and dishonor her vows."

Auld feels a stab of irritation. Why didn't James Armour say ought of this earlier? And what about Fisher and Lamie, leaving him ill-prepared for this interview? Or is Burns merely improvising? "These vows ye speak o'," he says. "What kind o' vows were they to be dishonored?"

Now Burns does look away from the minister's face. "They were irregular," he says quietly. "I wrote them mysel'." He looks again at Auld, his voice rising. "But they were fully binding by Scottish law. Until Armour had them mutilated."

"Mutilated?"

"Aye." Burns' voice drops again. "He got Bob Aiken to do it."

Auld considers this. It sounds just like James Armour to try to take matters into his own hands. And there's little doubt the Armours sent Jean to her aunt's in Paisley hoping that young Robert Wilson would solve their problem by wedding her. Sin is sin, however, and he must deal with the present situation first.

"That's as may be," he says to Burns. "But fine I ken o' such vows – that folk make and break as it suits them. And Scots law often enough has little to do wi' God's – more's the pity. And it's God's law that concerns me. Whatever the legalities o' your dispute wi' the Armours, you must answer to the ordinances o' the Kirk."

"It's the Armours that ha'e branded yon unborn wean a bastard," says Burns, with mounting anger. "If onybody should stand afore the Session, they should." He waves his hand. "But it's aey the same. The poor sin their sins and provide diversion for hirplin' hypocrites like Willie Fisher that ca' themsel's Kirk Elders – while the gentry tak their pleasure heedless and unheeded." He springs out of the chair, pointing at the window behind Auld. "And those wi' a wee bit siller to clink – like the Armours – "

"Mr. Burns!" Rising to his own feet, Auld glares at the young man. "Remember where you are and to whom you're speaking!" Looking subdued, Burns sinks back into his chair, and Auld proceeds sternly. "Mr. Burns, you are no mere ignorant sinner like the feck o' those that come before me. You are a man of uncommon gifts." Auld picks up several sheets of paper from his desk. "I ha'e read a number o' your poems, and I've heard ye plan to print a book shortly. Your 'Cotter's Saturday Night' I find both heartwarming and instructive. I wish I could say as much for 'The Holy Fair' and some others o' your verses that heap abuse on the Kirk."

"I've never attacked the Kirk," says Burns quickly. He glances meaningfully at the door behind which Fisher waits. "Only those that abuse its offices."

Auld clears his throat. "As I've said, ye're a man above the ordinary. A strong-minded man. And hence a man o' great power – for good or ill."

Burns snorts bitterly. "Ye can say that. And yet ye see me here as powerless afore the world as my unborn child!"

Auld moves around the desk to stand over the young man, conscious that if Robert Burns were rich or high-born he'd be universally admired and respected. But he knows, too, that one mauna rail against God's plan. "It is pride, Mr. Burns," he says, almost pleading, "pride ye must grapple with. And if ye dinna learn to curb it, ye will come to know the folly o' your headstrong ways." He bends to put a hand on Burns' shoulder, and feels him stiffen at the touch. "You think I ha'e ca'd ye here to humiliate ye to no purpose."

Straightening, Auld moves back around his desk and goes on. "A man o' your sense should know that self-love is at the heart o' a' other sins, and that I am merely doing my duty as God's priest to remind ye o' that, as forcefully as need be." He seats himself again. "I ha'e heard that ye plan to leave soon for the Indies. Is that true?"

"It is."

"And do ye intend pressing your suit further before the Armours?"

Burns is on his feet again. "Before a man that denies me a wife, but swears out a warrant to make me a father?"

"Just so," says Auld. "Well, then. Let's ha'e no more talk o' this marriage." He stops for a few moments to consider the solution that is forming in his head. "In view o' the special circumstances o' the case," he says at last, carefully keeping a neutral tone, "I think it richt to allow ye the privilege o' standing in your ain pew for the rebukes before the Session. If ye choose, ye needna take the cutty stool beside Jean Armour."

Burns sighs deeply. "Mr. Auld," he says. "I may say I canna agree wi' a' ye stand for. But I do recognize that according to your lights ye're a just man, and I respect ye for that." He looks again at the study door "There'll be those amang your elders that'll take this ill, I'm sure. No' to mention James Armour."

"I am quite able to deal wi' such questions, Mr. Burns." Auld thinks for a moment. "As for James Armour, the matter is simple. Having been rebuked three times before the Session, you will be given a certificate o' bachelorhood. That being so, I am sure I can point out quite easily to Mr. Armour the inconsistencies o' his legal position."

The young man's face creases in a smile. "I little thocht when I came here this morn that I'd ha'e cause to thank ye, Mr. Auld."

Now it is Auld's turn to sigh. "You trouble me deeply, Mr. Burns." Rising, he moves around the desk and takes Burns by the elbow. "I can only say I hope someday you will realize that the consequences o' your actions involve more suffering than yours alone, and that your soul hangs in the balance on more than your own account." As he speaks, Auld is uncomfortably aware of the "New Licht" ring of his own words; but he feels compelled to help this young man set higher sights for himself.

Burns extends his hand to the minister. "God knows how much thocht I do gi'e to such things, Mr. Auld."

Releasing Burns' elbow, Auld shakes the young man's hand. "I fear He does," he says dryly. "I fear He does." Then, nodding, he adds, "Well, good day to ye, Mr. Burns. Ye maun present yoursel' at Kirk next week for the first rebuke."

"I will," says Burns, opening the study door. "Good day to ye, Mr. Auld. I wish ye well."

Having watched Burns leave the Manse in glowering silence, Willie Fisher feels himself beset by dissatisfaction. He has heard almost nothing of what went on behind the heavy oaken door of Mr. Auld's study, strain as he might, though the sound of raised voices cheered him once or twice. He had counted on being in at the kill, so to speak, and he feels cheated. But now, as he considers the prospect of seeing Burns on the cutty stool, humiliated before the Session as he deserves, Fisher recovers his good spirits.

He chaps briskly at the study door and enters without waiting for invitation. As usual, the old minister is seated at his desk, fiddling about with some papers. "Weel, Mr. Auld," says Fisher. "We ha'e caught him fairly this time, ha'e we no'?"

Auld looks up at Fisher, his mouth set in a grim line, and waves some sheets of paper at him. "James Lamie has been gathering a wheen o' things for me," the minister says, and Fisher's stomach suddenly churns in discomfort. Auld takes up one of the sheets, holding it like a dead fish. "'Holy Willie's Prayer,' this is ca'd, Mr. Fisher. There are one or two lines here I would like to examine further." He looks pointedly at Fisher, who licks his lips in apprehension. "There's maybe more than Burns needs a session on the cutty stool."

Robert turns his horse up the High Street, a jumble of emotions quickening his pulse. Daddy Auld has given him a measure of freedom from anxiety – at least making the best of a bad situation – by keeping James Armour at bay. But he still feels a gnawing in his chest at the thought of Jean sitting now in her house at the Cowgate, a stone's throw away, with his child inside her. Not that he forgives her, or her parents; and, of course, he has Mary to think of now. But somehow he cannot bring himself to ride home to Mossgiel past the Armours' without seeing Jean, or inquiring after her health.

Robert reins in his horse at the Cowgate and dismounts, tethering the animal to the post outside Johnnie Dow's. He's fairly sure James Armour will still be out on some building site or other, but that leaves Mrs. Armour to stand guard. He takes a deep breath, then knocks at the door. As he stands waiting, he looks up the High Street and sees Jamie Smith standing in the doorway of his shop. He gives wee Smith a wave and then, turning back as the door opens, finds himself face to face with Mary Armour.

"Mrs. Armour," he begins, but gets no farther.

"You!" she says, a scowl disfiguring her plump features. "How ye can ha'e the face to present yoursel' at this door – it's ayont me!"

Craning his neck in a vain attempt to see past her into the house, Robert says, "I just wanted to see if Jean was a' right."

"How my lassie is will never be ony o' your affair!"

Mrs. Armour steps back and slams the door an inch or two from Robert's nose. He stares at the painted wood for a few moments, too stunned for anger, then walks slowly away to where his horse stands patiently, its tail swishing back and forth. As he unties the reins and prepares to mount, he hears a voice calling his name. Turning, he sees young Adam Armour running toward him from the direction of the Armours' back green.

"Mr. Burns!" Adam puts a hand on Robert's arm, then lowers his voice conspiratorially. "Jean says to tell ye she's a'right. She says she misses ye. She says if ye want to tell her something ye maun tell it to me and I'll gi'e her the message."

As Adam stops to catch his breath, Robert swings himself up into the saddle. He looks down at the boy. "Tell Jean I'm glad she's well. Tell her . . ." He pauses, at a loss. "Just tell her that." He starts his horse up the High Street, then turns to shout back to Adam. "Thanks, laddie! And ye can ca' me Rab!"

"The Cotter's Saturday Night"

My friend,

    I need not tell you the receipt of yours gave me pleasure. –

    O Jeany, thou hast stolen away my soul!
    In vain I strive against the lov'd idea:
    The tender image sallies on my thoughts,
    My firm resolves become an easy prey!

    Against two things however, I am fix'd as Fate: staying at home, and owning her conjugally. – The first, by Heaven I will not do! the last, by Hell I will never do! . . .

    A good God bless you, and make you happy up to the warmest, weeping wish of parting Friendship! –

    For me, I am witless wild, and wicked; and have scarcely any vestige of the image of God left me, except a pretty large portion of honour and an enthusiastic, incoherent Benevolence. –

    If you see Jean tell her, I will meet her, So help me Heaven in my hour of need!

    Farewell till tomorrow morning!

    ROBT BURNS

    letter to JAMES SMITH, Mauchline
    About 1st August 1786

Chapter Thirteen

"Order, if ye please!"

Bob Aiken, seated with John Ballantine and Gavin Hamilton at a table near the fire in John Simson's Brigend Inn, watches as Simson tries to quiet the noisy, good-natured crowd. Standing next to Willie Muir the miller, Robert Burns flashes a broad smile at the landlord, then turns and claps his brother Gilbert on the shoulder. The inn is full of Robert's friends and well-wishers: John Rankine of Adamhill is here, and wee Jamie Smith, and the Rev. John McMath, and Dr. John Mackenzie, and Tanner Hunter. Looking about him, Aiken is reminded of the far more somber gathering at Simson's nearly two years ago, after William Burns' funeral, when he first suggested that Robert consider printing his poems. And now here are those poems, cloth covers gleaming blue and white, fresh from Johnnie Wilson's in Kilmarnock, stacked on a table in the center of the room. And here sits Aiken, merely an onlooker.

"Order, I said!" Simson, a tall, grey-haired man with large ears and a beaky nose, waves his arms for silence. "Before the nicht gets ony older, I'd like to say this. I'm prood to ha'e sic distinguished folk on my premises, and prooder yet that ye're here to honor a man that'll like as no' end up to be the maist distinguished o' us a' – Rabbie Burns!"

A general chorus of assent rises at this. Aiken joins in, raising his glass and trying to catch Robert's eye. But Robert is too occupied accepting the plaudits of those nearest him, and Aiken finally sinks back in his chair, exchanging nods with Hamilton and Ballantine. When the shouting has died down a bit, Willie Muir's sharp voice cuts through the residue of talk and laughter.

"Thankee, John," says the miller, looking up at his taller host. "And now" – he turns to the crowd – "I'd like to ca' for a toast to the Bard. And I think we couldna do better nor ask a man wi' a gift o' gab equal to the occasion – a man that's as glib at readin' a poem as pleadin' a case – a man ye a' ken – orator Bob Aiken!"

Amid friendly laughter and outcries of agreement, Aiken pushes back his chair and gets to his feet. He raises his eyebrows at Hamilton, who says, "On ye go, Bob. Maybe this'll gi'e ye the chance to say a word to Rab."

Aiken smiles tightly, then makes his way across the room to where Muir stands and shakes his hand. "Thank ye, Willie," he says. He notes that Robert has moved away at his approach, but he puts it down to modesty, rather than hostility. He clears his throat and looks from face to face around him. "My friends," he says, and pauses for a dramatic moment before going on. "Tonight we ha'e the opportunity not only to pay deserved homage to a man close to our hearts" – he picks up a copy of Robert's book from the nearby table – "but to witness the distillation of that man's better part into a form to be enjoyed by countless others that canna number themsel's – as I hope we might – amang his neighbors and boon companions." Aiken holds the book up. "I refer, of course, to *Poems Chiefly in the Scottish Dialect,* printed in Kilmarnock in this year o' our Lord, 1786, and written by our ain Rabbie Burns." The company stirs and murmurs in reaction to this, but Aiken motions for quiet and raises his glass. "I gi'e ye a man o' great mind and greater heart, a staunch friend an' jolly compatriot, and aboon it a' a true poetic genius – Rabbie Burns!"

The assembly echoes Robert's name amid much clinking of glasses and whooping. Then, swallowing his whisky wrong, Tanner Hunter is seized by a fit of coughing, and by the time Jamie Smith has slapped his back and reduced him to red-faced panting, a measure of quiet descends on the room. Wee Smith looks up from his attentions to Hunter and, looking impish, addresses Aiken: "Ye're doubtless richt aboot what Rab's best part is, Bob. But I fancy there's a good few lassies aboot the countryside would fain dispute the point wi' ye!"

This elicits more laughter, even from the stricken Hunter, though Aiken notes that Robert joins in a bit ruefully, and Gibby Burns registers his disapproval by looking quietly into the depths of his pint stoup. Willie Muir, waving at wee Smith in mock reproach, says, "For God's sake, Jamie, can ye no' observe the solemnity o' the occasion?"

"Come on, Willie," says Smith, "the time for solemnity's by. It's an occasion for joy, man." He walks over to the book-piled table and picks up a volume. "Like welcomin' a new bairn – eh, Rab?"

Robert chuckles. "Aye, Jamie, it's like that, richt enough. Wi' a' the joy and pride and hope and fear a new faither can feel."

Aiken can see that Robert's words have veered too close to seriousness for Smith, who looks around him until he sees Simson's serving maid, a sonsie lass with a ready smile and an easy manner. "It's a song we're needin', then," says Smith. "And I ken just the one to celebrate this birth. Meg!" He crosses the room and takes the girl by the arm. "Let's ha'e 'Rantin' Robin'!" After no more than token protestation, Meg begins to sing in her strong, clear voice:

> "There was a lad was born in Kyle,
> But whatna day o' whatna style
> I doubt it's hardly worth the while
>   To be sae nice wi' Robin."

Meg motions for the company to join in the chorus, and many do, either already knowing this piece of musical autobiography, or quickly finding the words in the new book.

> "Robin was a rovin' boy
> Rantin', rovin', rantin', rovin',
> Robin was a rovin' boy,
>   Rantin', rovin' Robin!
>
> Our monarch's hindmost year but one
> Was five-and-twenty days begun
> 'Twas then a blast o' Januar' win'
>   Blew hansel in on Robin."

As she sings, Meg moves about the room from table to table and group to group, giving particular attention to the song's author, who smiles in embarrassed approval. Again, Aiken notes that Gibby remains aloof from the general merriment. Disapproval? Or envy? Hard to know, Aiken reflects, for Gibby Burns is a close lad, not given to unburdening himself. Aiblins he'd be happier if he could. Aiken takes a final swallow of whisky and gestures to Simson for another dram, then returns his attention to the song.

> "The gossip keekit in his loof,
> Quo' she, 'Wha lives will see the proof,
> This waly boy will be nae coof:
>   I think we'll ca' him Robin.

"'He'll have misfortunes great an' sma',
But aye a heart aboon them a',
He'll be a credit to us a'
     We'll a' be proud o' Robin.

"'But sure as three times three makes nine,
I see by ilka score and line,
This chap will dearly like our kin',
     So leeze me on thee! Robin.

"'Guid faith,' quo' she, 'I doubt ye'll gar
The bonie lassies lie aspar;
But twenty fauts ye may ha'e waur
     So blessin's on thee! Robin.'"

And as Meg launches into the final chorus, Aiken shakes his head in wondering approval at the acuteness of self-knowledge and the courage in self-revelation that the song displays, notwithstanding its jocular tone of self-celebration. Joining in the applause and enthusiastic outcries that follow Meg's effort, Aiken watches Robert laughingly cross the room to the girl and plant a kiss on her cheek.

Willie Muir thumps his stoup on a table for attention. "Weel, Rab," he says. "Now that we've gi'ed ye sufficient introduction, what aboot favorin' us wi' a poem, yoursel'?"

Robert gives Meg's shoulder a squeeze, then bows slightly to the company. "First," he says, "I'd like to thank ye a' for your warm sentiments." He looks at Aiken. "And you, Bob, for your words – and deeds." The ambiguity of this causes Aiken momentary discomfort, but Robert continues: "For this book wouldna be here now if it werena for so many o' ye that made up the list o' subscribers – Mr. Hamilton, Jamie, my ain brother Gibby – and a' the rest – ye a' ha'e my undying gratitude."

Robert picks up a copy of his book and leafs through it, finally finding what he is looking for. "And now," he says, "despite the joy o' the occasion, I think this catches my feelings best the nicht. It's one some o' ye may ken." He smiles mischievously, then begins to read:

"Ha! whaur ye gaun, ye crowlin' ferlie?
Your impudence protects you sairly;

I canna say but ye strunt rarely,
          Owre gauze and lace;
Tho', faith! I fear' ye dine but sparely
          On sic a place."

Aiken joins in the delighted laughter as he and the rest of the crowd recognize the opening lines of "To a Louse, On seeing one on a Lady's Bonnet at Church," Robert's satirical follow-up to his widely-loved but sentimental "To a Mouse." Aiken sips at his whisky as Robert continues:

"Ye ugly, creepin', blastit wonner,
Detested, shunned by saunt an' sinner,
How daur ye set your fit upon her –
          Sae fine a lady?
Gae somewhere else and seek your dinner
          On some poor body.

Swith! in some beggar's haffet squattle;
There ye may creep, and sprawl, and sprattle,
Wi' ither kindred, jumping cattle,
          In shoals and nations;
Whaur horn nor bane ne'er daur unsettle
          Your thick plantations."

Robert drops his voice to a dramatic whisper:

"Now haud you there, ye're out o' sight,
Below the fatt'rels, snug and tight
Na, faith ye yet! ye'll no' be right,
          Till ye've got on it –
The verra tapmost, towerin' height
          O' Miss's bonnet."

And as he continues, Robert adopts a tone of rising indignation, clearly savoring the vividness and pungency of his own language, and varying his rhythm with pauses obviously calculated to produce the greatest amusement in his audience.

"My sooth! right bauld ye set your nose out,
As plump an' grey as ony groset:
O for some rank, mercurial rozet,
          Or fell, red smeddum,
I'd gi'e you sic a hearty dose o't,
          Wad dress your droddum."

As Robert skillfully modulates the pitch of his delivery, Aiken can hear that the young man has indeed learned a thing or two about recitation these past months, and shows a new confidence in his own powers.

"I wad na been surprised to spy
You on an auld wife's flainen toy;
Or aiblins some bit duddie boy,
          On's wylecoat;
But Miss's fine Lunardi! fye!
          How daur ye do't?

O Jeany, dinna toss your head,
An' set your beauties a' abread!
Ye little ken what cursed speed
          The blastie's makin'
Thae winks an' finger ends, I dread,
          Are notice takin'."

And now, cutting through the laughter around him, Robert speaks to the gathering in his own voice, with heartfelt sincerity, reminding Aiken once more of the keen observer who lives within this extraordinary young man, who seems blind to nothing, not even his own failings:

"O wad some Power the giftie gi'e us
To see oursel's as ithers see us!
It wad frae mony a blunder free us,
          An' foolish notion:
What airs in dress an' gait wad lea'e us,
          An' even devotion!"

A moment of quiet follows the poem's conclusion; then the company breaks into applause and shouts of satisfaction. Aiken moves forward among others, including Willie Muir and Aiken's legal colleague David McWhinnie, who surge around Robert to offer their congratulations. Picking his way carefully, Jamie Smith steadies himself on Aiken's shoulder, then presses a glass of whisky into Robert's hand and says with a laugh, "Jeany Markland will never forgi'e ye for that ane, Rab."

Robert grins at wee Smith. "There's many a lass ca'd Jean," he says. "It could happen to ony o' them. And soon enough there'll be naebody that kens – or cares – whether it's real or whether it's made up." He lifts his glass and drinks to Smith. "We maun a' consider how we look to the world aboot us – especially the likes o' me, that parades his thoughts and feelings in print." Chuckling, he shakes his head. "Frae that point o' view I couldna say whether I'm the louse or the lass."

"We may weel worry aboot how others see us, Rab," says Aiken. "But one thing ye needna worry aboot is what ye've put atween the covers o' your book. And I daresay folk will still appreciate it when we're a' forgot."

He takes Robert by the arm and guides him to a corner of the room, then lowers his voice. "I wouldna bring this up now, Rab," he says, "but it's been on my mind for some time. Now and again the practice o' law puts a man in an awkward spot as regards his friends." Robert's shoulders stiffen, and his eyes take on a flat, guarded look, but Aiken presses forward. "I just wanted to say that if I've done ought to offend ye in the matter o' Jean Armour, I'm heartily sorry."

Robert appears to soften a bit as he digests this. "I canna deny I was a bit shocked at the time," he says. "And then, when ye sent word o' your subscription for the book, I didna ken what to think." He looks steadily at Aiken. "I canna tell ye how much I'm obliged to ye for that."

Aiken waves his hands, dismissing the subject of his subscription order. "It'll gi'e the world something to remember me for," he says. Then he returns to his main concern. "When Armour showed me those marriage lines, I couldna think but what ye'd want nothing less in your position than to be taigled wi' a wife and bairn. So I fell in wi' his wishes, thinking that way to please ye both." This sounds unconvincing, even to Aiken himself, but he goes on. "Had ye wanted it, of course, ye could've had the marriage vows recognized, right enough. But since ye've stood afore the Mauchline Session and been declared a bachelor, I suppose things ha'e turned out for the best, after a'."

Robert nods, a mere twitch of his head. "Aye, I suppose they have, at that," he says, sounding none too certain. Then he smiles at Aiken. "But never mind that now, Bob – it's a' by and done wi'." He takes Aiken by the hand and shakes it warmly, and the little lawyer feels relief flooding through his veins. "Now," says Robert, "let's enjoy oursel's like the friends we are."

Watching his brother and Bob Aiken in conversation across the room, Gibby feels empty, without substance, as if he might float away like one of those hot-air balloons the Italian daredevil, Lunardi, soared over Scotland in last year, firing the public imagination, even inspiring milliners to design the new style of hat Jeany Markland was wearing at kirk on the day Rab saw the louse on her neck. Aye, Gibby thinks, and wasn't it just like folk to go mad for the balloonist, instead of the balloon that enabled him to fly among the clouds? He realizes the thought makes little sense, that talent alone carries Robert above the ordinary; and yet who is always there, providing the foundation, taking care of what Robert's flights soar beyond? Angry at himself, Gibby takes a gulp of his whisky.

As he coughs at the unaccustomed burning in his throat, he feels a work-hardened hand slapping him between the shoulder blades. "Drink it, laddie," says Willie Muir, laughing. "Dinna snoke it up. It may be the Water o' Life, richt enough, but we canna breathe it."

Before Gibby can draw breath to respond, the miller starts across the room, shouting to Robert and Aiken. "Come awa' the pair o' ye and join the company!" As Robert and the little lawyer abandon their private conversation, Muir raises his glass and quiets the crowd. "Order! Order! I'd like to propose anither toast. This time to a man we see less often than yoursel', Rab. A rare fellow in every sense – your brither Gibby!"

Suddenly everyone's eyes are on Gibby, and he feels his face reddening. But before Muir can go on, Robert strides across to where Gibby stands. "That's a toast I can join in wi' every fiber o' my being, Willie." His eyes a bit wild with drink, Robert grips Gibby's arm tightly. "A better man nor a finer brither ever walked on two legs. We've rowed and chowed and rocht and focht wi' ill-fortune since ever we were bairns, and he's aey been there, dependable and sober and true. I wish could say the same for mysel'.'"

As Gibby forces a smile and fights the urge to shake Robert's hand from his arm, Willie Muir shouts, "To Gibby!"

The room echoing with his name, Gibby can only nod and raise his glass in acknowledgment. As he sips at the rest of his Kilbagie, he sees Muir approaching him and Robert. "And what do ye think o' havin' a published poet for a brither, Gibby?" says the little miller.

"It's a proud day, Willie," he replies stiffly. Then, impelled by Robert's obvious pleasure and by his own sense of occasion, he adds, "Though he's aey been a poet. But now maybe the world ayont Ayrshire will come to ken that as well."

Bob Aiken, who has followed Robert and Muir across the room, breaks in at this. "They'd ken it better," he says, "if he'd stay here in Scotland, Gibby, instead o' sailing away to Jamaica." The lawyer looks at Robert, his normally merry face bearing a solemn expression. "I've thought about this long and hard latterly, Rab, and I think ye're making a mistake."

Eyes widening, Robert glances at Gibby, then back at Aiken. "Ye ken it galls me to think o' leavin' kith and kin and country, Bob. But what can I hope for here?"

"A very great deal, Rab," says Aiken, "if I ha'e ony notion o' the power o' your verse."

"Bob's right, Rab," puts in Gavin Hamilton, who has joined the group. "I ken fine he is."

Gibby hears a murmur of agreement from John Ballantine, who stands at Hamilton's elbow.

"Edinburgh, man," says Aiken, his voice low and insistent. "Ye need only set your sights on Edinburgh. At the rate they're going, ye'll sell every copy o' your book within a month. Six hundred copies! That'll certainly make ye enough money to see ye off to Jamaica and maybe lea'e a bit for your family here and a'. But an Edinburgh edition o' your poems would make your reputation, and open the door to fortune and independence in the shape o' the Edinburgh gentry."

"I agree wi' ye, Bob." Hamilton nods vigorously and stabs a finger at the little lawyer. "Ye canna say the word too often." He turns to Robert. "Ye might be wise to try another printing in Kilmarnock first, just to be on the safe side. But Edinburgh's the place."

"But how?" Robert frowns, looking from Aiken to Hamilton. "A book canna provide a man wi' independent means."

"Aye, but think, Rab," says Aiken. "In Edinburgh ye ha'e the prospect o' a rich patron. And failing that, there's aey the idea o' the Excise commission I've mentioned to ye now and again. I'd do what I could for ye frae here on that score, but Edinburgh's where ye'd meet folk o' real power and influence."

"I could maybe lend a hand wi' sponsoring ye for the Excise and a', Rab," says John Ballantine, careful and soft-spoken. "And if ye choose to print a second edition in Kilmarnock, I'll stand good for the costs. Though I agree wi' Bob – Edinburgh's where ye maun make your mark."

"Aye, Rab!" Wee Jamie Smith shoulders into the group past Willie Muir. "Ye can stay wi' Jock Richmond at Baxter's Close. There's no' a poet in Edinburgh to match ye!"

"Aye, nor in Scotland," says Muir, not to be outdone in sentiment.

Aiken touches Robert's arm. "I'll be happy to write to Willie Creech whenever ye say the word, Rab. He's the most important publisher and bookseller in Auld Reekie."

Gibby sees bewilderment register on his brother's face. "Ye're comin' at me sae fast," says Robert, "I scarcely ken what to think."

What manner of man is it, Gibby wonders, who can find himself turned so quickly from one extreme course to another, who possesses a mind so far beyond the feck o' men as to warrant the name of genius, but whose passions seem to sway him regardless of intellect or common sense?

"It canna be, though," Robert murmurs. "My course is . . . set, . . . beyond my power to alter it." He looks down at the floor, then at the books on the nearby table. "Edinburgh," he says, his voice no more than a whisper.

Unable to define his own rush of strong emotion, Gibby feels the sudden need for fresh air. Setting his glass on the mantel over the crackling fire, he pushes through the crowd and makes his way out of the inn, not stopping until he finds himself standing on the old bridge, looking down into the broad slow flood of the River Ayr. He cannot tell how many minutes pass, aware only of the water below and the hard stone parapet under his elbows.

"It's no' sae easy, is it?"

Startled, Gibby turns to confront John Rankine, the burly master of Adamhill Farm. Rankine's broad, apple-cheeked face is flushed with drink, but his blue eyes are keenly focused on Gibby.

"It's no, sae easy," Rankine repeats, "havin' a genius for a brither. Is it?"

Gibby hunches himself again over the parapet and looks down at the dark water. For a time he cannot bring himself to reply. But then he feels Rankine's hand squeezing his shoulder and he says, "We maun a' live our lives as best we can, whatever we may be." Then he nods at Rankine. "But ye're richt, Mr. Rankine. There's times when it's no' easy."

Rankine smiles at him. "My lass Annie ance fancied she micht mak a wife for your brither. And that's what I hoped and a'." Rankine takes his hand from Gibby's shoulder and leans on the parapet beside him. "But it wasna to be. Rab's destiny will tak him far ayont what the pair o' us may imagine, whether it's to the Indies or to the great hooses o' Edinburgh. And the likes o' you and me maun just stand back . . . and watch."

Gibby makes no answer to this, for he knows there is none. And together the two men look down at the river's lazy, purling flow, listening to its hiss and whisper as if it might give them some hint of the future, some explanation of the past.

Wish me luck, dear Richmond! Armour has just brought me a fine boy and girl at one throw. God bless the little dears!

"Green grow the rashes, O,
"Green grow the rashes, O,
"A feather bed is no sae saft,
"As the bosoms o' the lasses, O."

ROBT BURNS

letter to JOHN RICHMOND, Edinburgh
3rd September 1786

Chapter Fourteen

Agnes, Nancy, Bell, and Isa are occupied with washing and mending when Adam Armour arrives red-faced and breathless at the open farmhouse door. "Where's Mr. Burns?" cries the lad.

Agnes looks at him through the steam from the laundry tub and wipes her hands on her apron. This will be news of the bairn, she thinks, and urgent news by the look of the boy. "He and the ither lads are muckin' the byre, son. But you come and sit doon a minute, for ye're pechin' there like a bellows." She turns to her youngest girl, who is sitting at the fire, darning stockings and watching wee Bess. "Isa. Awa' oot and tell Robert he's wanted."

Isa rises, a scowl darkening her usually sunny face, and makes her way out past the Armour boy. And as the lad sits at the kitchen table, Agnes notes that Bell and Nancy are glowering, too. Ever since James Armour swore out the warrant on Robert for child-support, forcing him for a while to lodge with several different friends, the girls have no time for any member of that family, especially Jean. Agnes herself has little use for James, but she does think that Robert should do right by the lassie. The present question, though, is one of hospitality. "Get the laddie a caup o' milk, Bell," she says.

Bell does as she's bid, but with an ill grace. As she sets down the milk with a thump before the boy, Robert and Isa walk in from the yard. Young Armour jumps up. "Mr. Burns! Rab! It's Jean – her time's come!"

"The hell ye say!" Robert starts across the room to the boy, then pulls up short at a disapproving sound from Agnes, who points down at his muddy boots. He pulls them off and throws them toward the door, then turns back to Adam. "Is it born yet, then?"

"It wasna when I left the hoose," says the lad. "But they said it was on the way. Ye maun come wi' me the now."

Robert's brows draw together. "Was it Jean that sent ye, lad? I'll no' go to be turned away at the door by your faither."

"No, no, Rab. It was him and my mither that sent me." The boy smiles, and Agnes can see in his rosy cheeks and dark hair the resemblance between him and his sister. "Since your book came oot," says the lad, "they seem to think mair o' ye."

"Aye." Robert grimaces sourly. "They'll likely no' ha'e read it, then."

The boy laughs at this. "No, they havena." Then, raising his eyebrows, he says solemnly, "But I've read bits o' it, Rab, and I think it's rare!"

"Thank ye, Adam," says Robert. "I'm glad ye do." He looks at Agnes. "I suppose I'd better go."

"Aye," she says. "But ye maun clean yoursel' up a bit, first, and put on your guid claithes – and clean boots an a'."

Laughing, Robert dips some water from the laundry tub into a basin, then climbs the stairs to his and Gibby's room to get himself ready. Agnes turns to Adam. "Sit ye back doon, laddie, and drink that milk. And ye'll tak a bannock and a whang o' cheese to go wi' it."

As the boy falls to his food and drink with good appetite, Agnes returns to stirring her laundry tub. Looking at the murky water, listening to the slosh and squelch of the sodden clothes, she wonders what effect this latest development will have on her eldest son's feelings, for they seem to change like the shift of light and shadow on the braes when the wind drives the clouds before it. Two women he's got with child, either of whom could have been – aye, and should have been – his wife. And then this notion of running to the West Indies, a place Agnes can scarcely believe in. And the book. His wonderful book, a copy of which lies on the kitchen table near wee Adam, its pages full of scenes and people and voices far more real than some green promise ayont the sea. She shakes her head and sighs, then looks up sharply as Robert clatters down into the kitchen.

Adam Armour rises from his chair. "Well, lad," says Robert, handsome in his blue coat, white breeches, and good riding boots, "I'll away out and saddle the mare. Then we'll gallop down the road and see whether ye've a nephew or a niece!"

When Adam leads him through the Armours' front door Robert prepares himself for a hostile reception. What he finds, instead, is James Armour, seated in his shirtsleeves in the parlor staring at nothing, a brown stain of snuff on his upper lip

Becoming aware of Robert's presence, Armour starts violently and rises. "Oh, it's you," he says, as if roused from sleep.

Robert nods stiffly. "Good day, Mr. Armour."

"I'm obliged that ye could come," says Armour.

This civility from a man who first drove him away, then set the bailiffs after him, alarms Robert. "Why?" he says anxiously. "What's the matter? Is Jean a' right? The child?"

Armour sits down heavily in his chair, then gestures vaguely at the door leading to the second floor. "Ye maun see for yoursel'," he says.

Without waiting further, Robert climbs the stairs and puts his head in at the room he knows Jean shares with her younger sister, Nellie. Jean is there, lying in the bed, eyes closed, her hair a tangle on the pillow and her face pale and damp-looking. Nellie, a smaller version of her sister, but with lighter-colored hair, is hovering at the head of the bed. Mrs. Armour is standing to one side, near a wooden crib, holding a swaddled baby in her arms. When she sees Robert, the corners of her mouth twitch in disapproval.

"Mrs. Armour," he says. "The child – Jean – are they a' right?"

Before Mary Armour can answer, young Nellie says, "Child? Mr. Burns, it's –"

"Nellie!" Jean, her eyes snapping open, cuts her sister off in a voice surprisingly strong. "I'll tell him," she says.

Seeing Jean's luminous eyes in her pallid but still beautiful face, Robert suddenly loses all sense of aggrievedness. He crosses quickly to the head of the bed and, as Nellie moves aside for him, falls to his knees and takes Jean's hand. "Are ye a'right, lass?"

Jean smiles wanly. "I'm fine, Rab."

"That's grand, Jean." He tightens his grip, gently kneading her fingers with his own. "When I saw your faither looking sae vexed, I thought – "

"Well micht he be vexed," puts in Mary Armour, scowling down at Robert.

Jean raises herself up on her elbows. "Mither!" she says sharply.

Robert rises and, loathe to approach Mrs. Armour, cranes his neck at the tiny red-faced child in her arms. "Is it a boy, Jean?" he asks, turning to her, feeling almost guilty at his own hope, and at the image his memory raises of Betty holding wee Bess.

Jean's eyes seem to cloud for a moment. "It's . . . a girl," she says, a tremor in her voice.

Robert cannot suppress a pang of disappointment. But he smiles down reassuringly at Jean. "A bonnie wee lassie," he says. "And I'll warrant she'll be as lovely as her mither." He senses Mrs. Armour's stare needling at the nape of his neck and moves uneasily back to the bedside, falling again to his knees, where he can smell Jean's natural fragrance mixed headily with the aromas of sweat and damp linen. He touches her bare arm. "How've ye been a' these months, Jean?" he says, his voice low.

Jean looks at him sidewise from her pillow. "Oh, I've been a' richt, I suppose." She must see his discomfort, for she suddenly says, "Mither. Nellie. We'd like to be left to oursel's for a minute."

Robert turns to judge the effect of this request. Mrs. Armour stares hard at him for a moment or two, then, still holding the baby to her bosom, walks wordlessly out of the room, elbowing Nellie before her.

When they are alone, Jean touches her fingers to his cheek. "I missed ye," she says quietly. "A' yon months in Paisley."

Robert looks at her dark eyes and the faint blue veins in the translucent hollow at her throat. "I thought o' you often and a' Jean," he says stiffly. And he cannot keep himself from adding, "You and Robert Wilson."

Jean withdraws her hand from his face as if burned. "He's never been onything to me, Rab!" she exclaims, her eyes wide with alarm. "Whatever my mither micht think." She takes his hand in both of hers, sending a shiver through him despite his resolve. "Oh, Rab," she says, "why do things need to be the way they are?"

This is too much, he thinks. He rises and moves away to the foot of the bed, then turns back. "Ye maun put that question to yoursel', Jean." Looking at him steadily, she begins to weep without a sound, her eyes and cheeks shining. He moves quickly to her and, kneeling, folds her in his arms. "Lass, lass, dinna greet," he says. "Wheesht. I dinna ken what I was thinkin', after what ye've been through." He holds her head to his shoulder, stroking her hair. "There, there. It's a' right. It's a' right."

They remain like this for a time without speaking, Jean sniffling now and again and Robert's mind full of conflict as he thinks of Mary waiting in Greenock, wind blowing her cornsilk hair as she looks out over the water where the *Nancy* lies anchored, poised to take them to the plantations of Jamaica. And beyond that he sees the shadowy outline of Edinburgh Castle, and hears again the voices of Bob Aiken and Gavin Hamilton whispering in his ear of the future he might find there.

"Rab?" Jean's voice is a mere whisper.

"Aye, lass?" he says.

"Look in the crib."

Robert settles her back on the pillow and looks at her for a moment, but he can read nothing in her eyes. He rises, crosses to where the crib rests near the room's far wall, and peers inside. There, asleep, is a baby, only its head and hands visible amid its swaddling. For a moment he merely looks at the fine dark hair, the miniature fingers curling and uncurling, the small bud of a mouth working away. Then he suddenly realizes what this means. "My God," he says numbly, turning to Jean. "It's another wean."

Jean beams. "Aye, Rab," she says, laughing. "And it's a boy!"

A surge of pure delight courses through Robert, and he claps his hands together. "Twins!" he says, and spins completely around, laughter bubbling out of him. He moves to the foot of the bed and smiles down at Jean. "My God, lass," he says, "ye've paid me back double! Two at one go! And one o' each, at that. Jean Armour, ye're a wonder, so ye are!" He moves back to the crib and looks down at his little son. "Aye, lad, ye're a rantin', rovin' Robin, right enough. And ye'll be a far better man than your faither."

"They're to be Jean and Robert," says Jean, a lilt of pleasure in her voice. Robert crosses to the bed, sits down, and hugs her tightly. "Faither doesna ken where to turn," she adds, her voice dropping.

Robert disengages himself from her arms and sits back. "I can understand his feelings," he says carefully. Then his resentment boils over. "Of course, it's something he took on himsel' months ago when he decided the likes o' me wasna fit for his dochter."

"I ken that, Rab," Jean says quickly. "I didna mean to press ye in ony way."

Looking at her, seeing the way her long dark hair frames her tear-wet face, Robert softens. "Och, Jean," he says, "I ken fine how it is. I'm just happy to see ye've come through it a' sae well. And the bairns are marvelous." He hugs her again, then sits back decisively. "If you're willing, Jean," he says, his thoughts taking shape no more than an instant before he speaks them, "and your folk are willing, . . . I'll tak responsibility for the wee boy. He can come and stay at Mossgiel when he's old enough to leave you." He puts a hand on her shoulder. "I wouldna have ye bear the whole burden, lass."

"Oh, Rab," says Jean, reaching out to him, "that would be wonderful!"

He presses his lips to hers and feels her mouth open and her arms tighten around him. Again he thinks of Mary and the two Bibles he gave her with his pledges of faith. He leans back from Jean, his mouth still feeling the force of her kiss. "Mind ye, lass," he says, "it can mean nothing mair than that. The decisions have a' been made where you and I are concerned."

Jean sinks back onto her pillow, her eyes averted from his face. "I . . . I ken that, Rab," she says softly. Then she does look at him and speaks with growing fervor. "I wish I had never done what I did to ye. But he's my faither, Rab, and I was frightened. Ye can see plain enough how I feel aboot ye." She lays a hand on his knee. "Do ye feel nae love at a' for me now?"

Robert covers her hand with his. "I didna say that," he says. "But now we've both committed oursel's to . . . other courses."

"Aye," she says, the word a mere breath. Then, after a time, she asks, "Are ye still minded to go to Jamaica?"

"Aye. I suppose I am." But as he speaks, the image of that green island amid a calm turquoise sea seems to fade in his mind like a dream he cannot quite recall.

Jean glances at the crib across the room. "But what aboot wee Robert, then?"

"He'll be fine," Robert says, though he realizes that the matter is by no means settled, especially since in turning over his affairs to Gibby he named wee Bess his sole beneficiary. That will need looking into. "I'll make provision for him at Mossgiel," he says. "Ye can tell your mither and faither and see what they think."

Hearing a sniff behind him, he turns and sees Mary Armour glowering at him from the doorway, the baby girl still in her arms. "I think it's time my dochter had a bit rest, . . . Mr. Burns."

Ignoring her reluctance to speak his name, Robert rises. "Aye, that's a fact," he says. He kisses Jean's warm forehead. "You rest, lass. We'll talk again."

At the sound of footsteps coming down the stairs, James Armour looks up from his chair to see Adam hovering near the door, followed by the appearance of Burns, who tousles the boy's hair, then nods shortly at James. "Well, Mr. Armour," says Burns, "I'm obliged to ye for the opportunity o' seeing Jean and the weans. And now I'll say good day."

"Aye," says James, torn between resentment and resignation. "Now that ye've seen them, ye'll want to be away."

Burns, careless blackguard that he is, either misses the sarcasm or ignores it, turning instead to shake Adam's hand. "Thanks for fetching me here, Adam," he says. "Ye're a good lad." And with little more than a nod to James, Burns is out the door and away, with Adam's goodbyes trailing him.

After glaring at his son, James rubs a hand across his mouth, then heaves a gusty sigh. He feels thwarted at every turn, even by Mr. Auld, contrary old curmudgeon that he is, ignoring the will of respectable parishioners to favor an upstart verse-maker. James knows, too, that his own actions have done little to improve matters, leaving him burdened with not just one, but two illegitimate grand-children; and that knowledge only sharpens his frustration.

As he opens his mouth to rebuke Adam for being overly friendly to Burns, Mary bustles into the parlor from upstairs and glances about her. "He's away?" she says.

James snorts. "Aye," he says sourly.

Mary approaches him, rubbing her hands. "Did he tell ye what he said to Jean?" she asks eagerly.

"He said nothing at a'."

"Weel, ye'd better hear this, then." Mary pulls a chair over in front of James and sits. "He's offered to tak the wee boy off our hands."

Startled, James sits upright. "What?" he demands. "Are ye serious?"

Mary clucks impatiently. "Of course I am," she says. "Do ye think I'd be haverin' aboot a Godsend like that?"

James reaches for his snuffbox and takes out a pinch, then sniffs, producing a sneeze that clears his brain a bit. He pushes himself out of his chair and looks down at his wife. "I canna understand it," he says at last. What can Burns be playing at? he wonders. He shakes his head. "There's just nae way to puzzle a man like that oot. Takin' anither wean into yon housefu' at Mossgiel. Legally, he needna ha'e lifted a hand to help us."

"Weel," says Mary, "ye canna say we didna ha'e some hopes when we sent for him." At a sound from Adam, who has been listening near the door, she shoots him a silencing look, then turns back to James. "Yon book o' his," she says. "Everywhere ye go folk are readin' it or gabbin' aboot it. He's maybe made oot better wi' it than we ken."

As James digests this, nodding, Adam pipes up. "Maybe he's just no' as black a rogue as ye thocht he was, Faither." Then, always quick, the boy dodges out of the front door and away before James can start for him.

"And when did ye agree to this?"

Nancy Burns hears an unusual note of panic mixed with the understandable exasperation in Gibby's voice. Like the rest of the family, who are ranged about the kitchen, she looks at Robert and waits for his reply.

"It was the day the weans were born," Robert says, shifting his weight from one foot to the other. "I couldna leave withoot telling Jean something."

Nancy puts her hands on her hips. "O'er a month ago," she says. "And this is you just tellin' us now?"

"It makes nae difference to the wee lad," says Robert. "And little difference to us, either, for he'll no' be able to lea'e Jean for a good while yet. And I've had a lot to think aboot these past weeks."

"Aye," Bell puts in, "like attendin' to your correspondence wi' the high and michty. And sittin' doon to your dinner wi' Lord Daer o'er at Catrine Hoose to hear your book praised. Nae wonder ye canna spare a thocht for the likes o' us."

Nancy sees Robert's eyes narrow as if in anger, but when he speaks his voice is calm enough. "Aye," he says. "And the book that's cost me sae much thought has already eased matters for us a' – for every copy's spoken for, as ye ken weel enough. And the high and mighty – like Lord Daer, and Professor Stewart that owns Catrine Hoose – might finally gi'e us the hope o' a better life – even wee Rab."

"How and ever," says Gibby, "it's askin' an awfu' lot, expectin' us to tak in anither bairn, and you thoosands o' miles awa'. Nae matter what financial provisions ye may be able to mak for it."

"Aye," says Agnes Burns, stirring a pot of broth at the fireplace with a wooden spoon. "It's the Paton business a' o'er again."

Once more Nancy can tell that Robert is straining for control. "It's hardly that, Mither," he says. "The Armours ha'e made ony ither solution impossible. And we canna let the bairn suffer for that." Turning back to Gibby, he says, "I know it would be better in some ways if I could stay here, instead o' sailing for Jamaica. Then I could maybe look into this idea o' an Edinburgh edition. Even Professor Stewart was on aboot it the ither day."

"Aye," says Gibby. "And it's maybe time ye gi'ed thocht to an Excise post hereabouts and a'."

Nancy hears her mother humming in agreement. "Weel may ye heed that," Agnes says to Robert. "For as lang as we've a king o'er us, there'll aey be a job for a tax collector."

Robert shakes his head. "I just canna do it," he says. "I've already postponed the voyage so I can help see in the harvest, poor though it may be. And I've a job waiting for me there at thirty pounds per annum."

"But ye ken nothin' aboot what kin' o' man this Dr. Douglas may be to clerk for," says Gibby. "And ye havena bound yoursel' to him, have ye? Ye're no' an indentured servant, for God's sake."

Robert sighs loudly. "I've made promises," he says, his voice low, and betraying a depth of emotion Nancy finds puzzling.

"What kin' o' promises?" demands Gibby, slapping his thigh in a rare show of frustration.

Before Robert can reply, wee Davie Hutcheson runs into the house from the yard. "Rab!" he shouts, then catches himself at a look from Gibby. "It's a letter," he says, dropping his voice and holding out an envelope.

The arrival of letters has become a frequent occurrence since the publication and enthusiastic reception of Robert's book. Nancy finds herself eager to know what fresh praise Robert may have won, and from what distinguished correspondent

"Who sent it?" Robert asks, voicing Nancy's question as he crosses the kitchen to the boy and takes the letter.

"I dinna ken," says wee Davie. "But the man said it was frae Greenock."

Gibby looks less than pleased. "It'll be news aboot your passage, nae doubt," he says to Robert.

As the family looks on, Robert opens the envelope, withdraws a single sheet, and begins to read to himself. Almost immediately, though, he recoils with a cry of shock. Then, crumpling the letter, he drops it on the floor and, coatless, staggers out of the house into the yard.

Nancy hurries over to the door and watches as Robert makes his halting way out of the yard, walking like a blind man in the direction of the high field. Then she turns back to see her mother standing open-mouthed at the fireplace, wooden spoon clutched to her chest. "My God, Gibby," says Agnes. "What is it?"

Gibby picks up the crumpled sheet of paper from the floor, handling it as if it were painful to touch. Gingerly, he smooths it out and reads aloud. "'Mary Campbell, my sister, died here this month twenty days with a bad fever. It was her dying wish that you should be wrote to which I have done. Robert Campbell.'"

Wide-eyed, Gibby looks from his mother to Nancy. Saying nothing, he crosses to the kitchen table and drops the letter. Then he moves to the door and, taking Robert's coat from a peg, hurries out of the house. Other members of the family stand, staring at each other in silence. Then from outside, Nancy hears Gibby's voice, already distant, calling, "Rab! Rab!"

Gibby walks up toward the crest of the high field at a slow, steady pace, with Robert's coat slung over his shoulder. On the ridge above him he can see Robert seated on a large round stone, elbows on his knees, head buried in his hands. Behind Robert the late afternoon sky shines with the pure luminous blue of a candled robin's-egg, and before him a cool wind moves through the thin pale crop of oats with a sound like running water.

When he reaches his brother, Gibby looks down at him for a

moment or two, then says, "Are ye no' comin' back to the hoose now?" Waiting for some response, Gibby feels the damp cold of the ground seeping up through the soles of his boots. "Ye'll freeze yoursel' oot here, man," he says at last. "Here, put this on." He drapes Robert's coat over his hunched form. "Was she ought to ye, then?"

Robert looks up, his face drained of color and his eyes bruised-looking. "I thought ye'd ha'e guessed it afore now," he says wearily. "I'd promised to take her wi' me to Jamaica."

Gibby stiffens. "I see," he says.

"And God forgive me," says Robert, a ragged sob breaking from him, "It was in my heart to stay here and abandon her."

Shocked by the raw edge of his brother's grief and remorse, Gibby touches Robert's shoulder. "Dinna lose your heid, man," he says. "Talk sense. It's no' ten minutes since ye tellt me ye were determined to go."

"But . . . I didna want to," Robert says, his voice shaking. "My God, Gibby – I didna want to." He covers his face with his hands and bows his head.

Gibby is shaken by the depths of his brother's feeling. Mary Campbell. How unlike Robert to have kept so quiet about a romantic attachment. And to have made such a promise, with Jean Armour carrying his child. His children, Gibby reminds himself, shaking his head. "Ye canna condemn yoursel' for what was in your mind," he says at last.

Robert remains silent, save for his hoarse breathing. Then, after a time, he drops his hands to his knees and rises, moving a few unsteady steps away from the large stone. "I ken what I maun do," he says. "I'll need to go to Edinburgh."

Discomposed by the sudden change of subject, Gibby says, "To see aboot your book, do ye mean?"

"Aye, . . . that," says Robert, looking at the ground. "I need to get away frae here. If I'm here I'll only dishonor her memory further."

Now Gibby examines the damp clay around his own feet, as if he might find there some clue to Robert's thinking. Finally looking up, he says, "What aboot Jamaica, then?"

Robert shakes his head. "I couldna go there now." He shivers suddenly. "But I canna live here, either." Then, squaring his shoulders, he says, "I'll write to Jock Richmond this very night. We can maybe share lodgings."

"Go to live in Edinburgh?" Gibby can scarcely credit this. "But damn it, man," he says. "Ye've less reason than ever to lea'e us now! We need ye here!"

"I've told you I canna stay here!" Robert declares, and for the first time since he came up the hill, Gibby sees his brother's eyes glint with passion. Then, as if attempting appeasement, Robert adds, "I'll send ye what I can."

This, at last, is too much for Gibby. "Money!" he exclaims. "Do ye think that's a' that matters?" He walks a few paces farther up the ridge, his back to Robert. Then his bitterness breaks forth again. "It's aey Gibby that stands by, isn't it? Whatever's left to be done, Gibby'll do it." He turns again to Robert, who is watching him open-mouthed. "After a', Gibby's got nothing else to think aboot. He's no' a genius like his brither!"

"Genius!" says Robert heatedly. "I've never used sic a word in connection wi' mysel'!"

"No," says Gibby, pointing at him, "but ye've stood by willingly and let ithers use it. And thocht that gi'ed ye license to act ony way ye wanted." Past checking himself now, Gibby finds words tumbling out that he realizes he's wanted to say for months – aye, or years. "Do ye think I've never felt like drownin' my troubles at Johnnie Dow's? Do ye think I've never had the notion o' a lass? I have. But I've had something else you're no' as weel-acquainted wi'. A sense o' responsibility. Something a genius doesna need."

"Genius? Genius?" Robert closes the space between him and Gibby to a hand's-breadth. Then he turns and moves away again, saying, "Don't whine aboot genius to me!" He faces Gibby once more, his brow now blotchy red with anger. "Damn it, man," he says, "we've sweated and broken our backs thegither in fields like this a' our lives! Ye saw nae bloody genius there, did ye?" He paces about for a moment or two, hands clenched in front of him. "I'll be damned if ye can name me the day I've shirked responsibility to this family – or onybody else, for that matter. And if I've sinned sins, by God I've paid for them, right enough! It's as if a poor man's very birth was a bloody sin – for he pays for it every mortal day!" He stabs a finger at Gibby. "And if you werena sae bloody strait-laced and narrow-minded, ye'd see for yoursel' we've nothing to hope for here except what each day brings. Genius!" – his voice grows harsh with scorn – "If I've got it, ye can well see what good it does me."

Gibby's heart feels swollen in his chest, and his breath comes in gasps. He cannot trust himself to speak, and fears that in a moment they will come to blows. And what good will that do? What good, for that matter, can come of further words? So he starts away down the hill, his eyes fixed on the farmhouse below. But before he has gone more than a few steps, Robert's voice, returned to its usual brotherly pitch, stops him.

"Gibby, Gibby! We shouldna be fightin'. We've too much that binds us thegither for that." Gibby turns slowly and looks back at Robert, who moves down toward him, adopting a cajoling tone. "I canna just visit Edinburgh," he says. "I'll need to live there. Ye ken as weel as me the book'll no' be enough to raise us oot o' poverty. As much as I hate the thought, we can only hope I'll catch the eye and the fancy o' whatever gentry might be inclined to do us some good. And I'll no' do that here." He takes Gibby by the shoulders, almost pleading, yet with a note of confidence in his voice. "Ye've read the notices for my book. And counted the sales. Ye've seen the work I've written these past months. Ye've heard Aiken and Hamilton. I'm at the height o' my powers, Gibby. I feel there's nothing I canna do wi' words or thoughts. I'll mak sic a mark in Edinburgh, we canna help but prosper."

Gibby detaches himself from Robert's grip. He feels calmer now, and he cannot deny the sense in what his brother has said. But he feels, too, that he must speak his own mind. "I havena got your power o' words, Robert," he says quietly. "Ye can argue me down wi' half your mind while the rest is busy wi' ither things. But the Edinburgh gentry are maybe no' just as eager to aid us as we micht hope. As Mither says, 'Praise is easy got, but gowd's anither man's matter.' There's many a country coof met his match in the city afore now. Ye'd maybe as weel watch they dinna send ye back wi' less than ye had when they got ye."

Robert smiles and nods. "I will, Gibby. Never fear." He extends his hand.

"I'll no' tak your hand," Gibby says, "till ye promise ye'll come back."

Robert ducks his head for a moment as if in prayer, then looks up. "Aye, Gibby," he says warmly. "Ye have my promise. I'll no' desert ye."

Gibby grasps Robert's hand tightly in his own. Then, looking about him at the waning light, he says, "We'd best be gettin' back." He gives Robert's hand a last squeeze and starts off down the hill; then, hearing no footsteps behind him, he turns back. "Are ye no' comin'?"

Robert looks down at him absently. "Aye," he says. "I'll no' be long." Then, as Gibby watches, his brother all at once hugs himself as if to keep from trembling. "My God, Gibby," he says in a voice distorted by pain, "what manner o' man can I be? To talk aboot prosperity wi' her no' cauld in her grave?" Racked suddenly by sobs, he seems about to fall. As Gibby moves to him reaching a hand out for his shoulder, Robert slumps into his arms. "Oh, Gibby," he says, "what can I do?"

Then, as if ashamed, Robert breaks away and sits back down on the stone where Gibby found him earlier, again hiding his face in his hands. And Gibby realizes that, for now, neither he nor anyone else can assuage his brother's pain. "God, Robert," he says, "I'm sorry." And turning, he begins the long walk down to the house.

When Robert finally raises his head, he sees the small figure of Gibby walking far down the slope of the ridge. He feels empty now, as if his very vitals had been scooped out of him. And he knows why. For beyond his sorrow for the lovely young woman whose beauty is now lost forever to him, to her family, to the world – beyond his guilt over his wavering resolve to meet her at Greenock and set sail for a new land – beyond those feelings, he recognizes one that damns him far more surely in his own eyes: relief.

And he looks around him at the fields and sees there the color of her hair; then he looks up and sees a sky darkening to the color of her eyes. "Mary," he whispers, though he knows there is no one to hear him. "Mary, forgive me."

Edinburgh Castle

Dear Patron of my Virgin Muse,

I wrote Mr Ballantine at large all my operations and "eventful Story" since I came to town. – I have found in Mr Creech, who is my agent forsooth, and Mr Smellie, who is to be my Printer, that honor and goodness of heart which I always expect in Mr Aiken's friends. – Mr Dalrymple of of Orangefield I shall ever remember; my Lord Glencairn I shall ever pray for. – The Maker of Man has great honor in the workmanship of his Lordship's heart – May he find that patronage and protection in his guardian angel that I have found in him! His Lordship has sent a parcel of subscription bills to the Marquis of Graham with downright orders to get them filled up with all the first Scottish names about Court. – He has likewise wrote to the Duke of Montague and is about to write to the Duke of Portland for their Graces' interest in behalf of the Scotch Bard's Subscription.

You will very probably think, my honored friend, that a hint about the mischievous nature of intoxicated vanity may not be unseasonable, but, alas! you are wide of the mark – Various concurring circumstances have raised my fame as a Poet to a height which I am absolutely certain I have no merits to support; and I look down on the future as I would into the bottomless pit. –

You shall have one or two more bills when I have an opportunity of a Carrier. –

I am ever with the sincerest gratitude, honored Sir,

Your most devoted humble servt

ROBERT BURNS

letter to ROBERT AIKEN, Ayr
16th December 1786

Chapter Fifteen

Robert stands in the middle of the Lawnmarket, a wide section of the narrow mile-long thoroughfare that climbs gradually from Holyrood Palace past the sooty walls and buttressed spire of St. Giles' Cathedral to the main gate of Edinburgh Castle itself. Less than a quarter-mile up Castle Hill Walk, the brooding fortress presents its least imposing view; for on all other sides the great grey Rock beneath it falls away in a sheer plunge, so that it looms over the town, dominating the landscape and facing down any threat with its aloof and impregnable aspect.

Robert shakes his head to clear it. Two days and sixty miles of riding through November's chill mists on a borrowed pony have left him sore and exhausted. And now he has just made the steep climb from the Grassmarket, where he left his pony at the White Hart Inn to be returned to its obliging owner, Geordie Read of Balquharrie, who had called himself privileged to lend the animal to "Scotland's Bard." Robert's lungs feel thick with phlegm from the damp cold and from the haze of smoke that gives Auld Reekie its apt nickname. The air swirls with warring smells – of produce and meat, both fresh and rotting; of excrement, both animal and human; of cooking and wet clothes; and more – more than his country-bred senses can take in without dizziness. And the din of the city – the clatter of hooves and wheels on cobblestones; the shrill outcry of voices clamoring to be heard amid the thronging crowds – numbs Robert's ears, as if the Castle might be a latter-day Tower of Babel, addling the brains of all who walk in its shadow.

Ten minutes ago, as he climbed to the Lawnmarket by way of the cramped and twisting West Bow, Robert felt threatened by the buildings that leaned over him from the great height of seven or eight storeys, where dripping laundry flapped and slapped directly above him from clotheslines strung between upper windows built close enough together for their tenants to reach across and shake hands. And now, almost reeling with fatigue and confusion, he crosses the cobbled street to Baxter's Close.

Jock Richmond will still be at work, copying letters and legal papers, but he has assured Robert that his arrival will be expected by the landlady, Mrs. Carfrae. As he picks his way between the high tenements that form the gloomy, ill-smelling close, and climbs a narrow flight of stone steps to what he hopes is the right door, Robert reflects that if Richmond is earning more here than he could back in Mauchline, he seems to be living little better. But perhaps both of them will prosper now, for Richmond has arranged that they might share lodgings for only sixpence above the half-crown a week he's been paying himself. Reluctant to breathe deeply, Robert raps on the door's scarred surface.

After a moment or two the door opens a crack and Robert sees a single bright black eye peering up at him. "What is it?"

The hard-edged voice, its diction precise in the Edinburgh way, resonates with a timbre that his mother would say could "clip cloots." And for a moment before answering, Robert imagines Agnes sitting at the ingle in Mossgiel, shears in hand, cutting cloth to make a smock for wee Bess. He swallows and sniffs, then says, "Mrs. Carfrae? I'm Robert Burns."

"Och, yes. Mr. Burns." The door swings wide and the landlady bustles out onto the cramped landing. A squat, middle-aged woman in mutch and long apron looks cannily up at Robert, black eyes squinting in her pale round face. "Mr. Richmond told me to look for ye any day now. Your belongings are here before ye, and steeked away in his room. Though it'll be your room as well, now. As soon as ye've paid your share o' the week's rent. One and six, that'll be."

Since she seems disinclined to do more until he crosses her palm, Robert fishes a shilling and a handful of pennies from his purse and hands them over. With a tight-lipped smile she tucks the money in a pocket of her apron. "Come now till I get ye settled in," she says, brushing past him and beckoning him to follow her through the door and down a dark hallway.

The room proves to be a pleasant surprise, dirty though it may be, with a double bed, a table he can write at, a fireplace that should keep them warm despite its chipped mantelpiece, and a small window looking out on what Mrs. Carfrae tells him is Lady Stair's Close. His trunk sits at the foot of the bed, looking as if it belongs there. And suddenly swaying with fatigue, he longs to throw himself down on the chaff-filled mattress.

But Mrs. Carfrae's penetrating voice commands his attention. "I hear ye're a well-read gentleman, like Mr. Richmond," she says. "A poet, is it no', wi' a book that folk seem to think a deal o'?"

Not wishing to encourage further conversation, Robert merely shrugs and smiles. But the little landlady goes on. "Ye maun take your inspiration from the Good Book," she says, "and from the hymns and psalms ye may hear just down the road at St. Giles." She glares balefully at the ceiling. "There's them under this roof that maun fear for their souls, Mr. Burns. No' Mr. Richmond, sober and carefu' as he is," she adds, to Robert's silent amusement. "Nor you neither, I'm sure." She points above her. "But ye maun watch yoursel' wi' the shiftless jades that live above ye. Loose women o' the worst kind. God Himsel' may ken what transpires up there, but I wouldna want to."

Despite his weariness, Robert cannot resist a question. "Could ye no' just put them oot in the street if they're as bad as ye say?"

The landlady's pinched mouth twitches. "I'm a poor widow-woman, Mr. Burns, that needs to watch every penny – aye, and every farthing. If they werena here, they'd just sin their sins some other place. But whiles they're here I maun pray for them down the road and maybe win their souls back to the Lord." She nods sharply. "It's my Christian duty."

And with that pious pronouncement, Mrs. Carfrae makes her departure. It's clear to Robert that Holy Willie Fisher would not lack for spiritual allies among the faithful in the wicked streets of Edinburgh. He chuckles sourly. Then, all at once, alone and exhausted in the room's relative quiet, he thinks of Mary Campbell, whose trust he might have betrayed, now lost to him forever, and of Jean, caring for the twins back in Mauchline, without a husband, her girlhood taken from her. And suddenly overcome, his legs trembling, his eyes brimming with tears, he sinks down on the bed as if he might never rise from it again.

Shivering a bit in the early December morning, William Creech looks out the window of his Lawnmarket bookshop at the crowds moving back and forth before the Mercat Cross, most on foot, some on horseback or in coaches, some borne in sedan chairs, all breathing steam into the raw wind sweeping south from the Highlands. As usual, Creech feels an inward stir of satisfaction at the view he commands of Edinburgh's geographical center. His shop's location, within sight of the Luckenbooths and St. Giles' to the north and Tron Church downhill to the south, allows Creech to keep watch on the comings and goings of the City's social and cultural elite. Such discerning folk naturally incline to stop at such a shop as his, where they can find intellectual stimulation from his books and from their own good talk. And of course, such custom can harm neither his own social position nor his purse.

"Sit doon, for God's sake, Willie." Creech turns at the sound of William Smellie's bass growl. Smellie, large hands propped on his knees, calves bulging like puddings in his white stockings, has wedged himself into a wooden armchair next to a table bearing a discreetly small display of books for sale. "It's only the Earl that's comin'," says the burly printer, "no' the bloody King."

Shocked as he often is by his colleague's coarseness and irreverence, Creech opens his mouth to utter a suitable rebuke. Just then, however, the outer door opens and his clerk, Peter Hill, bustles into the shop, speaking even before the bell stops its tinkling. "They're here, Mr. Creech!" says Hill, whose boyish demeanor hardly becomes a man of thirty-three, his cheeks glowing as much from excitement as from the snell wind outside.

"Calm yoursel', Mr. Hill," says Creech, ignoring Smellie's ironic snort behind him. "Be businesslike. Remember that and ye'll maybe rise in the world." He waves Hill back to the door. "Now mind ye let them in when ye see them mount the stairs."

Moments later the clerk ushers two men into the shop, and Creech advances, hand outstretched in welcome, with Smellie at his back. "My Lord Glencairn," says the bookseller. "A very good morning to ye."

"Good morning, Mr. Creech." James Cunningham, the elegant and frail-looking fourteenth Earl of Glencairn, is a frequent customer at Creech's shop. Former representative of the Scots Peerage in the House of Lords and a current member of the Caledonian Hunt, an association of sports-minded noblemen and country gentlemen, the Earl is at thirty-seven one of Scotland's most influential aristocrats.

And as he inclines his head deferentially, Creech knows well that Glencairn means to bring that influence to bear on him this morning.

Ah, well, he reflects, one may find a way to accommodate the Earl while preserving a prudent regard for one's own interests.

"This is Mr. Robert Burns, the Ayrshire Bard," says Glencairn, indicating his younger companion, who, though unmistakably of the lower class, appears sturdy and presentable enough in coat, breeches, and boots, with dark hair curling over his brow and tied at his neck in an old-fashioned queue. A bit inclined to affectation, Creech thinks, as the Earl goes on with his introductions. "And Mr. Burns, these two gentlemen are Mr. William Creech, Edinburgh's foremost publisher, and Mr. William Smellie, Edinburgh's foremost printer."

The young farmer, as Creech knows him to be, bows and smiles as they shake hands all around. "I'm honored to make the acquaintance of two such distinguished men o' letters," says Burns, with unexpected eloquence, and perhaps a vague touch of presumption.

But Smellie, in his usual impulsive way, tramples decorum and politesse underfoot. "Be damned, Mr. Burns," he growls, shouldering past Creech to pump the young man's hand, "if ye havena ta'en your place at the head o' the van as far as Scots poetry goes. That's if I'm ony judge o' the matter."

Burns smiles and shakes his head. "Ye're very kind to a humble petitioner at the Muse's knee, Mr. Smellie." A modest enough response, Creech notes, but hardly a denial of Smellie's assessment.

With the verbal formalities and handshakes disposed of, Glencairn addresses Creech and Smellie. "Gentlemen," he says, "I'll not give ye further cause to wonder what my errand is this morning. Ye both ken fine the notice that Mr. Burns has won for his poetry. Ye'll have read his praises in *The Edinburgh Magazine* and *The Monthly Review*. One way or another, there's scarcely a copy o' Mr. Burns' Kilmarnock edition to be found in the country."

"Aye, and wi' good reason," says Smellie, nodding vigorously. Creech keeps his own counsel for the moment, but notes both the Earl's smiling agreement and the flash of appreciation in young Burns' luminous dark eyes.

Glencairn presses on. "My kinsman by marriage, James Dalrymple of Orangefield, came to know Mr. Burns' work through Lawyer Aiken of Ayr, and wrote to me when he heard that the Bard meant to chance his arm here in Auld Reekie. I've had the pleasure of entertaining Mr. Burns to dinner, and my family and I have found both his poetry and his conversation convivial and perceptive to a degree far beyond the ordinary. Suffice it to say that his abilities far exceed the position Nature has placed him in."

Dinner with the Earl, Creech thinks. This young farmer has clearly played his natural gifts into some advantageous connections. Aloud, he says, "Aye, my Lord. Lawyer Aiken has written to me about Mr. Burns' knack as a versifier. I'm pleased to meet him at last."

"Knack be damned, Willie!" says Smellie. "Versifier be damned! Mr. Burns is a poet, and nae knack aboot it. And there's no' many poets onywhere could sell oot an edition o' six hundred copies in a month."

Creech flushes at this, but before he can speak the Earl nods and smiles. "I'm much inclined to agree with ye, Mr. Smellie," says Glencairn. "And your remark about sales o' the Kilmarnock edition brings me back to my reason for coming here this morning. I think it's only fitting that the obvious demand for Mr. Burns' poems be met here in Edinburgh – the seat o' Scots culture – and I propose that you and Mr. Creech are the very men for the job."

"By God," says Smellie, "it's a grand idea!" He looks at young Burns. "And what do you say to that, yoursel', sir?"

The poet, having stood quiet while Glencairn advanced his cause, seems reluctant to speak even now. Whatever the fellow's gifts, Creech thinks, and despite his earlier, no-doubt rehearsed, utterances, he cannot be used to civilized conversation. "I'm already much honored by My Lord Glencairn's kind interest," says young Burns to Smellie, "and I'd be more than grateful to see my poetry further distinguished by association with such respected businessmen as yoursel's."

Clearly Burns is no tongue-tied peasant. Fixed by the young man's penetrating eyes, Creech waves a hand uncertainly and chooses to address Glencairn. "Your Lordship's proposal holds much interest for me," he says. "But of course we must think of practical matters. Perhaps the sales of Mr. Burns' previous edition will have exhausted the public's demand for his poems. One way or another, we must assure oursel's that we can meet the considerable cost of a new printing before we can think of potential profits. And that, of course, means subscriptions."

The Earl chuckles. "I think you may rest easy on the question o' public demand," he says. "Why, I'll personally guarantee that each and every member o' the Caledonian Hunt will subscribe for a new edition. That's at least a hundred copies spoken for. And my mother and I will take twenty-odd copies oursel's. How's that for a start?"

Creech is taken aback. The Earl's liberality is well-known, as is his interest in the arts, and Creech himself cannot dispute the potential for sales in a novelty like this ploughboy poet; but such unbridled enthusiasm from the likes of Glencairn may mean that Burns is a valuable commodity indeed. Creech touches a finger to the bridge of his nose, then essays a cautious smile. "Your Lordship is most generous," he says. "I'm sure that, after suitable discussion, Mr. Burns and I should be able to come to some mutually satisfactory arrangement."

"Well, then," says the Earl, "I'll leave ye to it."

And after a brief flurry of farewells, and what Creech regards as polite but effusive thanks to the Earl from Burns, Glencairn makes his departure. Having closed the door solicitously behind the nobleman, Peter Hill turns to Burns and introduces himself with a grin and an extended hand. "I'm that glad to meet ye, Mr. Burns," says the clerk. "I'm a great admirer o' your poems. I wish I could write like that mysel'."

"Thank ye, Mr. Hill," says Burns. "My Muse is homely enough. Whenever she glances in my airt, I jingle at her."

Hill laughs in apparent recognition. "That's frae one o' your verse epistles, is it no'?"

"Aye," says Burns, looking pleased, "near enough. I penned something like it to another country poet – an old fellow ca'd Lapraik, that's married to the sister o' my good friend John Rankine."

"Mr. Hill," says Creech, keeping his voice low but firm, "do ye not have other business to perform?" Thus chastened, the clerk hurries away to his desk, and Creech regards Burns. "Well, Mr. Burns, you have a powerful patron in Lord Glencairn. You may think yourself lucky to have found him."

The corners of Burns' mouth tighten briefly. "I do, Mr. Creech," he says. "And I look forward to my association with you and Mr. Smellie, too." He looks about him. "Ought we to discuss the matter at hand? I can tell you now I propose to add some poems to the new edition. That way, the public's interest may be further stimulated."

Creech frowns and pulls at his lower lip, then sighs. "We need not rush headlong into this arrangement, Mr. Burns. It will need due consideration and careful planning. We can meet again and talk here after I've had time to think it out." Feeling the need to make a hospitable gesture, he adds, "In the meantime, I'm giving a small supper for some friends at my rooms in two days time. Perhaps ye'd care to join us. Mr. Hill will see to it that ye receive proper notice."

Burns accepts and begins to utter a civil enough thanks, but again the impetuous Smellie breaks in. "And now that business is laid aside for the nonce, what aboot a dram, Mr. Burns? We'll hie oursel's roond to Dawney Douglas', next door to my office in Anchor Close. Are ye comin' wi' us, Willie?"

"No, thank ye," says Creech. "I've many other matters to deal with this morning." And after bidding Smellie and Burns good day, Creech stands watching as they start on the short walk down the High Street to the tavern, exchanging animated talk as if they were old friends reunited. He nods thoughtfully. He must remember to send a note to the Earl, thanking him for the opportunity to publish this new literary phenomenon. The Ayrshire Ploughboy. Creech chuckles. Of course, Glencairn could scarcely have avoided choosing Edinburgh's foremost publisher. Nonetheless, the niceties must be observed, especially where there is money to be made.

"Dawney!" cries Willie Smellie. "Two drams o' malt here for Mr. Burns and me."

The printer leads Robert to what is obviously his usual table and bids him sit. When the landlord sets drinks before them, Smellie makes him aware that Robert is none other than the Ayrshire Bard.

"By God, Mr. Burns," says Dawney Douglas, wringing Robert's hand, "it's an honor to meet ye. And ye'll no' pay for your first drink in Dawney Douglas'. Welcome to Edinburgh!" Douglas looks at Smellie. "Ye'll need to see aboot inductin' Mr. Burns into the Crochallan Fencibles, eh?"

"Aye," says Smellie, "and you'll need to gi'e him a chorus or two o' the theme song."

When the landlord has left them to their drinks, Smellie explains to Robert the history of the drinking club. "I'm the founder, mysel'," says the printer, his broad face painted by amber highlights from the glass he holds before him. "I took the first name from an old Gaelic song that's a favorite o' Dawney's. And Fencibles has a rare regimental sound aboot it, eh?" He squints at Robert. "Of coorse, if we do induct ye, ye'll tak a sound drubbin' by way o' initiation. A verbal drubbin', that is – ye're o'er young and sturdy for the likes o' me." He laughs, a deep sound from his ample paunch, and raises his glass. "And now, as Dawney said, 'Welcome to Edinburgh.' May you and your work live to prosper, as it surely will, if I know ought aboot my trade."

Robert thanks Smellie and they drink off their drams, whereupon the printer orders up another round. Over the next half hour or so, Robert marvels at his drinking companion, who displays an erudition that belies his rough manner and plain speech. In response to a casual inquiry by Robert about Smellie's interests and past activities, the printer unexpectedly reveals that he was the first editor and principal writer of the *Encyclopedia Brittanica*.

"Mind ye," says Smellie, grinning and cocking his head, "I didna ken the half o' what's in it when I started, but I kennt well enough who to ask."

But as their discussion turns to the sciences, Smellie's animation grows, and before long Robert worms out of him the grudging admission that he is author of his own *Philosophy of Natural History*. ("I canna sum matters up in a couplet like you, Rab. I just plod forward in prose till I've had my say.") And not long afterward, when Robert laments the lack of opportunity to practice his slim knowledge of French, the printer – inadequate term! – offers to lend him not only a French edition of Buffon, but also Smellie's own published translation of the eminent naturalist's work.

And again the big man makes light of his accomplishment. "I couldna resist the chance to hear folk describe my book as the Smellie Buffon," he says with a throaty chuckle.

But for all his self-deprecation, Smellie possesses a knowledge of literature and science unmatched in Robert's experience. And beyond his wit and intellect, the printer demonstrates that a man can distinguish himself and keep a level head. Perhaps coming to Edinburgh will prove fortunate for Robert, after all, if such advocates as William Smellie take up his cause.

As if reading Robert's thoughts, Smellie leans across the table and lowers his normal thumping bass to a mere kettle-drum's rattle. "Dinna fash yoursel' lad. We'll do right by ye. Atween Creech and me we'll see your poems published in an edition that'll dazzle them a'."

He clasps Robert's arm, causing the whisky to tremble in his glass. "And ye needna worry aboot Willie, either. He's a hard lad to part frae a ha'penny, but he's honest enough, for a' that. And, by God, he kens how to sell books!"

Smellie laughs, returning to his normal booming tone. "No' that your poetry needs ony help finding buyers." He slaps the table, hand splayed so that Robert can see the ink under his fingernails. "Now, come on, Rab. Drink up and we'll ha'e anither!" He cranes his neck, looking about him for the landlord. "Dawney!" he bellows. "More whisky – and a verse or two o' 'Crodh Chailein'!"

Taking advantage of a brief silence, Robert takes a bite of currant cake and sips at his now lukewarm tea. He sits gingerly on a frail-seeming chair in William Creech's cozy oak-paneled parlor, balancing a delicate china cup and saucer on his knee. Ranged about him are several of Edinburgh's most prominent citizens: James Burnett – Lord Monboddo – judge of the Court of Session and author of *The Origin and Progress of Language;* Professor Dugald Stewart, youthful holder of the Chair in Moral Philosophy at Edinburgh University and Robert's host earlier in the year at his country seat in Catrine, near Mauchline; the Rev. Dr. Hugh Blair, Stewart's senior colleague at the University as Professor of Rhetoric; Patrick Miller of Dalswinton, a director of the Bank of Scotland; Willie Smellie; and, of course, Creech himself. The only guest approximating Robert's own humble stature is Bob Ainslie, a law student from Berwickshire, not yet twenty-one, whose youth and facetious mien make him seem an unlikely part of this distinguished gathering. Perhaps, Robert surmises, Ainslie represents an attempt by Creech to insure that an ignorant Ayrshire poet will not feel too far beyond his depth.

Feeling the need to distract himself from seeing slights where none may exist, Robert decides on a polite gesture of his own. "Professor Stewart," he says, "may I ask that you remember me to Lord Daer when next you find yourself at Catrine Bank? I recall your hospitality there – and his conviviality – with particular fondness."

Stewart, for all his academic distinction only a few years older than Robert, inclines his head and smiles. "I will, Mr. Burns. I hope you'll likewise convey my regards to my old friend Dr. Mackenzie when you return to Mauchline."

Robert thinks fondly of Mackenzie, wondering how goes the young doctor's shy and awkward pursuit of Helen Miller. "I will," he says to Stewart. "As ye know, he's my good friend, too, and I'll aey be indebted to him for bringing my work to your attention."

As Stewart waves a deprecating hand at this, Robert's eye falls on Creech. His slight frame garbed almost clerically in simple but elegant black, the publisher hovers near the door, lips pursed as if he is listening for something. His vigil is rewarded a short time later when his maid appears and whispers to him, followed by the entrance of another slim well-dressed gentleman in his early forties whose sober and ascetic aspect make Robert wonder if this might be a brother of Creech's.

"Speaking o' Mackenzies," says Willie Smellie, "here's anither one."

At this, young Ainslie grins conspiratorially at Robert, while Creech darts a reproving glance at Smellie. Then the bookseller motions the new arrival into the room. "Mr. Mackenzie," says Creech, "may I introduce you to the young farmer-poet of whom I'm sure you've heard? Mr. Robert Burns of Ayrshire." He turns to Robert. "Mr. Burns. Mr. Henry Mackenzie."

His heart racing, Robert sets down his cup and saucer and rises. "Mr. Mackenzie," he says. "I'm honored to meet ye." As the two men shake hands, Robert feels he must guard against staring open-mouthed at the sensitive face and quietly appraising eyes of the renowned novelist. "I am one of your greatest admirers, sir," he goes on, tightening his grasp on Mackenzie's hand. "Your *Man of Feeling* is a book I have prized next to the Bible."

Mackenzie, releasing Robert's hand, shuts his eyes for a moment as if savoring the compliment like a fine malt. "You are far too kind, Mr. Burns," he says in soft and cultured tones. "But I thank you for your generous sentiments. I am glad my little book has brought you pleasure." Then, before Robert can respond, the novelist smiles graciously and raises a delicate finger. "I myself am an admirer of yours," he goes on, "as you'll see if you read my review of your Kilmarnock poems in the latest issue of *The Lounger*."

Robert has, in fact, read Mackenzie's essay, which commended the new young poet's "uncommon penetration and sagacity," but described him as a "Heaven-taught ploughman . . . humble and unlettered." Ah, well, he thinks, so long as the gentry hold him in esteem, what matter that they prefer to ignore his obvious learning, such as it is, and see him as some prodigy of Nature? And besides, Mackenzie's review did declare that such talent as Robert's deserved to flourish free from want and called for some wealthy patron to come to his aid. Aloud, he says, "I am honored by the notice of one so clearly beloved of the Muse to whom we both pay court. I must thank you, too, for your concern over my economic well-being."

At this, Patrick Miller the banker clears his throat. He has already surprised Robert once today, for while he appears every inch the banker, canny, smooth-faced, and prosperous-looking, he warmed earlier to a disarmingly high pitch of enthusiasm on the subject of inventions, describing his own ideas for a drill plough and a new threshing machine. And now Miller says, "I'm glad you allude to Henry's suggestion, Mr. Burns, for I have a proposal that may interest you."

As Robert resumes his chair and Creech busies himself in seating Mackenzie and directing the maid to offer fresh tea and cakes, Miller continues. "I have recently bought Dalswinton estate, on the River Nith down near Dumfries. I'm in need of a gifted agriculturalist – someone who kens what he's about – to lease the farmland on the property. It occurs to me that my need and yours might be well met. I'd see to it that ye'd not lack resources to build a farmhouse to your satisfaction, and with the effort I know ye're capable o', ye might soon find yourself on the road to independence."

Aye, or on the road to ruin, Robert thinks, considering the succession of miserable farms he's worked. "It's an intriguing notion," he says aloud. "And I thank ye for your generous interest. I'd be delighted to discuss it wi' ye. And, of course, I'd need to see the land itsel'."

"Oh, aye," says Miller, passing a hand lightly over the thin fuzz of sandy hair on his head. "We wouldna wish to gallop into any such weighty arrangement. As you say, we'll need to find an opportunity for further conversation on the matter." He looks about him apologetically. "And this is neither time nor place, even for friendly business."

The Rev. Dr. Blair sniffs loudly, as if commenting on the intrusion of commerce into the gathering. In his late sixties, Dr. Blair is a stout, choleric-looking man with an orotund voice. He seems, at least in his own mind, to have attained the status of literary and moral arbiter, and his peremptory manner and apparently innate conservatism remind Robert more than a little of Mr. Auld.

As if to confirm Robert's judgment, Dr. Blair addresses him now. "Mr. Burns," he says, his chair creaking under him as he leans forward. "Like Mr. Mackenzie I admire your natural gifts. But I'm bound to observe that your fame might be wider if you'd consider casting your verse into formal English, so that a larger audience might enjoy it. Without the needless affectation of a local dialect, your chances of poetic success would be much enhanced, believe me." Blair smiles, evidently pleased by his own wisdom, then adds, "You may also wish to consider leavening the regional nature of your work by turning to subjects drawn from historical or even classical sources."

Aware that all eyes in the room are on him, Robert takes a sip of cold tea, hoping it will quell the flush he feels creeping over him. "I'm thankful for the suggestion, Dr. Blair," he says at last, setting down his cup without a clink. "I fear though," he continues, "that I'm incapable of writing in a voice other than the one the Muse grants me, or of subjects beyond my direct observation."

Before Blair can reply, Lord Monboddo slaps his thigh as if gaveling for order in his court. The elderly jurist, whose impatience and eccentricity Smellie has described to Robert at Dawney's, has apparently endured all he can of conversation that excludes himself. "Direct observation," says Monboddo, "is very commendable. It's at the heart o' the scientific method. And I see in your verse, Mr. Burns, that you are a keen observer o' Nature and local custom, particularly in poems like 'To A Mouse' and 'Halloween.'"

Whatever Monboddo's peculiarities may be, and however short his temper, Robert feels a surge of affection for the hook-nosed old man. "The poet," he says, "must aey acknowledge his debt to Nature, Lord Monboddo, for there is where poetry – like everything else – begins."

While Monboddo is beaming his approval of this, and Blair frowning in consternation, the dandyish young Bob Ainslie looks at Robert with a barely perceptible wink, then turns to the jurist. "I've heard, your Lordship, that you take a great interest in the sciences."

As if sensing something amiss, Creech raises a cautionary hand. "I think – " he begins.

But Monboddo ignores his host's would-be protestation. "That I do, Mr. Ainslie," he says. "Any man that ca's himsel' educated would be well-advised to look to his knowledge o' science. For it's science we maun place our faith in for the future."

Now Robert can see that Ainslie is evidently as mischievous as he looks, for Monboddo's remark has proved too much for Dr Blair. "My dear Lord Monboddo," says Blair, "you would do better advising a young man to place his faith in his Maker than – "

Monboddo cuts him off testily. "Ye needna fear, Dr. Blair, that I mean to attack the Kirk merely because I look forward to the advent o' an intellectual climate that gi'es science its rightfu' due."

Unimpressed, Blair gives another of his catarrhal sniffs. "If the moral climate o' Scotland were such as to give the Kirk its proper due, I'll warrant ye'd have fewer scoundrels up before your bench and leisure enough to pursue your scientific interests wi' greater zeal."

As Robert is struck again by the rhetorician's philosophical kinship with Mr. Auld, and as Creech again opens his mouth to make peace, Ainslie speaks quickly. "I understand," he says, his boyishly disarming voice all innocence, "that your Lordship's current interests are more inclined toward the past than the future."

Monboddo smiles and nods. "I fancy ye mean my theory o' man's origins." Robert notes Creech's increasing agitation, but imagines that the bookseller feels powerless now to interrupt.

Oblivious to Creech, Monboddo continues. "Well, Mr. Ainslie. It is my contention that man is descended" – he pauses for effect – "from the monkey."

"The monkey!" Blair is aghast.

"The monkey!" Monboddo repeats the words with triumphant glee, then looks about him to gauge the reactions of his listeners, some of whom, Robert knows, must be well aware of the jurist's theory. He notes Ainslie's open pleasure at having sown the seeds of discord and Creech's fidgeting distress. But the rest of the company seem calm enough, no doubt being used to the temperaments and foibles of both Monboddo and Blair. Willie Smellie, though, does catch Robert's eye and smiles at him with tongue in cheek. No doubt the science-minded printer will be closer to agreement with Monboddo than with Blair.

But now Robert's attention returns to Blair himself, who has gathered his wits sufficiently to make a pronouncement. "Your theory, my Lord," he says stiffly to Monboddo, "is hardly consistent wi' the tenets o' religion."

Monboddo shakes his head impatiently. "I make no quarrel wi' the Bible, Dr. Blair. But the evidence is as plain as the nose on your face."

"And what might that evidence be?" Blair demands, raising an eyebrow and squinting dubiously.

Monboddo seems disinclined to be pressed into further colloquy on the matter. "The likenesses between man and the simian tribe are too well-known to need recounting," he says, throwing his hands apart dismissively.

"Indeed," says Blair, adopting a tone of exaggerated patience. "And how, might I ask, does your Lordship reconcile the monkey's present state with our own?" He gestures toward the ceiling. "Why are we not now hanging by our tails about the tea table?"

Monboddo narrows his eyes cagily at this, and Robert can see that the old man feels his adversary has committed a fatal blunder. "Tell me," says the jurist, making a steeple of his fingers, "have ye ever heard o' a monkey sitting down?" Before Blair can respond, Monboddo answers his own question. "No," he says. "But here we all are – sitting on our" – he pauses a moment, then opts for delicacy – "our chairs."

Blair is unimpressed. "I fail to see how that advances your point," he says with one of his characteristic sniffs.

Monboddo shakes his head as if confronting a backward child. "It is simple," he says. "The monkey has a tail. Man has none. Monkeys are well-known for their lecherousness and foolishness, forever capering and swinging about wi' no time to think at a'." He stabs a finger at Blair. "I ask you – where does a man get most of his finest ideas? Why, sitting in his study, of course." Again he spreads his hands in satisfaction. "Therefore, man is obviously descended from a superior species of monkey that learned the value of sitting. And over the centuries" – he eyes each of his listeners quickly before returning to Blair with the coup de grace – "our tails have been worn off!"

This amazing declaration produces a brief silence, during which Robert finds himself hard put not to let out a great hoot of laughter. His condition is obviously shared by Ainslie, who has whipped a kerchief from his sleeve and is rubbing energetically at his nose, and Smellie, who has applied an ink-stained paw to his mouth as if he were lost in thought. Dr. Blair seems merely speechless with disgust, and Creech is fairly bouncing with discomfort. As they have through-out the contretemps, Stewart, Mackenzie, and Miller look on with enviable serenity.

Suddenly, though, Monboddo rounds on Robert. "Well, Mr. Burns," he demands. "What do ye say to that?"

With some difficulty, Robert composes himself sufficiently for speech. "Well, . . . your Lordship," he begins, playing for time to form a coherent reply, "I think" – and he pauses again – "I think . . . we can all be grateful to those learned monkeys o' long ago." He darts a glance at the troublemaking Ainslie, then continues. "I myself find it difficult enough to write even when I am sitting down, much less dangling from a tree."

Robert's sally finds its reward in a burst of choking and coughing from Ainslie and in the quiet but obvious trembling of Smellie's ample frame. Dr. Blair, however, is freshly outraged.

"Worn off our tails, indeed!" he says loudly. "I have never heard such stuff and nonsense!"

Lord Monboddo responds swiftly and contemptuously. "The ignorant are aey sair-taxed wi' new ideas!" he declares, folding his arms with a flourish.

Creech almost dances his way into the center of the room, looking from Blair to Monboddo and plucking at his waistcoat. "Gentlemen, please," he says, his normally high voice keening with anxiety. "Let us have no disputes."

Immediately, Monboddo rises. "I fear it's time I was away, Mr. Creech," he says testily. "I'll just slip out without ceremony." He looks around him at the company. "Good day to ye, gentlemen." And so saying, he starts for the door.

Trailing behind him, further discomposed, Creech says, "We are sorry to lose your company, My Lord."

Nodding shortly at his host, the jurist turns and looks at Robert, frowning as if about to pass an uncommonly harsh sentence. But when he speaks, his voice is warm. "You're a byornar man, Mr. Burns. Ye'll need to dine wi' me soon."

Robert rises and bows slightly. "Thank you, my Lord. Perhaps we'll be able to continue our discussion o' the sciences."

"Aye," says Monboddo. He shoots a venomous glance at Blair. "Under more advantageous circumstances. I look forward to it, Mr. Burns." With little more than a nod to the company, the old man takes his leave.

Pleased, Robert quietly resumes his seat. While Creech is out of the room seeing the jurist on his road, Bob Ainslie leans over to Blair, whose cheeks have blossomed with a purplish hue. "Lord Monboddo is a man with interesting ideas," says Ainslie. "Eh, Dr. Blair?"

"Indeed." Blair snorts like a bull about to charge. "The sort of ideas you'd expect from a man that's been known to send his wig home in a sedan chair to keep it dry – then walks home in the rain himself!"

Lying in the dark of the room in Baxter's Close, uneasily balanced between sleep and waking, Robert suddenly comes to full consciousness. He shifts to eye the dim moonlit square of window in the opposite wall, then the few dying embers in the fireplace, and feels Richmond stirring in the bed beside him. All at once Robert realizes that the cause of his disturbance has not been noise or movement, but silence. He looks at the cracked and dirty ceiling through which, until a few moments ago, came the barely muted nightly din of the bawds upstairs.

"Well, Jock," he says, sure that Richmond, too, is awake, "they've finally gi'ed up, I think. They've earned whatever they've made the night."

Richmond yawns, his breath a small white phantom in the chilly room. "Aye," he says good-humoredly. "They're energetic enough, a' right." He nudges Robert with an elbow. "We'll maybe need to pay them a visit oursel's sometime."

"I dinna ken, Jock." Robert exhales a frosty sigh. "There's times these past weeks when I'd sooner ha'e gotten a good night's sleep."

"That doesna sound like you, Rab." Richmond turns toward him. "Ye havena been at yoursel' at a' – for days. I thought ye'd be happier now that the new edition's been arranged for."

"Aye," says Robert, "it's arranged for, after a fashion. But God knows when I'll see ony money. Willie Smellie was right – yon Creech would wrestle a ghost for a ha'penny. I've had to turn a deaf ear on Gibby and my mither. They'll think I've abandoned them."

Richmond props himself up on an elbow. "What aboot the gentry? Are none o' them minded to help ye? I thought ye'd been a great success wi' them."

"Oh, aye." Robert chuckles bitterly. "'The Ploughboy Poet,' they style me. I'm in great demand at their tables and salons. But I canna help but think I'm just a nine day's wonder to the feck o' them. Willie Smellie's a grand lad – and Bob Ainslie's aey able to mak me laugh. But they're no' the gentry. And I've got little frae the gentry save tea and advice – usually the suggestion that I write in 'good English' instead o' the Scots." He runs his hands through his hair in frustration. "Ah, to hell, Jock," he says. "We're aey confounded, whatever we do. The pair o' us came to Edinburgh to mak our fortunes, and look at us – lyin' here like a couple o' damned souls."

"But it's no' Heaven that's above us, eh, Rab?" Richmond chuckles slyly. "Or is it?"

"Ye can joke a' ye want," says Robert, unsettled by his own churlish rejection of Richmond's attempt to cheer him, "but Gaw'n Hamilton spoke truer than he knew when he tellt ye Edinburgh wasna the far end o' the rainbow."

Richmond puts a hand on Robert's shoulder. "I dinna fancy ye'd ha'e found it in Jamaica, either, Rab," he says. Then, as Robert remains silent, staring across the room at the faint orange glow from the fireplace, Richmond speaks again, his voice low. "Are ye still thinkin' o' Mary Campbell?"

Robert's throat tightens and the light from the dying fire blurs before him. "I'll never forget her," he says at last. "No' in the depths o' my heart."

Richmond lies back, making the straw-filled mattress rustle in the room's silence. "One o' these days it's back to Mauchline for me," he says after a time, "and Jenny Surgeoner. If she'll still have me. Maybe ye should look back that road, yoursel', Rab. What aboot Jean?"

Robert shifts uncomfortably. "I don't know, Jock," he says. "I just don't know."

Richmond says nothing to this, and Robert lies on his back for minutes, eyes open, seeing nothing. Suddenly from overhead comes the sound of raucous female laughter, accompanied by indistinct male voices and the muffled thump of furniture being overturned. "For God's sake, Jock," says Robert, with a short burst of resigned laughter, "they're at it again."

He turns to his friend, expecting some of Richmond's usual ribaldry. But the only sound he hears from the shadowy form lying next to him is a loud snore.

❦ 1787 ❦

Sir,

    I have taken the liberty to send a hundred copies of my book to your care.--I have no acquaintance with Forsyth; and besides I believe Booksellers take no less than the unconscionable Jewish tax of 25 pr Cent. by way of agency. – I trouble you then, Sir, to find a proper person, of the mercantile folks I suppose will be best, that for a moderate consideration will retail the books to subscribers as they are called for. – Several of the Subscription bills have been mislaid, so all who say they have subscribed must be served at subscription price; otherwise those who have not subscribed must pay six shillings. – Should more copies be needed, an order by post will be immediately answered. –

    My respectful Compliments to Mr Aiken. – I wrote him by David Shaw which I hope he received. –

    I have the honor to be,

      with the most grateful sincerity,

      Sir, your oblidged & very humble servt

        ROBERT BURNS

letter to JOHN BALLANTINE, Ayr
18th April 1787

Chapter Sixteen

Robert **looks down** at the proof-sheet without really seeing the words of the poem before him. The narrow lines of verse keep suggesting to him the columns of figures in a ledger. Pounds, shillings, and pence. Pounds, shillings, and pence. The phrase sounds in his head over and over, its insistent rhythm drowning out the meter of his own poetry. Why should commerce keep intruding on the precincts of art? Why should the Muse be forced to go arm-in-arm with the likes of canny Willie Creech? But then Robert remembers Gibby toiling back in Mauchline, waiting for some relief from the family's chronic economic anxiety, and he realizes what an inescapable burden weighs on the flimsy pages in his hand.

Breathing deeply, he skims the final few stanzas of "Address to a Haggis," which he composed not long ago, and which both the *Caledonian Mercury* and the *Scots Magazine* were pleased to print.

Now "Haggis" will appear in the new edition, along with a number of poems he suppressed in deference to Johnnie Wilson's squeamishness, poems like "Address to the Unco Guid" and "The Ordination," that take hypocrisy to task. Here, at least, he has a printer willing to take risks – aye, and willing to take his part whenever Willie Creech's sensibilities look like being offended.

Robert lays the proof-sheet on the desk and shifts himself on his stool, cocking his head toward the rattle and clatter of Willie Smellie's printing press. And as he watches the large sheets accumulate, soon to be folded into octavo size, then gathered, stitched, and bound, he smiles with pride in despite of all his financial cares.

"It'll no' be lang, now, eh, Rab?" Willie Smellie says, picking his way among the machines and workers with a nimble-footed grace unexpected in so large a man. Standing before Robert, the printer folds his arms and grins. "We'll mak ye famous yet."

"It's no' fame I'm worried about the now, Willie," says Robert. "It's fortune. When I saw Creech yesterday, he said it might be months afore I saw a penny out o' the book. He's no' just so sure the likely demand justifies an edition o' three thousand copies. He says the costs –"

But Smellie cuts him off. "Stuff and bloody nonsense!" says the printer, clenching his fists and thrusting his large head forward as if he might bite Robert. "There's a list o' subscribers in the damned book that runs to thirty-seven bloody pages! I know, because I set the bloody type! There's no' a bugger'll need to worry aboot costs on this venture! And you can say I said it! You just beard Willie in his den and tell him that."

His outburst halted, Smellie stands there, chest heaving and eyes glinting with irritation. Smiling affectionately at the printer, Robert nonetheless reflects that bearding Creech is easier said than done, for the man is a master of evasion, always eyeing his timepiece and hinting at far weightier matters that demand his immediate attention. Aloud, he says, "I'll try, Willie. Though I think I might do better if you were there to mak him listen."

Smellie waves a hand dismissively. "Och, no," he says. "I'd only antagonize him, and that wouldna help ye at a'." The big man thinks for a moment or two, then snorts with satisfaction. "Henry Mackenzie, now – the Man o' Feelin' – there's the lad that's fit for Willie Creech. Ask him to go wi' ye, if ye feel the need o' somebody, for he's as sly an old stoat as Willie ony day, wi' his by-your-leaves and if-I-may-says. Aye," he concludes with a sharp nod of his head, "Henry Mackenzie's your man."

"Thanks, Willie," says Robert. "I'll maybe just see aboot that. But in the meantime I think I maun tak steps to find mysel' an Excise commission and a', for in the long run I canna mak a livin' oot o' poetry." And struck by a sudden pang, he adds, "I'm no' sure I'd want to. The Muse mauna be soiled in sic a way."

Smellie shakes his head impatiently. "Ye maun heed yon Englishman, Sam Johnson, that Jamie Boswell's made sic a great deal o'. Johnson says, 'Nae man but a blockhead ever wrote except for money.'" The printer squints at Robert. "Ye've been listenin' to o'er many o' the gentry, that wouldna foul their hands wi' honest work o' ony kind."

"Aye," says Robert, "ye're right there, Willie. They seem to think because I write poetry that I can live on fresh air and bugger a' else."

Smellie gives a bitter little laugh. "Of course, it's the same consideration they gi'ed to poor Bob Fergusson – and him an Edinburgh man born and bred – till they buried him down the road in the Canongate kirkyard – in a pauper's unmarked grave."

Smellie looks startled by his own vehemence, and his eyes widen as he sees the tears that have spilled down Robert's cheeks. Robert finally speaks with difficulty. "I've little enough to complain o', Willie, that I should forget a man like Bob Fergusson, that they let die in a madhouse. There's a wheen o' poems in the very book ye're printin' that would never ha'e got written but for him – like 'Scotch Drink,' and 'The Twa Dogs,' and 'The Holy Fair,' and 'Cotter's Saturday Night' – he gi'ed me the models for them a'."

Smellie shakes his head. "Fergusson was a grand poet," he says. "And he deserved better than he got. But you're alive now, Rab. The mair reason ye should think o' yoursel', and dinna waste regrets on the past."

Robert swallows hard, then forces a smile. He cannot quite bring himself to tell Smellie what he feels, that he is suddenly convinced of his and Fergusson's brotherhood, as if they are members of a secret lodge, not of Masons, but of poets, impoverished and dispossessed. He hands Smellie the sheets he's been proofreading. "There's 'To a Haggis,' Willie. I think I maun tak mysel' out into the fresh air for a while, for I canna seem to settle to the task."

Smellie takes the poem and glances at it. But he looks up as Robert stands to leave, and when he speaks his tone is serious. "I dinna ken what the answer may be for ye, Rab, but I hate to think o' ye as a gauger, gallopin' hither and yon on a pony in a' weathers, and a' to tax poor folk for makin' their ain malt and brewin' their drink."

"It's a job," says Robert quickly, "just a job." Why will no one understand? he thinks. But he goes on, trying to keep his voice calm, for he has no wish to fall out with Willie Smellie. "The gentry would rather see me ahent a plough forever, for that would keep their illusions alive aboot 'untutored genius' and 'Heaven-taught ploughboy.' But I'm just a man, for a' that. A man wi' responsibilities."

Smellie spreads his hands. "Ah, weel," he says, "ye'll ken best yoursel' what ye maun do, Rab." And, farewells by, he walks with Robert to the door and shakes the sheets he still carries in his hand. "We'll maybe need to ha'e a good platter o' haggis oursel's the night at Dawney's, eh?"

"Aye," says Robert, his good humor momentarily restored. "And wash it down wi' a dram or two and a'."

"Fergusson's grave, ye want?" The old beadle stands with Robert among the worn grey headstones and monuments of the Canongate cemetery, white hair lank on either side of his frowning brow. "There's Fergussons scattered a' roond the place. What ane are ye speirin' after?"

Robert looks down at the old man, wondering whether he's being subjected to some heavy Edinburgh humor. But the beadle stares back guilelessly enough. "Fergusson the poet," says Robert patiently. Seeing no flicker of recognition at this, he adds, "He wrote 'Leith Races' and 'The Farmer's Ingle.'"

Now the old man nods. "Och, aye," he says, chuckling hoarsely, "ye'll be talkin' aboot the young lawyer's clerk that died in the mad-hoose." He twists his mouth sidewise, thinking. "That'll be a guid ten year ago or mair. We dinna get many folk speirin' for him."

The beadle begins to hirple away across the kirkyard, beckoning Robert to follow him over the wet grass. At last, his breath rasping consumptively, the old man comes to a halt and points at a patch of trodden clay, bare save for the remains of a few dandelions and weedy stalks of grass. "There ye are, sir." As Robert looks down, appalled, at the unmarked and neglected grave, the beadle says, "Was ye ane o' the family, then?"

"No," says Robert tersely. Then, after a moment or two, he adds, "But I'm maybe the closest relation he has in this town." He hands the old man a copper and asks him, "What if I wanted to place a stone here?"

The beadle hums his thanks for the coin, then purses his lips and shakes his head. "I dinna ken, sir," he says. "I think ye'd maybe need to tak that up wi' the Bailies o' the Canongate." Then he brightens a bit. "But I canna see what objection they'd mak to it, if that's what ye're set on."

Robert takes this in, then says, "And is there a good mason aboot, somebody that could do a decent job cheap?"

The old man chuckles. "Och, aye, sir," he says, pointing vaguely at the crowds milling in the Canongate's broad thoroughfare. "Mr. Burn's the man ye want. Mr. Robert Burn. He'll do ye a rare job."

"Aye, Mr. Burns," says Robert's near-namesake, a stout, leather-aproned little man with a nose like a potato, standing in his yard amid an array of granite and marble monuments, some blank, some finished, and some in progress. "I'll be pleased to cut whatever ye like on a nice bit stane, just as soon as the Bailies gi'e ye permission to commence wi' it." Burn widens his eyes at Robert. "And what was ye wantin' on the stane, like?"

Robert unfolds the sheet of paper in his hand and glances over the words he wrote not ten minutes ago, seated on a headstone in the kirkyard. Hastily written or not, they say what needs saying. "On the one side," he says, "I want this." And he reads: "'Here lies Robert Fergusson, Poet, born September 5th, 1751 – Died 16th October 1774.' And under that, these lines:

'No sculptured marble here, no pompous lay,
No storied urn nor animated bust;
This simple stone directs pale Scotia's way,
To pour her sorrows o'er the Poet's dust.'"

He looks up at the mason, who smiles and nods approvingly. "And this is to go on the other side," Robert says, reading again: "'By special grant of the Managers to Robert Burns, who erected this stone, this Burial-place is to remain forever sacred to the memory of Robert Fergusson.'"

He extends the sheet to the mason, who slaps a cloud of white dust from his hands, then takes it and examines it for a time, lips working silently. Finally, Burn lays the paper next to a hammer and chisel on a half-cut slab of pink granite. Looking at Robert, he says, "Yon's a muckle screed o' words, but. Was ye ettlin' to put onything toward the job the day, like?"

Commerce again, Robert thinks, disconcerted. But he can scarcely take offense at the mason's caution, for Burn's fee, like so much else, must come out of future proceeds from the book. And in any case, he reminds himself, the mason, like any working man, is worthy of his hire. He fumbles in his pocket and withdraws a half-crown, which he drops into the little man's outstretched hand.

Burn looks down at the coin nesting in his palm, then squints at Robert. "I ken ye've a great name for your ain poetry, Mr. Burns. Mind ye, I havena read ony o' it." He gestures around him at the small forest of monuments. "I'm no' much for verses, for I spend o'er much time howkin' at them wi' my chisel, if ye ken what I mean. But I fancy when your new book's oot, ye'll ha'e nae need to bother aboot money."

Robert tries to smile, but he manages no more than a twitch at the corners of his mouth. "And you needna bother aboot your fee, Mr. Burn," he says. "If I owe a debt to you, I owe a far greater one to the man that lies o'er there in the Canongate kirkyard."

Burn nods, and his dust-covered face cracks open in a sudden smile. "Aye. Weel," he says, shaking Robert's hand and spitting to seal the bargain, "I'll pick oot the stane, then, Mr. Burns. And whenever the Bailies gi'e ye the nod, I'll mak a start."

Striding back up the Royal Mile to Baxter's Close, Robert feels elated, full of energy. In however small a way, he has begun to assure that Bob Fergusson's memory will be preserved in stone. And in doing so he knows he has reaffirmed a part of himself that he has had to keep in check during much of his time in Edinburgh, especially during his encounters with the gentry. Furthermore, seeing that forsaken patch of clay and weeds in the kirkyard has reminded him he is still alive, and that life had best be enjoyed while he can still draw breath.

Then, sniffing the air around him, thick with the mingled odors of smoke, overworked horses, hot grease, and human waste, he decides that breathing may be a mixed blessing, at least in the teeming streets of Auld Reekie. Grinning at the thought, he tries to pick his way through a crush of people in front of a stall selling hot bridies and other foodstuffs; finally, realizing that he could do with something to eat, he allows himself to be jostled unresisting toward the counter.

A short time later, having detached himself from the press of bodies, he sets out again for Baxter's Close. Just as he raises his purchase to his mouth, he hears behind him the soft, suggestive voice of a young woman.

"What aboot a wee bite o' your sausage roll, laddie?"

Amused, he turns to look at the source of this impudent remark. And there, smiling and looking askance at him is a lass of twenty or so, wearing a yellow muslin dress trimmed with green ribbons, and with an edge of matching green petticoat just visible at the hem. Her thick red hair is only partly hidden by a maidservant's white mutch, and her fair skin is sprinkled with freckles. She is a strapping girl, Perhaps a bit more substantial in the hips than is strictly to Robert's taste; but she has a full, pretty face and her wide green eyes hold the promise of a mischief that his life has sadly lacked for too long a time.

He holds out the sausage roll. "Well, then," he says, grinning, "here it is."

The girl moves toward him, never taking her eyes from his, and closes her mouth around the pastry, taking a bite that is far from dainty and chewing with obvious gusto. As Robert watches her, an involuntary shiver runs through him, and he feels a familiar and pleasurable emptiness in his chest.

"What's your name, then?" he says.

Still watching him steadily, the girl finishes chewing and swallowing her mouthful of sausage roll before she speaks. Finally, after wiping her lips with the back of her hand, she says, "Peggy Cameron. Meg to them that knows me." Then, raising her eyebrows, she says, "What's yours?"

"Rab Burns!"

Willie Smellie pounds the table in the Crown Room at the back of Dawney Douglas' tavern, sending a small fountain of ale up out of his tankard and onto the plate bearing what's left of his haggis. The talk has been good, but now's the time for song and bawdry. Smellie looks down the table to where square-jawed William Dunbar sits gulping his dram. As "Colonel" of the Crochallan Fencibles and a lawyer to boot – Writer to the Signet – Dunbar should be imposing order on the proceedings, not swilling down drink and sniggering.

"Lawyer Dunbar!" Smellie roars at him. "Colonel! Will ye no' listen here to me and mak yon versifier tak heed and a'?"

After signalling Dawney for another dram, Dunbar eyes Smellie. "What are ye on aboot, Willie?"

"We need a sang," says Smellie. "A sang frae Poet Burns." He punctuates this utterance with a fart like a beginner's first blast on a bugle.

"Aye," says Dunbar dryly. "Now that ye've sounded the martial trumpet, I'll warrant ye've caught the Bard's attention." The lawyer wags a finger at Robert. "Come now, sir. The founder has issued forth the call to arms. Ye maun gi'e us a sang."

Burns smiles broadly at Dunbar. "Certainly, your Colonelship," he says, much to the amusement of Jock Richmond and Bob Ainslie, the two young would-be lawyers who have come as his guests.

Then he turns to Smellie. "What's your pleasure, then?" he asks. "For anither blast like yon micht tumble the Castle itsel'."

Waiting for the laughter to subside, Smellie reflects that something has made Robert decidedly better-humored than he was earlier in the day. "I dinna care," he says at last, "as lang as it's aboot houghmagandie."

Before Burns can do anything with this request, though, Smellie catches sight of two men entering at Dawney's front door. "Hang on a bit," he says, and he peers through the smoky air to confirm his first impression. Then, rising, he gives a shout that carries across the tavern. "Nicol! Cruikshank! Come awa' in here for a dram and a sang!"

As the newcomers make their way to the Fencibles' gathering, Smellie turns to Burns. "Ye'll want to meet these fellows, Rab. Latin scholars, the pair o' them. Maisters at the High School. And baith ca'd Willie, and a'. The stout ane's Willie Cruikshank, and a kindlier lad ye'd never hope to find. The skinny ane's Willie Nicol. Brilliant man, and a good man and a', but wi' a temper like the wrath o' God when it's roused, and contrary and disputatious into the bargain."

With this for preamble, Smellie turns back to shake hands with Nicol and Cruikshank and presides over the formal introductions. Then he looks about him for the landlord. "Dawney!" he bellows. "Chairs for these gentlemen – and a couple o' drams!" And as Dawney hurriedly complies, Smellie adds, "Sit them doon next to Mr. Burns, so they can ha'e a bit crack after his sang."

When Cruikshank and Nicol are settled, with drink before them, Smellie waves to Robert, who stands and bows to the company. "Weel, gentlemen," he says, "the founder wants houghmagandie, so I maun do as I'm bidden." Burns raises his eyebrows at the new arrivals as if to disclaim responsibility. "I hope my wee sang'll no' gi'e offense to these distinguished scholars," he says with a smile, "for there's nought o' classical lore aboot it."

This innocent quip puts Smellie on the alert. Not on Cruikshank's account, for as usual he is smiling and nodding equably. But Smellie knows that Nicol's sensitivity rivals Burns' own, always attuned to possible slights and ironies. And indeed the classics scholar's dark eyes are glinting fiercely in his sharp-angled face.

"Just sing the bloody sang, Mr. Burns," says Nicol, "and ye'll ken soon enough whether we like it or no'." Before Burns can respond, the schoolmaster adds, "And ye needna mak apology for your voice, either, for as far as I can tell, there's no' a bugger that sings as ill as he fears nor as weel as he hopes."

Smellie shifts his attention to Burns, noting, too, that Richmond, the poet's Mauchline friend, is watching the exchange like a man at a prizefight. Smellie opens his mouth, hoping to interject some disarming sally, but inspiration seems to evaporate with the fumes from his Kilbagie.

In any case, Robert surprises him by smiling, perhaps recognizing a soulmate in the volatile schoolmaster. "Ye're richt enough, Mr. Nicol," says the poet. "I wrote this to the tune o' 'Cauld Kail in Aberdeen.'" And without further preamble he begins to sing:

"O gi'e the lass her fairin', lad,
O gi'e the lass her fairin',
An' something else she'll gi'e to you,
That's waly worth the wearin';
Syne coup her o'er amang the creels,
When ye ha'e taken your brandy,
The mair she bangs the less she squeels,
An' hey for houghmagandie.

Then gi'e the lass her fairin', lad,
O gi'e the lass her fairin',
And she'll gi'e you a hairy thing,
An' of it be na sparin';
But coup her o'er amang the creels,
An' bar the door wi' baith your heels,
The mair she bangs the less she squeels,
An' hey for houghmagandie."

As Robert finishes singing, the company, which punctuated the performance with laughter, breaks into warm applause, and Smellie cannot restrain himself from whooping with delight and drumming on the table. "By Christ, Rab," he says, "yon's a grand bit o' bawdry, a' richt!" He turns to Nicol. "And what d'ye say to that, Willie?"

Nicol glares back down the length of the table. "Ye're no' the only ane wi' ears, Mr. Smellie," he says. "And I can read and a', by God, as ye'll aiblins ken." The schoolmaster gets to his feet and raises his glass. "To Rab Burns," he says, "auld Scotia's finest bard!"

Amid the chorus of agreement with Nicol's toast, Robert sits abruptly. Though he looks pleased by the schoolmaster's approbation, Smellie can tell that something is troubling him. "What's up wi' ye, then?" he calls down the table.

Robert shrugs, then waves his hands as if to dismiss his own concern. "I dinna ken," he says at last, then turns to Nicol. "I'm honored by the toast, of course. But I'm just thinking that I've lived nearly a' my days in one poor wee corner o' the bonniest land on the face o' the world." He looks at Richmond. "You ken what I mean, Jock." Then he speaks more generally to the company. "My faither did his best to educate me. There's nae man can boast o' better folk than mine. And the heart's aey the best teacher in the end. I've maybe learned mair aboot life frae ahent a ploughshare than the feck o' scholars at their desks. But for a' that," he says to Nicol, "ye canna ca' me Scotia's bard if I havena seen ought but Ayrshire and Edinburgh. And I canna write aboot what I've never seen."

Nicol shakes his head in exasperation. "What's keepin' ye, then? Ye maun awa' to the Hielan's the morrow's morn if ye're so inclined."

"No," says Robert. "I'll need to see the book oot afore I can think o' travel."

Smellie breaks in, partly to forestall some caustic rejoinder from Nicol. "Your book'll be ready ony day now, Rab," he says. "Then ye can mak whatever travel plans ye like, for ye'll no' need to worry aboot how weel it'll sell." He looks around at the rest of the party. "The whole edition's damn near spoken for already."

"Nae doubt," says Nicol. Then, somewhat to Smellie's surprise, he adds, "I've been ettlin' to mak a tour o' the North, mysel', when school's by. So If ye can bide a while, ye maun travel wi' me." He eyes Robert challengingly. "That's supposin' ye can cope wi' a sharp tongue and a rude wit."

Smellie sees Robert's face light with interest at this. "I think, Mr. Nicol," says the poet, "that whatever tour we mak, ye'll find lang afore we lea'e the shade o' the Castle that wi' me it's a rude tongue and a sharp wit."

Nicol lets out a raucous laugh. "Weel spoken, sir!" he says. "We'll mak oor plans in the weeks to come, then. And for God's sake, ca' me Willie!"

"This way," Meg Cameron whispers. "An' dinna mak a sound."

Robert feels her hand close around his, and she pulls him gently along the dark entryway of her lodgings, past her sleeping landlady's door. His head is still swimming from the liquor he consumed at Dawney's, and his tongue seems to have grown too large for his mouth. Finally, Meg stops and turns to him, pressing her breasts against his chest, and he can smell the slight sour tang of sweat amid the perfume clinging to her skin.

"Here we are," she hisses. "In ye go."

She gives him a push through the narrow entrance to her closet-like room, where he stands swaying in the darkness while she closes the door. Then she puts her arms around him and draws his head down until her cool parted lips meet his. As her tongue probes his mouth, and he cups a hand over her warm breast, he is surprised when she suddenly reaches between their close-pressed bodies to rub her hand where his cock swells within his breeches. Though far from a bawd like those living above him at Baxter's Close, Meg is obviously no virgin.

"Ye maun ca' canny, lass," he murmurs, "or the bird will flee afore it finds its nest."

"Then lay ye doon here," she says, as they sink onto her straw-filled pallet, "and we'll see to it that they come thegither."

Meg indeed proves to be a practiced lover, her hands moving deftly over him, loosing his cock from its confinement and guiding it to the already wet depths of her cunt. Slipping into her, he shudders with pleasure, and the blood seems to course through his veins like brandy. And as he thrusts rhythmically, with her legs and arms tightening around him, the darkness itself seems to keep time, as if the room were a chamber in some great beating heart. But when release comes, both of them stifling their cries of delight in the quiet house, and they lie clasped together, breathing softly, Robert shivers in the cold air and his mind fills with images and sensations from other times and places: Mary's violet eyes; Betty's white breasts, with their faint pattern of blue veins; Jean's thick dark hair and heathery fragrance. He sighs, suddenly feeling empty, and swallows with difficulty.

At the sound, Meg shifts beside him and lays her head in the space between his neck and shoulder, so that her breath caresses his skin. "What are ye thinkin aboot?" she asks.

He tightens his arm about her for a moment. "The past, Meg. The past," he says. "And a' the days yet to come."

"I dinna ken aboot the past or the future, Rab," she says. "This day's a' I maun live in."

Robert chuckles ruefully. He's declared as much himself on other occasions. "Aye, lass," he says, "ye're richt."

"But I never thocht I'd meet the likes o' you," she says, touching his face as if he might suddenly disappear, "admired by a' an' sundry."

He kisses her hand. "So ye ken aboot my verses, eh?"

"Aye." Meg lies back and folds her hands over her breasts. "I ken aboot them, a' richt. And I've heard some o' them an' a'. But I canna read – nor write." She falls quiet for a time, then stirs again. "Could ye no' say ane o' your poems for me? Or maybe sing a sang?"

Robert brushes her cheek with his mouth. "I'll need to be quiet aboot it," he says, "or we'll ha'e your landlady in on the top o' us." He thinks for a moment, then raises up on one elbow and begins to sing softly:

"The heather was blooming, the meadows were mawn
Our lads gaed a-hunting ae day at the dawn
O'er moors and o'er mosses and mony a glen,
At length they discovered a bonnie moor-hen.

I rede you, beware at the hunting, young men,
I rede you, beware at the hunting, young men;
Take some on the wing, and some as they spring,
But cannily steal on a bonnie moor-hen.

Sweet brushing the dew from the brown heather bells,
Her colors betray'd her on yon mossy fells;

228

Her plumage outluster'd the pride o' the spring,
And O! as she wanton'd sae gay on the wing.

> I rede you, beware at the hunting, young men,
> I rede you, beware at the hunting, young men;
> Take some on the wing, and some as they spring,
> But cannily steal on a bonnie moor-hen."

He pauses after the second refrain, for the song is unfinished. Then, hearing the slow and even cadence of her breathing, he realizes that he has sung Meg to sleep.

He smiles in the darkness, then sinks onto his back again and closes his eyes. And suddenly, with no more provocation than the tune still sowthing in his head, he imagines the sun painting the low green hills of Ayrshire, and the wind whispering in the thorn trees. And as he lies there dreaming of that Western breeze, the melody rising fresh in his mind is no longer "The Bonnie Moor-Hen," but "Miss Admiral Gordon's Strathspey." Someday, he thinks, adrift in the space between sleep and waking, he must write Jean her song.

Lawn Market, Monday morning

. . . When you kindly offered to accommodate me
with a Farm, I was afraid to think of it, as I knew my
circumstances unequal to the proposal; but now, when by
the appearance of my second edition of my book, I may
reckon on a middling farming capital, there is nothing I
wish for more than to resume the Plough.

Indolence and Inattention to business I have sometimes been guilty of, but I thank my God, Dissipation
or Extravagance have never been part of my character. If
therefore, Sir, you could fix me in any sequester'd romantic
spot, and let me have such a Lease as by care and industry
I might live in humble decency, and have a spare hour
now and then to write out an idle rhyme. . . . I am afraid,
Sir, to dwell on the idea, lest fortune have not such happiness in store for me. . . .

letter to Patrick Miller
1st May? 1787

Chapter Seventeen

Seated easily in his favorite armchair, Henry Mackenzie makes a steeple of his forefingers and brings them to his lips, then closes his eyes for a moment. Opening them again, he looks from Willie Creech to young Burns. Creech's mouth is drawn down at the corners, and he sits on the edge of his chair poised as if for sudden flight. Burns, too, appears ill-at-ease, though Mackenzie supposes that his discomfort stems more from injured pride than from the press of business elsewhere. And one knows well what pride goeth before, especially for those who can ill afford it.

In any event, Mackenzie does not intend to be hurried. He leans forward and takes up a crystal decanter from the small table before him. "Brandy, gentlemen?" he inquires.

"Thank ye, no, Henry," says Creech. "No' while business lies before us."

Burns, too, declines the offer, and Mackenzie replaces the decanter on its tray beside the snifters' small shining globes.

"Very well," he says. "Perhaps when business is concluded." He picks up the copy of Burns' new collection that Creech brought along with him. "A handsome volume." He leafs through it languidly. "Willie Smellie has done ye both proud, I must say. And the subscription list seems more than ample assurance of success."

Creech coughs at this. "Eventually, perhaps," he says. "But as ye well know, Henry, it'll be some time till we see anything like profit from the venture."

"Mr. Creech," Burns puts in. "For mysel' I might not care. God knows I ha'e little mercenary zeal. But I fear that others must wait as well – others that depend on me, and feel the extremity o' need." He turns to Mackenzie. "And that is why I've asked for your assistance, Mr. Mackenzie, in the hope that you may advise me – and Mr. Creech – on how to meet this crisis into which family circumstances have plunged me."

Having spoken, Burns looks down at the carpet, his face flushed the color of sandstone. A proud man, indeed, Mackenzie thinks. Ah, well, to have such gifts yoked to poverty must be galling.

How infinitely preferable to find oneself fit for the lot one was born to. Still, something must be done. Mackenzie looks at the publisher. "And what do ye say to that, Mr. Creech?"

Creech cocks his head sidewise and shakes it, clicking his tongue. "There's no' much I can say, Henry, for the matter's in the hands o' the public now."

Before Mackenzie can respond, Burns looks up from his scrutiny of the pattern in the rug. "But the books are sold, are they no'?" he says. "The money's promised."

"Aye," says Creech, with a sharp look at the young poet. "But there's a good bit difference between promised and paid."

Burns folds his arms and sighs as if sorry he spoke. And Mackenzie raises a calming hand. "Come now, Willie. Three thousand copies, wi' ample guarantees. Might you not consider an advance to Mr. Burns against future sales? Such a – "

But Creech cuts him off. "Three thousand copies!" he says. "Aye, Henry. Three thousand copies, right enough. And if I canna arrange wi' Cadell o' London to take up some o' them, I maun bear the whole burden mysel'. And where's the advance on that risk?"

This produces a notable physical response from Burns, his body stiffening and his breathing becoming suddenly audible. But he says nothing, and Mackenzie goes on. "Surely some accommodation is possible, Mr. Creech?"

Creech eyes Mackenzie, raising one brow, then looks over at Burns. He makes as if to speak, then passes a hand across his lips, ending by rubbing his chin vigorously. "There is one thing," he says at last. Mackenzie notes Burns darting a glance at the publisher, who continues: "I canna see my way to taking further risk on books already printed. However" – he looks again at Mackenzie, as if to gauge his likely response – "there is a risk I might undertake, and that for two reasons only. First, Mr. Burns seems to require some immediate financial relief. And second, as a good businessman, I must see some possible return for my investment." He pauses, and regards the other two men, looking particularly hard at Burns. "Shall I proceed?" he says.

Burns unbends somewhat, unfolding his arms and placing his hands on his knees. "I'd be pleased to hear what ye propose," he says.

"Go on, Willie," says Mackenzie, wishing to retain some control of the proceedings.

"Well," says Creech, addressing both Burns and Mackenzie, "as I say, I have taken what risks I can on the present edition of Mr. Burns' poems. And such an extensive printing may well exhaust all demand for the foreseeable future. But I am prepared" – the bookseller pauses as if reluctant to commit himself even in the midst of commitment – "I am prepared to make an offer against the unlikely possibility that a subsequent edition might prove desirable."

Mackenzie sees Burns' dark eyes light with indignation. "An 'unlikely possibility,' you think," says the poet. "Whatever my needs may be, Mr. Creech, I'll take no mere charity."

"Tush, tush, Mr. Burns," says Mackenzie, "this is a business matter. Mr. Creech is a gentleman, of course, but a businessman, nonetheless. There's no question o' charity here." He turns to Creech, who looks a bit less than well-pleased. "Now, Willie," he says, "what do ye propose?"

Creech fixes both men with a hard look, then addresses Mackenzie. "If Mr. Burns is agreeable, I am prepared to purchase the copyright to his verse for a suitable consideration."

Mackenzie nods; he has been expecting something of the sort. Creech has always had an eye for a bargain, and he must have a shrewd notion of what Burns' book might make him. He smiles at the bookseller. "And what might that suitable consideration be, Willie?"

Now Creech shifts in his chair and pulls at his nose. Finally bringing himself to speak, he says, "Perhaps Mr. Burns will have his own thoughts on that subject."

Obviously flustered, Burns looks first to Mackenzie, who decides for the nonce to keep his own counsel, then back to Creech. "My copyright," the young man says. "Does that mean the poems would no longer be mine?"

"No such thing, Robert!" Creech's tone becomes fervid. "The poems are yours and aey will be yours." He lowers his voice somewhat. "But the right to publish any subsequent edition would be mine. And for that right, I stand ready to pay a fair price."

Creech eyes the poet expectantly, and Mackenzie finds himself growing a trifle impatient with the publisher's tactics. Burns again looks about him helplessly. "I am no businessman," he says. "I must place my trust in your knowledge of such affairs, and in Mr. Mackenzie's good counsel. I maun do what ye think right."

"Very well," says Creech, without waiting for any word from Mackenzie. "I am prepared to offer you forty – no, let us say fifty – pounds."

The publisher falls silent, as if shocked by the recklessness of his generosity, and Burns glances at Mackenzie. "Were I your Man o' Feeling," the poet says, "my heart might tell me what to do. As it is, I can only bow to your own wisdom."

"I'm honored by your trust," says Mackenzie. In fact, he feels a touch discomposed. He was prepared to arbitrate Burns' claim to some advance against future sales of the current edition; but sale of a copyright is a weightier business. Whatever he does now will have far greater effect on a man's future. Ah, well, he decides, Willie Creech can better afford the consequences of his overvaluing Burns' work than Burns can afford his undervaluing it. So he turns to the book-seller. "I think, Willie," he says, "that Mr. Burns can hardly think of surrendering his copyright so early, no matter what your own risk may be in the matter."

Creech gives Mackenzie a piercing stare. Then, suddenly, he says, "So be it. I wouldna ha'e ye think I'd take undue advantage o' another man's straitened circumstances. I'll increase my offer" – and here the publisher's words seem to stick in his throat – "I'll increase my offer to" – he pauses again, then goes on in a rush – "to . . . a hundred pounds! There," he says, looking from Mackenzie to Burns. "What do ye say to that?"

Noting that young Burns appears too stunned to speak, and feel-ing a bit heady at his success in moving Creech, Mackenzie says, "I say guineas, Willie. Make it a hundred guineas and I'll gladly advise Mr. Burns to accept your offer."

Creech's normal pallor has transmuted itself into a dull red flush, and he sits for a moment with his jaw working. "By God, Henry Mackenzie," he says at last, "ye're gey open-handed other folk's siller – aye, and gowd and a'."

Mackenzie can sense that he has carried the day, and he notes with further satisfaction that Burns is still transfixed in shock. "Well," he says to Creech, "what's it to be? Do ye agree to the figure? Shall I draw up the papers?"

Creech shakes his head and says nothing for nearly half a min-ute. Then, his voice full of disbelief at his own action, he says, "Aye. I'll rue this day, nae doubt. But aye. A hundred guineas it is." He looks at Mackenzie, the flush beginning to fade from his narrow face. "And now," he says, "I think ye'd best pour us a snifter o' yon brandy, for by God I need it!"

"We'll ha'e these oot o' your road in nae time, gentlemen."

Robert watches from his seat between Richmond and Ainslie as their host John Dowie supervises the clearing of dishes from their table. The three friends have just finished eating a meal of collops and gravy in the small back room known as "the Coffin" at Dowie's tavern in Libberton's Wynd, not far from Baxter's Close.

When the servingmaid has left with her tray of crockery and cutlery, Dowie fills three coggies from a bottle of Kilbagie. "There ye are, lads," says the landlord, arrayed as usual in three-cornered hat and with silver buckles at his knees and on his shoes. And now he raises the tricorne with a dramatic flourish that causes his thin hair to rise up around his head like a halo in the candlelight from the sconces. "I'll lea'e ye to it, then," he says, and moves off to stand near the front door, where he can tip the well-known hat to customers as they enter.

As he often does, Ainslie lets out a high-pitched giggle as soon as Dowie seems out of earshot, prompting Robert to give him a dig in the ribs. And Richmond, shaking his head in mock exasperation, looks at Ainslie and says, "Can ye no' haud your wheesht, ye daft wee bugger?"

"Och, dinna be sae thrawn, Jock," says Ainslie good-humoredly, with a dandyish flourish of his lace handkerchief. "There's that much noise in here, old Dowie couldna hear us if he wanted to."

"Aye." Robert frowns and rubs the back of his neck. "I suppose ye're richt, at that, Bob. It's a wonder he can manage to think, let alone hear."

He feels Richmond's hand on his shoulder and, turning, sees his friend's blue eyes narrowed with concern. "What's up wi' ye, Rab?" says Richmond. "For a man wi' a book that's the toast o' Edinburgh – aye, and the rest o' Scotland and a' – ye've been gey down-in-the-mouth these past weeks."

Robert throws open his hands. "It's aey the same thing," he says. "However much praise I get, and however much hospitality, I canna seem to see ony real gain frae it. I've scarcely made enough to keep mysel', much less help my mither and Gibby."

Richmond's look of concern modulates to puzzlement. "But did ye no' mak a good penny when Creech bought your copyright?"

"A good penny." Robert echoes Richmond, then laughs bitterly. "Oh, aye," he says. "Creech tells me he canna see his way clear to gi'e me an advance on sales o' the book, but he declares afore Henry Mackenzie that he'll pay me a hundred guineas for the copyright. What he didna say was that he'd delay paying me for that and a'. The only money I've seen up till now is the money I've managed to collect on copies o' the book I've sold for mysel'." Robert tips his coggie to his lips and lets the Kilbagie swirl on his tongue as if to burn away the taste of what he's said.

Richmond nods soberly. "I kenned that something had ye vexed," he says, "for ye've been tossing and turning at night as if the bed was on fire." He lowers his voice a bit. "I thocht maybe ye were wearyin' for Jean, but I didna like to ask."

Robert is touched by Jock's solicitude. "Aiblins I do think o' her," he says. "And God knows I worry enough aboot things back at Mossgiel." Then, feeling the need to lighten the conversation, he goes on, "But it's sma' wonder I canna sleep, wi' the noise o' yon crew up the stair."

"Aye," says Richmond, "they go their mile, a' richt. Though ye canna deny there's mony a time it can be better than a nicht at the theatre."

At this, Ainslie lets out a snicker. "What is it ye ha'e livin' o'er ye, Jock?" he demands. "A troop o' acrobats?"

"Na," says Richmond, laughing, "no' acrobats, Ainslie. But damn near it when a's said and done."

Robert turns to Ainslie, pleased for this diversion. "Dochters o' Belial is what the landlady aey ca's them."

"Aye," says Richmond, cheerfully ironic, "oor Mrs. Carfrae. As staid, sober, pious, and evil-abhorring a widow as ever rented a room in Edinburgh."

Catching Richmond's spirit, Robert continues. "The floors are that ill-plastered," he says to the grinning Ainslie, "we can hear everything the lassies do – whether it's eat, drink, or – "

"Say their prayers!" finishes Richmond.

Ainslie gives vent to a peal of laughter deeper than his customary giggle. "It's a wonder your Mrs. Carfrae doesna ha'e them oot on the street," he says at last.

Richmond drains his coggie and signals for another round. "Oh, she's developed a comfortable enough philosophy for dealing wi' them."

At this, Robert impulsively snatches the lace handkerchief from Ainslie's sleeve and holds it around his head like the landlady's mutch. "Heaven will tak care o' these dochters o' Belial," he says, mimicking Mrs. Carfrae's pinched tones. "We needna be uneasy because the wicked enjoy the good things o' life. For these base jades that lie up gandygoin' wi' their filthy fellows – drinking the best o' wines and singing their abominable songs – will one day lie in Hell, weeping and wailing and gnashing their teeth o'er a cup o' God's wrath!" Concluding this speech to the wide-eyed delight of the other two, Robert tosses Ainslie's handkerchief in the air and watches it flutter to the table.

"In short," says Richmond to Ainslie, "times are hard and the Dochters o' Belial pay well."

Robert clasps his hands before him in mock prayer. "So there they stay," he intones, "while Mrs. Carfrae wrestles wi' the Devil for their souls on a Sunday at St. Giles' Cathedral."

They erupt into full-throated laughter just as Dowie bends among them in his tricorne to pour more drink, joining in their merriment as if he was present from the start and knew what they were talking about. When the landlord has left to resume his post at the front door and their mirth has subsided, Robert cannot forebear a serious word. "A' the same," he says, "between Willie Creech's meanness and the noise o' the jades up the stair, I canna think to write." He looks at Richmond. "I'm sorry to say it, Jock, but much as I value your company, I think I maun look for other lodgin's."

Jock's face darkens. "I thocht ye were ettlin' to mak a tour o' the Hielan's?" he says. "Maybe if ye do that, it'll clear your heid a bit."

"I'd leave the morrow if I could, Jock," says Robert. "But I've promised Willie Nicol I'll wait till he can go wi' me, and I mauna go back on my word."

Downcast, Richmond sips at his whisky in silence. Robert wishes he could say something to cheer him. But while he thinks, Ainslie plucks at his arm. "Rab," says the little clerk, "what aboot a tour o' the Borders in the meantime? Ye said ye wanted to see mair o' Scotland, did ye no'? And if I can get a few weeks off, I'll go wi' ye, for my family live in Berwick, at Berrywell. I ken fine my faither'd mak ye welcome. What do ye say?"

Robert thinks for a moment. A tour could allow him to husband his meager resources more effectively, for living in Edinburgh is costly, and the Border folk might prove hospitable to a recently well-known poet. "Aiblins ye're richt, Bob," he says. "I'd be as well roamin' the howes and knowes o' Berwick and Selkirk as fidgin' and grumblin' here at Willie Creech's pleasure."

Ainslie is fairly bouncing with enthusiasm. "It'll gi'e ye the chance to look o'er yon farm on Mr. Miller's estate in Dumfries," he says. "Even if ye're no' keen on it, there's nae harm in seein' it."

"Aye," says Richmond, brightening, "and ye can maybe pay a visit to Mauchline and a'. A victorious return, richt enough, eh?"

Robert leans back in his chair, suddenly in good spirits himself. Perhaps the next few weeks may not prove so unpleasant, after all. "Mr. Dowie!" he shouts, waving to the landlord, who touches his hat by way of acknowledgement. This provokes Ainslie to more ill-stifled laughter. "Wheesht!" says Robert; then he turns and calls again to Dowie, "Three mair Kilbagies for me and my friends, if ye please!"

A blue-grey haze has descended on the City from its own high chimneys on this cool spring afternoon. Breathing with some difficulty in the smoky air, Robert makes his way past Merchant's Hospital toward Greyfriar's Churchyard and his tryst with Meg Cameron. He has just left Patrick Miller's fine house in Nicolson Square, where for the past hour or so the banker has plied him with good claret and tried to convince him that Ellisland Farm will assure his future economic independence.

"I couldna just tell ye aboot the soil, Mr. Burns," Miller said as he showed Robert out onto the street a few minutes ago, "but ye'll can judge that for yoursel' firsthand, of course, when ye mak your trip. We'll no' discuss terms for a lease till ye've seen the land, but we should ha'e little difficulty then, and ye can be assured I'll mak ye a suitable allowance to build a house to your satisfaction." And as Robert walked away toward Potter Row, the banker was still calling after him, "Mind, Mr. Burns – it's the land that made ye, and it's the land that'll mend ye!"

Robert knows well enough what the land has done for him until now, so Miller's assurances give him little confidence. As far as he can tell, the man knows far more about loans and investments than about soil and crops. Like all the gentry Robert has met here, Miller sees a pastoral vision of the rustic poet drawing his sustenance and inspiration from the land; and what Robert knows to his cost is that the land seems far more open-handed with inspiration than sustenance. Still, Miller evidently means well, and Ellisland Farm may prove an exception; a man can look at it, at least, and hope. In any case, the trip itself should prove pleasant, as should Ainslie's company; and he'll have a good steed under him, too, having put down four pounds sterling from the little he's collected on the book to buy a sturdy old mare. He's already made up his mind to call her Jenny Geddes, after the woman whose contrary zeal caused her to fling a stool at the Bishop of Edinburgh on a summer's day nearly a hundred and fifty years past. A woman much of his own mind as regards the authorities of the Kirk, he thinks, chuckling.

But now he sees Greyfriar's ahead, surrounded by slabs and more ornate memorials, crowded by mean tenements, with the Castle and the highest of its crags in the haze hanging beyond. And as Robert draws nearer, hearing the shouts of children playing amid the profusion of graves, and snatches of song and argument from open tenement windows, he catches sight of Meg's red hair and yellow linen gown. Seated on a table tombstone with a basket resting at her feet, she looks unaccountably glum.

Meg rises momentarily to meet him, then sinks back on the tombstone without speaking, hands clasped in her lap. "Are ye no' glad to see me, then?" he asks. "We havena trysted often, but ye canna be fed up wi' me already."

She compresses her lips briefly. "It's no' that, Rab," she says. "But I'm gey worried." She falls silent, twisting her apron between her fingers and looking at him from eyes that look bruised and a touch sullen.

Sensing her unwillingness to speak, and suddenly uneasy himself, Robert finally says, "What's wrang wi' ye, lass? Has your mistress gi'ed ye a through-puttin' aboot something?"

She looks at him steadily, with no hint of humor. "I'm late," she says. "Behind my time. Nearly twa month."

Robert closes his eyes for a few heartbeats. Here, with silent reminders of death and the din of bustling life surrounding him, he feels suspended, apart from it all. Or perhaps he only wishes to be. He opens his eyes and looks down at Meg. "It's early yet," he says, forcing the words. "Aiblins ye're mistaken."

Meg tilts her head, and something in her eyes and the set of her mouth reminds him of his mother. He braces himself for an angry retort, but all Meg says is, "No."

Suddenly Robert himself feels irritation bubbling up within him. Here he is with a new edition out, with the promise of substantial money to come, and the prospect of a pleasant trip before him, one that might even hold the key to his future. But as always Fate seems ready to trip him at every turn. If only the seed he bought for the rigs of Mossgiel had proved as potent as his own, and the land he ploughed and sowed it on had proved as fertile as the women in his life.

"And ye think it's me," he says, for want of anything wiser.

Meg rises, glaring at him, her green eyes ashine with furious tears. "And ye'd say that to me!" she exclaims. She turns and kicks the basket at her feet, scattering the odds and ends of messages she has evidently been sent out for by her mistress. Then, turning back to confront him, she says, "I wouldna ha'e thocht ye'd ha'e the face to do sic a thing."

His face hot, Robert stares back at her, torn between guilt and anger. "Neither o' us kenned much aboot the ither when we met," he says, "and I ken little mair aboot how ye spend your time when I'm no' there. Dinna forget, it was you that spoke first to me, and they werena the words o' an innocent young lassie."

His words seem to rob Meg of her own high feeling. Again, she sinks down, this time almost falling to the grass before the tomb, and Robert notes for the first time the skull and crossbones inscribed on its worn surface, though he cannot quite make out the Latin motto beneath it. Looking down at this young woman he scarcely knows, but within whom his child may be forming, he shakes his head.

"I dinna ken," he says at last, "whether it's mine or no', nor whether it's even there. But I've never evaded responsibility – aye, nor blame – in my life." He pauses, and Meg looks up at him sidewise, wiping the back of her wrist across her cheeks. He breathes deeply, a hollow sensation in the pit of his stomach.

"I'm away on a tour o' the Borders soon, and I'll be in Dumfries to see to some business. If it turns oot that ye're richt, ye can send word to me there. I'll see what I can do."

He reaches down and offers her his hand. "Now get up oot o' that," he says, forcing a smile as he hoists her upright. Then he bends, picks up her basket, and hands it to her. "For whatever troubles ye may need to face," he says, "ye're no' ready for the cold clay o' Greyfriar's kirkyard."

My ever dear Sir,

I slept at John Dow's, and called for my daughter; Mr. Hamilton and family; your mother, sister, and brother; my quondam Eliza, &c all well. I date this from Mauchline, where I arrived on Friday even last. If any thing had been wanting to disgust me completely at Armour's family, their mean, servile compliance would have done it.

Give me a spirit like my favorite hero, Milton's Satan –

"Hail, horrors! hail,
Infernal world! and thou profoundest Hell,
Receive thy new possessor! he who brings
A mind not to be changed by place or time!"

I cannot settle to my mind. Farming, the only thing of which I know anything, and heaven above knows but little I do understand of that, I cannot, dare not risk on farms as they are. If I do not fix, I will go for Jamaica. Should I stay in an unsettled state at home, I would only dissipate my little fortune, and ruin what I intend shall compensate my little ones for the stigma I have brought on their names.

I shall write you more at length soon; as this letter costs you no postage, if it be worth reading you cannot complain of your pennyworth –

I am ever, my dear Sir, yours,

ROBT BURNS

letter to JAMES SMITH, Linlithgow
11th June 1787

Chapter Eighteen

Seated at the kitchen table, pencil in hand, Gibby looks down at the sheet of paper before him. In ten minutes of sitting poised to write a letter to Robert in Edinburgh, he's produced nothing more than the date and the salutation. Across the table, his mother sits bent over a wooden bowl, kneading dough. The girls are in the bothy, making the sweet-milk cheese for which Mossgiel has become well-known, and keeping an eye on wee Bess; he can hear their song and chatter drifting in at the open door.

"I just canna settle to it, Mither," he says, throwing down the pencil. "Petitioning my ain brither again for the aid he's bound by blood and law to gi'e us. By his ain promise and a'. It galls me to have to do it."

Agnes looks up from her bread-making, one cheek glistening red with sweat, the other smeared white with flour. "Aye, Gibby, it's a sair thing to face, richt enough." She rubs her hands together to remove a few clinging threads of dough. "But Gaw'n Hamilton'll no' wait forever to be paid his back rent, never mind what good friends him and Rab are supposed to be. And Rab's our only hope o' relief."

"I ken that, Mither." Gibby shakes his head. "I just canna understand what made him refuse to sign yon guarantee Hamilton asked for in March on our account. Wi' a' his success in Edinburgh —"

Before Gibby can finish his thought, he hears the clatter of a horse's hooves in the yard outside. As he turns toward the sound, a shadow falls across the threshold, followed immediately by the figure of his elder brother, so familiar and yet strange from so many months of absence. Robert's hair is wild from galloping in the wind, his breeches, boots, and coat dusty from the open road. He stands there without a word, face split by a smile, dark eyes glinting with pleasure at the shock produced by his unexpected arrival. Rising, Gibby indeed feels bemused, as if he has conjured this vision out of his own mind.

"Oh, Robert!"

Agnes brushes past Gibby and all but collapses into her eldest son's arms. As Robert swings her off her feet with a cry of delight,

Gibby feels a sudden rush of anger. No matter what Robert may do, or fail to do, his charm seems to win everyone over, even their mother.

Robert sets Agnes down and holds her at arms' length. "Mither," he says, "it's good to see ye!" Then he looks over her head. "How ha'e ye been keeping, Gibby?"

Gibby moves away, his chest feeling tight, as if he cannot surrender his heart to its normal rhythm. "Weel enough," he says without warmth, "if it's health ye mean."

From the corner of his eye, he sees Robert release his mother's shoulders, then kiss her on the cheek and cross the kitchen floor. "Let me ha'e a look at ye." Robert reaches down to take Gibby's hand and shakes it vigorously, then slaps him lightly on the arm. "Never better, my lad," he says, winking. "Best o' health, eh?"

Gibby stares back at him, mouth set. "What brings ye here?" he says at last.

Robert laughs, but Gibby feels perversely satisfied to see in his eyes that he is a bit hurt. "To see ye a', of course." Robert gestures around him. "You and Mither and Willie and the lassies – and my ain wee Bess."

Suddenly, amid whoops of joy, the entire family bursts into the kitchen, and Gibby watches silently as Robert embraces each of the girls in turn, then tosses the plump little Bess in his arms and kisses her, finishing with a manly hug and handshake for Willie.

When the uproar has abated, Agnes seems to remind herself that the Prodigal has returned. "Nancy! Bell!" she says. "Ye maun see aboot a bite to eat for your brither." Then she turns to her youngest son. "And Willie – you'll need to move back doon here to the spence the nicht." She looks almost apologetically at Robert. "Willie's been sleepin' up the stair wi' Gibby since ye've been away."

Gibby feels another knot of irritation tie itself in his chest. But Robert holds up his hands. "No, no," he says. "I'll no' impose on ye for food or lodging. I'll put up in the village the nicht, at the Whitefoord Arms. Johnnie Dow'll feed me weel enough."

Nancy and Bell pause uncertainly and look to their mother, who scowls at Robert. "Ye may suit yoursel' aboot lodgin's, if that's what ye want. But ye'll tak a bite, even if it's only bannocks and cheese. I dinna ken what ye'd stay in Machlin for, when ye could be in your ain bed."

Robert moves to his mother and puts an arm around her. "I'll be pleased to taste some o' your cheese again, Mither, for there's nane to touch it in Auld Reekie. But I'll no' disrupt the hoose, nor add to your burden here. I'm used enough wi' inns lately, onyhow. I've been on a tour o' the Border country this past month, wi' a lad ca'd Bob Ainslie. He's a grand fellow, Gibby – ye'll need to meet him someday."

"Aye," Gibby says, determined not to be swept up in the general rejoicing, "I didna think the likes o' us would be enough to tear ye awa' frae Edinburgh."

Robert moves away from his mother. "Gibby," he says, frowning, "I'll have ye know I left Ainslie wi' his folk in Berwick so that I could pass through Mauchline before I went back to the City. I've been wearying to see ye these past seven months." He looks steadily at Gibby, who stares back at him without speaking. "What's up then?" he asks.

Gibby sits again at the table, glancing down at his barely-started letter. "What's aey up?" he says sourly.

Robert nods ruefully. "Aye," he says. Then he looks around at everyone. "I ken I havena done near enough in the way o' helping ye. But it's been oot o' my hands."

"What do ye mean?" says Gibby. "Your new edition's oot, is no'?"

A quick grin crosses Robert's face. "Aye. Three thousand copies. And in great demand and a'." Then, as if remembering how the subject came up, he says, "But ye may ken it took five months o' delays and wrangling wi' Willie Creech the publisher afore they saw the licht o' day. And I still havena seen mair than a pittance o' the money he agreed to pay, either."

Agnes, too, resumes her seat at the table. "But ye'll ha'e had a deal o' praise, nae doubt," she says acidly.

"I'll ha'e money enough soon!" Robert paces the length of the kitchen, then wheels around to face Agnes. "This Border tour will likely ha'e gi'ed Creech time to see to my claims." He glowers from his mother to Gibby. "But never fear," he says, "I'll gi'e ye something toward the rent afore I leave. God knows ye seem to care mair aboot that than seeing me."

At this, Nancy speaks quickly. "Robert!" she says. "Ye ken fine there's nothing we want mair than to see ye back here amang us!"

As Robert looks at Nancy, his mouth softening with the beginnings of a smile, their mother speaks from her seat across the table from Gibby. "How much longer will ye need to be awa' in yon place, onyhow?"

Gibby can tell the question has somehow unnerved Robert, for his eyes widen and he blows air through his lips. "I dinna ken," he says finally. "I ha'e other matters to press there besides my business wi' Creech."

He crosses to the table and sits as Isa sets down a plate of bannocks and a whang of cheese and Bell pours him a caup of beer. When he has settled himself, he looks again at his mother and Gibby. "I've just been inspecting a farm doon aboot Dumfries – Ellisland, it's ca'd. There's a banker in Edinburgh offered to rent me it." He takes a bite of oatcake and washes it down with a draught from his caup. "If I agree, I'll be able to ease your circumstances here a bit by taking wee Bess under my ain roof."

"So ye'll no' come back to us at a'?" says Bell.

Robert chews reflectively on a piece of cheese. "I maun do what I can to turn a penny," he says. "But it'll need a good bit thocht yet. And I still havena gi'en up on the idea o' an Excise commission, either." He smiles at Bell. "In ony event, I'll need to see to a' that back in Edinburgh."

"Ye'll no' be lettin' the attentions o' your fine frien's there go to your head, then?" says Nancy.

Robert folds his arms and laughs. "Little fear o' that," he says. "Every minute I spend in their company reminds me how far I am frae their wealth and station. I'm just a novelty to the feck o' them – and when that wears off I'll be back where I started. And some o' them nae mair than coofs wi' the advantage o' a rich sire or a wealthy bride."

Nancy cocks her head at him. "Ye'd be as well maybe to look to yon quarter yoursel'."

"Believe me," says Robert, his expression growing somber, "I've met lassies in plenty there – "

"Nae doubt," interposes his mother dryly.

Robert shoots her a sidelong glance, then continues. "I fear there's little prospect o' the dochters o' the gentry lowering themselves to the likes o' me."

"Lower themsel's!" says Nancy fiercely. "They'd be lucky if ye gi'ed them a second look – ony o' them!"

"Nae matter" – Robert smiles his sister – "I couldna wed for mere mercenary gain. It wouldna do wi' me at a'." He looks down at the

table for a moment or two, then speaks again with a show of uncon-
cern. "Do ye ever see or hear ought o' Jean . . . or the bairns?"

Bell snorts scornfully. "I wonder ye'd bother your head wi' that
ane – or onybody connected wi' her."

Gibby knows well enough that his sisters still squirm with
shame and anger each Sunday whenever they see Jean Armour, for
she reminds them not only of their own humiliation at Robert's
rebuke before the congregation, but also of the senior Armours' arro-
gant refusal to accept Robert as a son-in-law. Of course, the Armours
will more than likely have altered their opinion of Robert in propor-
tion to his growing fame, especially if they can smell money in the
offing. In any case, Gibby realizes that his own irritation has dis-
sipated in the face of Robert's concern for Jean and the children.

"I've seen Jean frae a distance now and again," he says. "She and
the bairns seem weel enough as far as I can tell."

"Aye," says Robert, still affecting nonchalance. "I'll maybe stop
and see how they're getting on afore I leave. I'll can send o'er frae the
inn, the morn, and gi'e the Armours word to expect me."

Nancy makes a disparaging sound, then says, "Ye'd just better
watch they let ye go, once they get ye."

Robert looks sharply at her. "There's nae fear o' that, Nancy, as ye
ken weel enough. But Jeany and Robert are my ain bairns, and Jean's
their mither."

"Aye," says Agnes, "and she should be your wife and a'."

"Mither!" Bell shakes her head in exasperation. "How can ye say
sic a thing, after a' the Armours ha'e done to Rab?" She looks at Robert
meaningfully. "Especially Jean Armour."

Before Robert or his mother can say more to add to the growing tension, Gilbert says, "Never mind that the now. Rab's back at
Mossgiel, and that's the main thing."

Agnes softens at this, and smiles at Robert. "Aye," she says.
"Finish your bite, son, and tell us aboot a' the grand folk ye've been
meeting. What like are they?"

"Och," says Robert, "there's many a good man and woman
amang them, Mither. But honest to God, a good few o' the gentry put
me in mind o' some auld wives aboot the countryside here – for they
spin their thread sae fine that it's neither fit for weft nor woof." He
glances around him, smiling. "It's a pleasure to be back where folk ha'e
a good Scotch tongue in their heads."

And despite his earlier resolve, Gibby finds the remains of his icy humor melting in the warmth of his brother's presence. He leans over and claps Robert's shoulder. "And it's a pleasure to see ye here in your ain kitchen," he says, "wi' your ain folk."

Robert covers Gibby's hand with his own, and the light in his eyes takes Gibby back to their days at the fireside in the old clay biggin their father built in Alloway, where John Murdoch taught them to love knowledge and the written word.

But now Robert chuckles and points across the room. "Willie Burns!" he says, snapping his youngest brother to attention. "Away oot to yon old mare o' mine, if ye please, and gi'e her some oats and water. And then bring in my saddlebags, for I've brought ane or twa odds and ends for everybody." At the mention of presents, Willie runs out into the yard without a second bidding, and Robert grins at the rest of the family. "There's a few copies o' my new book in there and a'," he says with gentle irony, "if onybody's interested."

James Armour looks dourly around the parlor, unable to relax even in his favorite chair, or to break the room's tense silence. Mary Armour sits across from him with a crib set on either side of her, and Jean hovers near the window in a beribboned mutch and a new blue dress trimmed with lace. The rest of the house is unaccustomedly quiet, for James has sent his other children away for the day.

Jean turns from the window to her mother. "Should he no' be here soon?"

"You come awa' frae yon window," says Mary Armour. "Ye ken weel enough when he's supposed to be here. Though I fancy now that he's amang the nabbery, he's less to be trusted than ever."

Stung by this, Jean says, "Mither!"

Before she can go on, though, James cuts her off. "That's enough, the pair o'ye!" he says, happy enough to find a focus for his own frustration. Then he wags a finger at his daughter. "Just you see that ye dinna let him get awa' afore he's made ye a pledge o' some kind."

Jean glares back at him with a defiance that has shown itself with irritating frequency since the birth of the twins. "He did that – once!" she says. "But you – "

James rises and takes a step toward her. "You watch your tongue, my girl, or – "

The threat goes unspoken, for at that moment a knock sounds at the door. "Be quiet!" says Mary sharply. "It's him!" She rises and crosses the room to her daughter. "You get up there!" She gives Jean a push. "Hurry!"

After a moment's hesitation, Jean moves quickly to the door that leads upstairs. As she closes the door behind her, James calls after the sound of her receding footsteps, "Mind what I tellt ye!" Then, at another sharp rap on the door, he turns to his wife. "Weel, answer it, woman," he says. "And for God's sake see if ye canna put a good face on for him."

Mary scowls at him, but hurries to the door and opens it. As Burns steps into the house, flamboyant as usual in breeches and coat, James sees Mary's face transform itself with a smile that reminds him for a moment of the lassie he married. "Oh, Mr. Burns!" she says. "How do ye do?"

James can see that Burns is taken aback by this unexpected welcome, and he hopes that Mary has not laid the charm on too thickly. But Burns responds civilly enough, bowing slightly. "I'm fine," he says. "I trust I find you and Mr. Armour well, too."

"Oh, aye, Mr. Burns." James moves to him and takes his hand, shaking it energetically. "Come awa' in, then, come awa' in." As he ushers Burns into the parlor, he notes the cribs before them. "Aye," he says, gesturing, "ye'll want to see the weans. Bonnie wee things."

As Burns drops to his knees and begins to prattle at the children, Mary motions to James, indicating the small cabinet against the wall nearest him. He clears his throat, then speaks. "Ye'll tak a drop' o' brandy, will ye no', Mr. Burns?" Then, as Burns rises, James forces himself to continue. "I ken we've had oor differences – but that's a' by now and best forgot."

Burns looks at him, eyes widening a bit. "Aye," he says. "I'll be glad to tak a drink wi' ye, Mr. Armour."

James tries to ignore what sounds like a trace of mockery in Burns' tone. "Mary," he says, nodding to his wife. And as she fetches brandy and two glasses from the cabinet, James rubs his hands with such good humor as he can muster, then indicates a chair. "Weel, sit ye doon, Mr. Burns." Burns sits and James tries to mask his anxiety by fishing out his snuffbox. "Will ye tak a pinch, Mr. Burns?"

"No thanks, Mr. Armour."

Again, Burns speaks politely enough, but his manner causes James unease verging on irritation. "Weel," he says, "ye'll no' mind if I indulge?" He opens the box and sniffs two healthy measures, then sneezes prodigiously. As he does so, Mary sets the glasses and bottle down on the small table near his chair, then hovers at his shoulder while he sits and pours brandy for Burns and himself. He raises his glass. "Here's to your health and continued prosperity, sir."

Burns lifts his own glass. "Cheers," he says, barely opening his mouth.

After both men sip at their drinks, a silence falls, during which Mary gives James a surreptitious nudge. He glowers briefly at her, then turns to Burns and flashes what he hopes looks a hearty smile. "Weel, weel," he says. "So ye're back frae the great world. And a huge success by all accounts."

Burns sets down his glass. "Weel, I'm no' just sure what accounts that would be," he says carefully, "but I've hardly made my fortune, Mr. Armour."

"Aye, weel," James says, adopting the knowing tone he uses in business dealings, "a man's no' wrang to be canny wi' regard to sic matters." He waves a hand at the bottle. "Mair brandy, Mr. Burns?"

But Mary stirs again at his elbow. "James," she says, "Mr. Burns will be wanting to see Jean. Is that no' richt, Mr. Burns?"

Burns looks first at her, then at James. "Weel, . . ." he begins, then trails off.

"Aye, that's richt." Mary points at the door to the upper story. "Awa' ye go, then. She's up there waitin' for ye now."

Burns rises and looks down uncertainly at James. "Weel, Mr. Armour," he says, "if ye'll excuse me . . ."

James gets to his feet, too. "Never gi'e it a thocht, Mr. Burns. On ye go. The twa o' ye will ha'e plenty to talk aboot."

He shows Burns to the door, then calls up the stairs after him,

"And ye needna worry. We've sent the rest o' the weans awa' for the day. Ye'll no' be disturbed." He shuts the door and quietly turns the key in the lock, then turns to his wife. "He could maybe ha'e done wi' anither glass o' brandy. Do ye think he suspected ought?"

Mary Armour looks at the closed door, her mouth twitching. "It maks nae odds," she says at last, "whether he did o' whether he didna. I only hope Jean has the wit to mak the best advantage o' it."

Jean is standing at the window in her room, looking down at the back green and remembering the old wooden spoon she used to dig there with as a child, when she hears Robert's footsteps on the stairs. Her chest tightens and breathing becomes difficult, but she wills herself not to turn around. Then, hearing the scrape of his feet on the threshold, she can tell he has entered the room, and she waits for the sound of his voice.

"Hello, Jean."

Again, she fights the urge to turn and run to him. Instead, she merely says, "Hello, Robert," hoping she won't sound too tremulous, hoping he will run to her.

"For God's sake," he says suddenly, his tone harsh with anger, "do they think I'm sic a gull as a' that – no' to see through their damned hypocritical scheming? Is that what you think?"

Jean does turn now, to see Robert standing in the doorway, sturdy and handsome as ever in breeches and boots, color high and dark eyes alive with indignation. "I think nothing at a', Rab." She moves away from the window, close to the foot of the bed. "I just ken I'm happy to see ye."

He stares at her for a long moment, then shakes his head and smiles, close-mouthed. "Och, lassie," he says, "I canna be angry wi' you. No' when ye stand there looking like my heart's dearest hope."

Unable to stop herself, Jean crosses the small room to stand before him. "Oh, Rab," she says, her nostrils tingling with the warm smell of his skin, like spiced wine, "I canna believe ye're here. It's been that long."

And now he gathers her into his arms and presses his open mouth on hers, making her feel as if her heart might rattle itself to a stop against her ribs. But just as she begins to hope that all will be well, that he has returned to her for good, he releases her and strides over to the window.

"Mind, Jean," he says, turning back to her, "there's nae question o' my obligation here. Wi' the turmoil my affairs are in, I canna see the future a fortnight in front o' me."

Sensing the need to be careful, Jean moves to the opposite side of the bed from Robert. She knows that railing or pleading will do nothing more than humiliate her, so she chooses a less direct approach. "Did ye see the bairns, Rab?" She sits on the bed, facing away from him. "Are they no' lovely?"

She hears Robert moving and sees from the corner of her eye that he is standing at the foot of the bed. "Aye, lassie," he says warmly, "bonnie enough to tak the heart frae me." Then his voice turns stern again. "But do ye understand me? I'm awa' to Edinburgh again in a few days, and I can mak ye nae promises. Now . . . or ever."

Again, Jean changes the subject. "Is Edinburgh a grand place, then?"

He remains quiet for a moment, perhaps surprised by the question, then says, "Aye, it is that." Going on, he gradually becomes more enthusiastic. "As grand as ye could ask for. Sights and sounds – aye, and smells – in sic profusion as ye've never dreamed o'." He begins to pace as much as the cramped room will allow. "Lords and ladies and coofs and gangrels and a'. A life o' the mind that thraws ye ane minute and delights ye the next. And the Castle watching o'er it a' like a grey giant."

Jean cannot help asking, "And are the lasses lovely there?" She can see from his guarded look that the question has troubled him in some way.

"As bright as the summer sky," he says at last, his voice distant-seeming, even a bit sad, "and sweet as the milk-white thorn." Jean's stomach gives a sudden lurch of panic and despair. But now he is standing before her and, taking her hands, raises her to her feet. "But there's nothing there to compare wi' you."

"Oh, Rab," she cries, throwing her arms around him, pressing her cheek to the warmth of his chest, "I love ye! Nae matter what else happens, I love ye."

"And I love you and a', Jean," he says tenderly, the side of his jaw hard against the top of her head. "Never mind a' the rest." Then he holds her back at arm's length and looks her in the face. "And never mind this matron's mutch ye've hidden yoursel' under, either."

He plucks the mutch from her head and throws it aside, allowing her hair to fall about her shoulders. "And now, lass," he says, eyes glinting with wicked wit, "as long as they've gi'ed us time and place" – he nods at the bed – "let's mak the best advantage o' it!"

Laughing, he sweeps her up in his arms and sets her down on the bed. And as she looks up to see him bending over her, Jean is aware that her parents' scheming has turned back on them, and on her, too, for that matter. But as Robert's mouth covers hers and her arms seem to embrace him of their own accord, she realizes with her last clear thought that she doesn't care.

Reading a pocket edition of Milton he has bought on his travels, Robert sits on the bed in his room above Johnnie Dow's tavern, vaguely aware of the creaks and groans of the old building and the rush of wind about its eaves. A letter from Meg Cameron, evidently written for her by a literate friend, lies beside him, begging for assistance in what by now is her obvious plight. Robert feels he must do something. He knows Bob Ainslie can be trusted to act for him in his absence from Edinburgh, for Ainslie will not only have returned there by now, but he has also confided to Robert that he, too, has fallen afoul of the same ill-luck with a servingmaid.

Taking up pencil and paper, Robert writes a hasty note to his friend, requesting that Ainslie give Meg ten or twelve shillings to see to her immediate needs, and that he advise her to leave the City and stay with friends on a nearby farm until her trouble is over. Then, thinking of Ainslie's reckless temperament, he adds to the letter an admonition that his friend not attempt to "meddle with Meg as a piece."

Finally, with the letter completed and ready for copying in ink, Robert lies back and covers his eyes with his hands. His head feels stuffed to bursting with cares about the future. Meg, of course, will manage; she is an experienced lass, and knew full well what she was about when she accosted him on the Royal Mile.

But just across the way from the Whitefoord Arms, Jean Armour lies in her own bed with his seed sown in her again, already the mother of his children, and far less wise in the ways of the world than the likes of Meg Cameron. Up the road at Mossgiel, moreover, the entire Burns family waits for the help only he can give them. And all he can do is depend on the goodwill of a man like Willie Creech. A sigh escapes Robert and he brings his fist down on the mattress.

Why is he cursed in this way? To know a world beyond the one he was born to. To be gifted enough to belong in that other world, but to be denied any right to it beyond that of a quaint visitor on sufferance of those who control it. To meet women of beauty and learning, who profess to be charmed by his appearance and his accomplishments and his conversation, but who would no more think of marrying him than he would think of plucking Racer Jess as his bride out of Poosie Nansie's tavern. What power does he have, save over words on paper or lassies of his own class? If only he could be like Milton's Satan, and spit his fury at all of those who stand indifferent above him.

Robert's body twitches convulsively with anger, and he flings paper and pencil to the floor. Then, after carefully laying aside his pocket Milton and snuffing the candle on his bedside table, he sinks back on the bed and closes his eyes, as if he might hope to lose himself forever in the void of sudden darkness.

Mauchline

My dear Sir,

I have been rambling over the world ever since I saw you, through the heart of the Highlands as far as Inverness and back by the North coast the whole rout to Dundee. – I have done nothing else but visited cascades, prospects, ruins and Druidical temples, learned Highland tunes and pickt up Scotch songs, Jacobite anecdotes, &c. these two months. – it will be a fortnight at least before I leave Edinr, and if you come in for the winter session when it sits down, Perhaps we shall have the mutual pleasure of meeting once more in auld Reekie – I lodge at Mr Cruikshank's, No 2d, St James's Square, Newtown . . .

I am busy at present assisting with a Collection of Scotch Songs set to Music by an Engraver in this town. – It is to contain all the Scotch Songs, those that have been already set to music and those that have not, that can be found. –

I long much to hear from you, how you are, what are your views, and how your little girl comes on. – By the way, I hear I am a girl out of pocket and by careless, murdering mischance too, which has provoked me and vexed me a good deal. – I beg you will write me by post immediately on receipt of this, and let me know the news of Armour's family, if the world begin to talk of Jean's appearance in any way. –

Farewell, my dear Sir!

ROBT BURNS

letter to JOHN RICHMOND, Mauchline
25th October 1787

Chapter Nineteen

At the tinkling of the bell above his front door, William Creech looks up from the ledger on his desk to see Robert Burns enter. Another confrontation, he thinks, and allows himself a small, precise sigh. He gives Peter Hill a look that stops the clerk from leaving his own desk. Then, rising from his seat, he walks out to the front of the shop.

"Mr. Burns. Robert," he says, stretching his lips into a smile. "What can I do for ye today?"

Burns remains impassive, and Creech braces himself for a serious onslaught. "Mr. Creech," says Burns, "much as it pains me to speak o' such matters repeatedly, I feel nonetheless that I must. When I was last in Mauchline, I promised my brother Gilbert I would soon be able to afford him relief from certain financial pressures that had him at a disadvantage." Burns looks increasingly grim. "That was some five months ago, sir. I must press ye for some settlement o' our accounts."

Damn the fellow and his impertinence, Creech thinks. A common farmer, and lucky enough to be taken up by his betters – and where is his gratitude for that? Aloud he says, "Mr. Burns, I'm sensible o' your position, as I ha'e said before. But ye must consider my own. I ha'e many other matters that concern me besides your own – matters that tax my resources to the utmost." He glances sidewise at Burns and risks another smile, then continues. "Patience, Mr. Burns, is the great virtue in affairs o' commerce."

Burns is no fool, Creech knows, and he has heard this explanation before. And indeed the poet sighs now and shakes his head. "If ye'll forgive my saying so, Mr. Creech, patience is a commodity o' which I ha'e expended a great deal. I ha'e troubled ye, I think, as little as could be expected o' a man in my circumstances. I've occupied mysel' wi' tours o' the Borders and the Highlands. I've changed my lodgings. I –"

Before Burns can go on, the doorbell jingles again, heralding the entrance of the Reverend Dr. Hugh Blair. Always pleased to see distinguished customers, Creech now feels a surge of relief at the rotund cleric's opportune appearance. "Ah," he says, beaming, "Dr. Blair."

Blair looks at both men, and Creech can tell that he has noted the tension between them. "I hope that I am not interrupting," he says.

Sure that Blair's presence will have closed the subject, at least for the present, Creech feels able to risk an irony. "Mr. Burns and I were just discussing the vagaries o' commerce."

Blair purses his lips and coughs, evidently a bit put out. "I do not wish to intrude, of course," he says. Then, brightening, he adds, "Unless I might offer assistance in the form of advice?"

"No, no, Dr. Blair," says Burns, making a belated effort to be pleasant. "I'm thankful for the offer, of course." He gives Creech an ironic look. "But I think Mr. Creech and I ha'e reached an understanding on the subject o' our discussion."

"I see," says Blair, undaunted. "But if I might speak to the subject o' finance for a moment?" The scholar's eyes narrow shrewdly. "I think, Mr. Burns, that ye should give serious thought to a London edition o' your poems." He smiles as if the idea could have occurred to no one but himself. "There is the road to advancement and prosperity," he goes on. "Especially if, as I've advised ye before, ye make an effort to work your verse into formal English. I hardly need say that I stand ready to assist ye in any way I can."

Blair looks from Burns to Creech with the expression of a man who has brought unexpected enlightenment to the benighted. Creech himself would never think of mentioning his own negotiations with Cadell of London concerning Burns' work, nor of shaking Blair's pride in his own perspicacity. But Burns is less reticent, or less politic.

"I'm thankful for your wise counsel, Dr. Blair," says the poet. "But the authority o'er further editions o' my poetry rests wi' Mr. Creech here – for he owns the copyright. My only role in the drama at present is to wait for payment." He looks meaningfully at Creech, who feels himself coloring. Then Burns nods to both men. "Now, gentlemen," he says, "much as it distresses me to quit such distinguished company, I must beg your leave to excuse me."

And so saying, Burns nods again and walks out of the shop, his exit punctuated by the bobbing and jangling of the bell on the door. Looking after him, Blair shakes his head. "A gifted man, that Burns," he says. "But an exceedingly strong-headed one."

"Aye," says Creech shortly, still rankling at the poet's rudeness, "and a bit too fond o' the less propitious things he writes about."

Blair's moist eyes gleam with interest. "What do ye mean, Mr. Creech?"

"I hear he's recently been forced to settle wi' some maidservant he's gotten in the family way. And I wouldna be surprised if he's impregnated that mason's lass again as well, back in Ayrshire." Creech sniffs. "Poet Burns may be, but I fancy he kens more about ploughing when a's said and done."

As Blair clicks his tongue disapprovingly, Creech feels his own good spirits recovering from the contretemps with Burns; and he reflects that a wee bit of embarrassment was, after all, small price to pay for having succeeded again in deferring the settlement of accounts for another day. Smiling with satisfaction, he claps Blair on the arm. "Now, sir," he says, "what can I do for ye?"

"Ye see, Mr. Burns, the process o' strikin' the music on pewter plates maks the printin' o' it a cheaper proposition a'thegither. No' that I'll see much profit on an undertakin' the size o' this ane. I thocht at first to print twa volumes, but there's that mony Scotch tunes it'll tak years to gather and print them a'. And there's damned few folk'll be able to afford sic a collection when it's finally done."

James Johnson pauses in his enthusiastic rush of words to glance at Robert, who stands beside him at the counter in the little engraver's Lawnmarket music shop. The first volume of Johnson's *Scottish Musical Museum* lies open before them, as well as one of the pewter plates that helped produce the book. Robert can scarcely bring himself to raise his eyes from the fascinating marriage of words and music on the printed page, especially since the page bears his own version of "Green Grow the Rashes," which Johnson asked him for just prior to his Border tour.

He does meet the little man's friendly gaze, though, and says, "An enterprise like this can only be ca'd patriotic, Mr. Johnson."

"Jeems," says Johnson eagerly. "Jeems, if ye please."

Robert smiles and nods. "And I'm Rab." Then he snorts in exasperation. "When I think on the sangs I've heard aboot Ayrshire. The tunes are only kept alive by a handfu' o' country fiddlers, and the words are half-garbled and half-forgot by every new singer. If somebody doesna lift a hand to preserve them, they'll a' be lost, eventually."

"Aye, Mr. Burns – Rab – ye see clear enough what moves me, a' richt." Johnson runs a hand over his high forehead and through his unkempt grey hair. Robert can see by the engraver's grimy cravat and wrinkled, greasy coat that here is a man driven more by love of music than of money. "But it's like this, Rab," Johnson goes on. "I ken music weel enough, but as for words, I'm an ignorant bugger – I canna spell worth tuppence, for ane thing. And it's words that you excel at."

Robert can scarcely credit the implication of Johnson's words. "Ye dinna mean ye'd want me to help ye wi' the ither volumes?"

Johnson laughs, bringing one of his small, surprisingly delicate hands to his mouth. "God, man," he says, "that's far mair nor I could hope for. Ye ken there's scores o' tunes wi' nae words at a', and ithers wi' just a verse o' twa. And withoot words, a sang's no' a sang. And if ever a man was made to gi'e voice to Scotch music, it's Rabbie Burns!" Again, Johnson seems to check his own runaway enthusiasm, and his voice drops. "Mind," he says, "this is a labor o' love wi' me. I've nae money to pay ye, so I'll understan' if ye canna see your way clear to do it."

"Mr. Johnson. James," says Robert, shaking his head. "I'd be honored to take part in sic a worthy endeavor. And I wouldna think to embarrass you – or mysel', for that matter – wi' selfish demands for siller."

He offers his hand to the little man, who clasps it warmly, his eyes glistening with emotion. Then Robert is struck by a genuine reservation. "I may as weel warn ye," he says, "that I can read music, and get it off by heart easy enough – but I canna write it."

Johnson grins and waves his hands reassuringly. "Dinna fash yoursel' aboot that, Rab. Stephen Clarke will gi'e ye a hand wi' the music. He's the organist o'er at the Episcopal Chapel in the Cowgate, as ye may ken. So what d'ye think, then?"

"I'm your man," says Robert, chuckling with pleasure. "And I'll start this very day!"

Robert looks back over the North Bridge at the Old Town, with its tall, cramped buildings stacked haphazardly along the high southern slope of the North Loch valley, and the Castle farther on, towering over the morass at the valley's west end.

Behind him in the shifting light of the cloudy autumn afternoon lie the neatly geometric streets and structures of the New Town, and he turns now toward its airy and spacious aspect, taking pleasure in the ever-changing shades of green that dapple the Calton Hill off to his right.

He strolls across Princes Street and past the imposing Registry Office on his way to his new lodgings in the attic of Willie Cruikshank's house at Number Two St. James' Square. Jock Richmond has unexpectedly left Edinburgh and returned to Mauchline to set up shop as a law writer there, where he can be near Jenny Surgeoner and his wee daughter, allowing Robert himself to forsake the noise and squalor of Baxter's Close. Therefore, the schoolmaster's offer of accommodation in his New Town home was an ideal solution. Cruikshank lives quietly with only his wife and their daughter Jenny, a rose-cheeked twelve-year-old charmer, so the attic at St. James' Square affords Robert a calm haven of his own; and now that he and Johnson have agreed to work together on the *Museum*, Robert can benefit from Jenny's skill on the spinet. In fact, he thinks as he nears the Cruikshank's door, he must soon write a song for wee Jenny as a thankoffering for the family's kindness; and if Johnson decides to print the song, it will represent a double gift.

The thought of his writing a song for a lassie, however young she may be, turns Robert's mind guiltily to Jean. Not only has he never produced a set of words to "Miss Admiral Gordon's Strathspey," but Jean is pregnant again. Gibby has already taken in two of Robert's bastard weans, Betty Paton's Bess and now Jean's wee Rab; there are limits, Robert knows, to what he can expect from his brother and the rest of the Mossgiel household. With Meg Cameron he could feel justified in settling with her for twenty pounds; after all, his responsibility for her condition is uncertain. And for James and Mary Armour and their hypocritical pandering, he cares not a fig. But Jean is different. Clearly, he must do something – but what, and how?

Silently damning Willie Creech for his tight-fistedness, Robert suddenly thinks of his own father's struggle in the courts over money with David MacLure, the dishonest Tarbolton landlord who drove

William Burns to a bankrupt's death. Robert shudders at the prospect of similar litigation with Creech, for what chance would an Ayrshire farmer have against one of Edinburgh's most prominent citizens?

Shaking his head, he lets himself in at the Cruikshanks' front door. Once inside the house, he is distracted from his sour thoughts by a cheery greeting from young Jenny.

"Hello, Mr. Burns," she says in her sweetly piping voice. She runs to the small mahogany table just inside the door and, picking up two envelopes, hands them to Robert. "These came for ye just a wee while ago."

Robert's spirits sink again at the sight of the larger envelope, for he can tell by the handwriting that it will contain another plea for assistance from Gibby, knowing too that each request has grown more and more querulous with his brother's increasing doubt that Robert means to help at all. The other envelope looks as if it bears an invitation of some kind. "Thank ye, lass," he says to Jenny, forcing a jocular tone. "I'll just ha'e a read at it up in my wee nest."

He climbs to the attic with Jenny's melodic laughter lingering in his ears; then, seating himself at his writing-table, he opens the smaller envelope. The note within is indeed an invitation, requesting his presence for tea a week hence at the home of Miss Erskine Nimmo and her brother William just off Potterrow on Alison Square. "Your friend Mr. Ainslie will be in attendance," writes Miss Nimmo, a stout, pleasant spinster whom Robert has met at several social gatherings, "and you will of course remember my brother Captain Nimmo from meetings of the Crochallan Fencibles."

Robert sets down the invitation, undecided as to how he will respond, and somewhat reluctantly opens the letter from Gibby. The first sentence strikes him like a blow to the chest. "Jean Armour has lost her little girl – and yours – to pneumonia after a fever." Robert stares at the words until they become a watery blur. After a time, he wipes a forearm across his eyes and reads on. "The Armours are still mightily displeased with Jean for her further indiscretions with you," Gibby writes. "If not for the child's death, I would not be surprised at their turning her out nor at their asking for another warrant against yourself. Your sisters, of course, can scarcely thole the mention of Jean's name. Since we are already obbliged to feed two extra mouths here at Mossgiel, and remain in the direst of financial straits, I doubt there is much more you can expect us to do."

Robert drops the letter. Mauchline. The name calls up so much that is dear to him; and yet it holds nearly all that makes his life a misery, too. Small wonder that Richmond left there, and that Jamie Smith has since departed to enter a new business in Linlithgow. Knifing through Robert's grief at the death of wee Jeany is a hard edge of anger: at Willie Creech for his meanness; at the Armours for their vindictive hypocrisy; at Gavin Hamilton for his landlord's mentality that supersedes friendship; at Gibby for his straitlaced disapproval; at Jean for her very helplessness. He can hear his mother's voice railing at him, too, for his refusal to live with the world as it is, to remain within the limitations placed upon him by birth. And he realizes that, given the chance, he could cheerfully bring down the entire corrupt and oppressive order of things, as the American colonists have done, as the French peasantry seem likely to do.

He rises and paces frantically, wishing he could smash something, but unwilling to disturb the Cruikshank household. He must do something. Creech is immovable. And he can take no action as regards Ellisland Farm without money to lease it. Only an Excise commission seems to offer immediate promise. But how to go about it? He sits and looks again at the invitation from Miss Nimmo. Her brother William is an Excise supervisor, is he not? Perhaps he can help. Robert lays out a sheet of paper, opens his inkwell, and takes up his pen.

Miss Erskine Nimmo is troubled. She looks across the room to where Robert Burns and her brother are standing tête-à-tête, apparently still discussing the Excise. That a man like Burns would consider such a mundane calling is bad enough, but that he should take time to talk about it at her tea party is all but intolerable.

And sitting next to her, Agnes MacLehose tugs at Miss Nimmo's sleeve and whispers, "Erskine – do something!"

Agnes – or Nancy, as she prefers – is the main reason for the gathering itself. Miss Nimmo's closest friend, she has admired Burns and has wanted to meet him since his arrival in Edinburgh, and now here he is, talking not to her, but to her hostess' brother. Miss Nimmo smiles reassuringly at Nancy and, not for the first time, wishes her own appearance could stir men's admiration as her friend's does. Nancy is elegant in a dress of lavender silk that displays her fine bosom to good advantage, and her golden hair frames her cleanly-modeled face in a mass of curls. How, Miss Nimmo wonders, could a man allow himself to fall to such dissolution as Captain MacLehose has, to desert such a lovely wife and roam to the feverish climes of far-off Jamaica?

Nancy plucks again at Miss Nimmo's sleeve and, nodding, she turns to Robert Ainslie, who is seated nearby, balancing a cup and saucer on his knee and munching at a slice of currant cake. "Robert," she says, "can ye not convince Mr. Burns to abandon business for more social pursuits?"

Hurriedly chewing the last bite of cake, Ainslie sets down his tea and rises. "Certainly, ladies," he says somewhat indistinctly, his tongue sweeping residue of the cake from inside his mouth. Then he crosses the room in his light-footed way to confront the two taller men. "Captain Nimmo. Robert. The ladies crave the pleasure of your conversation."

William clears his throat and nods reflexively. "Indeed," he says, "Mr. Burns and I ha'e concluded our business anyhow." He spreads his hands helplessly. "I fear I've been little enough help to ye, Mr. Burns, beyond a few scraps o' information about the onerous duties o' an exciseman. But if ye're set on such a post, I'd write to Mr. Robert Graham of Fintry, for he's a commissioner o' the Excise Board, and far more influential than a mere supervisor."

"I thank ye for the good advice, Captain Nimmo." Burns smiles at William, then turns his searching eyes on the two women.

Miss Nimmo feels herself blushing; but she takes comfort in noting that Nancy's bosom, too, has turned a more than healthy pink. To cover her momentary confusion, she says, "Mr. Burns, might we not have the privilege of hearing some o' your new verses?"

Nancy, her fan working away rapidly, adds her own voice to this request. "Oh, yes, Mr. Burns," she says. "That would be delightful." She fixes the poet with what Miss Nimmo can only think of as a bold stare, and goes on, "I must confess that I am a bit of a secret scribbler. I have long looked forward to meeting you and hearing your poetry at first-hand."

To Miss Nimmo's disquiet, Burns looks back at Nancy as if she were the only other person in the room. "I am flattered, Madam," he says. "And may I say how glad I am to be in your own company. I should be most happy to see your poetry someday soon." He takes a folded sheet of paper from his pocket. "I have recently finished a little song," he says, offering the sheet to Nancy. "I wonder if you might do me the honor of singing it for the company?"

Nancy's fan positively dances before her face. "Oh, I couldn't," she says, but Miss Nimmo can tell that her friend is merely waiting to be coaxed.

"The tune was composed by a friend from Ayrshire – Mr. David Sillar. But it's simple enough." Burns smiles at Miss Nimmo. "And I'm sure our gracious hostess will be well able to pick it out on the spinet for you. Is that not so, Miss Nimmo?"

Now Miss Nimmo plies her own fan, until she sees her brother glowering at the display. Face warm again, she says, "I fancy I can do something with it, Mr. Burns." And so saying, she plucks the paper from Burns' hand and sweeps across the room to the spinet, where she sits poised and waiting for the startled Nancy.

"Please, Mrs. MacLehose," says the wicked Ainslie, looking amused as usual at any discomposure in those around him

"Yes, Nancy," says Miss Nimmo, a trifle impatient with her friend's coyness. "Come on!"

"Forgive me, Madam" – Burns trains his dark eyes again on Nancy – "but I understood your first name to be Agnes."

Miss Nimmo notes that her friend does not avert her own eyes from Burns' gaze before answering. "I am Nancy to those who know me well," she says, her voice low and melodic.

Burns extends his hand to her. "Then if I," he says, "the newest of acquaintances, may count myself among your friends, . . . please, Nancy."

"Very well. I will try."

Nancy crosses to Burns and allows him to escort her to the spinet, where she peers over Miss Nimmo's shoulder at the words and music of the song. After a short time, she touches Miss Nimmo's arm and nods, smiling, to show that she is ready to perform.

Miss Nimmo improvises a simple introduction and Nancy begins to sing in her clear soprano, a bit tremulous and tentative at first, but then with growing assurance:

"A Rose-bud by my early walk,
Adown a corn-enclosed bawk,
Sae gently bent its thorny stalk,
    All on a dewy morning.
Ere twice the shades o' dawn are fled,
In a' its crimson glory spread,
And drooping rich the dewy head,
    It scents the early morning."

As Nancy completes the first stanza, Miss Nimmo notes that, while the rest of the company are obviously pleased by the song, Burns himself is clearly more taken with the singer, and that Nancy seems unaware of any audience other than the poet. Clearly her friend may need a gentle reminder that, deserted and wronged though she may be, she is still a married woman. But now Nancy looks down quizzically, and Miss Nimmo resumes playing.

"Within the bush her covert nest
A little linnet fondly prest;
The dew sat chilly on her breast,
    Sae early in the morning.
She soon shall see her tender brood,
The pride, the pleasure o' the wood,
Amang the fresh green leaves bedew'd,
    Awake the early morning.

So thou, dear bird, young Jeany fair,
On trembling string or vocal air,
Shall sweetly pay the tender care
    That tents thy early morning.
So thou, sweet Rose-bud, young and gay,
Shalt beauteous blaze upon the day,
And bless the parent's evening ray
    That watched thy early morning."

Nancy ends the song on a pure and steady note, and Miss Nimmo punctuates with a flourish at the keyboard. After a respectful moment, the company breaks into applause for performers and writer alike.

But Burns has eyes only for the singer. "Thank you," he says, nodding to Miss Nimmo. Then he seizes Nancy's hand. "Madam." He kisses her fingertips with a fervor bordering on the unseemly. "That was wonderful."

Nancy closes her eyes for a moment, then withdraws her hand and brings it to her bosom. "Thank you, Mr. Burns," she says at last, slightly breathless. "Your words inspired me." Then she looks him directly in the eye, her tone becoming arch. "I am sure they inspired the young lady lucky enough to be their object, too."

"Aye." Burns grins at her playfully. "A bonnie lass, right enough." He waits for a moment or two before adding, "Wee Jean Cruikshank, the daughter o' my new landlord. She's twelve."

This draws a high pitched giggle from Ainslie and titters from the rest of the company, including Miss Nimmo, who welcomes a bit of lightness in what she sees as a situation with potentially serious consequences. But far from dispelling the tension between Burns and Nancy, her consternation now causes him to take her hand and lead her to a pair of chairs near a window.

Miss Nimmo, feeling the need to reestablish general conversation, rises from the spinet and places a hand on Ainslie's arm. "Was that not the Reverend Dr. Blair I saw you speaking with on the High Street the other day?"

"Aye," says Ainslie. "He deigned to pass a minute or two wi' me – to offer instruction on how I might succeed at law, for all that it's no' meant to be his chosen subject."

"Yes," says Miss Nimmo, casting about for an opening. "I thought he looked as if he had put on a bit of weight." She calls across the room to Burns, who is seated next to Nancy, speaking quietly. "Mr. Burns! Do you not think that Dr. Blair has grown exceedingly fat these past few months?"

Burns looks up with the trace of a scowl, then smiles tightly. "Once you've said that, Miss Nimmo, you've exhausted the subject o' Dr. Blair – for as far as I can see, fatness is his only quality." He turns back to Nancy. "Perhaps, Mrs. MacLehose," he says, "we can discuss when I might pay a visit to examine your own verses."

William Cruikshank bounces painfully on the coach seat across from Robert Burns, who looks as appalled as Cruikshank feels at the bone-rattling pace of their homeward journey. The two men are returning to St. James' Square from a night's carouse with Willie Smellie and the other Crochallan Fencibles at Dawney Douglas'. And now Cruikshank begins to suspect that their coachman has imbibed pretty freely somewhere himself.

"The bugger must be drunk!" he says, shouting to be heard over the clatter of the wheels as the coach judders and careens over the North Bridge.

"Aye," says Robert, "ye're richt! I'll say something to him." He struggles around on his seat and shouts at the coachman's back. "Use your reins, man, no' your bloody whip!"

The coachman, a square-jawed fellow with bad teeth and pale hair like straw hanging out of a midden, turns to bawl an answer; but as he does so the coach reaches the sharp turn at the foot of the hill that ends at Register House.

"Mind what ye're aboot!" Cruikshank cries.

But the warning comes too late, for the coach suddenly tips, teeters briefly on two wheels, then tumbles over and spills driver and passengers alike on the cold wet cobblestones of Leith Street. Cruikshank loses track of where he is for a bit, but when his head stops whirling, he realizes he has escaped real injury, save for a bruised hip and elbow. Rising slowly to his feet, though, he becomes aware that Robert is still lying in the street, moaning in agony and clutching his left knee.

"My God, laddie," says Cruikshank, bending over him, "is it broken, do ye think?"

"I dinna ken." Robert can barely speak. "I dinna ken." He rolls back and forth, gasping. "Curse the bloody luck," he says.

"We're no' far from home." Cruikshank looks about him and sees the coachman sitting nursing a bump on his head, then notices some neighbors gathering to survey the scene. "Somebody away and get the doctor for Mr. Burns," he says. "Lang Sandy Wood up at the Exchange." And having dispatched a lad to fetch the physician, Cruikshank solicits the aid of two or three able men to carry his tenant to St. James' Square. "Ye'll be a' right," he mutters to the stricken Burns. "We'll ha'e ye in your bed in two shakes wi' a glass o' brandy. Then when Lang Sandy arrives he'll get some laudanum in ye. That'll dull the pain."

The mention of laudanum seems to stir Burns from his fog of agony. "Dinna let me forget!" he says. "Dinna let me forget!"

Cruikshank bends to him. "Forget what, laddie?"

Gasping with the effort, Burns says, "I maun write to Mrs. MacLehose. I was invited to tak tea wi' her the morrow. And now I'll no' be able, worse luck. Dinna let me forget to write."

"Never fear," says Cruikshank, clapping Robert's shoulder. "We'll set ye up in bed wi' paper and pen." Then he hurries ahead to open the front door of his house, reflecting that the prospect of a missed engagement with Agnes MacLehose seems to be causing Burns nearly as much distress as his injured knee.

1788

My dear Clarinda,

Your last verses have so delighted me, that I have copied them in among some of my own most valued pieces,
which I keep sacred for my own use. Do, let me have a
few now and then.

Did you, Madam, know what I feel when you talk of
your sorrows!

Good God! that one who has so much worth in the
sight of Heaven, and is so amiable to her fellow-creatures,
should be so unhappy! I can't venture out for cold. My
limb is vastly better; but I have not any use of it without my crutches. Monday, for the first time, I dine at a
neighbor's, next door. As soon as I can go so far, even in a
coach, my first visit shall be to you . . . Farewell!

SYLVANDER

letter to AGNES MACLEHOSE, Edinburgh
3rd January 1788

Chapter Twenty

With the aid of a walking-stick, Robert limps down the Bristow Port from Greyfriar's Kirkyard, his left leg throbbing in the cold January air. Several weeks bed-rest and the ministrations of Lang Sandy Wood have not entirely mended the dislocated kneecap, and Robert prefers not to walk anywhere if he can avoid it. Nonetheless, he has just discharged his sedan chair to avoid attracting undue attention in approaching Agnes – or Nancy – MacLehose's apartment in General's Entry off the Potterrow.

The risk means little to Robert, himself, but Mrs. MacLehose has several times expressed concern for her reputation in the numerous letters they have exchanged since his injury. At her behest, in fact, they have taken to conducting their correspondence under the pastoral pseudonyms of Clarinda and Sylvander. Tonight, however, they will see each other for the first time since they met at Miss Nimmo's tea, and Robert feels hopeful that his physical presence will lessen Clarinda's insistence on propriety. The thought of this lovely woman, educated and refined, with her pale skin, her tumble of golden curls, and her obvious interest in him, stirs a pleasurable flutter in his stomach.

Now he makes his way carefully across the cobblestones of General's Entry. He pauses for a moment outside Mrs. MacLehose's first-floor flat, then reaches out with his walking-stick and taps at the door. Almost immediately a young woman appears before him, wearing the mutch and apron of a maid-of-all-work. The servant's garb cannot conceal the lassie's appealingly slight figure and pretty face, however, and Robert gives her an appreciative smile. "Mr. Burns to see Mrs. MacLehose," he says, taking off his wide-brimmed hat.

"Is it true, then?" The girl widens her dark blue eyes coquettishly. "You are Mr. Burns, the poet?"

The ingenuousness of the question amuses him. "Aye, lass," he says, chuckling. "Does that mean ought to ye, then?"

She smiles, somehow managing to convey both pertness and deference. "It's an honor to meet ye, I'm sure."

"What's your name, lass?" he asks, intrigued.

This direct inquiry turns the girl suddenly shy, unwilling to meet his eyes. "Jenny," she says softly. "Jenny Clow, sir."

He laughs and chucks her playfully under the chin, his own skin suddenly alive as he touches the smooth line of her throat. "Here now, Jenny," he says, laughing, "I'm only a man. And as fair a flower as you needna shrink afore ony mere man."

"I'll tak ye in to Mrs. Mac, then," she says, flirtatious again. Then, as she turns to lead him into the flat, she adds slyly, "I'm thinkin' she'll no' need to shrink, either."

Robert follows Jenny into the living room, where a coal fire dances in a small grate set in a chimney that juts out from the far wall between two windows, now discreetly shuttered. He notes with satisfaction an arrangement of dried heather, both purple and white, on the mantel, and several carefully-placed candles that reinforce the fire's cheery glow. The air smells sweet with the scent of herbs, and a love-seat and chair stand invitingly on either side of the hearth, flanking a small polished table. Mrs. MacLehose is nowhere to be seen.

Jenny moves quickly to an open door on the right and calls out, "Mr. Burns, ma'am."

After a moment or two, Nancy MacLehose sweeps into the room, resplendent in a dress of blue satin, with a lace fichu around her milky shoulders and her hair, burnished by the fire, tied up in a black velvet ribbon. She gives her maid a prim nod. "Thank you, Jenny." Then, smiling, she turns her luminous blue eyes on Robert. "I am delighted to see you again, sir."

He strides to her and kisses her lavender-scented hand, then gives her a look emboldened by the elegant but fervid language of their correspondence. "And I am transported by joy beyond belief to be in your presence once more, madam," he says.

Then, turning from his blushing hostess, Robert hands his hat and cane to Jenny Clow who, from the sparkle in her eyes seems to be enjoying herself. "Will there be anything else, ma'am?" she says.

Still blushing, Mrs. MacLehose fidgets with the loose knot of lace at her bosom. "Mr. Burns and I will take tea," she says at last. "Thank you, Jenny."

"Very good, ma'am." The little maid makes a perfunctory curtsy, then leaves the room with a knowing smile.

Mrs. MacLehose looks after her with a small frown, then settles herself in the love-seat beside the fire. "Pray be seated, Mr. Burns," she says, then turns to look into the shifting flames.

Robert moves to sit beside her, then thinks better of it and takes the chair. "Thank you," he says.

She looks up from the fire, apparently startled not to find him next to her. Recovering her poise quickly, though, she says, "I fear, Mr. Burns, that Jenny is an all-too-accurate mirror of the world's view of our meeting like this. Though we are innocent, I am acutely sensible of the dangers to my reputation – and to yours for that matter."

Robert rises from the chair and moves behind it. Now is no time for reticence, he thinks. "Never fear on my account, madam – Clarinda – or Nancy, if I may be so bold. My only concern is for yourself. As for me, I am headstrong and careless to a fault, I know, and likely to act as my passions move me." He glances down at the red heart of the fire. "But in that event," he says, "I can willingly stand like Milton's Satan – against a' the blows and brands and flails that pious hypocrisy might torment me wi'."

He leans across the back of the chair toward her and speaks intensely. "The world is full o' those that would see intrigue in any tender regard a man might hold for a woman. But if you choose that we should remain the most brotherly and sisterly o' friends, I can only honor your wish." He draws himself upright, trying to gauge the effect of his declaration. "Then the world will find little to complain of."

Mrs. MacLehose raises a plump white hand before her. "Please, Mr. Burns – Sylvander – "

Quickly moving to her, he says, "Between us here let it be Robert and Nancy!"

She looks up and meets his eyes momentarily, then drops her gaze again. "Very well – Robert. But please do not upset me with declarations we cannot act upon." She pauses, then goes on more softly, "It disturbs me, too – and frightens – that you find Satan a fit object of praise."

Robert paces across the room, thinking quickly, then turns back to her. "What I admire in the Satan o' Milton," he says, "is his manly fortitude in bearing what canna be remedied – the wild broken fragments o' a noble mind in ruins. I meant no more."

Her expression softens. "I am sorry, then, to doubt you so quickly. Such admiration is itself to be admired." She gestures at the space beside her on the love-seat and goes on brightly, "But come, sir. I wish to know more of you, who are so worthy of regard yourself."

Pleased, he starts toward her. "I would much prefer," he says, "to discuss you – and your admirable verses."

In fact, though he admires Nancy's mind, he finds her poetry pallid and conventional; but what harm can there be in a bit of flattery? In any case, his words seem to have produced the desired effect, for she is now smiling at him openly.

Just as he begins to take his place on the love-seat, however, Jenny Clow enters suddenly from the other room with a laden tray. "The tea, ma'am," she says, with an impish smile.

Amused but a touch unsettled, Robert moves aside. And Nancy, somewhat discomposed herself, says, "Set the tray down on the table, Jenny." As the little maid does so, her mistress adds, "And please announce yourself more fittingly in future."

"Yes, ma'am," says Jenny, her eyes on Robert.

"That will be all, Jenny," says Nancy coldly.

"Yes, ma'am." With a last smile at Robert, the girl reluctantly leaves the room.

Nancy looks at the door for some moments after Jenny has disappeared. Finally, not without visible effort, she turns back to Robert and, once more beckoning him to take his place beside her, says sweetly, "Now, . . . Robert. Perhaps we can resume our discussion without further disturbance."

Bob Ainslie, seated in the Cruikshanks' parlor at St. James' Square, sips delicately at the claret that Rab Burns has just poured for him. Across the room Burns finishes serving Jock Richmond, who is back from Mauchline for the winter Sessions; then Robert resumes his seat, fills his own glass, and raises it.

"Your health, gentlemen."

Having observed the ritual, Richmond looks around the comfortable room and says, "Aye, Rab, I can see how ye'd be happier here than in Baxter's Close. We're both weel oot o' yon dark hole."

"Mind," says Burns, looking serious, "I dinna ha'e the run o' the hoose like this a' the time. But the Cruikshanks are grand folk, and they said I could entertain you two in the parlor the day while they were oot. And it's true I ha'e mair room here, and less noise and a'.

Besides, wi' you awa' back to Mauchline, Jock, there was nothing to keep me at Mrs. Carfrae's." He smiles at Richmond. "It's grand to see ye again."

Richmond takes a swallow of wine. "Aye," he says. "I wish ye were back in Mauchline yoursel', Rab."

"Aiblins I will be," says Burns, turning somber again. Then he grins suddenly. "I'd sooner be there than amang yon jades in Baxter's Close again! I wonder if Mrs. Carfrae has finally saved their souls for them?"

Richmond laughs. "I dinna think she could afford to save them. She'd sooner suffer their sin than lose their siller!"

Feeling a bit left out, Ainslie speaks up. "Talking aboot souls, Rab, ye'd best keep a watch on your ain, or ye'll be losing it to Agnes MacLehose."

"Nothing o' the kind," says Burns lightly. "For God's sake, man, I was laid up here wi' this damned knee for nearly a month after I met her. It's only days since I've been able to hirple o'er the doorstep."

"Aye," says Ainslie dryly. "But I was at Miss Nimmo's last month, and I ha'e eyes. Ye needna tell me ye havena written to her, . . . or arranged to meet her under . . . mair advantageous circumstances."

Burns smiles at this, tongue in cheek. "No, I couldna tell ye that," he says archly. "We've exchanged a number o' letters." Then a note of triumph enters his voice. "And I had the pleasure o' calling on her last week!"

"I kenned it!" Ainslie giggles, pleased by this confirmation of his own acuteness. "Damned but ye're a rogue, Rab Burns." He leans forward conspiratorially. "And how do matters progress?"

Burns pulls a much-handled sheet of stationery from his pocket and unfolds it. "Listen to this!" And he reads aloud. "'I will not deny it, . . . last night was one of the most exquisite I have ever experienced. Few such fall to the lot of mortals!'" He folds the letter and pockets it again, smiling with satisfaction. "I'd say I have her interest."

Ainslie cannot suppress another high-pitched snicker. "And how much mair?" he says. Then, probing more delicately, he adds, "It must ha'e been a delightful evening."

Burns shrugs. "We talked, I fear. Merely talked." Then he brightens. "But by Heaven she's a beauty. And as elegant a conversationalist as ye could wish for." He adopts a musing tone. "But I've scarcely begun my campaign. I think her inclinations bode weel. She's a healthy enough woman, God knows."

"Aye," says Ainslie, "and a determined ane, I fancy. But mind yoursel', though," he adds. "She's still married – and three weans into the bargain."

Burns snorts explosively. "Her weans are weel oot o' the road in Glasgow wi' relations. And her husband – if he still deserves the name – he's even further away – in Jamaica! I dinna ken how ye can ca' that 'married.'"

Richmond, who has been uncharacteristically silent, rises abruptly and glares at Burns. "That's what the law and the Kirk ca' it," he says. Then, stiffly, he asks, "And what aboot Jean?"

Burns, too, gets to his feet. "Jean's nothing to do wi' it!" he says sharply. "The Armours ha'e made their ain trouble." Then, lowering his voice, he adds, "I ken you still mean to wed Jenny Surgeoner, Jock. But your case and mine are different a'thegither. And I need to think o' my future."

Richmond's back stiffens and he drinks off his claret. "There seems damned little future in the likes o' Agnes MacLehose, if ye ask me."

"I'll provide for Jean, a' richt – never you fear!" Burns stares at Richmond, face suffused with blood, and Ainslie begins to wish he had never mentioned the subject. But before matters can go further, there is a knock at the front door, and Robert hurries away to answer it, leaving the other two alone in awkward silence.

When Robert returns, though, he bears two envelopes, one freshly-opened, and his mood has improved greatly. "Listen to this," he says, grinning. "It's a poem frae Clarinda. That's what Agnes ca's hersel' in our correspondence."

Ainslie chuckles. "Agnes. Nancy. Clarinda. She gi'es ye a whole trinity o' goddesses to worship."

"And what does she ca' you?" inquires Richmond, eyeing Robert sourly.

Burns reddens. "Sylvander," he says, his reply scarcely audible.

"God save us," says Richmond, shaking his head.

"Come," says Ainslie, unwilling to lose this opportunity, "let us hear the verses."

Still glowering at Richmond, Burns lays down the unopened envelope on a table, takes out the other letter, and begins to read: "'Lines from Clarinda to Sylvander':

Talk not of Love – it gives me pain, for Love
    has been my foe;
He bound me in an iron chain, and plunged me
    deep in woe!
But Friendship's pure and lasting joys my
    heart was formed to prove –
The worthy object be of those, but never talk
    of Love!"

Smiling proudly, Robert looks at the others. Richmond is visibly unimpressed, and Ainslie cannot find it within himself to praise the mundane language and sentiments. But Robert seems oblivious. "Ah," he says, "what a pleasure to meet a woman wi' the powers o' discourse as weel as beauty!"

Feeling a stab of envy that undercuts his ironic tone, Ainslie says, "She's a fortress weel worth the storming, richt enough."

Richmond picks up the unopened envelope from the table. "This is frae Mauchline," he says, "so I fancy ye'll be in nae hurry to read it."

Robert snatches the envelope from Richmond's hand, then stares at him for a few moments, obviously struggling to retain a semblance of good humor. "I'll ha'e a look," he says at last.

He slits the envelope with his penknife and withdraws the letter, a brief scrawl on a single sheet. Reading it virtually at a glance, he tosses it aside, breathing deeply and expelling the air with a hiss between clenched teeth.

"My God, Rab," says Richmond, his disapproval suddenly replaced by concern. "What is it?"

"It's frae Jean Smith." Robert looks at them with dull eyes. "The Armours ha'e turned Jean out into the street like a common whore!"

Obviously distracted, he paces away from his guests toward the mantelpiece. Ainslie hangs back, unsure of what to do, but Richmond follows him. "I'm heartily sorry, Rab," he says. "Will ye go to her?"

"I dinna ken," Robert says. "I suppose I'll need to, eventually." He shakes his head as if bewildered. "In the meantime I can aiblins send word to Willie Muir at the mill in Tarbolton and see if he'll tak her in."

"Aye," says Richmond, nodding. "But surely," he adds, "ye'll ha'e done wi' this MacLehose woman now?"

Burns wheels on him, mouth forming an angry retort. Then, catching himself, he says stiffly, "I couldna do that within the bounds o' courtesy!"

Richmond looks at him steadily for a time, and Ainslie holds his breath in apprehension. Finally, though, Richmond gives a curt nod. "Ye'll excuse me," he says shortly. "For I ha'e business up the road at the Sessions." He backs away a few steps, still looking at Robert, then turns and walks out of the parlor.

Ainslie expects Robert to follow, but instead he sits on a chair next to the fireplace and sighs deeply. Feeling out of his depth, Ainslie takes a sip of claret and swirls it on his tongue until he hears the front door close behind Richmond. Then, setting his glass on the mantel, he says, "What will ye do, Rab?"

"I dinna ken," says Burns softly. "But whatever it is, there'll aey be somebody to tell me it's the wrang thing."

"Robert – my dear Robert – we cannot seem to keep the word 'love' from our lips."

Nancy MacLehose stands at one of the shuttered windows in the living room of her flat, as if she would like to see out; but Robert knows she is more afraid of someone's seeing in. Rising from his chair at the fireplace, he says, "Nor should we shrink from it, Nancy. You have declared your fond regard for me. And never has any woman more entirely possessed my soul. How can that fail to raise the tenderest o' passions?"

Turning from the window, Nancy lifts a hand to the white hollow of her throat. "Your sentiments almost make me swoon into unreason, Robert." When Robert starts toward her, though, she retreats to a mirror hanging above the sideboard and begins fussing at her hair. "But you know I am bound by strictures of law and religion from any such lapse."

Robert moves behind her and is pleased when the reflection of her blue eyes meets his own urgent gaze for a moment before she looks away. "What passes between us here is a lapse in no other's sight," he says. "The God o' Love is blind – wi' good reason!"

Again Nancy breaks away from him, this time returning to the mantelpiece, where the firelight paints her pale skin in shifting hues of reddish gold. "But can love be genuine," she says, "if it hesitate a moment to sacrifice every selfish gratification to the happiness of its object?" As Robert moves back to stand near the chair he left moments before, she goes on: "When it would purchase one at the expense of the other, does it deserve the name of love" – she sinks onto the love-seat – "or one too gross to mention?"

Her language and her demeanor are like an acting-out of her letters, Robert thinks – an admixture of politesse and desire that remains suspended, like a goblet held by a statue, its contents never to be drunk. Driven by his own ill-suppressed passion, he crosses the room in a few strides and finds himself again before the sideboard. Seeing his image in the mirror, he notes that now, in the month of his twenty-ninth birthday, the dark hair seems to be thinning above his brow; and he tries without success to imagine himself in old age, weary and beaten like his father.

"I've told ye," he says carefully, "I must leave Edinburgh to deal with matters that call me back to Mauchline." He turns to look at her. "Jean Armour, to whom you know I once gave my heart, requires my assistance in a grave and delicate circumstance. All too soon I'll be denied the very gratification o' seeing ye – for God knows how long!"

"It wounds me to think of your absence," Nancy says, her eyes shining. "And of your caring for another."

Sensing that he has finally moved her beyond mere play, Robert once more crosses the room to stand over her. "She's no more to me than an obligation!" he declares. "And you are my very soul!" Guilt stirs inside him, but he pushes himself beyond it. "Think, Nancy," he says, pressing his body next to hers on the love-seat, "love's fond kiss? Could that be gross?" He embraces her, and she startles him by turning in his arms and kissing him, open-mouthed, forcing him back against the love-seat's wooden arm. Light-headed from the lavender scent of her, he breaks momentarily from the kiss and whispers in her ear: "Or love's caress?"

And moving his lips again on hers, he runs his fingers lightly over her cheek. She responds with a gasp and a low moan. By degrees he allows his hand to descend to her neck's silken curve and, finally, to the soft mound of her breast. She squirms against him, tightening her arms around his shoulders. Thus encouraged, he slips his hand into her dress, cupping the warm breast and kneading the nipple to hardness with his fingertips. Nancy looses a high-pitched cry of pleasure and rakes his hair with her fingernails. Almost without thinking Robert withdraws his hand from her bosom and drops it to her waist, stroking her belly and circling down to force her thighs apart, feeling the damp heat radiating from her, and all the while moving his tongue on hers.

Suddenly, though, she breaks from his embrace, her breathing rapid and shallow. "Robert! Robert!" she gasps, pushing him away. "What can we be thinking of?" She waves a hand before her mouth. "We cannot let such things occur between us!" She turns away, unwilling to meet his eyes, several strands of golden hair clinging to the corner of her mouth. "I must ask you to go now, Robert," she says, "for fear we may fall prey again to our baser instincts."

Robert rises and looks down at her, then sighs with barely controlled exasperation. "Aye," he says.

Nancy MacLehose pulls the shutter open a fraction and watches Burns cross the frost-rimed cobblestoned court of General's Entry, still limping slightly from the injury to his knee.

What torture to send him away at such a time, she thinks. But what would the Reverend Kemp, her minister and confidant in most things, say of such conduct as tonight's? Or Lord Dreghorn, her cousin and sometime benefactor? No, she must not yield, however importunate Robert may be, however insistent the urgings of her own heart and body.

As Robert disappears around the corner of the adjoining tenement, Nancy pushes the shutter to and stands there for a moment or two, breathing deeply. But a soft rustling behind her fills her with a sudden rush of guilty panic, and she turns to the sound.

Jenny Clow stands at the door, her lips curved in a tiny smile, looking wise beyond her years. "Will ye be wanting anything more, ma'am?" she says.

Nancy gives her a look and considers reprimanding the girl for her forwardness; but she finally decides that any such response would be unwise. "No, Jenny," she says. "I am perfectly content."

Silhouette of "Clarinda" (Agnes MacLehose)

My ever dearest Clarinda,

I make a numerous dinner-party wait me while I read yours and write this. Do not require that I should cease to love you, to adore you in my soul; 'tis to me impossible: your peace and happiness are to me dearer than my soul. Name the terms on which you wish to see me, to correspond with me, and you have them. I must love, pine, mourn, and adore in secret: this you must not deny me. You will ever be to me

"Dear as the light that visits those sad eyes,
"Dear as the ruddy drops that warm my heart."

. . . Farewell! I'll be with you to-morrow evening; and be at rest in your mind. I will be yours in the way you think most to your happiness. I dare not proceed. I love, and will love you; and will, with joyous confidence, approach the throne of the Almighty Judge of men with your dear idea; and will despise the scum of sentiment and the mist of sophistry.

SYLVANDER

letter to AGNES MACLEHOSE, Edinburgh
3th February 1788

Chapter Twenty-One

Robert sits alone in John Dowie's tavern, finishing a meager birthday meal of bread, cheese, and mutton stew, which he washes down with an occasional swallow of ale. He has just come from a brief meeting with James Johnson at the music shop, where he gave the engraver several new songs for the *Museum*. As he mops up the remains of his stew with a crust of bread, his head rings with the strains of a freshly-written lyric called "Clarinda, Mistress of My Soul."

And the thought of Nancy reminds him that in his pocket is a letter to which he must compose a persuasive reply. After passing his coat sleeve over the tabletop, he takes the letter out and spreads it before him. Then he drains his pint stoup and signals Dowie for another. While waiting, he reads the first line or so in Nancy's constricted hand: "Sylvander, the moment I waked this morning, I received a summons from Conscience to appear at the Bar of Reason." Then follows a somewhat labored description of the various personified virtues who admonish her against passion. This concludes, mercifully, with a return to plainer language: "Sylvander, to drop my metaphor, I am neither well nor happy today."

"Here ye are, Mr. Burns," says Dowie, placing a full stoup of ale at Robert's elbow. The landlord then gathers up the remains of the meal. "Will ye want anything else, then?"

Robert glances down at the letter. "Aye, Mr. Dowie," he says. "I'd be grateful for something to write on, if ye please."

Dowie touches a finger to his tricorne hat. "Nae bother," he says, and hurries away, returning shortly with pen and ink and several sheets of writing-paper. "There ye are."

After thanking the landlord, Robert again glances over the opening of Nancy's letter. Clearly, his reply will need to strike a similarly extravagant tone. He takes up the pen, dips it into the inkwell, and begins to write: "Clarinda, my life, you have wounded my soul. Can I think of your being unhappy . . . without being miserable?"

Having penned these lines, he returns to Nancy's elaborately troubled sentiments: "My heart reproaches me for last night. If you wish Clarinda to regain her peace, determine against everything but what the strictest delicacy warrants."

Robert shakes his head, reflecting that Nancy has far less to reproach herself for than he could have hoped. But again he recognizes the need to answer in kind. "Oh Love and Sensibility," he writes, "ye have conspired against my Peace! I love to madness and I feel to torture! Clarinda, how can I forgive myself, that I have touched a single chord in your bosom" – and here he cannot suppress a smile at his own wit – "with pain!"

He pauses, pen suspended above the inkwell, and rereads another of Nancy's effusions: "Delicacy, you know, won me to you at once; take care you do not loosen the dearest, most sacred tie that unites us."

"Would I do it willingly?" Robert writes. "Would any consideration, any gratification, make me do so?"

"I do not blame you," says Nancy's letter, "but myself. I must not see you . . . unless I find I can depend on myself acting otherwise. . . . Remember Clarinda's present and eternal happiness depends upon her adherence to Virtue. Happy Sylvander! that can be attached to Heaven and Clarinda together. Alas! I feel I cannot serve two masters. God pity me!"

Robert can nearly hear Nancy's voice in her letter's closing lines, can sense her almost theatrical enjoyment beneath the throb of emotion. Well, he thinks, he is equal to the game, and he begins to write rapidly: "Oh, did you love like me, you would not, you could not, deny or put off a meeting with the Man who adores you; – who would die a thousand deaths before he would injure you; and who must soon bid you a long farewell!"

A few more lines aimed at arranging a rendezvous on the following evening, and Robert signs the letter decisively. Then he drinks off the last of his ale and calls to the landlord, "Mr. Dowie! I'll tak a dram o' Kilbagie now." He may as well drink a solitary toast to his birthday, for as the years go by he feels more and more alone, even in the midst of the social throng. And as he waits for Dowie's to pour his dram, he looks down again at the two letters. "Damn it to hell." he mutters. "If I had her on a straw pallet for five minutes, I'd touch a chord in her, a' richt!"

Seeing Dowie draw near, Robert hurriedly gathers up the letters. The landlord sets the dram of Kilbagie on the table, then says, "Will ye still want the pen and ink, Mr. Burns?"

Robert's first impulse is to let Dowie remove the writing imple-
ments, but then he waves him off. "Och, just lea'e them, Mr. Dowie.
Aiblins I'll think o' something else yet."

Alone again, he lifts his glass and takes a sip, congratulating
himself silently on entering his thirtieth year and idly imagining what
life might be like on Ellisland Farm with Nancy MacLehose. But, as
the whisky fumes rise in his nostrils, the tune that haunts his memory
is not "Clarinda, Mistress of My Soul," but "Miss Admiral Gordon's
Strathspey." And, bringing pen to paper once more, he finds himself
writing four unexpected lines:

> "Of a' the airts the wind can blaw
> I dearly like the west,
> For there the bonie lassie lives,
> The lassie I lo'e best."

He takes another swallow of Kilbagie and smiles, hearing the
words in his head. Perhaps something will come of this.

Nancy MacLehose stands beside the mantelpiece in her flat,
rereading the letter that Robert sent her yesterday. Robert himself is
looking at her from the love-seat, his face flushed, evidently from the
port he says he consumed earlier in the evening with Bob Ainslie. He
seems far from intoxicated, though, and he looks manly and handsome in his blue coat, buckskin breeches, and riding boots.

"Your letter pierced me to the heart, Robert." Nancy folds the
single sheet of paper and lays it on the mantelpiece. "I could not deny
you a last visit before you leave Edinburgh – no matter what the risk
to decorum and propriety."

"As much as I could wish to deny it for your sake," says Robert,
"I must admit again that I am a passionate man. Where my heart
goes, my body must follow." He fixes her with that extraordinary dark
gaze. "And I long to possess you, as any man must wish to possess the
woman he loves."

Unable to restrain herself, Nancy moves toward him. "You say
you are passionate." She touches his arm, her voice husky. "Can you

doubt that I, too, am swayed by such forces where you are concerned?" He places a hand over hers and she steps back, her breath quickening. "But it cannot be," she says. "Not in such a world as this, where my very welfare, and that of my children, depend upon the good opinion of men who see passion as ruinous!"

Robert reaches out and takes hold of her wrist, and she gasps, pulling instinctively against his powerful grip. Gradually, though, she allows herself to be drawn down beside him.

"No more talk, Nancy," he says. "Not now."

He leans to her and touches his tongue to her lips, and she feels her nipples grow taut and a moist softening between her thighs. Then he kisses her more deeply and crushes her to his chest, so that she can smell around her the harsh spice of wine and sweat, and feel the coarse fabric of his clothing on the bare flesh at the neckline of her dress. She sinks back weakly against the arm of the love-seat, and he bends over her, his mouth moving to her neck, then to the swell of her breasts. She cannot seem to catch her breath, and as his hands caress her with feathery lightness, she hears a low humming from deep in her own throat.

Then she feels his fingers plucking at the laces of her bodice, and at length her breasts fall free, deliciously vulnerable in the warmth radiating from the fireplace. Now his lips cover one of her distended nipples, and as she squirms in response to his touch her hand brushes the front of his breeches, where the movement of his swollen organ causes a dizzying whirl in her brain. Then, suddenly, his fingers scrabble at her belly and push between her thighs, and even through layers of dress and petticoat his touch is like a red-hot brand.

The shock makes Nancy realize that she must do something, or else be lost, and she struggles beneath him and pushes at his shoulders with both hands. "No!" she says, and then more loudly, "Please, no!"

He sits back with a start, breathing heavily and staring at her with sullen eyes. She sits upright and begins to adjust her clothing. "I am sorry, Robert," she says at last. "More sorry than you can know. But I must not grant that one request that destroys my very life."

At this, he rises and turns his back on her. "And I must leave, madam," he says, his voice brusque.

"Madam!" She can feel him slipping from her, and the thought stirs both panic and anger. Why can he not understand her position? "You wound me with formality," she says, her voice trembling, "and lessen yourself in doing so."

And now he kneels before her, his hands clasping her thighs. "Forgive me, Nancy," he says. "I am so distracted I scarcely know what I'm saying."

Her panic subsiding somewhat, Nancy leans forward and kisses his hot forehead. "Robert, Robert," she says, "of course I forgive you. We mustn't part in anger." She covers his hands with her own. "I must own that I am distracted too, for fear that Jean Armour will make you forget me."

"Never!" he says with satisfying fervor. "With you beyond reach, I could never think to love or wed another!"

Her confidence returning, Nancy takes Robert's hands and looks him in the eye. "I am almost agreed with you on the subject of marriage," she says. "Unless a woman could be companion, friend, and mistress, she would never do for you. Only such a one could keep you."

He covers her hands with kisses, then looks up at her again. "And where would such a one be found, with you debarred from showing the third facet of the jewel you are?"

She drops her eyes and speaks softly. "Nowhere, I hope."

"And nowhere else, I fear," he says. He rises, and Nancy follows suit. "Farewell for the present, Clarinda, till I return."

He envelops her in his arms, and she returns his kiss warmly, feeling satisfaction in her successful negotiation of a difficult passage. If only she had never married James! If only he might fall prey to some tropical fever! She feels her face growing hot with shame at her own selfish desire, and breaks out of his embrace.

"Promise you will write to me, Robert," she says at last, her voice quavering with emotion.

"I will," he says.

"And that you won't forget me."

He shakes his head. "That could never be."

She smiles at him. "Then you leave me happy in my sadness." She holds open her arms. "Goodbye, Robert."

He kisses her once more, a lingering kiss that takes away her breath and threatens her resolve. Then, abruptly, unsettlingly, he stands away and looks down at her. "Goodbye, Nancy."

When he is gone, Nancy stands looking at the doorway for a time. Then, sighing, she crosses to the mantelpiece. Feeling the heat of the fire suffuse her body, she picks up the letter she left there, unfolds it, and begins to read again Robert's desperate plea.

Standing outside in the wintry gloom of General's Entry, leaning on his walking stick, Robert takes a deep breath and gives vent to a shuddering sigh of frustration.

"I fear ye found little satisfaction o' the kind a man needs, Mr. Burns."

Turning, startled, at the sound of the soft voice, Robert sees little Jenny Clow, in coat and bonnet, smiling at him from Nancy's front door. "Oh, it's you, Jenny," he says. "And what do you ken o' the satisfactions a man needs, eh – and you just a bit lassie?"

Jenny moves toward him, her expression shy, but her voice a seductive whisper. "I could show ye."

"What?" Intrigued, Robert looks askance at her. "How?"

"At my lodgings," she says, her eyes hooded. "It's my nicht to leave early."

Robert glances nervously at Nancy's shuttered windows and, motioning to Jenny, leads her into the shadow of the adjoining building. Then he smiles down at the little maidservant. "Weel, weel," he says. "So ye'd like to mak love wi' a poet, eh?"

She puts a hand on his arm, sending a thrill through his body. "Wi' you, Mr. Burns," she says softly.

Robert closes his eyes for a moment or two. Is his life always to be like this? Will he never be truly acceptable to women beyond his own class? Or will they always regard him as a mere curiosity, fit for conversation and a bit of amorous byplay, but nothing more? Well, he thinks, to hell with them. And he opens his eyes and takes Jenny's hand. "If that's how ye feel, lass," he says, "it's high time ye stopped ca'ing me 'Mr. Burns.'"

Jenny gives him a wicked smile. "Should I ca' ye Sylvander, maybe?"

Robert chuckles ruefully. "No, Jenny," he says. "I fear the likes o' Sylvander wouldna ha'e the mettle to cope wi' a willing lass." He bends to kiss her small cool mouth, then adds, "Rab's the name for me."

Sitting room of Burns and Jean Armour at Mauchline

My dear Friend,

I am just returned from Mr. Miller's Farm. . . . On the whole, if I find Mr. Miller in the same favorable disposition as when I saw him last, I shall in all probability turn farmer.

I have been through sore tribulation, and under much buffeting of the Wicked One, since I came to this country. Jean I found banished like a martyr – forlorn, destitute, and friendless; all for the good old cause: I have reconciled her to her fate: I have reconciled her to her mother: I have taken her a room: I have taken her to my arms: I have given her a mahogany bed: I have given her a guinea; and I have f----d her till she rejoiced with joy unspeakable and full of glory. But – as I always am on every occasion – I have been prudent and cautious to an astounding degree; I swore her, privately and solemnly, never to attempt any claim on me as a husband, even though anybody should persuade her she had such claim, which she has not, neither during my life, nor after my death. She did all this like a good girl, and I took the opportunity of some dry horselitter, and gave her such a thundering scalade that electrified the very marrow of her bones. O, what a peacemaker is a Guid weel-willy p---le! It is the mediator, the guarantee, the umpire, the bond of union, the solemn league and covenant, the plenipotentiary, the Aaron's rod, the Jacob's staff, the prophet Elisha's pot of oil, the Ahasuerus' sceptre, the sword of mercy, the philosopher's stone, the horn of plenty, and Tree of Life between Man and Woman.

I shall be in Edinburgh the middle of next week. My farming ideas I shall keep quiet till I see. I got a letter from Clarinda yesterday, and she tells me she has got no letter of mine but one. Tell her that I wrote to her from Glasgow, from Kilmarnock, from Mauchline, and yesterday from Cumnock, as I returned from Dumfries. Indeed, she is the only person in Edinburgh I have written to till this day. How are your soul and body putting up? – a little like man and wife, I suppose.

Your faithful Friend,
R.B.

letter to ROBERT AINSLIE, Edinburgh
3rd March 1788

CHapter Twenty-Two

John Burns, 1769-1785.

Robert looks down at the inscription on his brother's tombstone and stamps his feet in a vain attempt to warm them on the hard frost-rimed ground of Mauchline Kirkyard. The impact sends a twinge of pain through his left knee, so he soon stops and glances about him at the kirk and at the back stairs of Nanse Tinnock's tavern. The day, though cold, is unusually bright for late February, with a scud of clouds blowing like scattered petals across the sky.

"So ye'll be awa' o'er to Tarbolton the day, eh?" says Gibby, who stands a few paces from Robert, his breath flying from him in miniature versions of the clouds overhead. "I must say I'm surprised it's ta'en ye this long to get back here."

"I couldna travel till my knee recovered a bit," says Robert. "It's still no' richt," he adds, flexing his leg. "But at least I was able to provide for Jean in the meantime, thanks to Willie Muir and his wife."

"Aye," says Gibby. "Nancy and Bell would as soon ye'd left her to the relations she went to in Ardrossan after the Armours turned her oot."

"They wouldna ha'e kept her long," says Robert, silently marveling at his sisters' continuing animosity toward Jean. "No' at the risk o' James Armour's displeasure." He looks over in the direction of the Cowgate. "Besides, I couldna ha'e left things like that – whatever Nancy and Bell may think." He chuckles ruefully. "At least Mither'll be pleased."

"Aye." Gibby smiles crookedly at Robert. "Ye're sure ye'll no' come and stay at Mossgiel?"

Robert shakes his head. "You've enough to deal wi' there," he says. "And I'll ha'e ample business here as weel. No, I'm fine at the Whitefoord." He claps Gibby's shoulder. "I'll be up the road to visit ye a' when I get things squared away, never fear."

"It's grand to ha'e ye here again, Rab," says Gibby. "And I thank ye for the money ye've brought. God knows it'll be put to good use. But I ken how hard it must be to deal wi' a tight-fisted so-and-so like yon Willie Creech."

Robert smiles at his brother, realizing how glad he is to see him. "I'll try to get the rest soon, laddie," he says. "Then we can maybe get past a' this worry aboot landlords and leases."

Gibby embraces him awkwardly, then stands back and says, "Weel, I'd best get on my way to Mossgiel, for there's plenty there to do. I'll tell Mither we'll be seeing ye afore lang."

"Aye."

With a last silent look down at John's grave, the brothers leave the kirkyard and walk together along the Backcauseway, nodding to folk as they pass, and leaving the hiss of whispers in their wake. Robert knows his return to Mauchline has excited a good deal of comment, for now Jean Armour's situation is well-known, if not a subject for open discussion. So be it, he thinks. Let them talk, and may Hell mend them.

Stopping outside John Mackenzie's surgery, diagonally across the street from Gavin Hamilton's house, Robert reminds himself that he'll have to call soon on Hamilton, too. "Weel, Gibby," he says, "I'll just ha'e a look in here."

He and Gibby shake hands and exchange a last word or two; then Gibby trudges away on the road toward Mossgiel, and Robert watches until his brother disappears around the bend near the Carriers' Quarters. Now the old Tower catches Robert's eye, and he feels a tightening in his chest as he thinks of his last tryst there with Mary Campbell. Sniffing, he passes the back of his hand across his face, then turns and enters the surgery.

Jock Richmond picks his way down Mauchline High Street, shivering in the keen bright February air. Finally reaching the Whitefoord Arms, he enters hurriedly and stands for a few moments just inside the door, blowing on his hands and enjoying the sudden warmth. Then, looking across the room, he sees Johnnie Dow bending to pour a stoup of ale for Robert Burns, who sits alone at a table with pen in hand and paper and ink before him.

Though they have exchanged letters cordially enough since then, Richmond has not seen Robert since his visit to Edinburgh for the winter Sessions, when he walked out of Willie Cruikshank's house in St. James' Square in irritation over Robert's relationship with the MacLehose woman. But now Robert is here in Mauchline and, fired by a surge of joy at his friend's return, Richmond crosses the room to Robert's table.

"Weel, Rab," he says, smiling down at him uncertainly. "Here ye are at last."

Robert snorts ruefully. "Aye. It's an infernal bloody tangle, and I suppose there's naebody to straighten it oot but me. "

Richmond waves a hand at Robert's writing paraphernalia. "I'll be disturbing your correspondence, nae doubt," he says, feeling awkward. "Ye wouldna tak a drink wi' me, eh?"

Robert leans forward, grinning, and slaps Richmond's leg. "Sit doon, ye daft bugger. When ha'e ye seen the day I wouldna tak a drink wi' ye? Especially here!" He shuffles the papers before him. "I'm just going o'er some sangs for James Johnson and" – he flashes Richmond a look – "penning a letter or two."

Richmond settles himself on a chair and calls to Johnnie Dow for two drams. Then, turning back to Robert, he says, "Ye've been living your whole damned life in letters these past weeks, I fancy." Robert looks back at him opaquely, and Richmond reminds himself that he wishes to end one quarrel, not begin another. Thinking to change the subject, he gestures at the sheets near his hand. "Can I ha'e a look at your sangs?"

Robert indicates his willingness with a shrug, and Richmond picks up the top sheet and begins to read aloud:

> "Clarinda, mistress of my soul,
>   The measured time is run!
> The wretch beneath the dreary pole
>   So marks his latest sun.
> To what dark cave of frozen night
>   Shall poor Sylvander hie;
> Deprived of thee, his life and light,
>   The sun of all his Joy."

Before Richmond can go on, Dow arrives and sets two drams on the table. Relieved, Richmond pays the landlord and raises his glass to Robert. When the two have drunk each other's health, Richmond realizes he can read no further and, despite his placatory intent, he replaces the song-sheet atop the others.

"Weel," says Robert, obviously nettled. "What do ye think?"

"Dinna tak offense, Rab," says Richmond. "It's just that this" – he waves at the song – "isna you talking. It's somebody else." He can tell that things are going wrong, but he cannot stop himself. "And it's no' about life, either," he says, his vehemence increasing. "Ye ken that as weel as me! It's aboot some dry, sapless corner o' the mind. No' aboot folk wi' good Scots blood in their veins – aye, or good Scotch whisky in their gullets!"

"Dinna be daft, Jock," says Robert defensively. "Ye're making o'er much o' it. It's just a bagatelle. It was never meant for onything mair than that."

Again unable to stop himself, Richmond says, "And what else ha'e ye written o' ony account since ye left Mauchline?"

Robert drinks off the remains of his dram at one swallow. "I've been occupied wi' ither matters, as ye ken weel enough!"

"Aye," says Richmond scathingly. "Like the accomplished Mrs. MacLehose."

"Now watch yoursel', Jock," says Robert, glowering at Richmond. "I'll no' listen to ony abuse o' that lady – by you or onybody else!"

Richmond waves his hands in the air. "For God's sake, Robert," he says, wishing he could shake his friend into good sense. "I ken fine the depths o' your regard for her – though I fancy ye havena plumbed them, if I ken her kind. Ye'll likely ha'e done a damned sight better wi' her maid!"

Enraged, Robert leans across the table and grasps a handful of Richmond's shirtfront. "God damn ye, Jock!" he says. Then, suddenly aware of where he is, he releases Richmond and sits back on his chair, still red-faced with emotion.

Richmond stares at him, unflinching. "Can ye deny it?" he says.

Robert looks back for a moment, then turns away, his anger replaced momentarily by shame. "No," he says, his voice barely audible.

Richmond feels suddenly sorry for his friend. "Ach, Rab," he says, "I wouldna talk to ye like this. But Christ, man – ye canna throw Jean aside. She's worth ten o' your bloody Clarindas."

Turning back to glare at Richmond, Robert slaps the table with the flat of his hand. "I'm here, by God!" he says. "And what the hell can you know aboot it, onyhow?"

And now Richmond feels a surge of anger, himself. "I ken weel enough," he says, "how ye lay aboot at Baxter's Close wi' your face tripping ye when ye first left here. Only then ye were mourning the death o' Mary Campbell."

"And what aboot it?" Robert demands, trying to keep his voice low. "I never thocht I'd see the day when ye'd tak the confidences o' friendship and fling them back in my face!"

"Ye ken me better than that," says Richmond. "It's you I'm thinking o'. Ye've lost Mary Campbell forever. Do ye want to lose Jean as weel? And a' because ye're after a life ye can never hope to live – a life ye wouldna even want!"

Robert looks at Richmond as if he might strike him. "Can ye imagine what it's like to sit at the tables o' the great and mighty – and listen to them deign to gi'e ye advice? And to know a' the time they arena fit to sole your boots?" His voice drops almost to a snarl. "If I could marry a fortune, I'd maybe ha'e the chance to help my mither and Gibby – aye, and Jean – and tak the measure o' the bloody gentry as weel!"

Richmond shakes his head. He feels now as if he can lose no more by going on, and he begins to speak calmly. "I'll warrant there's nae fortune tied to Agnes MacLehose," he says. "And onyhow, ye hardly need me to tell ye what ye'd be in for wi' a woman like her. Ye've written lines enough yoursel' on the life o' the gentry: 'Days insipid, dull, an' tasteless, . . . Nights unquiet, lang an' restless.'"

Robert's face registers a mixture of outrage and disbelief, but he makes no move to interrupt, so Richmond continues. "If ye mak it up wi' Jean now, ye'll maybe forfeit the trappings o' high romance. And ye'll say goodbye to polite tattle, and modish manners, and fashionable dress. But ye'll no' be sickened and disgusted wi' boarding-school affectations, either." Richmond leans toward his friend and takes him by the wrist. "And what ye will have," he says, "is beyond price. The handsomest figure, the sweetest temper, and the kindest heart in the country!"

William Fisher, having made his daily calls at Mr. Auld's manse and the Sun Inn, rounds the corner from Bellman's Vennel onto

Loudon Street just in time to see two unpleasantly familiar figures emerging from Johnnie Dow's. Unwilling to face them together, he waits until Jock Richmond has started away up the High Street; then he hirples along the road as fast as his rheumatic legs and two gills of Ferintosh will allow, and reaches the Whitefoord before the other blackguard has mounted his horse or even noticed the Elder's approach.

"Ooh, aye," says Fisher, voice thick with sarcasm, "so the celebrated writer's back amang us."

Burns turns, startled, then curls his lip in a sneer, uncivil as always to his betters. He passes his hand along the horse's neck. "As ye can see, I'll no' be amang ye for lang," he says. "So may it please ye, Mr. Fisher."

"Aye," says Fisher. He lays a finger against one nostril and clears the other onto the cobblestones at his feet. "It'll please me richt enough to see how sic a fine upstanding bachelor" – he stresses the word viciously – "will manage to twist the Kirk aboot his finger this time." Fisher grimaces contemptuously. "I wouldna ha'e thocht to see ye forsakin' your fine Edinburgh frien's for sic a trifle as the droppin' o' anither bastard. Though I can see" – he gestures toward Richmond's receding figure – "ye've found your richt level o' companionship soon enough."

Burns steps toward Fisher. "You damned sniveling crowl," he says.

Fisher flinches at the younger man's intimidating reaction, but stands his ground. "Ooh, aye, Burns," he says, his voice steady, though pitched higher than he could wish. "Ye can threaten and ye can slander – but ye canna deny it."

Burns' face darkens, and he stabs a finger before him. "Damn the time I've ever slandered ye, Fisher," he says, "wi' your sly tipplin' and your secret lechery!"

Fisher draws himself up and fills his chest with air. "I'm an Elder o' the Kirk!" he says, expelling his breath in outrage.

Burns curls his lip again. "It taks mair than words to mak a saint, Fisher."

"Aye," says Fisher bitterly, wishing he could see this ruffian humiliated as he deserves, instead of praised on every street corner. "And it's words will surely pave your way to Hell, Burns."

So saying, Fisher turns his back on the impudent scribbler and starts away up the High Street, moving hastily, but with a gait he hopes will bespeak enough dignity and scorn to infuriate the blackguard without provoking him to violence. Finally unable to resist a fearful glance behind him, though, he is disappointed to see Burns mounting his horse and riding off down Loudon Street toward Tarbolton, looking as blithe as if their confrontation had never occurred. Fisher stops to look after horse and rider for a time, then draws out his handkerchief and blows his nose loudly. Thrusting the handkerchief back into his sleeve, he shakes his head at the man's brazen effrontery. Then, sighing, he begins walking again. Perhaps he'll meet with a bit more respect for his person and position at Nanse Tinnock's tavern.

Jean Armour sits alone in her small room at Willie Muir's mill in Tarbolton, a shawl drawn about her against the wind that seems to whistle through the very walls. Looking around at her spare though scrupulously clean accommodations, she feels a dull ache in her chest. How simple life was in her own house when she was a child, her father's favorite, and how cozy she and her sister Nellie were in their own room, with nothing more to worry them than Adam's mischief or their mother's half-hearted scolding. And now, to be a mother herself, swollen with child, sick and alone in a world that cares nothing for her – Jean bows her head and feels her eyelashes grow wet with tears.

"Hello, Jean."

She looks up, startled, her movement spilling the tears down her cheeks. There, framed in the door as if she conjured him from the pain in her heart, is Robert. "Rab!" she says, unable to keep her voice from trembling. "Is it really you? Oh, Rab, I thocht ye'd never come!"

He moves quickly to her and kneels, embracing her as best he can as she sobs with relief. Then he draws back and looks at her. "My God, lassie," he says, "ye're in an awfu' state. It's no' to be twins again, is it?"

"I dinna care, Rab. I dinna care." Jean shakes her head, still marveling at his sudden appearance, and at his dark handsome features, almost more striking than she remembered. "Just as long as ye're here."

"Aye," he says. "Weel, here I am. And here I stay till I see ye richt." He puts his arms around her again and draws her to his body, and the smell of him makes her head so heavy on her neck that she lets it sink to his shoulder. "And ha'e ye no' had a soul to stand by ye here at a'?"

She looks up and meets his dark, penetrating stare. "Mr. Muir and his wife ha'e been kind since ye wrote asking them to tak me in. And Jean Smith comes to see me now and then. But my mither and faither want nothing to do wi' me."

His face grows suddenly red. "To hell wi' them, then!" he says. But when Jean flinches and looks away, he turns her back and cradles her face gently between his hands. "Och, lassie," he says, "I ken how ye feel. They're your ain flesh and blood when a's said and done." He traces the line of her jaw with a finger, sending a shiver through her. "I'll try to talk wi' your mither and see if I canna bring her round a bit." He looks about the cramped room. "But meantime," he says, "ye'll no' stay here. I've spoken wi' Dr. Mackenzie in Mauchline, and rented a room for ye above his surgery. He'll attend your lying-in, and a'. Ye'll no' be banished like a Pariah if I can help it."

"Oh, Rab," she says, her heart almost too full for words. "I dinna care where I am – as lang as it's wi' you!"

At this, Robert breaks from her and rises, turning his back. "Lass, lass," he says, "I can promise ye nothing ayont decent care till the bairns come. I ha'e obligations . . . and entanglements . . . in Edinburgh that mak onything else impossible."

"Aye," she says softly. "I can see that a simple lassie like me could never be enough for a man like you, that belongs in the great world. It's just" – she pauses, trying to think of the right words, words that won't anger him – "it's just that . . . I dinna ken what's to become o' me."

He looks down at her for a long time, making her feel like a mouse under the eyes of an owl, and she holds herself still, waiting for his fury at her weak-willed betrayal of her vows so many months ago. And when at last he speaks, his voice does sound angry. "No!" he declares, and her heart sinks. But he goes on, "I'll be damned if I say that to ye again, Jean. It's time to live instead o' scribble aboot it. By God, lass, we'll do it!"

She looks up at him, puzzled. "Do what, Rab?"

He smiles at her. "Get married," he says softly.

"Married?" Jean cannot believe she has heard him clearly.

But now he is grinning at her and waving his arms. "Aye!" he says. "Richt and proper this time – to please the law and the Kirk as weel as us." He begins to pace excitedly. "By God," he says, "I'll tak yon farm at Ellisland – and I'll press for an Excise commission and a'! They'll hardly deny me as a married man." He points at her, and she can tell his mind is working even as he speaks. "Mr. Miller said he'd mak a reasonable allowance so that I can build a decent house. When it's done, you and the bairns will be under your ain roof. And I'll go back to Edinburgh and a' – as soon as your time's by – and wring my money oot o' that damned Creech whatever way I can!" He pauses in his restless pacing and looks down at Jean. "Weel? What do ye say to a' that, lass?"

"I dinna ken what to say, Rab." Jean shakes her head. "It's like a dream come true."

"No, Jean," he says solemnly, moving to her. "It's nae dream. No' this time. It'll be life – our life – wi' blood in its veins – our blood. And whatever joy or sorrow we mak will be ours as weel."

Jean reaches up from her chair and clasps his hand. "I ken I've disappointed ye and hurt ye in the past, Rab," she says haltingly. "And I ken since ye've been awa' ye've maybe met ither lasses grander and lovelier and better-schooled. But I love ye for what ye are, Rab, though I canna say things the way you can. I've aey loved ye. And I always will."

Robert looks down at her, his eyes shining, and squeezes her hand tightly. "Aye, Jean," he says with difficulty. "Ye've stuck by me better than I've stuck by you." She tries to speak, but he silences her with a wave of his hand. "But ye've aey been there in my heart and mind and a', Jean. Even when I didna ken it!"

He sinks down beside her and rests his head in her lap, his arms clasping her knees. Jean looks down at him, torn between disbelief and delight. But finally, despite the growing discomfort in her belly, a sense of calm descends on her, and she begins to stroke his hair and to hum softly the tune of "Miss Admiral Gordon's Strathspey."

After a few moments, Robert looks up at her. "Jean?" he says.

She stops humming. "Aye, Rab?"

He smiles at her. "I've got a surprise for ye."

She can imagine no greater or happier surprise than he's given her already, but her heartbeat quickens all the same. "What, Rab?"

"I've written your sang," he says. Then, with tender irony, he adds, "I tellt ye when we knew each ither better I'd ken what words to write." He takes her hands and, looking her in the eyes, begins to sing, his voice – despite all his modest denials – clear and steady and melodious:

> "Of a' the airts the wind can blaw,
>   I dearly like the west,
> For there the bonnie lassie lives,
>   The lassie I love best:
> There's wild-woods grow, and rivers row,
>   And mony a hill between:
> But day and night my fancy's flight
>   Is ever wi' my Jean.
>
> I see her in the dewy flowers,
>   I see her sweet and fair;
> I hear her in the tunefu' birds,
>   I hear her charm the air:
> There's not a bonnie flower that springs
>   By fountain, shaw, or green;
> There's not a bonnie bird that sings
>   But minds me o' my Jean."

And as the last notes fade from the air, as they will never fade from her mind, Robert rises and pulls Jean to her feet; then, placing his hand tenderly on her swollen belly, where even now she can feel the tiny life stirring inside her, he kisses her open mouth, and soon she scarcely cares for parents, for children, for anything at all save Robert.

Ellisland

... I am not entirely sure of my Farm's doing well. – I hope for the best: but I have my Excise Commission in my pocket; I don't care three skips of a Cur-dog for the up-and-down gambols of fortune. . . .

from a letter to ROBERT AINSLIE, Edinburgh
18th October 1788

Epilogue

Robert sits by himself on the broad grassy plateau above the River Nith, writing a new song and looking around him from time to time at the hundred and seventy acres of Ellisland Farm. Down at the south end of the property he can see young Adam Armour, promising mason that he is, digging the new well with several day-laborers. The ground slopes sharply down from the flat stretch of land where the farmhouse will be, and Robert thinks with pleasure on the breathtaking views Jean will have of the Nith and the green Dalswinton hills beyond.

Fine views aside, though, he cannot shake off his sense of trepidation about his future in this place: running a farm is chancy enough at the best of times, but doing so while working as an Exciseman will be doubly difficult. He is certainly grateful to Lang Sandy Wood, the doctor who tended to his dislocated knee, for influencing the Excise Commission on his behalf, just as he is grateful to Patrick Miller for leasing him the farm on reasonable terms. But when he thinks of the labor that awaits him, he cannot keep his heart from quailing just a bit.

About Jean he has few doubts. Even now she is at Mossgiel, on better terms with his family at last, learning the domestic arts that will make her a good farmer's wife and caring for Bess and Robert. She is healthy again, too, having recovered both physically and emotionally from the loss of her second set of twins. Furthermore, she is as bonnie and complaisant a lassie as a man could ask to begin married life with, and he looks forward eagerly to sending for her when the house is ready. For all that, Robert realizes that his existence will never be quite what he might hope for. His settlement from Creech – won at the cost of considerable, if temporary, ill-will on both sides – is now nearly gone or spoken for, consumed by the needs of his family at Mossgiel and by the costs attendant on establishing a new household at Ellisland. Nancy MacLehose, though she still corresponds with him, has never quite recovered from Jenny Clow's pregnancy, despite his having settled with the girl and her being quite content to keep the child; the world of Clarinda and Sylvander is an all-but-forgot-ten dream, and one that Robert now concedes to himself may be well-lost. And Nancy has apparently found solace in the company of Bob Ainslie, in any case. But when Robert thinks of romance and intellectual stimulation, he knows that Jean cannot supply them both; and he knows, too, that he will likely continue to be swayed in years to come by the witching voice of his own passions.

Even now, watching the Nith sweep on its westerly course through the lush June greenery toward the Solway Firth, he can hear in his mind the pious caviling of hypocrites like Willie Fisher and moralists like Mr. Auld. He can even hear his own mother admonishing him to live with the world as it is, and to abandon both his dreams and his attempts to distract himself from reality. Well, he will live in the world as it is, all right; but he refuses to surrender his innermost self to it, even at the price of essential loneliness. "A fig for those by law protected!" he thinks. "Liberty's a glorious feast!" And then, "Courts for cowards were erected, Churches built to please the priest."

He stares at the blank sheet of paper on his knee and, taking up his thick stub of a pencil, writes quickly and surely to the insistent rhythm of an old tune he's been playing with for days. When he finally finishes, he reads over the lyrics and makes one or two corrections. Then he rises to his feet and, standing alone, with no one to hear him, he begins to sing:

> "I ha'e a wife o' my ain,
>   I'll partake wi' naebody;
> I'll take Cuckold frae nane,
>   I'll gi'e Cuckold to naebody.
>
> I ha'e a penny to spend,
>   There – thanks to naebody!
> I ha'e naething to lend
>   I'll borrow frae naebody.
>
> I am naebody's Lord,
>   I'll be slave to naebody;
> I ha'e a gude braid sword,
>   I'll take dunts frae naebody.

> I'll be merry and free,
> > I'll be sad for naebody;
> Naebody cares for me,
> > I care for naebody."

Chest heaving and the words of the song still buzzing in his ears, Robert looks down at the sparkle of the sun on the river and the tiny figures working away on the site of his future home; then he surveys the flat green field around him, noting here and there the grey stones that push through the earth, awaiting the careless ploughman. And, thinking of the wind among the thorn-trees of Ayrshire, and the cacophonous streets of Edinburgh, he wonders for a time where his right place may be. Then, breathing deeply, he sinks back down amid the long grass; and, smoothing a fresh sheet of paper across his knee, he begins again to write.

Finis

Appendix A

The Characters

The following alphabetical list includes all persons, historical or imaginary (boldface), who appear or are mentioned by name in *The Witching Voice*, with a brief identifying phrase and relevant Chapter numbers.

Aiken, Robert (1739-1807), lawyer, Ayr, Chapters 1-2, 5-8, 10-16

Ainslie, Robert "Bob" (1766-1838), law student, Edinburgh, Chapters 15-22, Epilogue

Allan, Robert "Bob" (c. 1760-?), RB's cousin, ploughman, Mossgiel, Chapters 2, 5

Armour, Adam (1771-?), Jean's brother, Mauchline, Chapters 6, 10, 12, 14, 22, Epilogue

Armour, James (c. 1735-1798), Jean's father, master mason, Mauchline, Chapters 6-7, 10-11, 14, 18-20, 22

Armour, Jean (1767-1834), spinster, Mauchline, Chapters 5-6, 8-12, 14-22, Epilogue

Armour, Mary (c. 1740-?), Jean's mother, Mauchline, Chapters 6, 10, 12, 14, 18-20

Armour, Nellie (c. 1770-?), Jean's sister, Mauchline, Chapters 14-22

Auld, The Reverend William (1709-1791), minister, Mauchline, Chapters 2-3, 5-9, 12, 15, Epilogue

Ballantine, John (1743-1812), merchant and banker, Ayr, Chapters 1, 11, 13, 15-16

Beadle (c. 1715-?), Canongate kirkyard, Edinburgh, Chapter 16

Blair, The Reverend Dr. Hugh (1718-1800), minister and Professor of Rhetoric, Edinburgh, Chapters 15, 19

Blane, John (c. 1770-?), farm laborer, Mossgiel, Chapter 2

Campbell, Mary (1763-1786), Gavin Hamilton's maidservant, Mauchline, Chapters 2-3, 5-8, 10, 12, 14-16, 22

Carfrae, Mrs. (c. 1725-?), RB's landlady, Baxter's Close, Edinburgh, Chapters 15, 17, 20

Clarke, Stephen (c. 1760-1797), musician, Edinburgh, Chapter19

Clow, Jenny (c. 1770-?), Agnes MacLehose's maidservant, Edinburgh, Chapters 20-22, Epilogue

Creech, William (1745-1815), bookseller and publisher, Edinburgh, Chapters 13, 15-19, 22

Cruikshank, William (c. 1745-1795), Latin master, Edinburgh, Chapters 16, 19-20, 22

Cruikshank, Jenny or Jeany (c. 1775-?), William's daughter, Edinburgh, Chapter 19

Cunningham, James, fourteenth Earl of Glencairn (1749-1791), Edinburgh, Chapter 15

Dairymple of Dangerfield, James (1752?-1795), landowner, Ayrshire, Chapter 15

Dalrymple, The Reverend William (1723-1814), minister, Ayr, Chapter 5

Douglas-Hamilton, Basil William, Lord Daer (1763-94), Selkirk, Chapters 14-15

Douglas, Daniel "Dawney" (c. 1740-?), innkeeper, Anchor Close, Edinburgh, Chapters 15-16

Douglas, Dr. Patrick (?-?), planter, Jamaica, Chapter14

Dow, Johnnie (c. 1730-?), innkeeper, Whitefoord arms, Mauchline, Chapters 4-5, 7, 10, 12, 18, 22

Dow, Mrs. (c. 1735-?), Johnnie's wife, Mauchline, Chapter 7

Dow, Alexander "Sandy" (c. 1760-?), Johnnie's son, coachman, Mauchline, Chapters 4, 7

Dowie, John (c. 1740-1817), innkeeper, Libberton's Wynd, Edinburgh, Chapters 17, 21

Drunken coachman (c. 1750-?), Edinburgh, Chapter 19

Dunbar, William (c. 1740-1807), lawyer, Edinburgh, Chapter 16

Fergusson, Robert (1750-74), poet and law clerk, Edinburgh, Chapters 2, 6, 10, 16

Fergusson, William (c. 1730-?), physician and Provost, Ayr, Chapter 1

Fiddler (c. 1735-?), Poosie Nansie's Inn, Mauchline, Chapter 4

Fisher, William "Holy Willie" (1737-1809), church elder, Mauchline, Chapters 2-3, 6-8, 12, 15, 22, Epilogue

Gibson, Agnes "Poosie Nansie" (c. 1740-?), innkeeper, Mauchline, Chapters 4, 18

Gibson, George (c. 1735-?), Nansie's husband, innkeeper, Mauchline, Chapter 4

Gibson, Janet "Racer Jess" (c. 1760-1813), Nansie's daughter, Mauchline, Chapters 4, 18

Graham of Fintry, Robert (1749-1815), Excise Commissioner, Forfarshire, Chapter 19

Gravedigger (c. 1730-?), Alloway Kirk, Alloway, Chapter 1

Hamilton, Gavin (1751-1805), lawyer and landowner, Mauchline, Chapters 2, 4-8, 11, 13-15, 18-19, 22

Hill, Peter (1754-1837), bookseller's clerk, Edinburgh, Chapters 15, 19

Hunter, William "Tanner" (c. 1760-?), shoemaker, Mauchline, Chapters 4, 5, 7, 13

Hutchieson, David "Davie" (c. 1770-?), farm laborer, Mossgiel, Chapters 2, 14

Johnson, James (c. 1750-1811), engraver and music-seller, Edinburgh, Chapters 19, 21-22

Johnson, Samuel (1709-1784), author and lexicographer, London, Chapter 16

Lamie, James "Jeems" (c. 1735-?), church elder, Mauchline, Chapters 2-3, 7-8, 12

Lapraik, John (1727-1807), farmer and poet, Muirkirk, Chapter 15

Lunardi, Vincenzo (1759-1806), balloonist and diplomatic secretary, Lucca, Italy, Chapter 13

MacGill, The Reverend William (1732-1807), minister, Ayr, Chapter 15

Mackenzie, Henry (1745-1831), novelist and lawyer, Edinburgh, Chapters 6, 15-17

Mackenzie, Dr. John (c. 1755-1837), physician, Mauchline, Chapters 5, 8, 13, 22

Markland, Jean (1765-1851), spinster, Mauchline, Chapters 5-7, 13

MacLehose, Agnes Craig "Nancy" "Clarinda" (1759-1841), Edinburgh, Chapters 19-22, Epilogue

MacLehose, James (c. 1755-?), law agent, Jamaica, Chapters 19-20

McLure, David (c.1740-?), landlord, Ayr, Chapters 1-2, 19

McMath, The Reverend John (1755-1825), minister, Tarbolton, Chapters 1, 3-5, 9, 13

McWhinnie, David (c. 1750-1819), lawyer, Ayr, Chapter 13

Meg (c. 1768-?), servingmaid, Whitefoord arms, Mauchline, Chapter 4

Meg (c. 1765-?), servingmaid, Brigend Inn, Ayr, Chapter 13

Meldrum, Hughie (c. 1730-?), innkeeper, Elbow Inn, Mauchline, Chapters 3, 5

Meldrum, Sarah (c. 1740-?), Hughie's wife, Mauchline, Chapter 3

Millar, Archie (c. 1760-?), blacksmith's apprentice, Mauchline, Chapter 6

Miller, Elizabeth "Betty" (c. 1765-?), spinster, Mauchline, Chapters 5-7

Miller, Helen (c. 1765-?), spinster, Mauchline, Chapters 5-6

Miller of Dalswinton, Patrick (1731-1815), banker and landowner, Edinburgh, Chapters 15, 17-18, 22, Epilogue

Milton, John (1608-1674), poet, London, Chapters 18, 20

Montgomerie, Captain (c. 1740-?), brother of Hugh, twelfth Earl of Eglinton, Ayrshire, Chapters 3, 5-7, 8

Moodie, The Reverend Alexander (1722-1799), minister, Riccarton, Chapter 5

Morton, Christina "Chrissie" ((c. 1765-?), spinster, Mauchline, Chapter 6

Muir, Mrs. (c. 1725-?), Willie's wife, Tarbolton, Chapters 4, 22

Muir, Robert (1758-88), wine merchant, Kilmarnock, Chapter 11

Muir, Willie (c. 1720-1793), miller, Tarbolton, Chapters 1, 4, 13, 20, 22

Murdoch, John (1747-1824), schoolmaster, Ayr, Chapters 9, 18

Nicol, William (1744-1797), classics master, Edinburgh, Chapters 16-17

Nimmo, Miss Erskine (c. 1750-?), spinster, Edinburgh, Chapters 19-20

Nimmo, Captain William (c. 1750-?), Excise supervisor, Edinburgh, Chapter 19

Paton, Elizabeth "Betty" (c. 1762-?), maidservant, Mossgiel, Chapters 1-7, 9, 16, 19

Paton, Mrs. (c. 1735-?), Betty's mother, Lairgieside, Chapters 2-4

Paton, William "Willie" (c. 1730-?), Betty's father, farmer, Lairgieside, Chapters 1-4

Patrick, William (c. 1770-?), farm laborer, Mossgiel, Chapter 2

Ramsay, Allan (1686-1758), poet and master wigmaker, Edinburgh, Chapter 6

Rankine, Anne "Annie" (c. 1760-1843), John's daughter, Adamhill, Chapters 3, 13

Rankine, John (c. 1735-1810), farmer, Adamhill, Chapters 1, 3-4, 13, 15

Read, George (1762-1838), farmer, Barquharie, Chapter 15

Richmond, John "Jock" (1765-1846), law clerk, Mauchline and Edinburgh, Chapters 2-5, 7-8, 10-17, 19-20, 22

Ronald, William (c. 1740-?), tobacconist and ballroom proprietor, Mauchline, Chapter 6

Russell, The Reverend John (1740-1817), minister, Kilmarnock, Chapter 5

Shenstone, William (1714-1763), poet and landscape gardener, Shropshire, Chapter 2

Sillar, David (1760-1830), schoolmaster and grocer, Lochlea, Chapter 19

Simson, John (c. 1740-?), innkeeper, Brigend Inn, Ayr, Chapters 1, 3, 13

Smellie, William (1740-95), printer and scholar, Edinburgh, Chapters 15-17

Smith, Capt. Andrew (c. 1740-?), master of the *Nancy*, Greenock, Chapter 12

Smith, James "Jamie" "Wee" (1765-c. 1823), draper, Mauchline, Chapters 4-9, 11-13, 18-19

Smith, Jean (1768-1854), James' sister, Mauchline, Chapters 5-7, 18, 20, 22

Soldier (c. 1735-?), Poosie Nansie's Inn, Mauchline, Chapter 4

Stewart, Professor Dugald (1753-1828), Professor of Moral Philosophy, Edinburgh, Chapters 14-15

Surgeoner, Jenny (c. 1760-?), spinster, Mauchline, Chapters 3, 5, 7-8, 15, 19-20

Tinker (c. 1745-?), Poosie Nansie's Inn, Mauchline, Chapter 4

Tinnock, Nanse (c. 1740-?), innkeeper, Sorn Inn, Mauchline, Chapter 22

Wilson, Agnes "Aggie" (c. 1755-?), servingmaid and prostitute, Mauchline, Chapter 4

Wilson, John (1751-1821), printer and publisher, Kilmarnock, Chapters 11, 13, 16

Wilson, Robert (c. 1760-?), weaver, Paisley, Chapters 10, 14

Wodrow, The Reverend Dr. Patrick (1713-1793), minister, Tarbolton, Chapters 3-4

Wood, Dr. Alexander "Lang Sandy" (1725-1807), surgeon, Edinburgh, Chapter 19, Epilogue

Woodrow, Hughie (c. 1740-?), blacksmith, Mauchline, Chapters 6, 12

Appendix B

Poems and Songs

The following list includes the titles of all poems and songs by Burns quoted or mentioned in *The Witching Voice* and the chapters in which they appear.

"A Prayer in the Prospect of Death," Epigraph (frontis)
"Epitaph on My Ever Honoured Father," Chapter 1
"My Father was a Farmer: A Ballad," Chapter 1
"Green Grow the Rashes," Chapters 2, 14, 19
"No Churchman am I," Chapter 3
"Epistle to John Rankine," Chapter 3
"My Girl She's Airy," Chapter 4
"The Fornicator," Chapter 4
"The Jolly Beggars" Chapters 4, 5, Epilogue
"John Barleycorn: A Ballad," Chapter 5
"The Twa Herds; or, The Holy Tulyie," Chapter 5
"O Leave Novels!" Chapter 5
"Epitaph for James Smith," Chapter 5
"A Poet's Welcome to his Bastart Wean," Chapter 6
"The Mauchline Lady: A Fragment," Chapter 7
"Tall Todle," Chapter 7
"Holy Willie's Prayer," Chapters 7, 8, 12
"Of A' the Airts the Wind can Blaw" ("Miss Admiral Gordon's
        Strathspey"), Chapters 7, 16, 21, 22
"Tho' Cruel Fate Should Bid Us Part," Chapter 9
"To a Mouse," Chapters 9, 15
"Man was Made to Mourn: A Dirge," Chapter 9
"The Ordination," Chapters 10, 16
"Scotch Drink," Chapters 10, 16
"The Cotter's Saturday Night," Chapters 10, 12, 16
"Address to the De'il," Chapter 10
"Will ye go to the Indies my Mary?" Chapter 12
"The Holy Fair," Chapters 12, 16
"O Jeany, thou hast stolen away my soul!" Chapter 13

APPENDIX C

Works Consulted

Barke, James. *Immortal Memory*, five vols. Glasgow: 1946-1954.

_____, Sidney Goodsir Smith, and J. DeLancey Ferguson, eds. *The Merry Muses of Caledonia.* London: 1965.

Burns, Robert. *The Poems and Songs of Robert Burns*, three vols., ed. James Kinsley. Oxford: 1968.

_____. *Robert Burns's Commonplace Book*, eds. J.C. Ewing and D. Cook. Glasgow: 1938.

_____. *The Letters of Robert Burns*, two vols., ed. J. DeLancey Ferguson. Oxford: 1931.

Carswell, Catherine. *The Life of Robert Burns.* New York: 1931.

Daiches, David. *Robert Burns.* New York: 1950.

Fitzhugh, Robert T., ed. *Robert Burns: His Associates and Contemporaries.* Chapel Hill: 1943.

_____. *Robert Burns: The Man and the Poet.* New York: 1970.

Hartley, Dorothy. *Lost Country Life.* New York: 1979.

Lindsay, Maurice. *The Burns Encyclopedia.* New York: 1980.

McLehose, W. C., ed. *The Correspondence Between Burns and Clarinda.* New York: 1843.

Murray, James. *Life in Scotland A Hundred Years Ago.* Paisley: 1900.

Skinner, Basil. *Burns: Authentic Likenesses.* Edinburgh and London: 1963.

Snyder, Franklin Bliss. *The Life of Robert Burns.* New York: 1932.

Strawhorn, John, ed. *Ayrshire at the Time of Burns.* Doonholm: 1959.

Appendix D

Illustrations

Frontis: Charcoal and watercolor by Bryce Milligan, after the portrait by Alexander Nasmyth (1758-1840). The original portrait is held by the National Galleries of Scotland.

Page 13: Sketch of the Alloway Kirk and graveyard. After an anonymous photograph.

Page 27: "Mossgiel," sketch by D.O. Hill, in *Land o' Burns*.

Page 71: "Mauchline," engraving. W. H. Bartlett / H. Allard

Page 85: "The Kitchen at Mossgiel," sketch by Sir William Allan. National Gallery of Scotland. Through the door at the left, the stairs to the loft are visible. The door at right led to the milkhouse.

Page 101: Silhouette of Jean Armour, often reproduced. No images are known of Jean as a young woman. She was in her mid-50s when this silhouette was taken.

Page 113: "Last May a Braw Wooer," from a painting by Erskine Nicol.

Page 126: First edition of *Poems, Chiefly in the Scottish Dialect*.

Page 143: "The Betrothal of Burns and Highland Mary," by W.H. Midwood. The original hangs at the Burns Monument, Ayr.

Page 167: "The Cotter's Saturday Night," engraving by David Allan. Allan used Burns as a model for the figure next to the elderly reader.

Page 195: Edinburgh Castle. Anon. engraving.

Page 255: "Mauchline," from an anonymous painting. National Gallery of Scotland.

Page 283: Silhouette of "Clarinda" (Agnes MacLehose)

Page 291: Sitting room of Burns and Jean Armour at Mauchline, where the couple began their married life.

Page 303: Ellisland, engraving. Burns occupied the farm from 1787 to 1791.

APPENDIX E

Glossary of Scottish Terms

A': all; each one
ABREAD: abroad
ABOON: above; overhead
AFF: off
AFORE: before
AFT: oft
AGLEY: askew
AHIN or AHENT: behind
AIBLINS: perhaps, possibly
AIN: own
AIRT: a direction
AJEE: ajar
ALANG: along
AMAIST: almost
AMANG: among
ANCE: once
ANE: one
ANITHER: another
ASKLENT: awry
ASPAR: spread out
A'THEGITHER: altogether
ATWEEN: between
AULD: old
AUMOUS: alms
AWA: away
AY: always
AYE: yes
AYONT: beyond

BABIE-CLOUTS: baby clothes
BACK-YETT: back gate
BAILLIE: a magistrate
BAIRN: a child
BANNOCK: oatcake
BAUDRONS: a cat

BAWBEE: halfpenny
BAWK: a pathway
BEHINT: behind
BEN: within; inner room or parlor
BENMOST BORE: farthest crevice
BIG: to build
BIGGIN: a building
BIRK: birch tree
BIRKIE: a conceited person
BLASTIT: blasted
BLASTIE: a blasted or damned creature
BLATE: shy, timid
BLAW: blow; to boast
BLEERIE: bleary-eyed
BLEEZE: blaze
BLETHER: to talk nonsense
BLIN': blind
BLUID: blood
BLYTH: cheerful, gay
BOCK: vomit
BOGLE: hobgoblin, ghost
BONIE: beautiful, handsome
BOORD-EN': board (table)-end
BOW-HOUGHED: bow-thighed
BRACKEN: fern
BRAE: hill, slope, steep bank
BRAID: broad
BRAK: broke, broken
BRATTLE: scamper
BRAW: brave, handsome
BREEKS: breeches
BRENT: smooth, unwrinkled
BRIG: a bridge
BRITHER: brother

BROCK: a badger
BROSE: oatmeal mixed with water
BRUNT: burnt
BUGHT: a sheepfold
BUMMLE: a drone, a useless fellow
BURN: a small stream
BUSK: to dress
BUT: the kitchen
BUT AND BEN: the kitchen and parlor; back and forth
BYORNAR: extraordinary
BYRE: a cow-shed

CA': to call or summon; to knock or drive
CADGER: a hawker
CAIRD: a tinker
CALLAN, CALLANT: a stripling
CALLER: fresh
CANNA: cannot
CANNIE, CANNY: cautious, knowing, shrewd
CANTIE, CANTY: cheerful, merry
CANTRAIP: magic
CAUP: a wooden cup with handle
CARL, CARLE: a churl, a fellow, a clown
CAUDRON: a cauldron
CHAPMAN: a peddler
CHEEP: to chirp
CHIEL: a young fellow
CHIMLA: chimney
CHITTERING: shivering; teeth-chattering
CLACHAN: a small village
CLAES: clothes
CLAITH: cloth
CLAMB: climbed
CLASH: idle talk; to tattle
CLATTER: noisy disputation
CLEEK: a hook; to snatch or seize

CLOOT: a hoof; auld clootie (the devil)
CLOSE: an enclosed passage
CLUE: a ball of yarn
COG, COGGIE: a small wooden dish without handles
COOF: a blockhead
CORBIE: a raven or crow
CORE: a corps; a chorus; a cheerful company
COUP: to capsize or tip over
COUTHIE, COUTHY: kind, pleasant
CRACK: conversation; to converse
CRAIG: a crag or rock; the neck
CRAMBO-JINGLE: rhyming
CRANREUCH: hoarfrost
CREEL: a woven basket or hamper
CROUSE: cheerful, cheerfully; brave, confident
CROWDIE: oatmeal gruel; breakfast
CROWL: to crawl; one who crawls
CUTTY: short
CUTTY-STOOL: a low stool (used for repentance in the kirk)
DADDY: father or old man
DAFFIN: idling (romantically)
DAIMEN ICKER: a single ear of corn
DAUNTON: to intimidate or frighten
DAUR: to dare
DAURNA: dare not
DEAVE: to deafen
DEIL: the devil
DINNA: don't
DOCHTER: daughter
DODDLE: maidenhead
DOITED: stupid or senile
DOO: a dove
DOOL: to sorrow or lament
DOUCE: sedate; smug
DOWF: weak; spent
DOWIE: dull; sorrowful

DRAP: a drop
DREICH: dull
DRODDUM: buttocks, arse
DROOKIT: soaked
DROUTHIE: thirsty
DRUMLIE: muddy or discolored
DUB: a puddle (muddy or slushy)
DUNT: a blow or injury

E'E: eye
EEN: eyes
EERIE: sad; weird or ghostly; to feel fear or foreboding
ELDRITCH: unearthly
ENOW: enough
ETTLE: aim or plan

FA': a fall; to fall
FAEM: foam
FAIN: fond
FAIR-FA': good fortune
FASH: to annoy or trouble; to worry
FAULD: a fold
FAUSE: false
FAUT: a fault
FEART: frightened
FECHT: a fight; to fight
FECK: the greater portion
FELL: keen, fierce, relentless
FERLIE: a marvel; a shock; to marvel
FIDGE: to fidget
FIDGIN-FAIN: eager
FIN': to find
FIT: foot
FLAE: a flea
FLAINEN: flannel
FLEECH: to wheedle or cajole
FLEG: a fright; a blow
FLINDERS: splinters; pieces
FLYTE: to scold
FOGGAGE: foliage
FORBY: besides

FOU: full; drunk
FRAE: from
FRIEN: a friend
FU': full
FYKE: to fidget
FYLE: to dirty or soil

GAE, GANG: to go
GANGREL: a vagrant or tramp
GAR: to make or cause
GASH: wise or shrewd
GAUN: going
GEAR: goods, property
GEY: very
GI'E: give
GILL: a half-pint glass; a quarter-pint glass of whisky
GIN: before; until; unless; if; whether; should
GLAIKIT: foolish, thoughtless
GLIB-GABBIT: smooth-tongued
GLOAMIN: twilight, dusk
GOMERAL: a dolt, an idiot
GOOMS: gums
GOWAN: a daisy
GOWD: gold, money
GOWK: a fool or simpleton
GREET: to weep
GROZET: a gooseberry
GRUN: ground
GUDE, GUID: good; God

HA': hall
HA'E: have
HAFFET: temple (of the head)
HAIL, HALE: whole; healthy
HAIRST: harvest
HALD: possession, e.g. "house an' hald"=house and holding
HANSEL: to use for the first time; a gift or earnest-money
HAP: to cover or wrap
HAUD: to hold

HAUF: half
HAVENA: haven't
HAVER: to speak nonsense
HECHT: a promise or offer
HEM-SHIN'D: bow-legged
HERRY: to rob; to ruin
HIRPLE: to hobble or limp
HIZZIE: hussy, brazen wench
HODDEN: homespun cloth
HOUGHMAGANDIE: fornica-
tion
HOWE: hollow
HOWFF: house, inn
HOWKET: dug
HOWLET: an owl
HURDIES: the loins or buttocks

ILK, ILKA: each; every; the same;
kind or sort
INGLE: the fireplace; a chimney-
corner
ITHER: other

JAD: an old horse; a woman of ill-
repute
JIGGERY-POKERY, JOOKERY-
POOKERY: dishonesty
JUIST: just

KEBBUCK: cheese
KEEK: to look or peer
KEN: to know
KIRK: church

LAITH: loath
LEEZE: endear
LOOF: palm (of the hand)
LOUP: to leap

MAILEN: a farm; equipage
MAIR: more
MAK: make
MAUN: must

MAUNA: mustn't
MISHANTER: mishap
MENSE: tact, discretion
MOU': mouth
MUCKLE: much

NA: not (often added as in "werena")
NAE: no
NEIST: next
NO': not
NOO: now

ONY: any
OXTER: armpit

PAITRICK: a partridge
PEELY-WALLY: pale, sickly
PLACK: fourpence
POOSIE: to disarray
POUTHER: powder

REDE: to warn or advise
REEKIE, REEKY: smoky
ROZET: resin

SAIR: sore
SHAW: a wood
SHOON: shoes
SIC: such
SILLER: silver; money
SKELP: slap, smack
SMEDDUM: a powder
SNELL: keen, biting
SONSIE:, SONSY: pleasant, comely
SPLORE: horseplay; boasting
SPRATTLE: to scramble
SQUATTLE: to squat
STRAIK: to stroke
STRAVAIG, STRAVAGE: to wander
or ramble
STRUNT: to strut
SYNE: since, ago

TA'EN: taken
TELLT: told
TENT: to heed; to care for
THOWLESS: useless, lazy
TINT: lost
THOLE: endure
THRAW: to oppose
THRAWN: resistant
TULYIE, TULZIE: a squabble or
tussle
TWA: two

UNCO: unusual

VENNEL: a narrow passage or alley

WAD: would
WALIE, WALY: large, healthy
WAUR: worse
WEAN: a child
WEEL: well
WHANG: a large slice; the mouth
WHEEN: a few
WHEESHT: hush
WHINGE: to whine
WI': with

YON: that

About Arnold Johnston

Scottish-born **Arnold Johnston** lives in Kalamazoo, Michigan, where he was chairman of the English Department at Western Michigan University (1997-2007). A long-time faculty member in and co-founder of the creative writing program, as well as founder of the playwriting program, he has now left WMU to concentrate full-time on writing. His poetry, fiction, non-fiction, and translations have appeared widely in literary journals. His books include a collection of poetry, *What the Earth Taught Us* (March Street Press, 1996), *The Witching Voice: A Play About Robert Burns* (WMU Press, 1973), and *Of Earth and Darkness: The Novels of William Golding* (University of Missouri, 1980).

Johnston is an actor-singer, having performed nearly 100 roles on stage and radio, as well as many concerts. He has made numerous presentations on the life and work of Robert Burns in the U.S. and Canada, including performances of Burns' many songs and poems. He has produced two well-received commercial recordings of Burns' work, one for WMU and one for CMS Records, Inc. His play about Burns, *The Witching Voice*, has met with enthusiastic response from audiences and reviewers alike, and has enjoyed many successful productions and readings.

Johnston's plays, and others written in collaboration with his wife, Deborah Ann Percy, have been produced and published across the country. Their translations (in collaboration with Dona Roşu) of two long one-acts – *Night of the Passions* and *Sons of Cain*, by Romanian playwright Hristache Popescu – were published in Bucharest (1999) by Editura HP, as was an English-Romanian edition of his and Percy's full-length play *Rasputin in New York* (with Romanian translation by Dona Roşu and Luciana Costea). Johnston and Percy also edited *The Art of the One-Act* (New Issues Poetry and Prose, 2007). A collection of their own one-act plays, *Duets: Love is Strange*, appeared in 2008 from March Street Press. Another Johnston-Percy-Roşu translation – of Popescu's one-act, *Epilog* – will appear in 2009.

On his 1997 compact disc recording *Jacques Brel: I'm Here!* Johnston performs his translations of songs by the noted Belgian singer-songwriter. Four revues featuring his Brel translations have been staged in New York, as well as others in Chicago (recognized by four Jefferson Award nominations) and Kalamazoo; another Chicago production, *Jacques Brel's Lonesome Losers of the Night*, played to rave reviews and packed houses in 2008. Johnston is a member of the Dramatists Guild; he has been a resident playwright with both the Off-Off Broadway theatre company AAI Productions and Kalamazoo's Actors and Playwrights Initiative, and is an Artistic Associate with Chicago's Theo Ubique Theatre Company.

Wings Press was founded in 1975 by Joanie Whitebird and Joseph F. Lomax, both deceased, as "an informal association of artists and cultural mythologists dedicated to the preservation of the literature of the nation of Texas." Publisher, editor and designer since 1995, Bryce Milligan is honored to carry on and expand that mission to include the finest in American writing – meaning all of the Americas, without commercial considerations clouding the choice to publish or not to publish. Technically a "for profit" press, Wings receives only occasional underwriting from individuals and institutions who wish to support our vision. For this we are very grateful.

Wings Press attempts to produce multicultural books, chapbooks, CDs, DVDs and broadsides that, we hope, enlighten the human spirit and enliven the mind. Everyone ever associated with Wings has been or is a writer, and we know well that writing is a transformational art form capable of changing the world, primarily by allowing us to glimpse something of each other's souls. Good writing is innovative, insightful, and interesting. But most of all it is honest.

Likewise, Wings Press is committed to treating the planet itself as a partner. Thus the press uses as much recycled material as possible, from the paper on which the books are printed to the boxes in which they are shipped.

Associate editor Robert Bonazzi is also an old hand in the small press world. Bonazzi was the editor and publisher of Latitudes Press (1966-2000). Bonazzi and Milligan share a commitment to independent publishing and have collaborated on numerous projects over the past 25 years.

As Robert Dana wrote in *Against the Grain*, "Small press publishing is personal publishing. In essence, it's a matter of personal vision, personal taste and courage, and personal friendships." Welcome to our world.

WINGS PRESS

Colophon

This first edition of *The Witching Voice*, by
Arnold Johnston, has been printed on 70
pound paper containing fifty percent recycled
fiber. Titles have been set in Scotford Uncial
type, the text is in Adobe Caslon type. All
Wings Press books are designed and produced by Bryce Milligan.

On-line catalogue and ordering
available at
www.wingspress.com

Wings Press titles are distributed
to the trade by the
Independent Publishers Group
www.ipgbook.com